After the Crumble

by

Devon Porter

Dystopian Fiction & Survival Nonfiction

www.PrepperPress.com

After the Crumble

ISBN 978-1-939473-20-2

Printed in the United States of America.

Prepper Press Trade Paperback Edition: November 2014

Prepper Press is a division of Kennebec Publishing, LLC

For MGS

The Nez Percé Indians say that no one ever dies unless they are forgotten.

If that is the case, you will live on for at least as long as I do.
We will never forget you.

This is a work of fiction. Characters and events are products of the author's imagination, and no relationship to any living person is implied. The locations, facilities, and geographical references are set in a fictional environment.

Chapter 1

Autumn was setting in and the air smelled like rain. Gavin's target made a rustling noise nearby and he held his breath. He'd been lying in the reeds for hours, stalking his prey. He knew if he spooked the creature now it could escape into the nearby woods, potentially costing him another day or more. He was tired and wanted to get home. As he waited, it made another noise, closer now. He'd left some venison jerky out as bait, and he could hear the creature sniffing at it as he hid in the reeds, slightly out of sight.

Gavin expelled his breath and exploded out of his hiding spot with a net. Missing the ugly little thing completely, he managed to grab one of its hind legs. It yelped and tried to bite him, but no matter now. After he confirmed he'd found a female, Gavin allowed himself to relax. He had what he came for and could finally start heading back home.

He smiled to himself, thinking how unbelievable it was that he had found the creature, much less a female. He couldn't wait to get back to the farm to show his brother. Aidan had thought he was crazy.

"All you have to go on is a rumor," Aidan told him before he left. "They've all probably died out by now anyway. You just heard that a family of them might be living down in Eastchester. I can't let anyone go with you because it's harvest time. You'll be all alone out on the road; it's a suicide mission! And for a dog? I don't care how rare it is!" Aidan had tears in his eyes, worried for his younger brother.

"I have to go now; they may be dead or gone if I wait any longer," Gavin had said. "I know you don't understand, but maybe one day you will. I can take care of myself, and this is something I need to do. I haven't gone more than a few miles from the farm in years. I have to do this."

On the day Gavin left, Aidan said goodbye to his younger brother as if it were for the last time.

As Gavin looked down at this little dog he'd gone through so much trouble to find, the mangy thing shivered and snarled at him. She was ugly, dirty, and covered with dreadlocks. She continued to bare her teeth and growl. It broke his heart a little bit looking at her. This little one was not made for the wild, and must have had a very difficult life.

He stuffed her in a canvas sack, slinging it across his chest. As she struggled and snarled at being imprisoned, he ruefully thought this wouldn't be an easy ride. He adjusted his rifle and the sack, fiddling with his gear. His daypack and sidearm posed no trouble but he liked to have immediate access to his rifle, so he fashioned a sling with his extra gun belt that allowed her to hang off to his side. Even though she was dry now, she'd started to shiver and shake, probably more from fear than the chill in the air. *Shiver*, he thought. That would be her name.

As he swung up on his horse, an older but well-kept chestnut mare on loan from his brother, he saw that he could ride fairly comfortably that way and still have access to his weapons. He wanted to get in as many miles toward home as he could before sunset. As he was returning home following the same route he had come, he could mark his progress by the landmarks that he'd seen on the first leg of his trip.

I remember passing that Denny's on the way in, Gavin thought. *I used to hate the place, but I'd rather have a meal from there than more salted ham and hard biscuits. Too bad, it doesn't look open.* He laughed to himself.

The entire front of the building was caved in, with a moldering pool of water inside. The sign still stood proudly, however.

Shiver finally calmed down after the first hour. He admired her grit; he would have quit fighting long before she did. Gavin was already taking a liking to her just for the fact that she'd managed to survive this long. As he rode, he periodically looked around with his monocular, a remnant of the old days that had become one of his prized possessions. Binoculars were bulky and hard to carry around when you were carrying a gun too, but Gavin's monocular was so small that he could keep it in one of his vest pockets. This area was familiar to him now. Not only had he passed the same way just a few days ago, but he'd been through this area many times before. That had been years ago, though, and by car.

This part of Virginia got hit pretty bad by the Crumble, he mused to himself. While he kept to back roads as much as he could, where the

2

damage from the Crumble was less evident, he periodically had to use major roads and intersections. In those spots, the scenery was marred by burnt, crumbling buildings covered with graffiti, and wrecked and abandoned vehicles. Grass and weeds grew out of control, slowly reclaiming the roads as well as the buildings, breaking through the pavement in many places. The Denny's had been in fairly good condition compared to most of what he passed.

He rode, continually scanning the area, and after a few miles he saw he was coming to a bend in the road. It hadn't seemed as severe when coming from the other way. He started to look closely at the little bend, and even though he didn't see anything, he felt the hair go up on the back of his neck. That little spot would be great for an ambush. He didn't ignore that feeling. In order to survive, he had to rely on every little piece of intuition that he had. He looked again, and as he zoomed in closer he saw the glint of metal up on the hill facing towards him. Damn.

"No way," Gavin muttered to himself. "No way."

Despite Gavin's skill with the M4 rifle he carried, he would never risk trying to break through. He had no idea where they were or how many. He didn't know what weapons they had. *For all I know they could be sighting in on me right now*, Gavin thought as he hurriedly turned the mare around and started back in the other direction.

He had known taking this trip was risky, and he had reservations he didn't express to his brother. Maybe he deserved to die. It wasn't just Aidan; his whole family thought he was out of his mind. Now that he'd accomplished his goal, he sat with this shivering, skinny pile of dreadlocks in a sack, completely alone and exposed. This was what he had to show for five days of travel, three days of searching and chasing rumors, and maybe five or six days back. The horse he rode was one the farm could afford to lose. She'd recently lost a shoe and might go lame unless he could find a blacksmith, and now there was a potential ambush on the same road that he'd gone through just a few days before. He was lucky he didn't get attacked on the way there; they must have just started using that spot in the last couple of days.

Frowning, Gavin rode a couple miles back the way he had come. He found a suitable spot and finally started setting up camp as dusk descended. He hobbled the mare, set up his tent, and sat down to eat a quick dinner of salted pork, biscuits, hard cheese and raisins.

Once he was settled in and full, he brought the wriggling sack over to the tent. He opened the bag gingerly, throwing in some venison jerky. The dog was as ravenous as he expected, and by the fifth piece he decided to stop feeding her so she didn't get sick. She'd probably never tasted anything so good in her life; it looked like she had been hunting frogs in the reeds when he found her. She was skin and bones.

Once her belly was full, she quieted down considerably, and even poked her head out to look around. He kept a firm grip on her and she briefly went to snap at him, but soon rested her head on his leg. Since he had found her in the wild, she couldn't have had much experience with humans, and yet she was growing comfortable with him after just a few hours. His heart swelled. He forgot where he was.

"Do you want to go to sleep, honey?" He kept up a soft patter of whispers to her as he stood up and carried her to his little pup tent.

As he reached the tent, he heard the snap of a twig and saw motion in his peripheral vision. Quickly tossing Shiver into the tent, he threw himself to the ground just as he heard a loud gunshot.

His ears rang and a cold panic descended. He'd fallen to the ground hard and he couldn't tell if he was hit or not, but he realized that he'd already reflexively drawn his pistol and assumed a prone position facing where the shot originated.

His rifle was too far away to reach, so he fired a shot to get the other guy's head down, and raised himself to his knees, continuing to fire toward where the shot originated. As he fired, his panic ebbed and his anger began to rise, threatening to consume him. He stood up.

"Die, motherfucker!" he screamed. He saw movement by a thicket of bushes and directed his remaining shots there, yelling at the top of his lungs as he lost himself to rage. He came back to his senses a moment later and heard his own ragged breathing and the repetitive clicking of his pistol as he dry fired. Gavin looked down at his pistol like he had never seen it before, and finally stopped pulling the trigger. In the fading light, he looked back up to see a crumpled figure fall out of the thicket.

Blood was spreading on the ground beneath the thicket, dark and oily looking. After loading another magazine and checking for other attackers, Gavin walked over. A skinny, teenage boy lay on the ground, half tangled in the bush. He was shirtless; with baggy pants so dirty you couldn't discern their original color. The kid looked even dirtier than his clothing, and his face and torso looked like he'd recently taken a beating. He had an old revolver in his hand, which Gavin grabbed and tossed away. The kid had been hit in his stomach and Gavin saw he'd gotten one in his shoulder, too. But the shoulder wound didn't even matter when there was a gut shot. These days, a gut shot was fatal. Gavin's anger melted away and his racing heartbeat started to slow.

"I wanted to show them," the kid said, coughing quietly. "Santiago kicked the shit out of me when I gave us away. He said we couldn't surprise you now, and we couldn't get your rifle." He was panting. Sweat glistened on his forehead.

"That was you I saw on the hill?" Gavin asked. He was horrified. This poor kid had messed up. Not only had he gotten beaten for it, but now he had lost his life as well. Gavin didn't see how he could have handled it any other way, but that didn't change the fact that he'd killed him.

The kid was quiet. "What's your name?" Gavin asked.

"Santiago calls me 'Stain', but my mom called me Andre." His face cracked into a visage of extreme grief.

"Why did you come here, Andre?" Gavin asked. "You should have just taken the beating." Tears misted in his eyes. He absently pushed his glasses to the top of his head, crouching down and leaning in to help the kid into a more comfortable sitting position.

"They don't even know I'm here. I stole the pistol from Santiago; I figured if I could get your gun it would get me in good. You know how it is out here, you gotta get yours!"

As Andre spoke, his eyes wandered down to the mess below his ribcage. Gavin didn't say anything, just looked sadly down at him.

"I'm not gonna make it, am I?"

"I don't think so. Can I do anything for you?" Gavin figured he would either ask for water or his gun back to finish things off.

"Is that a dog you got? Could I see it?"

"I don't think it's too friendly yet. I just found it," Gavin answered.

Andre was starting to bleed more heavily now, but stayed coherent. "I remember when I was just a little kid, we had this old pit bull named Bella. She was the sweetest thing. I can't remember those times much since it was so damn bad, but I remember that dog!" He was losing it now; his eyes were glazing over; spit and blood were bubbling out of his mouth. He was working himself into a frenzy.

"Hey man, calm down," Gavin said. "I'll get her, you can see her." He went and grabbed Shiver, who had barely moved in the tent. Gavin wondered what she thought of all this commotion. *For all I know, she's seen worse*, he thought to himself.

"Here she is. I'm calling her Shiver." He knelt down and held her out to him. She surprised Gavin a bit when she nuzzled Andre's hand and started licking it. Andre brought his hand up and stroked her, speaking baby talk to her. He got her bloody with his hand, but her tangled dreadlocks were already dirty anyway.

"What kind of dog is this? It's really weird looking," Andre asked, his breathing growing more ragged.

"She's a rare and special dog," Gavin said. "I've spent a lot of time out on the road searching for this little one."

Despite his condition, the kid looked up at Gavin with wide eyes, amazed. "You came out here just to find a dog?" Shiver continued to lick his face and had started whining.

Gavin sighed. "Okay, man. It's time for her to go to sleep now."

The kid looked at him. "I could have thrown in with you; I bet you have a better crew than these assholes I was with. You were nicer to me than anyone has been in years, and I was trying to shoot you! Are you some kind of religious nut or something?"

"Nah, man. I'm just a regular dude." Gavin was talking through tears now. He took Shiver and put her in his tent, then walked back to kneel next to the kid again. "I wish you'd come up and just said something. We could have worked it out. You didn't have to make me shoot you. Who the hell is this Santiago guy anyway? Why would you need to risk your life just to prove yourself?"

The kid laughed, snot and blood continued coming out. "You look like you've had it good; you don't know what it's really like out here. My little brother and I were on our own and almost dead when we met up with Santiago. He fed us and kept us safe. We would have done anything for him. As we got older, we killed for him and helped his crew set traps for people."

His eyes were glazing over, and he coughed for a little while before continuing. "But a few months ago, Santiago found a woman, and he had her in the back of this big truck. He'd done that before but I was never a part of it. This time was different, though. Santiago said it was time for me to become a man. He brought me into the truck and the woman was in there, tied up and beaten. She had this sad look in her eyes. The next thing I know, Santiago is telling me to do whatever I want with her."

Gavin sat and listened in sadness and horror. The kid was getting worse; the bleeding was increasing and his face was losing color.

Andre started to cry, his shoulders softly heaving. "I couldn't do it. I tried, but I couldn't get excited for that poor lady. Santiago got mad and called my little brother, Manolo, to the truck, saying that if I wasn't a man then my little brother needed to do the job for me." Tears were streaming down the kid's face.

"Poor little Manolo, he was too young to do anything, anyway. Santiago put a knife in his chest on the spot. He looked at me and said, 'I need *men* on my crew, not boys. Get your shit together or you're gonna end up like your brother.'"

Gavin was horrified. It had been more than eight years since the Crumble ended; not with a bang, but with a whimper. First, the lights started to flicker, and then the periodic outages became commonplace. When the electricity finally went off for good, most people barely noticed because they couldn't afford it by then, anyway. Gavin was glad when the worst of the violence died down, but he fooled himself into thinking it didn't exist anymore. He'd heard stories like Andre's before from refugees he'd taken in at the farm over the years. Some of the groups out there were brutal, living such a hard life that any perceived weakness could be punishable by death.

"So that was why you came after me?" Gavin asked. "You wanted to prove to Santiago that you were a man?" He said this softly, horrified that he already knew the answer.

"That doesn't matter now," Andre said. "Listen; watch out for Santiago's crew. Go around them; there are three more besides me. Essie is in a tree stand right past the bend, and Santiago's cousin walks up and down at night on the south side. Go around," he repeated.

"Okay. Thanks, kid. Do you want some water or something?"

"Yeah," Andre said. He was looking down at his stomach. "How long do you think I got?"

Gavin gave him his canteen and tried to pull himself together.

"Well, you're bleeding pretty badly, but it's not spurting, so probably an hour or more. I have to break camp and get out of here, although I doubt Santiago will come after me at night like this, especially since he was smart enough not to chase me the first time." *Although*, Gavin thought, *if Santiago had caught me slipping like this kid did, I'd be dead right now.*

"Okay. You know what I'm gonna ask you next," the kid said. "And I promise, it's the last thing."

Tears began falling down Gavin's face. He felt torn between sadness for the kid and rage at the evil in the world. He looked him in the eye.

"Listen to me carefully, Andre," Gavin said in a breaking voice. "There is a spark inside you that will live forever. When you leave your body on this earth, all the pain and shit will all be gone. You'll be pure energy then, and you'll be with Manolo. You'll be with God. Your soul goes on forever."

Andre closed his eyes. His breathing was shallow and fast. A smile formed on his face.

Gavin turned around and cocked the hammer on his pistol as quietly as he could.

"I'm sorry. I love you, man," he whispered. "The universe loves you." He put his pistol behind Andre's ear and pulled the trigger.

Chapter 2

After Gavin was able to collect himself, he looted the body. It was heartbreaking to see what Andre had. Broken shoelaces, a moldy piece of bread, and a battered Swiss Army knife were all of his worldly possessions. Even the piece of crap .38 revolver only had two bullets when he fired it at Gavin. Gavin pocketed all of it anyway, including the worn pair of boots. No one wasted things anymore.

As he broke camp and put Shiver back in her sack, a cold sweat broke out on his forehead and he felt sick to his stomach. Gavin knew that killing had to be done sometimes, but that didn't mean he always dealt with it well. He'd seen so much death in the past few years.

He smoked half a joint to calm his nerves. These days a lot of people grew their own weed, and Gavin knew how to grow the best. That was one of his biggest farmer's market products, along with his famous Marinara sauce and blueberry jam. Gavin loved pot since he was a teenager, and he loved not having to look over his shoulder when he smoked now.

As the joint kicked in, he felt the familiar sensation spread through his body. He'd brought plenty of homegrown with him on the trip, and developed this particular variety himself, naming it Afghani after an indica he'd once tried in Amsterdam. It gave a great body buzz but didn't cause the munchies or a lethargic feeling.

He finished packing up his camp, sighing as he picked up his spent brass. *That's a lot of bullets for one kid, crazy man*, he thought to himself dully. As he started traveling away from the campsite, Gavin looked forward to lying back down for some decent shuteye, and hopefully an uneventful trip the rest of the way home. He could circle down south for about ten or fifteen miles and connect with an adjacent road.

Even if it took another day or two, it would be worth it to avoid more trouble. He had enough jerky and dry goods for him and Shiver to last another couple of weeks if necessary. In spite of the weed buzz, the hangover-like feeling from the violence still plagued him, a feeling he was more familiar with than he liked. His head was pounding and his throat was dry, although the nausea was thankfully starting to subside. Despite all of this, he knew he'd be able to sleep; that had never been a problem for him.

After another mile or so, he saw a spot that looked good, a big clearing off the road with a rock face on one side. He got back off his horse, and went through the motions of setting up camp again. A light drizzle had begun to fall.

Gavin finished setting the tent up and put Shiver inside, and found himself reloading his weapons, grabbing his brother's worn bulletproof vest from his saddlebags, and zipping the tent shut with a small opening near the entrance. *If I don't come back, she can get her head out and wriggle her body through the opening,* he thought detachedly to himself. He left a pile of jerky in there with her and some water in the battered Frisbee he used as a traveling plate.

Gavin also had another exotic item besides the vest; Aidan had loaned him a pair of vintage night vision binoculars. Their batteries were recharged by a small solar panel. Gavin hadn't charged them for a couple of days, never thinking he would use them. He checked and they still had nearly full power. His luck was holding.

I thought I decided to go around, he thought to himself.

He left the mare hobbled by his new campsite and broke into a jog towards the bend in the road.

Chapter 3

The moon was out, so Gavin didn't need the night vision. He only had a few miles to hike and he found himself enjoying it at first, but after the first mile his body quickly remembered it was supposed to be sleeping. He slogged out the rest of the way in a less genial mood.

As he approached, he knew the sentry would have to be taken out quietly or he'd have no chance. When he reached the same spot he'd stopped at before, he brought out the binoculars and looked around. Through the greenish tint of the night vision, he watched the area where the kid said the sentry would be. Sure enough, after a few minutes, the sentry appeared, walking to a burned out car a couple of hundred feet from Gavin, before turning back and walking the other way. Gavin was glad to see that the drizzle wasn't getting any worse. It would give him more camouflage and keep him cool, but it wasn't coming down hard enough to make the ground slippery.

Gavin let the sentry make his round once more, and he turned back at the same spot a second time. *Yes, a pattern*, Gavin thought excitedly. Patterns were mistakes. Gavin felt the left side of his waist where his K-bar hung, and checked the pistol strapped to his thigh. He'd also put his little backup piece on his ankle, just in case. Hopefully he'd only have to use his knife.

He laughed to himself. *This is still better than my old corporate job*, he thought. He'd been a VP at a large software company before the Crumble reached his part of the world. The security software they made and serviced had luckily been important enough that his company was one of the last ones to go under. When Gavin realized how grim everything was becoming, he prepared as well as he could, learning skills and sharing them with friends and family, and working on the family farm.

While the Crumble began so quietly that few people noticed, it grew like a snowball rolling downhill. The ever-growing demand for global oil production was prescient of things to come. The problem that industrial civilization faced was the same one that brought down all the empires that came before it: too many people and not enough resources. But this collapse was special, and it happened much faster than the ones that came before. While all the previous empires on the planet stripped the land around their cities of nutrients and water leaving only deserts behind, it took hundreds of years for them to fall.

The fall of industrial civilization was different for one reason. Oil. As it started to run out, it became more expensive to get out of the ground, and prices would climb. But the price of oil never stayed very high for long, because demand would quickly drop. When people and businesses had finally cut out all of the discretionary energy use that they reasonably could, the slow moving collapse of the machine began to accelerate.

Gavin wished that he would have had more time and foreknowledge. A million times, he wished that he could go back to 'past Gavin' and tell himself things that he learned only after the long, slow ride of the Crumble. But overall, he had ridden everything out pretty well, despite the fact that things got a lot uglier than he had anticipated.

Better than the old days and all that silly bullshit we had to deal with. Our culture was so in love with the machine we built that we didn't look at the price tag, Gavin thought.

Shaking his head, he looked through the night vision again and saw that the lookout had almost completed another circuit and was about to walk out of sight again. He had to be ready to move. He checked his gear reflexively, making sure there was nothing that would make noise and give him away. As the lookout left his line of sight, Gavin dashed over to the car and crouched behind it.

It seemed like it took hours for the lookout to walk back around, and the wait was torture. *What the hell am I doing?* Gavin asked himself as his heart threatened to beat out of his chest. The hairs on the back of his neck were standing up and he felt like he wanted to cough his lungs out. His breath was ragged in his chest as he tried to breathe as quietly as he could. *Screw it,* he thought to himself. *I can't not do this.*

Gavin finally heard him come back. As he got close, Gavin circled around as quietly as he could and came up behind him. He wrapped his left hand around the sentry's face and stabbed his jugular with the knife in his right as fast as he could, pulling the knife out just as quickly. Gavin gripped him tightly as he struggled and bled, finally lowering the lifeless body to the ground.

Gavin had blood all over his hands and arms and he already

felt sick. The sentry had bitten his hand, which hurt like hell. After patting down the body, Gavin realized that he'd only been armed with a long, rusty kitchen knife. It seemed that this guy was only supposed to yell a warning. Luckily, Gavin had prevented him from doing his job.

Moving away from the corpse, Gavin pushed in closer toward the bend in the road. He couldn't see anything with the night vision yet, but he figured he'd see something as he crept closer. The moon was out but the clouds had thickened, so he felt fairly comfortable with the level of darkness concealing him. After crossing another few hundred feet of ground, Gavin saw a tree stand up on the hill above the road where the woman would be, just like the kid said. She would be next. He still couldn't see where Santiago was, though, and Gavin figured he was the most dangerous of the bunch. He couldn't tell if the woman in the tree stand was asleep or awake, and he didn't want to get much closer for fear of being seen.

If she was awake and paying attention, she'd notice when the lookout didn't come back around the corner within the next couple of minutes. Gavin instinctively moved closer, crossing the road in a hurry and staying as close to cover and shadows as he could. He got to a distance where he could hit her with his rifle, but that would ensure Santiago would know he was coming.

As Gavin came closer, he was amazed at his luck. Loud snores were emanating from the tree stand. He quietly ran over and leaned his rifle against the tree, climbing the pegs with his knife between his teeth. *Just like a pirate*, Gavin thought wryly to himself. He scraped his foot once and heard the snoring falter briefly, but it quickly resumed.

Essie. The kid said her name was Essie. She must have thought she was protected by the lookout. As Gavin reached the top, he saw a dirty looking middle aged woman with short hair sitting with her back against the tree. Still thinking too much about her name, which sounded like that of a sweet old grandmother, Gavin reminded himself that she must have known what Santiago was doing with the women in the truck.

He slithered onto the platform and clapped his hand over her mouth, stabbing at her throat. He had to come in from a difficult angle and she struggled a bit, but he got the job done. This one seemed messier, and he felt sicker still. He breathed in great, quiet gulps of air, and struggled not to retch. He thought of Andre, and quickly focused his anguish to a fine point of anger. His breath calmed and he tried to listen for any nearby movements, thinking of Santiago.

Gavin decided to wait in the tree and for a few minutes while he caught his breath. He sat down, looking around with the night vision and still not finding him. He waited a little longer.

That's when the first bullet hit him.

Chapter 4

September 2037
Hollis, Virginia

Richard Spiegel was enraged. He'd taken his regular morning nip of scotch, but it did nothing to alleviate his stress. What should have been a routine operation had become a nightmare. His group had been performing a standard 'security check' on a farm in the Hollis area, which was to say a shakedown. They would show up with their guns, vehicles, and their official looking uniforms, and approach an isolated house or farm. Knocking on the door, they would say they were with the government and had to check their premises for contraband. Once Richard and his team were inside the house, the gloves came off. They took anything they could use and would terrorize the people as much as they felt like. If there was an attractive woman, they would sometimes take her with them for a week or two, dropping her off when they tired of her.

If Uncle Sam hadn't cut me loose, this wouldn't be necessary, Richard thought to himself, not for the first time.

That was when his day changed for the worse. He heard a loud "crack" and saw one of the men closest to the house go down. He flung himself to the ground and aimed his rifle at the source of fire, squeezing off shots but unable to see much of anything. Richard had been standing back by one of the Humvees and he was glad of it; as he peered out from under the vehicle, he saw a second man go down.

"Everybody down!" Longhurst yelled. Longhurst was Richard's right-hand man. He was a born fighter with balls of steel, and extremely loyal. Richard was thankful for him now, as he looked back and saw that Longhurst was already assembling a three-man team to go after the shooter. Just as the remaining men who had been in front of the farmhouse were able to make it back to the cover of the vehicles, Richard saw that the shooters had multiplied. Fire now came from at least three separate locations, all obscured by cover. This was an easy decision.

"Pull out!" he yelled. *Damn farmers and their deer rifles,* he thought. Their shakedown strategy had worked well until now, and they had lived very well on the remaining fat of the city as they crossed out of and through the suburbs, and then the farms that were on their fringe. But they had come out pretty far into the country now, and Richard figured they'd have to rethink their methods.

He scrambled into the Hummer and peeled off, racing back to their meeting point. He stopped to pick up Longhurst and two of his men, only to see one picked off in front of his eyes as he tried to enter the vehicle. Not satisfied with letting Richard's men leave in peace, the farmers seemed intent on killing as many of them as they could. A fourth rifle fired now, and Richard saw another man go down. He slammed his foot on the pedal, hearing shots "ping" the back of his vehicle. He didn't lift his foot from the pedal until he got to the rendezvous point.

Chapter 5

Gavin had been shot a couple of times before, but both of them had just been grazes. This one, however, hit him like a freight train and knocked him back into the tree, dazing him. He must have made more noise than he thought. It felt like he'd been punched in the shoulder by an iron fist. Looking down, he saw that the wound had already begun to bleed. The vest, old as it was, had only partially stopped the bullet, which looked to be a pretty big caliber. As the pain hit him like a wave, he threw himself off the tree stand, coming down hard on his ankle as he did. He limped as fast as he could toward the nearby woods, knowing he'd have to find a way to circle back around to pick up Shiver and the rest of his stuff.

He heard another shot that kicked up dirt a few feet away from him, right where he had landed. He scrambled away, thinking that he was really developing a strong dislike for Santiago. He reached for his rage but didn't find it. The pain and worry from the wound was heavy on his mind, and it was bleeding more now. A couple of decent sized shards of the bullet must have broken through and gotten in deep. He needed to stop and treat it, but as he saw another bullet hit a tree beside him, he wisely decided to keep moving. He reached a spot where the woods opened up into a meadow. As he looked across to the other side, he saw that he had a good shot at getting away if he could make it across the little clearing. He didn't.

As he felt another shot hit him in the back, he was propelled forward a few feet and landed in a crumpled heap right under a tree on the other side of the clearing where a cold puddle was forming. It took him a few moments to clear his head, and by the time he did, he could see that Santiago was approaching, and the look on his face told Gavin that this was personal. *Essie must have been someone close to him*, Gavin thought detachedly.

Not saying a word, Santiago fired his sidearm at Gavin as he walked closer. The first couple of shots missed, and the third hit so close that the ricochets raked the back of Gavin's head and neck. That finally propelled him into action. Cornered like this, he could feel his rage building again. He needed it, because otherwise he could barely maintain consciousness. Gritting his teeth and moaning, Gavin rolled over a couple of times to get behind a rock, and reached for the Ruger strapped to his thigh. It was gone. It must have dropped out of its holster when he had fallen from the tree stand. Gavin now remembered that, while he had been fleeing into the woods, he had felt a curious lightness at his waist. Not paying attention to things like that often got people killed. He had taught his nieces and nephews the same thing. Notice everything.

Gavin saw Santiago raise his gun again, only about ten feet away now. Gavin went for his backup .380 pistol down by his ankle, thinking that his ankle hadn't felt light at all. The little backup piece was still there. Grabbing it, he wildly fired the first shot just to get Santiago off balance. Aiming carefully, he fired again, just as Santiago was raising his gun toward him.

Yes. Gavin had gotten him in the chest that time. He knew that he might pass out soon, and so gritting his teeth, soaked to the bone and almost screaming from the pain, he lurched to his feet and went over to where Santiago had fallen.

Santiago was as dirty as Andre had been, only older and harder. He wore a torn, white t-shirt and common tattoos covered his neck and arms: a crude dragon wrapped around his neck, arms, and chest was covered with tribal designs. As Gavin saw the teardrops below Santiago's left eye, he raised his pistol again.

"Wait, Wait! Espera…" Santiago stammered.

Gavin shot him twice more; once in each eye. He sank heavily to the ground.

"Teardrop tattoos mean you were an assassin, right?" Gavin said to Santiago's corpse. "Well, that was for Andre and Manolo, fucker." The words surprised Gavin even as he spoke them aloud, and helped him feel justified for his violent actions.

He felt so tired all of a sudden. He worried that if he slept here he would never wake up. He couldn't let himself do that. He had to get back to his family, and more immediately he couldn't let his brother's horse, or that poor dog, starve to death. The rain had now decided to come down harder, which was a blessing. It felt great on his face and it kept him awake. He removed the vest and his shirt, welcoming the rain on his bare skin.

Gavin struggled back to his feet, trying to assess his situation.

He was still bleeding fairly heavily, which he figured explained the fatigue he was feeling. The profuse bleeding had to be dealt with first. He grabbed the first aid kit which he always kept in his day pack, and pulled out a packet of coagulant powder. This was one of the last ones that his family had. Taking shelter under a tree, he proceeded to shake out the powder onto the worst of the holes in his shoulder. The bleeding slowed substantially after a couple of minutes, and he was getting his head back together and feeling more focused. He had a lot to do. He looted Santiago's body, finding a couple of silver dimes and a decent knife. Santiago also had a 1911 pistol on him, but it had been damaged on a rock when Santiago fell. Gavin took it anyway. His boots came, too.

Limping back over toward the tree stand, Gavin realized that he was going to have to collect the loot, hide it, and come back for it in the morning. Although he was in pain and exhausted, he knew he had a fighting chance at surviving if he still had the energy to do all of this. He finished collecting all of their guns and food, pocketing a couple more silver dimes. It turned out the sentry had been smoking homemade cigarettes and not weed, but Gavin immediately lit one up anyway. Screw it. He'd been a smoker for years, although cigarettes didn't come around very often anymore. He only got a couple of drags off the cigarette before the rain put it out, and he finished covering the pile of loot with branches and leaves. He couldn't wait to get back to camp. At this point, he didn't even care if the loot was found and stolen. He just wanted to sleep.

When he got to the tent and dried himself off, he burrowed into his sleeping bag. He wasn't sure if he was dreaming, but he thought he felt Shiver licking his face.

·

Chapter 6

As Gavin awoke the next day, he realized he couldn't even remember the walk back to camp. He looked out through the tent flap and saw that it was late afternoon; he had slept for a good part of the day. He peaked around. Shiver was sitting next to him in the tent. She had eaten all of the venison jerky that he had left out and was now staring at him curiously. She had also left him a little present in the back of the tent. Realizing his own thirst, he drank half of the canteen down, and then poured more water into his Frisbee for Shiver. She went right for it.

Gavin noticed a few things then. He'd gotten up to a kneeling position to reach his gear outside the tent, and saw that his lower leg was grossly swollen, although it looked like he could still walk on it. He could move his toes and it didn't hurt all that badly, so he assumed nothing was broken. His shoulder didn't look all that bad in the light of day. There was one wound that was pretty big and would need looking at when he got home, but he thought that if he was careful not to reopen it, he could make it without stopping. His back didn't seem to have bled at all, although with his little shaving mirror he could see where the bullet had hit the vest. There was a huge red welt, and the majority of his back was turning that sickly yellow color you only ever see on bruises. Breathing through his mouth, he cleaned up Shiver's mess in the back of the tent. Gavin began to slowly break camp, feeling sore all over, especially in his back. His luck seemed to be holding out, though; the rain from the night before had cleared out and the afternoon was breezy and beautiful, with a piercing blue sky.

Gavin fashioned a leash for Shiver out of a couple of belts. He chuckled, thinking that he had ridden a hundred miles looking for a dog, and he'd forgotten to bring a leash. He walked her as best he could, although she had no idea what to do on a leash and eventually sat down and stared at him as he tried to pull her around. He tied her to a nearby tree so she could get some air before she went back into the sack.

He gave the mare some supplemental feed, although he had hobbled her by a patch of grass and a creek the night before. It looked like she'd been grazing all night because she only halfheartedly went for the feed. Regardless, he left it for her and brushed her down a bit. Gavin wasn't a horse guy, but he loved animals in general. There were several horses on Millwood Farm, but none of them belonged to Gavin. The few times he left the farm, he preferred to walk, although he did borrow a horse once in a while when the weather was bad.

He packed the rest of his stuff onto the mare, feeling bad about putting Shiver back in the sack and trying to figure out a better way to carry her. He finally settled on slinging the sack across his torso off to the side, but this time letting her head hang out. He figured he owed her that much; she could at least see where they were going this way.

With his myriad wounds, he was slow getting on the road, but when he finally did he started feeling pretty good. He'd accomplished his goal, and also taken care of a problem that would have hurt or killed others. That was the kind of thing that his brother would normally do, although Aidan would probably had planned it out and been more sensible about it. Aidan wouldn't have gotten shot in the process.

Approaching the now-familiar bend in the road, he managed to retrieve the cache of loot and get it all on the horse, breathing hard from the exertion. Luckily, his pack had been half empty because of all the food he'd eaten on the first leg of the trip. Traveling that way would make him vulnerable, and he kept a sharp eye out for anything unusual and held his rifle at the ready. He only made it about five or six more miles past the ambush site before dusk set again and he had to make camp. As he dismounted, he noticed that his shoulder had begun to bleed again. Not wanting to waste any of the remaining coagulant powders, he soaked a rag in water from his canteen and stuffed it in the biggest hole. He kept pressure on it, going about the routine of setting up camp one-handed.

Shiver was beginning to get the hang of things and was starting to like Gavin. He assumed it was probably because of the jerky. She seemed to be perpetually ravenous, and he wondered if he left her with the entire chunk that he still had in his pack, whether she would be able to eat all of it in one sitting. From the look of things, she'd certainly try. He made sure to give her a lot of water since the meat was so salty.

Although Gavin kept his spirits up, the next few days were

exceedingly difficult. He never quite managed to stop the bleeding in the worst of his shoulder wounds, and by the third day, he had taken to just riding with one hand applying pressure to his shoulder, and the other with his pistol cocked and held across his chest. The mare was well-trained enough that he could steer her with his legs.

Shiver had adjusted well and caused him no trouble, but his right foot had become almost too large to fit in the stirrup, and his back ached in a way that he had never felt, worsening by the day. He was a mess.

As the days progressed, his pain and soreness continued to increase, and the daily traveling on horseback didn't give him a chance to rest and heal. The mare was still missing a shoe and he was afraid that she would go lame if he pushed her too hard. He went as slowly as he could, his progress less than ten miles per day. At that pace, he would have trouble making his food last long enough. The one thing he did not want to do was stop in a place where he didn't know anyone, especially not in this weakened condition, which made him prey.

After the ambush, he stayed on back roads even more than before, luckily encountering few people. The ones he did pass, he saw at a distance. They took in his guns and dark expression, and looked away and passed him by. He could imagine what he looked like. Gavin was in his mid-forties with dark hair starting to go gray. He wore dirty glasses and had a full beard. He wore his usual outfit of canvas pants tucked into long boots, with a dark green utility vest over a black t-shirt. He donned his trademark brown duster, which was now scuffed and battered from years of abuse. He kept his expression grim and didn't open his mouth, so as not to expose the fact that his teeth were so well kept.

Gavin once heard a story about a couple of guys who decided to hitchhike around the American West for a summer off from college back in the 1980s. They were from families that were well off financially, but they didn't want to get robbed (or worse), so they dressed in the oldest clothes they could find, stayed in the worst hotels, and took public transportation. Gavin imagined that it was sort of like visiting a theme park for them, as they got to see how the other half lived but didn't have to lose everything in the process. Their strategy seemed to be working pretty well until they were sharing a bottle with a homeless guy one night. He asked them where they were from and made it clear that he knew they came from a soft life. They asked him how he knew and he said, "You're both wearing your class rings. If you were really that hard up, those would be the first things you pawned." After hearing that story, Gavin tried to pay attention to the small details that would mark him as well off. When he knew he was going to pass through a more populated area, he even spread some mud on the horse, disguising the quality of his transportation. His guns, however, he kept clean. There were certain limits to these things.

While he was on the mare, it was easy to disguise his injuries, but if anyone saw him try to walk, they would immediately know what kind of shape he was in. His plan for the return trip was changing in his mind, and it had morphed to just getting to one of the outlying towns around his farm and asking for help. If he could make it to the town of Ramsey, he knew people there and he thought Doc Ball was still practicing medicine nearby. He was pretty sure there was even a farrier, too. Ramsey was only about thirty miles from him. *I can make that*, he thought, as he wrung blood out of the rag and pressed it back into the shoulder wound.

As he rode, he sank into a daze. The scenery began to blur and the mare was thankfully able to stay on the road with little guidance from him. He passed the detritus of industrial civilization: broken down rows of townhouses, and huge, empty, industrial chicken buildings along the side of the road. At one point, he passed a little area that looked to be well-maintained. An old train depot sat on the edge of a busy little town, and the building had been freshly painted. A seesaw cart sat on the tracks next to the building. As Gavin passed by, skirting the main street of the town, he saw snipers on the roof of the town hall, and glints of metal behind the windows of the train depot. He was being watched closely. He laughed to himself. *I'm not a threat to anyone right now,* he mused.

He occasionally took a break to smoke a joint to ease his pain, although it didn't seem to help his state of mind.

"You know something, cutie-pie?" he said to Shiver as she hung her head out of the sack, looking at the passing landscape. "You don't look so hot right now. All that pretty fur is all matted and dirty. I used to have a guy; he was the best groomer in Virginia! He would have made you look like a princess." Cold sweat beaded on Gavin's forehead and he opened his coat and vest, suddenly feeling hot.

"I wonder what happened to him… Don. That was his name. Do you know?" He looked at Shiver and cackled crazily.

"Hell, when did I last see Don? 2028? I don't think I was doing much driving by then. What year is it now, anyway? It must be past 2036 because my brother keeps track of presidential elections. I remember he kept trying to find out who was running, and that must have been more than a year ago now. Can you imagine? Trying to find out who's running for president? Ha!" Gavin laughed so loudly that Shiver perked up her ears and turned her head around in the sack to look at him.

Two days and several conversations with Shiver later, Gavin rode into Ramsey and could go no farther. The weather had held. It was in the 70s and only slightly breezy, but he was freezing and bundled up as best as he could. He pushed hard for the last few miles because he knew he was cutting it close. The mare was drooling and pulling her head back, her neck covered in a thick sweat. His wound had been slowly but steadily leaking for the last two days. He was eating and drinking as much as he could, but he knew his body couldn't make blood as fast as he was losing it now.

Gavin rode right up to the Ramsey Town Hall and took his left foot out of the stirrup. He fired his pistol into the air twice and slumped off his horse onto the broken pavement of the parking lot. An older woman rushed out with a pistol of her own, and as she saw him, warily went over.

"Can you please call Doctor Ball? My name is Gavin Collier. I'm from Scotville. I know the Rockwells over in Bradenton, they can vouch for me, and also James Milton in Cherry Hill. I'm injured and I need help, and I have silver to pay. There is a dog in the bag hitched to the saddle, please give her some jerky." Gavin thought his words sounded curiously slurred.

"Okay, son, jeez! You scared the heck out of me there! Let me get the Doc." The woman came into slightly better focus.

Hmm, nice rack for an older lady, Gavin thought to himself as he lost consciousness.

It's funny the things you think of as you're dying.

Chapter 7

Ramsey, Virginia

As Gavin awoke, he looked around at where they had brought him. It wasn't bad. In fact, except for the smell, his room could have been in one of those old TV commercials for clothing detergent where there were fresh breezes blowing around everywhere. He was upstairs in what must have been the doctor's house. It was an older building; the walls were a sturdy whitewashed plaster and the floorboards were done in a beautiful hard pine. Pictures of placid and soothing settings covered the walls.

The smell was a problem, though. Doctor Ball must have had many patients in there over the years and it's not like people could go out and buy cleaning products and new mattresses anymore. They did the best they could, he was sure, but it wasn't the same as the old days. Gavin didn't dwell on it and immediately tried to get up, seeing a mirror over the wall opposite the bed. His head spun with the effort and after bracing himself on the bed for a moment, stood and faced the mirror.

He saw that his shoulder was bandaged and clean; the doctor had already gotten to him. The swelling was down in his leg, and he craned his neck to look at his back but didn't see much change. He still hurt like hell but felt much better rested, and his mind was at peace now that he was among friends. He saw that his pack and all his gear had been placed respectfully on a bench in the corner of the room. He peed in the chamber pot and climbed back into the bed, sighing contentedly. It was only as he was drifting back off to sleep that he wondered where Shiver was.

The next time Gavin awoke, it was because the doctor was prodding at his shoulder. It hurt like hell and Gavin sucked air in through his teeth.

"Sorry," said Doctor Ball. "I thought I could sneak a look while you were still out." He was a short and thick man with wire rim glasses just like Gavin's, which weren't that common anymore. Doc had the traditional old man ears, overflowing with tufts of hair, and big bushy eyebrows, too. He looked to be in his seventies.

"No problem. Listen, Doc, thanks a lot for taking me in like this. I already feel a lot better."

"Well, you were right on the edge when you first got here. It looked like you were down a couple pints of blood, which is extremely serious. The worst problem you had was that a piece of shrapnel lodged itself near one of your arteries. Your other injuries aren't life threatening. I assume you noticed that the wound was bleeding a lot more than normal, and you were feeling light-headed?" Doc had gone back to prodding at the shoulder wound, but this time more gingerly.

Toward the end of the ride, Gavin had been in a perpetual daze, now only half-remembering the trip at all. The memories of that last day were a blur. He remembered firing his gun into the air a couple of times, and he wondered how that alone hadn't gotten him shot. Again.

"Yeah, I tried to keep pressure on it, but it didn't stop the bleeding all the way. When you pulled out the shrapnel, how did it look?"

"You look good; I got everything that I could see in there. Even if there is something left inside you, as long as it doesn't press up against that artery again, you'll be okay. Your main issue is going to be fighting off infection. The rag you had in the biggest wound looked to be pretty clean and your shoulder wounds don't look like they'll get infected, but your leg had some cuts on it that looked pretty nasty. However, you're in good condition for your age and look to be fairly strong. If you made it this far, you shouldn't have any major problems with the recovery. I also have some old antibiotics. Sometimes that can help, even now." The doctor started to move toward the door, making notes on his pad.

The doctor's comment about how strong he was to make it this far reminded him of Shiver. "Hey, how is my dog doing?"

The doctor's face lit up. "She's fine and so is your horse; my wife has her now and my grandkids have been giving her a lot of affection. How did you find her? And what were you doing out on the road like that, anyway?"

"It's a long story, and I've been calling her Shiver. Thanks for taking care of her. I can pay extra if you need me to. How many days do you think I should wait until I can travel again?"

"For your recovery, you should stay here for at least a week, probably longer," said the Doc. "You won't be bedridden, but I wouldn't recommend doing any riding or anything else strenuous until you've healed up some. After a couple of days, you'll need to start getting regular exercise; it will help you recover more quickly. You'll feel pretty exhausted for the next few days, though. My granddaughter is my apprentice; I'll ask her to make up some of her herbal concoctions for you. They can really be a big help in the healing process. She'll probably be in to take a look at you later."

Doc paused. "It's no trouble at all on the dog. Is she a Poodle or something? My wife Beatrice has really taken a shine to her."

"She's a Bichon Frise," Gavin said.

The Doc gave him an odd look. "A what?"

Gavin laughed. "They used to be a popular breed before the Crumble, but they all but died out in the years after. People don't really need dogs like that anymore; everyone wants pit bulls and German Shepherds now. But I still have one old Bichon stud named BoBo. He's fifteen and is in good shape for his age; I think he can still breed. We took in a young refugee at Millwood a while back. When he saw BoBo, he said he'd seen a group of dogs like that before in Eastchester, only with long dirty dreadlocks. Supposedly they were mostly feral, but an old hippie woman would feed them sometimes. When I got to Eastchester, I found the woman's house, but she wasn't there anymore. It looked like she'd been gone for a while. It took me two more days to catch Shiver by a nearby pond. There might be more of them still living there, I couldn't say for sure."

The Doc was silent for a moment. "You're from Scotville, right?"

Gavin nodded.

"You're telling me that you went all the way from Scotville to Eastchester and almost got killed… for a… Beechun Freese?

Gavin laughed until it made his shoulder hurt. "Yeah, I get that a lot." And he went back to sleep.

Chapter 8

The next morning Gavin was woken up again, but this time it wasn't by Doc. He felt pressure on his shoulder and smelled something odd.

"What the hell is that smell?" he mumbled, eyes bleary from sleep.

"It's a rosemary and lavender poultice," a woman's voice answered.

Gavin opened his eyes all the way and saw an amazing sight. A beautiful woman stood next to his bed, putting a wrap on his shoulder. She was average height, about two inches shorter than Gavin, and had long, dark hair pulled back in a ponytail. Her face was striking, with almond shaped eyes, high cheekbones, and long eyelashes. She looked young; in her early twenties, maybe. She was wearing a vintage pair of colorful scrubs and had a calm and capable manner that belied her beauty. He could now smell the rosemary, which he knew was an antibiotic.

"It actually smells pretty good," Gavin mumbled, trying to think of something to say, some kind of angle. "I'm Gavin, by the way."

"I know," she said. "The Doc told me your story. He didn't tell me how you got this, though," she said as she finished the wrap.

"I got shot," Gavin said with a smile.

She looked at him, nonplussed. "No shit, Sherlock. What did you do to get shot?"

Gavin paused. He could make a joke and be cocky, but this woman didn't seem like the type that would respond to that. He sighed.

"It's a long story."

"I have time," she said. "I still need to change your sheets and bedpan, and I want to look at that bite on your hand, the cuts on your leg, and the bruise on your back, too." She helped him move into the chair next to the bed and started changing the sheets, and Gavin began to speak. He closed his eyes and lay back in the chair, feeling tired and sore.

"I'm kind of eccentric, you know? I was always that way. But after the world changed, I didn't get to be eccentric anymore. I just had to fight and survive. Now that things have calmed down somewhat, I went and did something eccentric again." Gavin looked at her as she ruffled the new sheets for the bed, not looking at him. A loose lock of hair had fallen out of her ponytail and his heart felt like it was going to burst. He hadn't even looked at her body yet. He wondered if she thought being eccentric was charming.

"Yeah, I heard that part of the story. But how did you get shot in the process?"

She was so direct, Gavin didn't know how to respond.

"What's your name?" he asked.

"Lea," she said.

He began to speak again, and this time he told her the right story. She came and sat next to him, wiping salve on his cuts and checking the bruise on his back. When he got to the part about how Andre died, she patted him on the back as he choked up. When he told her about killing Santiago, her mouth tightened into a thin, angry line. As he finished the story, she stood back up.

"Good riddance to bad rubbish, as the Doc likes to say. But don't expect any accolades from me other than that. I've spent my whole life doing exactly the opposite of what you did to those raiders." Lea took the bedpan to the door of his room and paused, looking back at him. She gave him a smile for the first time, which made her even more beautiful. "You're going to need to get some exercise soon. The day after tomorrow, you'll be well enough to start taking walks."

As Lea left, Gavin's head was spinning. In just the few minutes they had spent together, she had turned his world upside down. She wasn't like anyone he'd ever met before. *The thunderbolt,* he thought. *Finally, after all these years, I got hit by the thunderbolt!*

Chapter 9

The next day was as pleasant as could be. Gavin felt like he was in a hotel from back in the old days. He had breakfast and dinner brought to him by the Doc's sister, Ann. For lunch he walked over to the little diner that had managed to stay open and chatted with a couple of the locals. With no work to do, he took full advantage of this restful time, reading a book from the Doc's library and sleeping a lot. He looked around the house for Lea but didn't find her.

Shiver was becoming the talk of the town. There seemed to be something about a dog of that breed, or Gavin guessed likely any of the old companion breeds, that got people misty eyed and nostalgic. Beatrice had cleaned up Shiver and groomed her the first day she arrived while Gavin was still unconscious. She'd done a bang-up job of it, too, cutting off Shiver's dirty dreadlocks and giving her a bath. While Shiver didn't look like she could go to the Westminster Dog Show, she looked cute and cuddly enough to break the heart of many women in the town.

A few of the local woman had already found excuses to visit and see the dog, bringing pies and cakes over, or asking the doctor to look at imagined ills. There were a couple of men, too; Gavin was surprised at how many. One of the women who visited became very emotional, holding Shiver for almost an hour and cooing baby talk to her. Gavin was later told that the woman and her husband had raised dogs before the Crumble. Both the husband and the dogs were now gone, lost like so many other lives in the violence of the worst years.

Right after sunrise on the morning of the second day, he finally saw Lea again. He was up early and sitting at the kitchen table, holding an affectionate Shiver and drinking mint tea. Since the shooting he was constantly tired, and he dozed fitfully in the chair, feeling his age and the general soreness of his wounds.

"So this is the famous Shiver? She looks like a walking cotton ball."

Gavin looked up and saw Lea standing there with a smirk on her face. She wasn't wearing her scrubs that day. She had on a nicely tanned buckskin outfit, and to complete the image, she even had a bow and arrow. The buckskin showed her body better than the scrubs had, and Gavin saw that she had a small chest, wide hips, and was in great shape. The whole look really suited her. She looked like an Indian princess to him.

"Look here, Pocahontas," Gavin retorted flirtatiously. "I'll trade you the dog for that little toy bow and arrow you have hanging on your back." He chuckled as he said this, finally thinking to glance at her left hand. She wasn't wearing a wedding ring.

Grinning at him, she said, "I'll make you a bet. If I can shoot an apple off your head, then I will get the dog. If I miss and hit you in the head, then you get to keep it."

Laughing loudly, Gavin found himself at a loss for words, and thankfully they were interrupted by a visit from the Doc's sister. *Thank God*, Gavin thought. *It's Ann!*

Since Ann had been bringing Gavin his meals, he'd had the chance to get to know her a bit. An elderly woman in her late eighties who walked with a pronounced stoop, Ann had wispy white hair and a lively, expressive face. Gavin had loved her as soon as he'd met her. She was a real firecracker. A middle aged woman who'd gotten too much sun visited the previous day as well. Ann had pulled him aside and whispered to him, "That one looks like she was ridden hard and put away wet!" Gavin struggled not to crack up on the spot, and had a great laugh about it later that day. Ann had also given him some of her apple butter, which was delicious. She probed him about how he had gotten there, seemingly fascinated by why Gavin would risk so much and go so many miles chasing after a dog. His explanation had seemingly satisfied her though, and she'd taken a liking to him in return.

"Ann, it's good to see you!" Gavin gently hugged the elderly woman, feeling her physical frailty but also a deeper, resolute strength. She gripped his arm with one hand and held onto her cane with the other.

"Lea, I heard you from the other room, you know my ears are still good for my age. Don't you call my little baby a cotton ball!" Ann raised her cane and poked at Lea, and then sat down at the table, reaching her arms out to Gavin. Gavin handed the dog over, smiling innocently up at Lea.

Looking suddenly sheepish, Lea said, "I'm sorry, Auntie Ann!

You know I'm just teasing. Besides, you're going to love me this afternoon when I bring back a deer!"

"Bring back some purlsane and witch hazel, too," Ann murmured as she petted Shiver. "We're low." She looked at Lea. "You'd better be nice to this man here so we can get one of her first litter! Everybody has been buttering him up since he got here because they all want her babies, but he loves me the most. Don't you, Gavin?"

"Yes I do, Ann," Gavin said. "And for enough of that apple butter and a few more hugs, I'll take you anywhere you want to go."

Lea and Ann laughed in unison.

"Okay, Auntie Ann, I have to get going before it gets too late," Lea said. "We're going to feast this winter!"

"Bye, Pocahontas! See you soon," Gavin said and she punched him on the arm, which made his heart quicken. Lea paused and turned back to him.

"Have you walked yet today?" she asked.

"Not yet. I think I'll go this afternoon," Gavin replied. "I'm going to help Ann do some canning, at least until lunch."

"If I'm back here by the time you leave, maybe I'll go with you," Lea said as she walked away.

When she was gone, Gavin started helping Ann with the canning preparations, carrying the pot of water to be boiled and snapping the tips off the endless pile of beans on the table. While they worked, Ann gave him the scoop on Lea. She was the doctor's oldest granddaughter, and had just turned twenty-four. She'd gotten married young to a local boy, although from the outside it seemed like an unhappy union. They never had children, and her husband was killed in a raid two years ago. Her main trade was healing, having learned conventional medicine from the Doc and natural healing from Ann.

"Her true love is nature, though," Ann said. "I think she would stay out in those woods all day hunting and picking herbs if she could. But we need her here sometimes, too. The Doc and I have trained a couple of other apprentices, but she's still our best healer." Ann paused and poured a fresh pile of beans onto the table from a basket. Gavin groaned and Ann swatted him from across the table.

"Don't complain," Ann teased. "Cheer up! Have I told you that Lea hasn't shown any interest in remarrying since the death of her husband?" She winked at him.

"I'm a little old for her, don't you think?" Gavin asked, trying to keep his voice calm despite his pounding heart.

"These are different times now, young man," Ann said. "And besides, Lea has always been fickle about men, and for some reason she seems to like you. Stranger things have happened," she said, winking at him again and kissing him on the cheek. "Now get to work. And trim that beard the first chance you get, you hairy man!"

Rolling his eyes in mock horror, Gavin laughed with Ann and reached for a fresh pile of beans.

Gavin had never married, having several long-term girlfriends but never settling down. As a young man, he'd been in love with his career, and then later, with his obsession for preparing for the Crumble. As the Crumble worsened, he often regretted not having someone to lean on for support. He loved his brother's kids, and Aidan's oldest son, Mike, was very close to Gavin. It wasn't the same as having his own, though. Needless to say, once the electrical grid finally failed and the gas stopped flowing, Gavin didn't have much time for dating.

Now that the thunderbolt had hit him, he was glad he'd waited. She was smart, capable, beautiful, and funny. More importantly, she appeared to like him as well. He just needed to be sure he didn't screw it up.

Chapter 10

When he finished helping with the canning, he had a lunch of a sumptuous bacon and tomato quiche he helped Ann make. After eating, Gavin went outside and unpacked his gear, putting it all out on a blanket in the Doc's backyard. He started cleaning his guns and getting organized, hoping to catch Lea on her return from hunting. He also did some personal grooming, trimming his hair and beard, and putting on clean clothes. He hurt all over, with his shoulder throbbing and his other wounds making him sore, but despite that, he felt on top of the world. Escaping death and then meeting a beautiful woman would do that to a man. Besides, the pain was now a good kind of pain; the healing kind.

Shiver was still with him and was doing her level best to sit directly in the middle of all of his stuff. She'd quickly come to love human attention and petting, and was starting to demand it. While still rail thin, she was eating everything they gave her. She'd already learned to hang around the kitchen and get little tidbits of food.

After spending a couple of hours cleaning his guns and sharpening his knives, Gavin saw a shadow over him. He looked up to see that Lea had ditched the buckskins. She was wearing a pre-Crumble dress from the looks of it, and it was a beautiful blue. While it was slightly ill fitting, it made her breathtaking. She had a thin gold necklace around her neck, and Gavin couldn't help but admire her small, but pert, breasts below it. *Pervert*, he thought to himself as he smiled.

He shaded his eyes with his hand and squinted up at her, into the sun. "Did you get anything?" he asked.

She showed him her hands. Even though she'd clearly washed up and changed, he could still see the remains of blood on her palms. "What do *you* think?" she asked with a grin.

She looked down at what he had laid out on the blanket. "Wow, look at all this stuff! Hi Shiver!" Lea stooped down to give Shiver a pat on the head, her hair brushing against Gavin's cheek.

"Yeah, I'm trying to get organized now even though I have a few more days until I leave," Gavin said.

"Can I look at your books?" Lea asked, grabbing one and thumbing through it. "Oh my God, this is so cool, I love Italy. In school I used to read about it all the time! Have you ever been there?"

Gavin had carried a few books on the trip with him. Although they added weight, they were well worth the trouble. He had brought a picture book of a place he loved in Italy, an old favorite novel called *Replay* that he had read many times, and one of his Foxfire books. Foxfire was a magazine that focused on preserving old time traditions and the rural way of life, and their book compilations had proved invaluable. To Lea, however, the book with the pictures of Italy was the star of the show.

"Those pictures are of a town called Tropea, in Calabria, in the south of Italy. The food is excellent, the people are very warm and friendly, and the town sits right on the most amazing beach. It's beautiful; I still miss visiting there sometimes. I must have gone there ten times in the years, before the Crumble made things so bad I couldn't fly anymore. Even when things were close to falling apart, I still took the risk and visited Tropea every August, for as long as I could. My mom's family is from near there, and she and my father Bob had a little vacation house near the beach. Over the years, we got to know a lot of people in the area. There was one particular family, named the Valerios. We became very close to them."

Lea was quiet for a while, and she continued to look at the pictures, mesmerized. "You know, I was married once, and my husband, Danny, had no interest in things like this. I used to bring books back from the Doc's house and show them to him, but he refused to even look. The only books he read were about farming, and few enough of those. He said that things like that didn't matter now, and he would either go to sleep or change the subject. All he cared about was our twenty acres and his weapons, even when we had enough food put up for the year already. It's ironic that his guns still didn't save him in the end."

Gavin didn't say anything, he just sat listening.

It seemed like the longer she looked at the pictures of Italy, the more her melancholy mood deepened. She looked at Gavin, saying, "He was right though, wasn't he? I'll never be able to see those places, will I?" Shiver sat quietly at Lea's feet, who reached down to pet her periodically.

Gavin couldn't think of anything to say right away. He looked down at the meager possessions that he had with him, and thought of how good he had it compared to most people. He thought of the things that he'd been able to do that she would never be able to do, like using a cell phone, flying on a plane, or driving across whole states in just a few hours. And he thought of *why* that was.

"You see all these cool gadgets I have here? I was what was called a 'prepper' before the Crumble came. Have you ever heard of those?"

She nodded, still looking sad, but she smiled briefly and made a twirling motion against her forehead with her index finger. "Craaaaaazy..."

Gavin thought that was hilarious and laughed himself silly. "You know, I used to be really sensitive about that." She smiled at him again, waiting for him to go on.

"I guess I was like your husband in some ways back then," Gavin continued. "All I cared about was getting ready to survive what was coming, and after I did that for a while, I realized I'd forgotten how to enjoy my life, too. There were some people who saw the Crumble before it came, and what you said has a bit of truth; a few of those were a little nuts. For the most part though, we were just people who cared so deeply about our families and communities that we would do anything to protect them. Different people prepared for different things, but it all boiled down to something very simple.

"Humanity made a grave mistake. We were given the gift of fossil fuels, but instead of using them to explore the galaxy, we used them to pamper ourselves. We built whole cities in deserts, because we thought we could afford it. We used energy for the silliest things, like shipping tomatoes across the country in the middle of winter, and making so many useless entertainment devices it would boggle your mind. We built whole communities based on the idea that every single person would always have a car and access to cheap gas, even though it was common knowledge that oil was a finite resource. When we used up all of the cheap energy, we were left with a bunch of machines that wouldn't run anymore, and lots of communities and infrastructure that couldn't work anymore either. So nowadays, pretty much no one gets to travel to other countries like that, not like we used to do, at least."

Lea looked glum. "I've heard it explained a lot of ways, but never quite like that. It doesn't really matter though; the end result is the same."

Gavin immediately regretted making her unhappy. "Look at it this way," he said. "Back before we had airplanes, people still went to places like Italy. It just took a lot longer. In fact, I know a place where there used to be a lot of big sailboats; it wouldn't be impossible to make a trip like that with a year or two of preparation."

Lea's eyes lit up, but she quickly hid her excitement.

"I even know of a way to get there," Gavin said. "On the way here I passed something that gave me an idea…"

"That's all great, Mr. Prepper Man, but it's time for you to take a walk," Lea interrupted. "You can finish cleaning your manly guns and give me more of your worldly wisdom later." She gave him a grin and helped him get up as he groaned mightily. After a few moments, he noticed something. He was smiling and hadn't even realized it.

Chapter 11

Gavin tried not to show it, but as his stay approached a week, the walks with Lea became the highlight of his day. The first couple of times they went out, they kept to short walks in the town. But as he got stronger, Lea started taking him into the woods, and Ann was right. The forest was Lea's element; she knew the names and uses of every plant they saw, and she came even more alive when she was surrounded by nature. As they talked and got to know each other, Gavin came to respect how direct she was. Back in the old days, when someone said, 'I tell it like it is,' it usually meant they were about to say something mean. That wasn't the case with Lea. She was also very curious, asking him about his travels and the books he'd read.

One day, her curiosity finally got the better of her.

"So why aren't you married?" she asked, batting her eyelashes at him. She wasn't doing it quite right, which made it even cuter. His heart melted and he felt something in the pit of his stomach that he hadn't felt since he was a teenager.

Gavin was breathing heavily from the walk. He was getting better and his wounds were healing, but the longer hikes still got to him.

"I never felt the thunderbolt," Gavin said, chuckling and still out of breath.

"The what?" Lea asked.

"It's from an old movie called The Godfather. In Italian, they have a saying that when someone falls in love, it's like getting hit by a thunderbolt. I've done my share of dating but I never felt anything like that, and part of it was because it took me a long time to grow up. Until I got older and wiser, I wasn't ready for the thunderbolt anyway. On top of that, in the later years of the Crumble, I was so obsessed by it that I could barely think about anything else. I was really angry that so many people refused to see it. That affected some of my relationships. I spent so many years being angry!" Gavin laughed sardonically.

"You don't seem angry now," Lea said as she playfully poked him in his side. "Come on, pick up the pace!"

"Torturer!" Gavin shouted as he hurried to keep pace with her.

"So what made you stop being angry?" Lea asked.

"I finally let go of my anger when I realized that most people just aren't made to think that way," Gavin said. "It isn't in our nature to look that far ahead. Besides that, the machine made all of us pretty soft. Most people were in a cocoon of processed food, prescription drugs, and technology. I was, too. It was really hard to wake up from that."

Lea looked thoughtful and pointed to a bench. "Let's rest before we go back."

Gavin heaved a sigh of relief and sat down. Lea sat next to him, closer than she needed to. Gavin's heart skipped a beat. She turned and looked at him.

"So, by 'cocoon of processed food and technology,' you mean everyone was clean and warm, and had enough to eat?" Lea asked.

Gavin stammered for a moment, taken aback by her question, and then took a deep breath. "Yes, that's true," he said. "It was a great time to be alive. We had the whole world at our fingertips. But we ignored the fact that we were using everything up, and killing off the whole planet in the process. Yes, we had enough to eat; enough to eat for almost eight billion people at one point. But look at what that left us."

Gavin pointed to a building across the street; a seemingly ancient, dilapidated real estate office, covered with graffiti.

"I see it," Lea said. "I've been seeing it for all of my life. I guess I'm reacting negatively because you sound so much like the resistance did. Do you see that big red tag on the door, the one that says, 'Break the Machine'?" She pursed her lips, looking at him. When she was concentrating, a little line appeared between her eyebrows. His heart fluttered.

"That's a pretty common one," Gavin mused. "I've seen those before. It's just one of the slogans that the resistance used."

"You say the Crumble happened because we ran out of juice, but the resistance destroyed so much! The rebellion is why so many people died," Lea said angrily. "The rebellion is why I can't travel. If they hadn't started blowing everything up, we might have been able to save a lot of people. When they shot up a substation, who suffered? Us, not the government. When they tore up the highways, we paid the price! And I know they directly killed people out west when they blew up those dams. They made everything fall so much faster than it had to. If we'd had more time, maybe we could have found a solution to the energy problem!"

Gavin sighed and edged away from her. She wasn't going to like this.

"I understand why the rebels did what they did," he said quietly.

Lea scowled at him.

"Just give me a few minutes to explain," Gavin said imploringly. "I know that people died because of them, and I know it might seem like they were the ones who pushed it over the edge. But it would have happened anyway, and if they hadn't sped up the collapse, we might be living in a very different world right now."

Lea's face softened. "I lost my cousin when she was at the hospital during one of the rebels' substation attacks. The hospital's generator was out of fuel and she was really sick. When the power died, my cousin did, too. That's one of the reasons I've been so dedicated to learning about healing from Ann and my grandfather." She looked away.

"I'm so sorry, Lea." Gavin took her hand and looked into her eyes. He sat quietly for a moment, not wanting to say anything else and feeling the warmth of her hand in his.

After a few moments, she said, "Well, I've always told myself that I want to know the truth, even if I don't like it. I've heard so many different explanations for what happened; it's hard to make sense of it all. So go ahead, explain to me why you think the rebels were so mad at 'the machine.' What did that even mean, anyway?"

Gavin took a breath and plunged in.

"It dates back farther than either of our lifetimes. At the beginning of the industrial revolution, human beings started building the machine. For more than a hundred years, we made it larger and larger until we lost control of it." He chuckled. "It's funny. We kept on building new parts of the machine right up until the end, even as other parts of it fell apart. The machine gave us processed food, electricity, and clean water. It gave us clothing, entertainment, and all the products we could ever want. It warmed and cooled our homes. Some people even started using it to raise their kids, putting them in front of screens for hours on end. As the years went by, it became bigger and bigger. Every time the machine did something new for us, we slowly lost the ability to do that thing for ourselves. We forgot how to grow our own food; we forgot how to make our own clothes and tools, and even how to entertain ourselves. The machine took all of those activities away from us, and we allowed that to happen. We even encouraged it. It used to be that a majority of the people in the country were involved in producing food; by the end it was less than two percent of the population.

"The worst of it was right as the Crumble was beginning, right around the first decade of the twenty-first century. In the twilight of our industrial civilization, the machine even started to communicate for us. There was a whole generation that forgot how to talk to each other without it. That was my generation, and like I said before, I was no different from the rest. I loved junk food, TV and video games. I constantly looked at my phone and computer just like everyone else. I loved the comforts that the machine provided.

"Despite the fact that the machine hurt us in some ways, we loved it anyway. A lot of us even knew it was making people sick and killing the planet. But it was so pervasive and powerful that even the people who knew what was going on could barely get away from it. I had a very hard time with it myself. I didn't fully get away from the last pieces of the machine, things like the electrical grid, until they were pulled away from me. The problem was that it did so many good things for us. High technology gave us unbelievable powers to heal in the medical field, unsurpassed abilities to store information and crunch data, great communications, and the ability to travel long distances. You know, like being able to fly a plane to Italy in just a few hours. When the machine crumbled, it made it so we couldn't do those things anymore."

Gavin leaned back on the bench and let go of Lea's hand. She was looking into the distance with her brow furrowed, listening intently. She turned to him.

"I don't remember much about the early days of the Crumble," she said. "I was fairly young when it started to get bad. I recall that, for some reason, life just kept getting harder. After a while, I didn't have to go to school, and I got to play in the woods a lot more. I actually liked it at first. I was twelve or thirteen when the power finally went out for good, but by then we couldn't afford to use it much anyway. My parents were farmers and you've already met some my other relatives. We did as well as anyone could through the hard times; we fought and survived. I saw a lot of the aftermath of the violence that happened; even when I was really young I'd already started helping my grandfather. My schooling was spotty for what should have been my middle school years, but my family had taught me to love reading, so it wasn't too bad for me. My mom eventually started teaching a group of the local kids again and I got a semblance of a high school education, but even then we didn't learn very much about the Crumble itself. I've heard older people talk about it over the years though, and all they kept talking about was debt. They said there was too much debt, and their money wasn't worth anything anymore. If everyone was in all this debt, who was it owed to? And what did that have to do with the machine?"

Gavin was so deep into the conversation that he didn't notice her softening toward him as their rapport grew. He did notice something else, though. Lea spoke so easily about early memories of the Crumble, even the bad ones. He'd noticed the same thing with the kids at home at Millwood. The younger generation that grew up after the Crumble seemed tougher, and more in the 'now' than their elders. They were also more accepting of the way life was; they had no sentimentality about the times before the Crumble. In that sense, they were freer than Gavin.

"That's the crazy thing," Gavin responded. "It seemed like most of the debt was ultimately owed to just a few people, either directly or indirectly. A group of several hundred extremely rich and powerful individuals controlled the largest economies and governments on the planet through the corporations they owned. A lot of those people came from families that had been obscenely rich for generations. Those few people managed to subvert the governments of the world! Their companies, and the governments they controlled, made up a big part of the machine itself. All of the debt owed to them, or to anyone else, for that matter, was based on the idea that it could be paid back. But without our supply of cheap energy, the entire world's economy went into decline. It got a lot harder to even pay the interest on the debt, much less the balance. That's when the money supply started to destabilize. Just those few hundred people, the 'elites,' were worth so much it was incomprehensible. Their combined money and property was almost equal to the money and property owned by *everyone else*. A lot of that was in the form of debt."

"You sound like my dad," Lea scoffed. "He always says there was a conspiracy to break the system, and that the elites were the ones who had control over everything. But with him, it somehow always turns into how the Jews were in on it, too. Of course, that part only comes out when he's been drinking."

Gavin marked that information to be processed later, wondering how Lea could come from a man such as that. He continued, sensing that she didn't want to discuss her father any further at the moment.

"Yeah, I would see that kind of thing in my research sometimes," he said. "There was an ugly underbelly to some of the movements that existed back then. And when you consider the idea of an elite few controlling the lives of so many, I'll admit it is hard to believe. It was clear that they had huge sums of money, but sometimes I wonder about it myself. Did the elites really have the control they thought they did? Did they have the control that *we* thought they had? For one thing, they were doomed to fight amongst themselves, but I think they were ultimately slaves to the machine just like the rest of us were, and that they lost control over it. One of the machine's biggest problems was that it could only do one thing, which was to feed. And the machine's favorite food was oil.

"When crude oil was discovered, it was like humanity had found heroin. A single barrel of crude oil gave us so much energy that it was the equivalent to, say, what a hundred men could do in a day. When we found it, it would have been unthinkable not to use it. In the beginning it was so easy to get that it would literally just start flowing out of the ground in certain places. The U.S. found some big deposits very early on and it added to our prosperity even more. But as we started to figure out all the wonderful things we could do with the substance, something started to happen that no one saw coming. The profits from the oil and the technologies it helped develop started to make corporations richer, larger, and more powerful than anyone could have ever imagined. In fact, some of the companies that started to get big early on were the oil companies themselves, along with the railroads that moved the stuff. As these companies got bigger and more powerful, their technology became more and more advanced. While the technologies of the corporations were starting to make people softer and dumber, those same large corporations were simultaneously infiltrating the governments of the world with huge amounts of cash."

Lea pulled a knife from her boot and began to sharpen it. Gavin's practiced eye could tell she was a skilled sharpener. He liked that, and his attraction to her grew even stronger. She looked thoughtful for a moment and said, "I've heard a lot of talk over the years about how the corporations were evil, and how they had a big part in causing the Crumble. But that doesn't make sense to me. If I do a bad job as a healer, then people just won't use me anymore. It's the same for the butcher, the dressmaker, or really anyone who sells something. If all they were doing was making things and selling them, how could that be so evil? Even if they controlled the government, people could just stop buying their stuff, right?"

"Unfortunately, when a company gets to a certain size, all of those rules go out the window," Gavin replied. "When a corporation gets large enough, it gains a measure of control over their customers as they become dependent on that product." Gavin didn't want to talk about the machine anymore. He wanted to kiss her. But he saw the fire of curiosity in her eyes, and that was sexier than kissing, at least for right now. He continued.

"The size of the corporations was supposed to be restrained by the monopoly laws, but by the 1990s, those were barely used anymore," he continued. "By then, corporate money had fully conquered all branches of the government. Toward the end, the Supreme Court even declared that corporations had the same rights as human beings, which allowed them to subvert the political process even more." Gavin inched back toward her on the bench.

"But, isn't that the fault of the people for letting themselves become dependent?" Lea asked.

"To a certain extent, yes," Gavin answered. "But because of the design of the machine, an odd phenomenon happened. It came to be that mostly greedy people were running it. Unfortunately, the sociopathic personality turned out to mesh very well into the corporate model," Gavin said.

"The only thing the corporations could do was increase profits and keep growing, by any means necessary. The companies that were traded publicly were even bigger slaves to growth. They were responsible to their largest shareholders, who would sell their stock at any sign of a decrease in their fortunes. Corporations could grow faster and larger than a government ever could. Because of the way they were designed, they had no other choice. After a while, the largest of them became richer and more powerful than the governments of the world.

"What the machine really was, at its essence, was large corporations using their money and technology to run the world. Of course, the people that *owned* those corporations ultimately held more power than anyone else. That wasn't what was supposed to happen. The governments used to answer to their people, but as the machine took full control, that stopped completely. By that point it was impossible to restrain it. It just got bigger and bigger, and used up more and more energy, and destroyed the planet faster and faster."

"And that's when the machine started to run out of juice?" Lea asked.

"Exactly," Gavin said. "By starving the machine of oil, Mother Nature gave humanity a beautiful gift that saved us from ourselves. She gave us a second chance, and may have kept mankind from a future of complete environmental desolation and utter tyranny. Did you ever read *1984*?" he asked her.

"Of course," she said. "So that was supposed to be a kind of warning about the machine?"

"Exactly," Gavin said. "But Orwell never asked himself what would be *powering* all of the surveillance technology that he described in the book. The machine began its slow death when the planet finally started to run out of crude oil. By 2006, we'd already used up about half of the oil on the planet, and it became harder to keep production at its current rates, much less increase it. We started to go after extreme oil, which cost a lot more to get out of the ground. We started drilling miles under the ocean, in the Antarctic, and anywhere else it could still be found. We even got to the point where we started smashing up rocks and gravel that had oil sludge mixed in it, just so we could get a little more. We called that 'fracking,' an exercise in institutional insanity if there ever was one. That was the only thing that made it look like we were producing more energy in the years after the peak, but those gains were illusory and the price proved to be too high, even for people as addicted as we were. The oil you got from fracking wasn't crude oil at all, but instead a thick, toxic sludge. It burned through pipelines and train cars, and the chemicals used in the fracking process poisoned the water tables in whole regions. The wells, or 'plays,' as they called them, lasted just a few years before they were depleted.

"Despite all these desperate efforts, it was all we could do just to keep oil production at about the same level. Since the entire world's economy was based on the stuff, a strange period began. From 2006 to 2018, the world produced roughly the same amount of crude oil every year, as the growth in production levels began slowing down. The gains from fracking gave us a 'bumpy plateau' effect for a few more years, but even that didn't last long. The whole planet was in a kind of limbo. By then, Mother Nature had started to fight back in other ways besides just starving the machine of oil. The climate got more aggressive and seasonal changes became more extreme. Volcanoes erupted more frequently, earthquakes increased, and massive storms slowly started taking out infrastructure and production centers. Small pandemics started to pop up in places where the world was the most overpopulated. Wildfires and massive droughts increased all over the world, particularly in the American west where the aquifers and fresh water sources had been almost used up.

"In 2020, a perfect storm began. A lot of the massive debt you were asking about started to come due. A large part of that debt was directly caused by the existence of the machine. As the machine grew, it replaced workers with robots. The first ones to go were the factory workers, replaced by machines that never had to rest and never made mistakes. It accelerated with computers and the internet, and more and more jobs were eliminated. Travel agents, independent bookstores, and record stores all went away quickly. The friendly guy at the video rental store became a vending machine that dished out DVDs with the swipe of a credit card. The nice old lady at the checkout counter in the grocery store became a self-checkout aisle. Your banker became an ATM. It went on like that until there were more than a hundred million people displaced from work. The government had to feed and take care of all those people, and the only way they could afford it was to *borrow and print more money*. The worst of it was, every time they fed or took care of someone, they stole so much more for themselves, or spent it on useless bullshit. Lots of the taxes they took in went right back to the largest corporations by one means or another, mostly through subsidies. A big part of the U.S. debt came from that."

"You said earlier that the debt was based on the idea that it could be repaid. How did anyone ever think all that money could be paid back?" Lea asked.

Gavin smiled at her and tapped his nose. "That's a very good question, lady. The American people themselves were the collateral, especially the young ones. Everything was based on their future earnings and growth. As some of these youngsters started to realize what was going on, they joined in the fight against the machine along with Mother Nature. Youth all over the world started pushing back. They were the ones being asked to pay the impossible price of keeping the machine in motion, and they knew they had to stop it. That's when the resistance began."

"That's what I don't understand about the resistance," Lea said. "What would have been the harm if we just waited a few more years for it to fall naturally? If the machine was going to collapse on its own, why did the rebels feel like they had to speed up the process? My generation didn't even have a chance to fix it, much less enjoy it." She frowned, finishing with her knife and putting it back in her boot.

"There were two hundred species going extinct every single day," Gavin said. "The oceans were, and still are, filled with trash and plastic. The atmosphere, the water, and the land were filled with poisonous chemicals and getting worse every day. I could go on, but suffice it to say that if the machine had lived for just ten more years, there would have been no clean water or land left. In many parts of the U.S., the rebels were trying to force the slow shutdown of the nuclear plants. They would sabotage the grid wherever they could find a dangerous nuclear power plant so the plant had to run on generators and slowly shut down. That prevented a bunch of Fukushimas from happening all over the country when the power grid started failing on its own, because by that time, some of the plants wouldn't have been able to get fuel for their generators. I know you might not like to hear this, but they saved a lot of lives that way."

Lea was quiet for a long time, and when she finally spoke again, she didn't sound angry with him. Gavin breathed an internal sigh of relief.

"Since you understood what was happening, it must have been

interesting for you to watch, right?" Lea had progressed to another knife, and this one seemed to have come from nowhere. He didn't respond for a moment, imagining where that second knife had been hidden. As he watched her, the sunlight hit her face in a way that projected a soft glow. He was struck by how stunning she was. He cleared his throat and coughed.

"It was actually terrible for me, especially in the early years when I hadn't had much time to get used to the idea," Gavin replied. "It was like watching a car crash in slow motion. I started keeping a journal to track of all the events related to the slow collapse of industrial civilization. Writing in that journal helped me see the bigger picture as it happened." Gavin sighed. "I still have that journal somewhere."

"Why bother to write it down if people weren't even paying attention?" Lea asked. "But I'll admit that what you're saying makes sense. It fits with what I've heard already; so many people have told me about what was wrong with the economy, but if the energy was running out, of course it would affect the economy, too."

Gavin smiled at her. "I guess that was the point. So few people were paying attention, I wanted to write down my own version of the news, since I felt like I saw it more clearly. And you're right about the economy. When the energy got scarcer, the economy started to sputter, and as people became poorer, they bought less oil, keeping its price down. That just prolonged the agony. Any time the economy tried to grow again, the demand went back up and oil got too expensive, smacking the economic growth back down. There wasn't enough oil being produced to meet anything other than the existing demand. It was the lack of cheap energy, combined with insurmountable debt, that made the machine start to crumble.

"Many attempts were made to find suitable replacements for crude oil, but nothing could really take its place in the world economy. The dirty secret of the machine is that it was only built for certain types of energy input. Cars could only use gas, power plants could only use coal, etcetera. The machine couldn't subsist on alternative power sources even if they *could* produce enough energy; they were too intermittent and unreliable. Ethanol was a bust; it cost more energy to make it than it produced. So suffice it to say that we tried. But when worldwide oil production began declining in 2017, it dropped off sharply after that. By then, the planet's population had become so large, and our appetite for energy was so huge, that all of the solar, nuclear, wind, natural gas, and coal in the world wasn't enough, even if it could be efficiently used by the machine's existing infrastructure. The alternative methods of producing energy didn't provide nearly as big a return on investment as crude oil, and others carried a terrible environmental price. Look at what happened to Japan.

"We did everything we could to keep it going, so it took almost twenty years for the thing to starve to death, even with the rebels helping it along. The worst time was near the end during its final death throes. The governments of the world took more and more from their people, most of whom were destitute by that point. Entire communities had been ruined by the slow buildup and subsequent decline of the machine. Even the giant corporations started to reach plateaus in their growth, as their extractive natures hollowed out the very communities they were trying to sell their products to. The corporations couldn't grow anymore, so they consolidated to give the appearance of growth. They also used their government stooges to regulate their smaller competitors out of existence, which gave them more market share, and another way to pretend that the economy was growing for a while longer. By the end only the largest corporations in each industry were left, as they ate each other like starving animals.

"You describe it like everyone was a bunch of zombies," Lea joked. "So everyone just sat around and let it happen? I mean, even toward the end? That seems so strange. I'd like to think I wouldn't have been like that."

There's no way you would have been a sheep. You're an angel, Gavin thought to himself.

"I know, it seems suicidal and insane," he said. "And it was. Everyone played along, for the most part. We pretended that everything was okay as long as we possibly could, because we had to keep it all going. We couldn't possibly imagine the alternative. It was only a few people in the resistance who actually fought, although as you said, they did help the machine die an early death." Gavin took a deep breath.

"But... jeez, Gavin! If the machine was that bad, and if even half of what you say is true, then how could most people still want to keep it around so much? How come more people didn't fight back?"

Lea looked at him curiously.

"Well, it was the only life we knew, and like I said, it did all those things for us. Wouldn't you try as hard as you could to protect your food and water supplies, and how you made your living?"

She looked down, seeming to be in deep thought. She finally looked back up at him. "So you were a prepper, right? And now the thing you were preparing for has already happened. Does that mean you're not a prepper anymore?" Lea grinned. She had him.

"Hmmm." Gavin scratched his chin. "You might be right!"

Chapter 12

Excerpt from Gavin's Journal:

February 2005 - In a publication that comes to be known as the 'Hirsch Report,' Robert Hirsch examines the peak oil theory first espoused by M. King Hubbert in the 1970s. Hirsch shows that peak oil is an unprecedented geopolitical problem with severe consequences, even if well managed by society. His studies lead him to project that global oil production will start to decline by 2015.

Gavin and Lea continued with their walks as his wounds healed. He managed to draw Lea into telling him more about her life. She talked about her hopes, dreams and passions, and opened up about the struggles with her marriage and what she had gone through when her husband was killed. Gavin told stories from his travels and found that Lea was a voracious reader. Being the same way himself, he was able to discuss books with her.

During a brief rest halfway through one of their walks, Lea continued with the conversation they'd started the previous day.

"I don't agree that Orson Scott Card is the god you seem to think he is," Lea said, as she rested against a tree. "I read the Ender books and they were alright, but they didn't really speak to me. There was one that I did like, though."

"Let me guess," Gavin said. "The romantic one about Sleeping Beauty?"

Laughing, Lea said, "No, I don't think the Doc had that one, but I'll admit it sounds pretty good."

"Which one, then?" Gavin asked, stretching his tight shoulders.

"It was about a future society that could look into the past, and then they went back in time to the days of Christopher Columbus. What was the name of that one?"

Gavin was bent over now, stretching his back. He stood up abruptly, with his mouth open.

"That may be one of my favorite books of all time. It's called *Pastwatch*."

"Yep, that's the one!" Lea said with a smile. Her hair was back in a ponytail with a few errant locks gracing her forehead. She was wearing a homemade yellow sundress with a blue belt. Her beauty made him lightheaded.

He walked toward her and took her in his arms. She looked up expectantly.

Gavin leaned in to kiss her, and she pulled away with a twinkle in her eye.

"That's not how it works anymore, buddy. I've heard about what it was like in the old days, with everybody watching porn and sleeping with a bunch of different people, but that's not how things are now."

"So how does it work now?" Gavin asked flirtatiously.

"You figure it out, prepper man," she said with a wink.

"I'm not a prepper anymore, remember?" He winked back.

The next morning was drizzly and chilly, a typical fall day in Virginia. Gavin decided to teach Ann and Lea to make his special marinara sauce since they had a surfeit of tomatoes. The hardy heirloom breeds that had survived could produce well into fall. Ann's garden had many of the same breeds that Gavin knew and loved, like Yellow Pear, Roma, and San Marzano. As he explained the process to Ann, Lea interjected: "How is this different than just plain old spaghetti sauce?"

"Marinara is tangier and sweeter. You do the process differently and it has some red wine and sugar in it to sweeten it up. The composition of herbs and spices is also different. I always put in some freshly chopped basil at the very end; it adds that final bit of sweetness you need."

Obviously enjoying playing devil's advocate, Lea said, "We don't have any sugar, only honey."

Gavin grinned and held up an object in his hand.

"Oh boy, a prepper gadget!" Lea exclaimed, snatching it from his hand. "Oh wow Ann, look at all these spices!"

Gavin had a camper's spice wheel with dried herbs, salt, and of course, two wheels full of sugar. He still had a sweet tooth after all these years and paid dearly in trade for the delicious substance. He laughed and said, "See? Not so crazy after all!"

"Did you learn how to make that sauce in Italy?" Lea asked as she tasted the sugar. Her eyes widened with the taste.

"Actually, no," Gavin said. "My mom, Stella, is Italian and she taught me when I was a kid."

"You don't look Italian," Ann said, turning back to look at him.

"Technically she isn't my real mom, she's my stepmother. But I think of her as my mother now. When I was very young, my parents split up and my father met Stella and remarried. She and I have been really close ever since."

"A lot of times you hear kids don't get along with their step parents," Ann said. "Stella must be a great lady; I wish I could meet her."

"Stella and I liked each other from the start," Gavin said. "I remember the first time we met; I was five years old. We went to a Chinese restaurant, and I remember that my dad had a new woman with him, and she was beautiful. I was really nervous until she started making funny faces at me from across the table. We clowned around all through that first dinner, and we got closer as time went on. We had some tough times together when I was really young, too, so that brought us closer."

"What kind of tough times?" Lea asked. Since she had already opened up to him about her marriage and the grief from her husband's death, he felt he owed it to her to do the same.

"When my dad got remarried, I was still living with my biological mother," Gavin said. She's not a mean person, but she wasn't emotionally stable. I could sense that even when I was really young. I could do the same thing on two consecutive days and get a completely different reaction both times. I guess the shrinks would have called her 'bipolar' or something like that, but as a very young kid, all I knew was that I really liked being with my dad and Stella, and I was full of anxiety when I would go back to my real mom. Because of that, eventually there was a big court battle over who I would live with."

Gavin checked the pot and stirred the sauce's base, and then walked over to help Lea chop the tomatoes. She looked at him. "So is Stella still alive? And what do you mean there was a court battle? Your parents fought over you?"

"Yep, Stella is alive and well, living at Millwood and looking as beautiful and classy as ever."

"Millwood?" Ann asked. "Is that the name of your farm?"

"Yep," Gavin said. "And Stella runs Millwood with an iron fist.

She controls the finances and the cooking, and leaves everything else to my dad, my brother, and me." Gavin chuckled. "She's a very strong woman but she secretly has a soft side, too. And yes, there was actually a battle in the courts over who would get to have custody of me. I was the one who started it." Gavin continued to chop tomatoes and would flirtatiously bump Lea with his elbow once in a while. She smiled at him, and his heart melted.

"I was nine years old and still living with my biological mom, and she was getting more and more unstable. The only good thing about my life at that time was the fact that I got to spend every summer with Dad and Stella at Millwood. I had such a great time there, riding horses and taking walks, just generally being a farm kid. As I was leaving at the end of one summer, I looked back from the rear window of the car and started crying my eyes out. I wasn't a particularly emotional child, so Dad and Stella pulled the car over and asked what was wrong. Through my tears, I told them that I wanted to live with them and not go back to my mom.

"Little did I know what I was setting into motion. In those days, everything was so much more complicated, and for the next year of my life, there were whole days spent in court and shrink's offices. I got to know the first names of social workers and lawyers. My mom, who I still had to live with, was more impossible to deal with each day, and toward the end of the year, she started threatening suicide. She would berate me every night about changing my decision, using guilt and every other manipulative tool in her arsenal. I was a nine-year-old kid and I had to live alone with this woman. My brother was so much older than me that he was already in college at that point and couldn't help me. That was a hard time.

"Through it all, Dad and Stella tried so hard, especially Stella, who fought for me with the fierceness of a banshee. They saw me as much as they could, but the courts didn't allow much time. Whenever anyone asked me, whether it be a lawyer, judge, shrink or social worker, I would tell them forcefully that I wanted to live with Bob and Stella and not my mom. I told them so many times for so long, and still nothing happened. A year of the fighting had gone by, and I came to realize that not a single one of them cared. They were just cogs in the machine, hardly real human beings at all.

"It all finally ended when my mom dropped me off at a new

boyfriend's house for the weekend and left town. This guy was a real douchebag and he sat me down and told me that I had to stop this craziness, and that my mom loved me very much. He said that she had gone out of town to get away from the stress and that if I didn't change my mind, she would kill herself over the weekend. Of course, I changed my mind and said I would stay."

Lea was looking at him with pity and compassion in her eyes, and he wanted to tell her that the pity, at least, was misplaced. Sometimes, adversity can build character.

"Don't worry, Pocahontas, I turned out great! Maybe a little... craaaazy though." He grinned and made the same twirling motion on his forehead she had done a few days before.

Lea smiled back and said, "So how did you end up with Stella and your dad, then?"

"It was the fact that, out of all the assholes involved, there was one good guy. I called Stella and Dad the Monday after that weekend and told them in a dead voice that I had changed my mind and didn't want to live with them after all. Stella knew something was up, and they both dropped everything and got on a plane. Before the school day was out, Stella and my dad had picked me up in a rental car. Basically, what they had done was kidnapping. They took me straight to the office of one of the many shrinks I had seen, the only one who we all thought was somewhat of a human being. They left me alone in his office and I broke down and told him everything.

"You've got to hand it to this guy. Even though he was a shrink, which I considered to be somewhat of a bullshit profession, he saved my life. He flipped out and started making phone calls. He called all of the other assholes and threatened them, cajoled them, and basically forced the machine to spit me back out. After that day, I went to live at Millwood farm, and it's been my home ever since. My life wasn't perfect after that, and I was still a messed up kid, but I never for one second regretted the choice I made. And to this day, I'd take a bullet for Stella. I wasn't her blood and she didn't have to, but she's been the greatest mother in the world to me; she *chose* to love me and take care of me. That has made a big difference in my life ever since." Gavin choked up saying that last part, and he was quiet for a while.

Lea stopped processing the tomatoes and took his hand. "Thanks for telling me that," she said. "I think it's really sweet how you feel about Stella."

Gavin went back to chopping and for the rest of the day they talked of inconsequential things. He had never told anyone that whole story before. He knew he was madly in love with this woman. She was giving him all the right signs and he only needed to figure out what to do with them.

Chapter 13

August 2005 – Hurricane Katrina hits the Gulf Coast. For the first time in recent memory, Americans are reminded that their government isn't omnipotent. We can only fool Mother Nature for so long, and when she strikes back, the results can be disastrous. New Orleans is below sea level and when the levees fail, it is a catastrophic disaster. Many of the poorer areas that are destroyed lack the resources to rebuild.

On the sixth day of his stay, Gavin was sitting on the Doc's porch, taking a break from another day of canning. As he absentmindedly stroked Shiver in his lap, it dawned on him. He finally understood what he had to do.

He got up from his chair and walked back inside. Lea and Ann both looked at him expectantly, and he said, "Ann, I would like you and your family's permission to formally court Lea. As you know, I have to leave soon. I'd like to invite Lea to visit my farm in Scotville with a chaperone within the next month, and the month after that I'll come back here to visit. We'll keep doing that until we either decide to break it off or to get married." He could see Lea's eyes widen at that, and he looked straight at her.

"Lea, you obviously have the final word in this. I just want to say that I've really enjoyed spending this time with you and you're a beautiful, incredible woman. I hope you and your family will consider it."

Before anyone could reply, he walked away, strolling down the driveway toward their little stand of fruit trees. He guessed that he was giving them time to discuss it. His heart pounded. *What the hell am I doing?* He thought to himself. *Was that even the right way to approach it?*

He'd taken a chance at interpreting the situation. Years ago, if he had done something like that, he probably would have been looked at like a weirdo or religious fundamentalist. But for some reason, this just felt right. He finally understood why Lea hadn't been willing to kiss him; he hadn't made his intentions clear. So he had just gone for it. He lay down under an apple tree and tried to nap. He'd been there for less than an hour when he heard Lea approach.

She stood there smiling, and Gavin got to his feet slowly, feeling a bit awkward. He looked around while trying not to be too obvious about it, trying to see if there were any family members around. He saw no one.

"I said I would come and get you and tell you the news, so we only have a minute." Lea walked over and looked up at him, and before Gavin knew it she was in his arms. He kissed her and it was like he had never really, truly, kissed a woman before. He was awkward about it and so was she, but it was incredible. The kiss must have lasted a couple of minutes, but to Gavin it felt like less than a second. As they broke away, he could sense that she had also enjoyed it. He knew not to push his luck, so he threw his arm around her shoulder, and they began walking slowly back to the house. That single kiss was more erotic than anything from the internet porn he had ever watched in the old days.

"So I'll take that as a yes, then?" Gavin asked teasingly.

"Well, there was some resistance because of the age difference, but frankly I think that they were just happy to see me with anyone. I'm a bit choosy, you know," she said as she bumped him with her hip.

"They're right; I'm a lot older than you. I couldn't fight the thunderbolt, though!" He gave her a sideways grin and she smiled back, her eyes twinkling. "I do wonder though; you're beautiful and smart and spunky. You could have had any man you wanted. Why pick an old man like me?" Gavin asked.

"Spunky?" Lea asked incredulously. "I hate that word, what does that even mean? It sounds like I'm a baby chipmunk or something. Is that what you think of me, Gavin? Am I a baby chipmunk?"

Gavin's mouth dropped open until he saw the twinkle in her eye. He began to laugh, and rolled his eyes.

"Oh man, is this what I'm going to have to deal with?" Gavin asked, his eyes crinkled with laughter.

"You know it, buster!" Lea said. "But seriously, you're not *that* old. Not too old for some things, I hope!" Her joke quickened his blood. She stopped walking and looked at him.

"When I was married to Danny, I realized that I wanted more out of my life than to just survive. All we cared about was making it through the next season and defending what we had, and it seemed like we forgot why we were alive in the first place. Like I told you, my husband wouldn't think about anything other than that. That isn't even unusual; most people are like that now. It just wasn't how I wanted to spend my time on earth."

She reached up and stroked his beard, and she hugged him and nestled her head against his chest.

"I'd resigned myself to doing my work and nothing else. I had dreams I knew could never come true, but overall, I'm very lucky to have a great life. I do things that are needed, and things that I love. I have a great family. But after my marriage to Danny, I promised myself I would never again settle for someone who didn't understand and respect me." She kissed him on the cheek.

"And then one day, I heard that some strange guy had gotten himself shot and made it to Doc's doorstep, and that he had a peculiar kind of dog with him. The story I heard was that he had traveled more than a hundred miles to find it and gotten injured in the process, all because he liked that kind of dog and wanted to breed it."

Gavin laughed and said, "Well, jeez, when you say it like that it really sounds like I *am* crazy!"

"But don't you get it?" Lea exclaimed. "You're doing more than just trying to survive. You are trying to do something new, or to bring back something old, anyway. That was different than anything I had ever heard, so I had to see you for myself. And when I met you, you turned out to be handsome, charming, interesting, and sort of funny, too, so the rest is history."

"*Sort of* funny?" Gavin asked incredulously.

She smiled and kissed him again, and they walked back to the house.

Chapter 14

February 2008 - The average sales price of new homes sold in the U.S. drops significantly for the first time since the 1960s, as the housing bubble finally bursts. Uncle Sam had wanted everyone to own a home, even those who couldn't afford them. As the housing bubble got bigger, people started using their homes to over-leverage themselves, borrowing 120% of the home's value or more. Banks are blamed for lending the money and the government for encouraging it. Increased unemployment causes foreclosures to accelerate.

The night after Gavin and Lea's engagement, a few family members came by to celebrate. One uncle brought a bottle of pear brandy and another neighbor brought over a side of ribs from a hog he had just butchered. The crisp fall air still had a way of making people want to gather and celebrate, and soon there were twenty or thirty people and a bonfire in Doc's backyard. The party was a joyous occasion and old Ann presided like the Grand Dame that she was. Gavin eased into a comfortable manner with Lea. While he wasn't glued to her side, he made sure that every once in a while he joined in with her discussions. It was clear that she loved being with her friends, talking about books and telling stories about hunting and foraging in the wilderness.

He found himself possessively touching the small of her back when he asked her if he could bring her anything, or when he made a little joke or teased her. It seemed that he was being fairly well accepted. As the party went on, a guy pulled out a guitar and started playing. Gavin noticed that he was pretty good. In fact, the guy was *really* good, the best Gavin had heard in years. He had a decent voice, but his guitar playing was excellent. After about an hour, he took a break, Gavin approached him. "Mind if I play a couple?"

The guitar player was a young redheaded man who introduced himself as Scott, and Gavin could see that he was cool. In fact, his eyes were bright red and he looked high as hell. Gavin made a mental note to seek him out for a smoke later in the evening. Scott handed the guitar over and said, "Play on, man!"

As Gavin took the guitar over to the chair, he launched into 'Dust in the Wind.' His voice was pretty good, and his guitar playing was passable. He got some nice looks from Lea, who hadn't known he could play. As he finished the first song and got some polite applause, he spied Ann and yelled over at her, "Hey Ann, remember this one?" He started playing 'Shady Grove,' giving it a fast little rhythm:

Peaches in the summertime, apples in the fall,
If I can't find the girl I love, I don't want none at all
Shady Grove, my little love, Shady Grove I know
Shady Grove, My little love, going down to Shady Grove
Some come here to fiddle and dance, some come here to tarry,
Some come here to fiddle and dance, I come here to marry
Shady Grove, my little love, Shady Grove I know
Shady Grove, My little love, going down to Shady Grove

Ann started dancing a little jig, and toward the end of the song, she started shaking her ass towards the crowd, eliciting hoots and hollers from everyone. As he wound the song down, he asked Ann if she had any requests.

"Something we can dance to!" she shouted.

Gavin yelled, "Scott! We need you!" As Scott came over smiling, Gavin asked if he had another guitar. It turned out that Doc played a little bit and had one in the house. Gavin and Scott practiced for a minute and then launched into a blues medley of 'Hands to Yourself' and 'Johnny B Goode,' with Gavin on rhythm and Scott on lead. The whole party was on their feet dancing. Knowing that they shouldn't overdo it, he and Scott did a couple more and then brought things back down, finishing with a hilariously melodramatic 'Purple Rain' that had the whole group loudly singing along. He gave his guitar back to Doc, patted Scott on the back, and went to find more of the pear brandy. He found it in a circle with Lea and a couple of middle-aged women. When they quieted as he approached, he figured that they must have been talking about him. He hoped it was all good.

"Can I have a swig of that?" For some reason, the exhilaration of playing music always made Gavin want to drink, which he didn't do often. On most days, he would rather smoke. Lea handed him the bottle, and she had a gleam in her eye that he hadn't seen before. The two other ladies found a reason to wander off, and he sat down next to her.

"You're full of surprises today," she said. He felt her hand on him, rubbing his knee through the worn denim of his jeans, and the hair on the back of his neck stood up. Lea was incredible to him. Before long, other people wandered over and the little moment ended. He thoroughly enjoyed the rest of the night. By that time, he and Lea were inseparable and the people at the party sensed the glow around them and gravitated towards it. As the evening ended, he sat with Scott and Lea and passed around a joint of Scott's Northern Lights, which was pretty good, like it always was. As Gavin took his first hit, he looked over at Lea, worried at her reaction.

"Well, look at my bad boy rock star!" She smiled at him. "I don't really like pot myself, it just makes me tired. But it doesn't bother me if you smoke. Scott is always smoking, anyway, so I'm used to it. Isn't that right, pothead?" she called over, smiling, as she teased her cousin.

Scott put on an exaggerated stoner impression. "Whaaat? Oh, man, what's going on?"

Gavin laughed and joined in. "Oh maaaan, I can feel the oneness, brother. Whoa, look at your *hands*, man." Lea smiled and rolled her eyes at the two men. As the night ended and everyone said their goodbyes, Gavin thought that he wanted to stay there forever.

These people hadn't survived quite as well as his family on the farm had, judging by the dirty hair, slim figures and ragged clothing of the party attendees, but they had maintained a sense of community that Gavin's family hadn't quite achieved with their neighbors. When the Crumble began to accelerate, there had been great unrest. The worst time had been when the electrical grid finally failed in 2027, and a migration started from Washington, D.C. Hordes of refugees flooded south and west of the city, picking clean all of the homes and communities that were close to the highways. Gavin's family had survived by putting large berms around their farm, which were still there to this day, and blocking off the end of their road with burned out cars. That was a period of time that Gavin didn't like to think about. There were lots of raiders and refugee groups that had to be dealt with, and he lost close friends because of it. He had also killed more people than he would have liked.

That difficult period had brought him and his family closer, but it had also made them more insular. They managed to provide for themselves quite well, with various types of poultry and livestock, and Gavin's garden was second to none. While they had struggled with staple crops in the first couple of years, the trial by fire had eventually made them good crop farmers as well. They traded when they needed to, but otherwise didn't mingle much with their neighbors. Gavin had always thought that that was the safest way to be, but his experience with Lea's community had made him question that assumption.

Gavin woke the next morning with his head in a fog and his stomach still pleasantly full, even after a night's sleep. He knew that he couldn't dawdle any longer. His injuries were almost fully healed, and he didn't even want to think about the medical bill he had racked up. While he had been busy healing, courting Lea, and playing music with Scott, his brother and the rest of his family would be worried sick about him, and Gavin knew that Aidan would probably be slightly pissed off, as well. He'd been gone during harvest time, and he had managed to injure himself to boot. Gavin didn't regret it though. He had gotten what he came for, and now maybe he had found a wife as well. The trip had definitely been worth it. He only hoped his family would agree.

He got ready quickly, and approached Doc first. He was holding his bag of silver, and Doc waved his money away as soon as he saw it. "You don't think you're getting off that easy, do you? You owe us pick of the litter. That's all there is to it!"

Doc Ball wouldn't hear of anything else. When Gavin asked what happened if Shiver couldn't conceive, the Doc said, "We'll cross that bridge when we come to it. I know you're good for it, and I assume we'll be seeing you soon?" Judging by the twinkle in his eye, he expected Gavin's courting of Lea to go well.

Gavin assured him that it would, and saying his goodbyes to Doc, he loaded up his horse as Lea stood by his side, holding Shiver for him in a special sack Ann had sewn. They discussed when her visit would be and made pleasantries as she absently brushed dirt from his worn duster and straightened his vest. She tried to put on a stoic exterior, but Gavin could see she was holding back tears. He assured her, saying, "It's just a month away, and you're going to love the farm. We have the best food, and wait until you meet BoBo, you'll love him. If he and Shiver get along, maybe we'll have two marriages!"

He kept her laughing, and after a long kiss, Gavin reluctantly got on the mare. He took Shiver from Lea and started down the road toward home. He looked back several times. She was achingly beautiful to him.

In the old days I'd have been texting her already, he thought as he hurried home. He hoped to make it back in two more days. The territory was getting more familiar, making his progress faster.

Chapter 15

The last leg was mercifully short, as Gavin had hoped. He passed the time daydreaming and thinking about Lea. He could afford to be less alert now that he was closer to his home turf. He passed acquaintances on the way, waving at them as they went about their chores, but thankfully none came close enough to engage in conversation. That would only have slowed him down.

As he approached the front gates of the farm, Gavin again reflected on the fact that it had been several years since he had been away from Millwood for this long. He saw it with new eyes on his return. The pond was on his right as he entered the driveway, filled with ducks and a few wild geese. Cattle filled the field on his left; it looked like Aidan had just rotated them out of the back field. The place looked pretty good. The livestock kept the grasses manageable, although it didn't have that nice, trim look that Gavin had liked so much back in the old days. Mike, his oldest and favorite nephew, saw him first and ran over, embracing Gavin with a loving hug when he got off the mare.

"We missed you! Dad said you wouldn't let us down, and that he was sure that you were coming back. Everybody got really worried, though." Mike's excitement shone through in his voice. He was a handsome kid, already Gavin's height at just sixteen, with short, black hair and soulful eyes.

Gavin pondered this, gaining some respect for his older brother. Aidan had told him several times before he left what a fool's errand this was, and that he was going to get himself killed. But he'd backed him up when it counted.

"I have something for you, buddy." Gavin untied the sack and gently grabbed Shiver. She was totally in love with him now and she tried to lie on her back in the nook of his arm, like she had often done during the last leg of the trip. She was still so light, not quite skin and bones anymore, but still needing to put on more weight. He handed her to Mike, who was glowing.

"I can't believe you actually found one! How did you get her so trimmed and clean on the road?"

Laughing, Gavin started to head up the driveway. "That's a long story, and I have some big news, too." Gavin let Mike lead the mare, and he managed to keep carrying Shiver, too. Mike's mother had left the family when he was young and when Aidan moved them to Millwood, Mike had gravitated to Stella as a mother figure. He also looked up to Gavin, who played the part of the cool uncle to the hilt.

Like all teenage boys, Mike had the characteristic obsession with girls, but Gavin had noticed an iron core in him that he hadn't remembered seeing in young people before the Crumble. Gavin, himself, surely hadn't had it. Mike was integral to the farm and he knew it. He had his chores, his schooling, and he had started raising rabbits as his own special project, providing a different and easy-to-produce meat for the families on the farm. As he led the mare to the Big House, he strutted a little, like Gavin was a special prize he had found. *He's a good kid. He deserves to strut a little*, Gavin thought.

As they approached the Big House, he saw that Xavier and his brother, JB, had been working on one of the chicken coops and were coming over. Xavier and JB were Jacksons. The Jacksons and the Colliers had known each other for a long time, and got along well. In the 1980s, the Colliers had hired Coretta Jackson to help with the house and the pets. As time went by, Coretta had become like part of the family, bonding with young Gavin. After a few years, Bob and Stella bought a modular home for Coretta and her husband and had it placed in the back of the farm. They placed it in a small hillock near a grove of pines, with the porch facing out toward a small pond. Gavin remembered that Coretta cried that day; the new house was like a dream to her. She had six kids who were grown, and from time-to-time, different ones would come to stay and work on the farm for a while. As Gavin and Aidan grew up, they became close to other members of the extended Jackson family, and Gavin was always Coretta's favorite. Before she died many years later, she asked that at her funeral, Gavin and Aidan's names be listed when they read the names of her own children. After the funeral, the Collier family had given the house to Coretta's husband Earl, and as the years passed, several of the Jackson children and grandchildren came to work at Millwood, too. When the Crumble came, they proved invaluable. As Gavin grew up, he and Xavier, Coretta's grandson, developed a close friendship, and Xavier had managed Millwood since before the

Crumble.

"Xavier! JB! What's up, fellas? Come on back to the house, so I can fill in everyone at the same time," Gavin said. Both brothers had been big guys before the Crumble and had managed to keep on more weight than many people, mostly in muscle. Both were in their early forties now. Both tall, black men with distinctive dreadlocks and tattoos, the brothers were well-known and popular in the area, being more social than the Colliers.

"Hey, boss," Xavier said, clasping Gavin's outstretched hand and hugging him. "Alright, now we can get back to doing the *real* shit." When Xavier said 'alright,' it sounded more like 'iight'. In fact, when he and Gavin used to text each other in the old days, he spelled the word that way, too, teasing Gavin, who was a stickler for grammar. Gavin was happy to see his old friend.

"Yeah, buddy! I have some stories to tell, too. I did the Outlaws proud, know what I mean?" Gavin slapped his friend on the back.

It had become a parade now, with JB and Xavier bringing up the rear, Mike holding Shiver, and Gavin leading the way. BoBo was sunning himself on one of the stone walls, and immediately ran up to Gavin, panting, to say hello. Once he noticed Shiver, though, all bets were off. He followed Mike right on his heels, jumping up to try to get a closer look at her. BoBo was fifteen and still had great energy. Constant exercise and lots of venison had kept him very healthy, and with their small size, Bichons generally had a decent life expectancy. Mike was sent to get Aidan, who was working in the back garden.

Bob and Stella, now in their late seventies, but still in good condition, were sitting out on the stone deck in the back of the big house. Renee was with them, helping Stella with the family books. Renee was also a Jackson, and a younger cousin of Xavier's. She was in her early twenties with light skin, dark hair, thick eyebrows and inquisitive eyes. Renee and Stella had grown close during her schooling, as Renee had shown great promise in business and accounting. She now ran their farmer's market booth and helped Stella with the farm business in general. Renee also had a strong mothering instinct, and fluttered around Stella and Bob, making sure they got their rest and ate enough. In fact, a bottle of wine, a plate of biscuits, and a jar of honey sat on a table next to them.

Stella and Bob were a handsome picture. Stella was decked out in a lovely black and white dress and wore a simple gold necklace, and Bob had on his traditional corduroys, button up shirt and hunting vest. All three smiled broadly as he walked up. Gavin had missed his parents greatly, and after giving everyone big hugs, he waited for everyone to arrive so his parents wouldn't have to get up. Mike had gone to find his father and Gavin could see the two of them approaching, Aidan now holding Shiver.

"Little brother, I knew you would make it! And this little creature Mike brought me, what am I supposed to do with this?" Aidan had a shit eating grin on his face and his eyes had that glassy look he got when he felt emotional. He gave Gavin a bear hug and whispered, "Missed you, little brother." Ten years older than Gavin, Aidan was always the solid one, physically, as well as emotionally. He was close to six feet tall, with a thick shock of straight black hair, dark eyes, and an aquiline nose. He was clean shaven, having learned to use a straight razor because he didn't like facial hair. Aidan had the sturdy physique of a farmer, although he hadn't always been that way. When he had finally realized that Gavin was right about the Crumble coming, he had moved Mike and his younger siblings from New York to the farm, and Gavin had teased him at first about his physique. Aidan had been a successful real estate attorney in Manhattan, which hadn't allowed much time for exercise. Years of work outside had hardened him up nicely since then, however.

Gavin laughed, feeling emotional, too. "I missed you, too, Cashmere." Gavin's nickname for his brother came from those early days, when Aidan would try to hunt in his cashmere overcoat before finally realizing that what was fit for the streets of New York might not necessarily work for Virginia farmland. Gavin's heart soared as he looked at the group that had assembled. These were his people. This was his family. He responded to his brother, saying, "Well, I'm sure she'll be useful for something. If she can't breed with BoBo we'll use her to mop the floor."

Everyone laughed. They all sat down and Gavin did as well, relishing the chance to tell a new story. Gavin hadn't had the chance to practice this one yet, but he knew it would be good. Everybody on the whole farm, except the people who were on sentry duty, had come out, and it was getting towards late afternoon, so most of the work was finished for the day. Anything else could wait for a good story or news.

New stories like this were now one of the best forms of entertainment.

He started in a funny vein, telling how he had to get used to wiping his ass in the woods and how he was glad he hadn't encountered any poison ivy. He quickly got to the part about how he had to stalk Shiver for so long, getting more laughs as he described her bedraggled appearance and her first snaps and snarls toward him. As Shiver was being passed around to happy murmurs, followed by a very attentive BoBo, Aidan said, "Well, she is a sweetie pie with everyone else, what does that tell us about you, brother?"

Gavin's father spoke up. "We knew you would eventually go back to your first career, Gavin." Bob smiled and looked at the group. "I don't know how many of you know this, but Gavin started selling Bichon puppies at twelve years old. We were well known breeders in the area, and every year or so, we would have a litter. Gavin raised the puppies and handled putting all the ads in the paper, so we gave him a cut of the proceeds. Back then, Stella and I would travel for business sometimes, and Gavin would be at the Big House on weekends with Coretta taking care of him. People would come by to see the puppies we had for sale. Gavin, what was the story?"

Smiling, Gavin gestured at his father. "You tell it, Dad."

"One time, Stella and I were out of town and Coretta had gone to do errands. Gavin was alone at the house and had set up a viewing of a puppy. Can you imagine you are going to buy this expensive puppy with fancy papers, and you show up and there is nobody but a twelve year old kid? You should have heard him talk at that age, though. He could sell ice cubes to an Eskimo. We have no idea what happened to those slick, street talking ways as he grew up," Bob said, smiling and winking at Gavin.

"So this couple shows up and Gavin gives them the whole spiel, and of course they love the puppy. They ask when his parents are going to get home, and he says, 'Not for a while. You can take the puppy now, or you can wait. But you should know; another buyer is coming this afternoon.'" Bob laughed along with the group. "Of course, they ended up buying the puppy. So that's why he went to so much trouble for this dog; it was the first business venture that ever made him any money!" To general laughter and applause, Bob bowed to the group and sat back down next to Stella.

Laughing at the memory, Gavin continued on with his story.

He realized on the spot that he couldn't tell them how he had deliberately gone after the remaining raiders after the first attack in the woods. He was embarrassed by the fact that he had taken such a big risk for no immediate, pressing reason, and he didn't want to relive the killings he had done. So he spun the tale, saying that there were only two of them and that they had surprised him. He reshaped the event pretty well, although he saw in Aidan's eyes that he noticed something was amiss with that part of the story. It didn't seem like anyone else did, though. While they hated raiders, they weren't surprised by them, and had dealt with many different groups over the previous years.

When he said he had been wounded, everyone wanted to see the scars, which were still healing. After this had diverted their attention for a few minutes, he got back on track, telling of how he managed to get to Ramsey and Doctor Ball. When he reached the part about meeting Lea, the hoots and hollers came so loud that he turned red in the face. He yelled at everyone. "Shut up, you all will jinx me! She's coming here soon and you all had better not screw this up for me!"

The group threw things at him and everyone laughed and had a good time at his expense. While they ribbed him, he could tell that they were all happy for him and excited to meet her. Bob and Stella already doted on Mike and his younger siblings, and wanted more grandkids. Their lives were very different now. They had lived all of their formative years in the old days, and many of their generation had trouble accepting things when the Crumble came.

Gavin's parents, however, had adapted remarkably well. They enjoyed the authentic fulfillment that this new life gave them, and they occupied themselves with cooking, gardening, teaching, and handling the family library. They were the family resource for all wisdom. Bob and Stella spent lots of time with Mike and the other kids on the farm. They were the best teachers around, having lived as long as they had. The kids liked doing classes with them much more than Gavin and Aidan's 'labs,' which, while very instructive, were also hard work. Most of the labs involved the kids digging holes for fencing or doing some other hard labor, while Aidan and Gavin explained such things as when to rotate livestock, which cover crops to plant and when, and how to turn the compost pile.

Having finished his story, Gavin went silent. Aidan asked,

"When do we get to meet her?"

"A month from now. I want to get the pool house up to speed pretty quickly, and set it up with a bed and furnishings. All the stuff stored in there can go to my room in the Big House." Another thing that Gavin had done as the Crumble progressed was set up solar-powered hot water heaters, as well as a solar system to run the well. This proved to be a great idea when the electrical grid finally failed. There was enough energy left over to allow them to run a refrigerator and freezer in the Big House. The pool house had water and Gavin had wanted to move into it for quite some time, but he never had a pressing reason to make the move until now.

"Cool, I knew you were thinking about that anyway." Aidan was silent for a moment. "So, what was it like out there, just in general?"

The whole group erupted in laughter, with Bob and Stella leading the way, pounding on the table.

Gavin grinned from ear to ear. "Let me guess. You guys took bets on how long it would take Aidan to ask me for news?"

Stella stood, shushing everyone. Xavier, meanwhile, was reaching into his back pocket, sheepishly giving a silver coin to his brother.

"Now, we tease Aidan about being a news junkie, even nowadays with no computers or cell phones in sight," Stella said. "Even the few people who still have working devices can never get a signal. But he's right; we need to know what's going on in the outside world to keep us safe." Stella patted Aidan on the arm, and he gratefully put his arm around her. He made a funny face at Gavin, but he wasn't really mad. They all enjoyed playfully teasing each other.

"I didn't see many people while I was on the way to Eastchester. I kept to back roads and stayed away from towns, and I kept my guns handy. I probably only passed twenty souls the whole way, mostly at a distance. The landscape is trashed; there is crap everywhere. I saw lots of burned-out cars and buildings, and even piles of bones in some places. But that was only when I passed the old, big intersections. When I was deep in those unpaved back roads, there were still signs of life. There are lots of little farms, and lots of ingenious fencing arrangements. I saw one place where they had pushed around twenty cars into a big circle, and they were keeping livestock in there."

"Did you talk to many people?" Aidan asked.

"Besides the ones I killed, and the people I met in Ramsey, not really." Gavin sighed. "Everyone I saw was armed with a bow or a gun, and the people I passed didn't seem interested in making new friends. But according to what I saw, your estimates are about right. Over the last twenty years, if this trip was any indication, it seems we've lost more than two thirds of our population."

Aidan looked pensive for a moment. "God, that's sad. I hate to think of all those people... people we knew, people we did business with..."

"We can't dwell on that now, though," he continued, taking a deep breath. "That does tell us something new, however; that Ramsey is a going concern now. It sounds like they really have it together. I would have liked to ask the people in town what they've heard, especially the doctor. I did get some news from someone passing through Scotville who said there is still a functioning government in D.C., which isn't a surprise. When the lights went out, they concentrated all their efforts on the mid-sized cities and military bases."

"Good fucking riddance," Gavin spat. "Towards the end, we were better off without them. They had too much power, too many rules, and too many guns. Too many damn sociopaths working for them." Xavier and the Outlaws grunted their agreement.

Aidan smiled. "I'd be inclined to agree with you there. When the grid finally failed, there was an upside. No more bills. *No more taxes*. I figure they're still keeping D.C. out of pride, though, because there are a lot of other places that would make more sense as the capital now. Either way, nowadays D.C. might as well be on the moon, and just as dangerous to get there. And since I've also recently heard rumors about armies forming in the Deep South, I think a relationship with a more southern neighbor, like Ramsey, could be very promising. At the very least, we could set up a trading arrangement with them."

"Speaking of which," Gavin said, "I also passed a well-maintained little train depot. Someone had found one of those little seesaw carts and it looked like it was in use. One thing that still works is the train tracks."

Aidan's eyes blazed and he started to speak, but Stella shushed him. "He's tired, Aidan. Let him unpack and settle in." Stella paused and smiled. "Oh, and by the way…"

She walked over to a smug-looking Bob, and gave him two pieces of silver. She looked back at Aidan. "I bet that you'd ask him for the news within the first five minutes."

The crowd roared with laughter and Aidan grinned and turned red. Gavin hugged his brother again.

"See you at dinner, little brother," Aidan said as he walked over to laughingly cuff Xavier and Mike, who were still chuckling. Aidan and Xavier walked toward the back of the farm, evidently planning to get in a bit more work before dinner. Mike joined Gavin to help him unpack. The crowd of fifteen or so that had accumulated gradually dispersed, with everyone who hadn't said hello to Gavin doing so on their way back to various jobs on the farm.

After Gavin gave Shiver to his parents, he and Mike went back to unpack the mare, who would get a nice rest and some extra hay now that she was home. She had gotten her missing shoe replaced in Ramsey and was well taken care of there, so she made the last leg back to Millwood with ease.

Gavin led the mare to the front of the pool house and handed the reins over. Mike genuinely wanted to help, although from the gleam in his eyes, he wanted to see the loot too. He knew he would have to work for anything he got, but he was willing to do it. He was getting to the age where he was going to want his own gun. He probably wanted his own guitar, too, as he was becoming fairly good, but Gavin wasn't going to give him one of his. Not yet.

When Mike returned from putting the mare away, Gavin had him start emptying out the pool house while he unpacked the loot onto the grass and spread it out on a blanket. As Mike walked by carrying a box of Mason jars, he said, "Look, you have four pairs of boots; I thought you said there were only two of them."

"They must have attacked someone recently, because they had a pile of stuff already there. Now finish your work and then maybe I will let you look through this stuff." Gavin good naturedly cuffed Mike on the ear, who smiled and ducked away. The lie came easily to Gavin, as lying always had. That worried him sometimes. He had once seen a documentary about an experiment that showed the best liars also made the best natural leaders, which disturbed him a great deal more than the first because of the societal implications. That might be part of the reason why everyone was fond of looking to him for guidance, despite his older brother's strong personality and position. After the first couple of years following the Crumble, Gavin had shirked any leadership roles that came his way, deferring to his older brother on most decisions. They tended to agree on the major issues anyway.

Besides the boots, there were three pistols. The .38 that Andre had on him was probably only good for trade, and Santiago's pistol had been damaged in their battle, but the last pistol looked okay. It was a silver Taurus .22 revolver. Those types of guns lasted a long time, and a pistol of that size was a perfect first gun. It even looked to have been kept fairly clean. It was the gun he'd taken from the woman in the tree. He shuddered as the memory went through his mind.

There was some assorted junk, like the broken Swiss Army knife and some other broken and bent knives. This would all go to Xavier, who had a knack for reusing things, and loved knives and swords. Xavier always wore a sword on his back to use as a last resort during any battles. During the later years of the Crumble, their families had fought side-by-side many times to defend the farm, and even now that the violence had mostly subsided, they still had to fight every so often.

Gavin fully expected that the pieces of the Swiss Army knife would show up as new tools. The only other things of value were the holsters and a decent backpack. Gavin figured that Mike could have that stuff too. It was unfortunate that they hadn't had a rifle, but Gavin also knew that if Santiago had been armed with a decent rifle, he probably wouldn't have survived the first shot.

He left everything laid out and went to help Mike finish clearing out the pool house. All of their jars and canning implements were temporarily laid out on the lawn, and Gavin marveled at how many jars were needed to support a decent-sized group of people. There were jars of all types, mostly glass. While some plastic was still around, most of it had corroded and degraded in unpredictable ways. Gavin was glad that he'd had the foresight to get a few Tattler reusable canning lids, which made things a lot easier.

The work lasted until it was dark. They heard the dinner bell but ignored it, knowing that there would be plates left out for them. As they finished up, Gavin had Mike go over to the blanket and showed him the .22 and holster. The way that Mike's face shone almost made it worth the trouble it had taken to get it, and Gavin said, "Now don't shoot yourself in the foot. I have lots more work for you to do tomorrow. And we can both go shooting on Sunday afternoon; I need to re-sight my rifle, anyway."

After scarfing down a quick dinner with Mike, he went to bed in the pool house, and as he settled in to sleep, Gavin wondered why he hadn't moved into it earlier. He must have been waiting for Lea.

Chapter 16

The month-long wait went by painstakingly slowly, but Gavin worked like a madman to make the place as nice as he could, knowing that the work would also help pass the time. He mended fences, cleared brush, and made sure that his own projects looked the best they could. His chicken coops and turkey houses had never looked so good, and while they never really smelled bad because he allowed them to range on good-sized pasture, the wood chips he put down gave everything a fresh and rich odor. Now that autumn was setting in, chores were winding down anyway, and he could focus on cosmetics. Aidan was amazed at how much work Gavin was putting in, and told him so.

"You're normally no slouch when it comes to work, little brother, but this is amazing. This chick must be something special. I wish she would wait longer to come visit, maybe we could get even more work out of you!" Aidan had walked up while Gavin was fixing the wire on one of his chicken coops as BoBo stood nearby, studiously avoiding looking at the chickens.

Gavin laughed aloud, knowing it was true. Then he got serious. "Listen man, I didn't tell the real story to the group. The part about my fight with those raiders."

"I figured that," Aidan said. "Let me guess, it involves you doing something dumb?"

"Pretty much. Basically, I got surprised by a young guy trying to prove himself, and I killed him. I could have gone around and avoided the rest, but I attacked them instead. I killed three more the same night, which is how I got the wounds. From there, I managed to make it to Ramsey."

Aidan wasn't laughing now. "God damn it, man, you could have gotten yourself killed! We need you around here – and leaving for three weeks in September like that left me shorthanded! I love Shiver as much as everyone else does, but what's the point? Was the whole trip even worth it? People need working dogs now; I still don't even see how you think we're going to sell any of her pups, assuming BoBo can even do the job!" BoBo looked up at the mention of his name, walking over to stand at Gavin's side.

"I don't know, man, something just came over me. I knew that group might kill someone else and I was feeling angry from the first encounter. Maybe I wanted to prove I was as tough as you and Xavier. I don't know. Either way, I did survive and I'm here now. I know it seemed crazy for me to risk all that just to find Shiver, but I just had, and still have, a feeling people will want her pups. Besides, who knows? Maybe we're the last people in the whole state that even have any Bichons!" Gavin looked down at BoBo and then back up at his older brother.

"You know, you've been out here for all these years, and I don't think you have ever asked about this breed or what their story is," Gavin said.

Aidan smiled and rolled his eyes at his younger brother. "No, I haven't. But let me guess: You know all about it, and you're going to tell me."

"Of course I know!" Gavin put on a serious face and imitated a deep, professorial voice.

"Bichon Frises originated in the fourteenth century, and were originally bred by mixing standard Poodles and Water Spaniels, better known as Barbets."

Aidan laughed. "Barbets? Oh lord, that sounds fancy. And I knew they had at least some Poodle in them!"

Slightly offended and not enjoying being reminded of the connection, Gavin picked up BoBo and held him sitting up in the crook of his arm. BoBo liked to be held that way so he could see everything that was happening. Gavin also thought it made him feel human for a minute.

"They were originally used on ships for Portuguese and Italian sailors, and they love water, even to this day."

Aidan laughed again, reaching over and scratching BoBo behind the ear. "That's true; I've seen BoBo swimming in the pond a million times, and I know you get mad about it because you're the one who has to groom him. At least they were useful for a while though, right? Were they mousers on the ships or something?"

"Not really. Even then, these little guys just got by on their charm. The sailors loved them for their company. Isn't that right, handsome little man?" He made a kissing noise and BoBo licked him on the mouth, causing Gavin to sputter for a moment. Chuckling, he said, "Anyway, they eventually became the favorites of French and Spanish royalty. There are a bunch of Goya paintings with Bichons in them.

"The bottom line is that people wanted companion dogs way before the industrial revolution even started," Gavin said. "So why wouldn't they want them now? I was right about the Crumble, wasn't I?" He loved using this on his brother. Gavin had seen it coming first and started preparing, and Aidan had taken a few years to catch on. As the younger brother, it wasn't very often Gavin had a chance to play the wise sage.

"The Bichons are a nostalgic part of the old days to me," Gavin said. "I feel like sometimes you've done better in this new world than I have, even though I was the one who saw it coming first. It seems like I miss a lot more about those days than you do."

Aidan said, "Well, I have my kids to worry about; the life of a single dad isn't as glamorous as it's cracked up to be. Like I've told you so many times, it really does change things. I never really felt like I had the option to dwell on the things we've lost. When Janine left me, I knew my life would never be the same. Less than a year later, I'd moved back to the farm. That whole process really changed me, and Mike was old enough that it really affected him, too."

Gavin nodded at his brother. When Aidan had first brought Janine to meet the family, they had all liked her. She seemed to have a bright and energetic personality. It was only when she and Aidan had kids that her dark side began to emerge.

"I know what you mean," Gavin said. "You were fairly serious before, but that experience seemed to make you even more so. And with Mike, I know he seems so strong, but I think he misses her sometimes. Sometimes I think he feels responsible for some reason."

"I know Mike feels that way, but he was too young to understand what she was really like. And there's no reason for him to feel guilty. It obviously had nothing to do with him," Aidan said. "After she left, I realized that it was for the best. She was so concerned with appearances and possessions that I wonder if she ever really loved us at all. Sometimes, though, I still wonder where she is now."

"I'm sure she's fine," Gavin said. "She always had a way of coming out on top."

"Despite that, I think Mike is generally well-adjusted. Being able to grow up here made all the difference," Aidan said. "And you know he looks up to you. Besides, you were always the dreamer, anyway. These days, you just read your science fiction books and daydream about ordering pizza on a Friday night. You need to find a new dream now. And from the way you talk about Lea, I think you might have found it." He paused for a second, looking down at the pool, which had now been filled in to make the front garden.

"I remember it was right before Christmas in 2021 when I finally started to believe you about what was coming. I was in the supermarket, and there were several things on my list that the store either didn't have, or were so expensive that I didn't want them after all. I was already frazzled with Janine gone, and I turned on the car and noticed I was low on gas. I thought about how damn expensive it was going to be to fill up again. I drove out of there and went over some new potholes in the road, and somehow it just hit me. It was exactly like you said. 'A Crumble, not a collapse'." Aidan looked introspective for a moment, absentmindedly stroking behind BoBo's ears.

"Watching the news was a horror show," he continued. "Those smug, well-fed newscasters were so flippant when they described the slow decay of society, acting like it was all just a passing difficulty. It seemed like every day there was a story of riots, wars, or economic collapse somewhere in the world. The machines started breaking down, and they didn't always get fixed. Planes got lost and landed on the wrong runways, small pandemics started popping up, cruise ships caught fire, and glitches in the financial trading algorithms started screwing up the markets on an almost weekly basis. Storms and forest fires started getting worse and the damage from those didn't get fixed, either. Unemployment was through the roof all around the world. I finally understood what you'd been saying. The machine was becoming too big and complex to sustain itself, especially without the cheap energy to run it. That's why I agreed to come to the farm."

"And you never regretted it! So trust me on the dog, too, it's going to work out great."
Gavin slapped his brother on the back and went to wash up for dinner. He thought of those heady times when he had started to learn the truth himself. It had been exciting, stimulating, and above all, terrifying.

Gavin couldn't deny how helpful his brother had been, and he sometimes thought he wouldn't have survived without Aidan's help.

Gavin had taken the lead at Millwood at first because he knew so much more, but he had gradually acceded authority to his brother over time. He didn't have the patience for being the leader and administrator like Aidan did.

Gavin's 'awakening' had happened more swiftly than Aidan's. It started when he was still very young. He was just barely into high school on September 11th, and it affected him deeply. He began questioning the events surrounding that day, sensing something amiss about the official story. The attack on the Pentagon in particular confused him. If a plane had hit the Pentagon, where were the wings? Where was the fuselage? The most damning fact about 9/11, however, was that the resulting wars were so convenient. If the majority of the hijackers were from Saudi Arabia, then why did the U.S. attack Iraq? It seemed quite the coincidence that Iraq was one of the few countries in the world with a majority of their crude oil in still-untapped reserves.

After researching the subject, Gavin came to the conclusion that, while he would never know the full truth about what happened on that horrible day, he *had* discovered several incontrovertible facts that couldn't be disputed. The U.S. military industrial complex did, in fact, exist, and exerted significant power on the world stage. Whether or not they knew the attack was coming, they were more than ready to use it as a pretext to strengthen their power when it did occur.

Gavin discovered the existence of the elites and the control they had, and saw how they had hijacked the world's governments. The machine was putting on a puppet show every four years for the benefit of the masses, with two bought and sold candidates who mouthed a few platitudes. Any real differences in the platforms of the two parties were social issues designed to keep the electorate polarized into two easily controlled blocs.

At that point, Gavin purposefully went back to sleep. Ignorance was bliss. He couldn't take the knowledge anymore, and for the next few years he submerged himself in typical American narcissistic activities. His career was taking off and he enjoyed the money he earned, while borrowing even more. But he never forgot what he had learned and no matter where he lived, he always planted his garden every year, just in case. From then on, he always looked upon the 'official narrative' with suspicion

Gavin was still blissfully dreaming when the financial crisis of

2007 hit, and it took a near death experience in 2011 to wake him back up. After several months in the hospital and a serious surgery due to a stomach illness, the doctors told Gavin he was cured. His stomach didn't bother him again until the early 2020s, when the condition struck once more. He knew that if it ever came back again, this time there would be no hospital to go to.

As he was healing from his surgery, Gavin started wondering why someone as young as he was would get such a serious digestive condition. A friend of Gavin's suggested that junk food and processed meals could have contributed to the weakness of his system, allowing the illness to grow undetected. This led him to start research on processed foods and their effect on health. After reading Michael Pollan's *The Omnivore's Dilemma*, Gavin discovered the food movement. He devoured more than a hundred books about natural farming, the industrial food system, and the depletion of the world's fossil fuels, water, and other natural, non-renewable resources.

At one point, he read that in the Midwest in the 1940s, most farms had an average of six feet of black loam topsoil, and that many of those same areas were now down to just six *inches*. Industrialized farming was destroying the very soil itself, from which all life was based. At that point, Gavin's research into peak energy and the fragility of the world economic system intensified until he reached the conclusion that he would see much of industrial civilization crumble in his lifetime. There was no way around it. While he didn't know if the Crumble was in the plans of the elites or not, he knew their actions were helping to bring it about. Either way, he decided to survive, and be one of the people that kept the light of human freedom and knowledge alive during its darkest time.

Chapter 17

September 2008 – Lehman Brothers, the fourth largest investment bank in the U.S., files for Chapter 11 bankruptcy protection. Lehman's failure sends an already distressed financial market into a period of extreme volatility. The carnage and chaos that follows is a perfect storm of economic distress factors. Eventually, a $700 billion bailout package called the Troubled Asset Relief Program (TARP) is put into place, essentially shifting the downside risk from the large financial firms to the taxpayer.

October 2037
Millwood Farm

Gavin watched the hand-carved, wooden calendar as the one month mark approached. Now that mass-produced junk was no longer available, people had begun to return to the rich artisanal traditions of their ancestors. Gavin enjoyed carving in the winter, mostly making wood spirits and animals. His Santa Claus carvings were very popular around the holidays.

Looking closely and cleaning off his glasses, he saw that tomorrow would be a month from when he left Ramsey. He planned to go into Scotville the next day to wait for Lea and her chaperone. They'd agreed to meet there a month to the day from when he left. He felt his heart soar as he thought of being reunited with her.

This time, since he wasn't travelling far, he took one of Aidan's other horses, a big, strong gelding named Buck. On his trip to get Shiver, Aidan would have never let him take as good of a horse as Buck, thinking that if his brother didn't come back, at least he didn't have to lose a good horse, too. Gavin made great time on the ride to Scotville, letting Buck get some exercise.

Although he had planned on bringing Shiver as a fun gesture, at the last minute he decided to leave her at the farm. Shiver had been adopted by the kids at the farm, and he hadn't seen much of her except at night when she slept at the foot of his bed. BoBo and she now got along famously and she forgave him for being so aggressive at first. BoBo spent a lot of time with the kids as well, though he didn't like their incessant playing as much as Shiver did.

As he approached the town, he noticed that someone was coming out on the road towards him at quite a good clip. As he got closer, he saw that it was Pastor Dennis Hastert from the Episcopalian church in Scotville. He sped up, hoping that Dennis had another reason for riding so fast that had nothing to do with Lea's arrival.

"Gavin, thank God! I thought I was going to have to go all the way to your place! You know someone named Lea, right?"

"Yeah, she is my fiancé. What's going on?" Gavin was starting to panic, but the fact that Dennis knew her name meant that she had been able to talk to him. ·

"We have her in the church. She got attacked by someone out on Route 88 and she is hurt. It looks like she fell off her horse and got dragged. She came in on a big horse that had been shot a couple of times. We had to put it down. She asked for you first, and then she said that she lost her cousin at Gilbert's Crossing."

Dennis had barely finished his sentence when Gavin took off toward the church. Dennis was close behind, and as Gavin's thoughts raced, he was filled with gratitude that she had made it to the church. He couldn't fathom the alternative. While Gavin didn't know Dennis very well, he knew his reputation well enough to know he was solid. His congregation had made it through the Crumble as well as anyone could hope, and Aidan and his kids went to his services as often as they could, although Gavin rarely joined them. Dennis had the reputation as a rock in the community and this was proving to be true now.

They got to the church in no time, and as Gavin ran through the front door, he saw that Lea was sitting in a pew with her pack and bow in a heap next to her. She was calmly applying a poultice to a scrape on her leg, with tears streaming down her face.

Gavin's heart leapt into his throat, and as he went to her, he could see that none of her injuries appeared to be life threatening. She was scraped all to hell on the side of her face, her shoulder, and her knees. It was concentrated on one side of her body.

"Hey," he said, with tears in his eyes. "How are you feeling?"

She lit up when she saw him, and she quickly wiped her eyes. "Hey, stranger! I've been better, that's for sure." She struggled to get up and hug him, and he gently embraced her, knowing how much pain she had to be in, and how much it must hurt to be touched. He was moved that she wanted to hug him anyway. As she calmly and quickly recounted what had happened to her, he found his love and admiration for her grow even more.

"Scott and I had made pretty good time. It was our third day on the road. We were on Broad Rock Road and getting close to the exit for Scotville, and we just came up on this group. They were camped out right in the road and saw us coming. It looked like there were about ten or fifteen of them that I could see, with big guns and vehicles. They were stupid though, they had set up their ambush right by a clump of trees and a field below the road, down about a fifty foot drop. Scott and I could see a glimpse of another road at the other end of a field adjacent to Broad Rock, and, we kind of looked at each other and just knew what we had to do, no words exchanged." Lea stopped and took several deep breaths, calming herself as Gavin softly massaged the back of her neck.

"We immediately broke right and started towards the trees for cover," she continued. "That must have surprised them. The shots started pretty soon after we started galloping, but by then we were down the hill and in the trees. I saw one hit a tree by me, and I ducked down in the saddle. At this point, I couldn't see much, but I know Scott was still with me because I could hear his horse next to mine. I also heard some of them chasing behind us. I realized that, to merge with the road, we would have to turn and expose our sides to them for a couple hundred feet. As I turned, I tried to hang off the side while I rode, holding on for dear life. I could hear one of the bullets hit old Sally, and..."

She choked up. Gavin held her and stroked her hair. She obviously didn't care about the pain; she just wanted to feel safe. His thoughts raced. He felt responsible for all of this. He should have never let her come to see him; he should have gone back there and escorted her. They had sent her with Scott, for God's sake! He was a great kid and a good guitar player, but not exactly what Gavin would consider to be a seasoned traveler or bodyguard. He needed to fix this, and quickly.

As he held her, he asked, "When was the last time you saw Scott?"

Regaining her composure, she continued her tale. "When Sally got hit the first time, I lost my grip and started being dragged. That old horse saved my life; she just kept going on the road and finally stopped after about a half mile. The last I saw Scott was right around when Sally got hit. I managed to ride the last mile to town and I saw the church and just went straight towards it. Did they put Sally down? I couldn't believe she made it that far."

"Yeah, she was too far gone. I'm so sorry, Lea. Okay, sexy lady, you rest here, and let me go talk to Dennis and get a couple people together to go find Scott."

"Make sure you get my saddlebags," Lea said. "The rest of my healing stuff is in there. It looks like I'm going to need it for myself."

Lea paused for a moment, looking down. "I don't think Scott made it."

She looked up at Gavin with shimmering eyes and he embraced her again.

Gavin's mind was whirling with anger, grief, and shame. *I should have gone back to Ramsey to get her myself*, he thought wretchedly. He softly walked back out the door. Dennis was out in the front of the church with the dead horse.

"I have Mike Stanwell coming over with his Clydesdale to help pull this out of here. What do you think? It's the first I have heard of a group near us, and if she is talking about the spot I think she is, they are less than two miles away from Scotville."

Gavin tensed. This situation felt different than previous confrontations. When he'd fought before, there had been so much less to lose. He had Lea now, and the fact that she had been so battered and had suffered so much in his town, a place that he felt protected and safe in, made him angrier than he had ever been in his life.

Dennis said, "Let's go look for Scott, and we can at least check out who we are up against before we start getting a group together. We don't even know how many people they have yet."

Dennis and Gavin hadn't gotten more than a mile out of town when they found Scott's pierced and broken body.

Chapter 18

Two miles outside of Scotville, Virginia

Richard grimaced as he sipped the coffee from an MRE ration, and looked around before adding some brandy from his flask. He sipped again, liking it better this time. Before the Crumble, he'd enjoyed a nightly beer or two, but as the years progressed he came to depend on alcohol more and more, until he woke up one day as a full-blown drunk. *One of these days, I'm going to hole up somewhere for a week and kick this thing for good,* Richard thought. He'd been telling himself that for years, but he knew deep down that he needed the alcohol to dull the pangs of his conscience.

Richard's team had parked their vehicles in a box, right in the center of a large four lane road with an overgrown grass median in the middle. That setup allowed them to watch both sides of the road, and to quickly pull a Hummer out in any direction if it became necessary to chase someone. He took a longer sip of the coffee and stepped out of his Hummer, signaling for Rodriguez to come over.

"Has Longhurst's team gotten back yet?" Richard had sent Longhurst and four other men to scout the town nearby, a little place named Scotville. After a regrettable incident, his team had lost two travelers, shooting down one while the woman escaped. From what Richard saw, the woman had been attractive and would have given his team the morale boost they desperately needed. *Maybe I'll even keep her to myself for a little while,* he thought detachedly. *When she's still fresh this time. Let the men wait a couple of hours for once. This time I'm going to have some fun first, before Longhurst breaks another one.* He needed to get a closer look at her to decide.

"Yep, they came back a few minutes ago. She managed to get to the church in that little town, but we couldn't follow her after that. They had at least three snipers on the rooftops that we could see. These little shithole villages are getting too smart for their own good," Rodriguez said, spitting out the last words.

Richard nodded. They knew better than to chase their prey too far into the villages or towns. A group of four soldiers chasing a fleeing woman into a church would probably have a very short lifespan in an enclosed little town like that one. *Soldiers*, he thought. *Well, technically we aren't soldiers, but they don't know that, now do they?* Richard's team had worked for Blackhawk Enterprises, which had cleaned up in the government protection racket since the Crumble began. Politicians were being blamed for the miserable state of affairs in the country, and since the military was almost exclusively occupied with trying to keep the government's last sources of crude oil locked down in various foreign countries, companies like Blackhawk took up the slack.

Richard started his job as a security guard for Blackhawk in 2018. He did well but didn't excel, not until a life-changing incident that occurred in 2022. By the end of that year, a nonviolent movement had evolved out of Occupy Wall Street, called simply 'The Resistance.' Their Modus Operandi appeared to be the destruction of the machine itself. They started with small acts of nonviolent resistance, such as the destruction of traffic cameras and the sabotage of corporate property. One of their favorite things to do in their early years was ripping up the pavement in the parking lots of big box stores, and offices of large corporations. They called that 'bleeding the machine.'

On one fall day in November, Richard had been leaving after his shift ended at five in the morning, just as the sun was starting to rise. He caught glimpse of a group of masked teenagers mostly concealed behind some parked cars, and it looked like they were trying to tear up some of the Blackhawk parking lot. As he got into his car, he quietly pulled out and turned to face the teenagers. Gunning the engine and driving straight toward the group, surprising and scattering them, he managed to hit three of them with his car. His heart was beating faster than it ever had before, and he realized that he had an erection. He'd done it on the spur of the moment with no forethought, and now he was worried that he would lose his job for it.

Blackhawk's reaction to what he did taught him a lot. The scene was quickly cleaned up. He hadn't killed any of the teens, but one was seriously injured and would potentially be in a wheelchair for life, although Richard had never asked afterward. Catching some of these teens had been a coup for the company. There were reprimands, but the tone seemed somehow gentle, and all of a sudden, more senior people at the company knew his name. Once, the CFO passed him in a hallway and looked at him closely, giving him a smile and a wink.

Termination was never even mentioned. A few months later, he was assigned to a Peace Patrol, which were two-man teams that patrolled around large corporate office buildings and housing complexes for the rich. They carried better weapons than the police and were subject to fewer restrictions. Richard had finally found his calling.

As he ruefully thought of his meteoric rise, Richard brought himself back to reality. He hadn't even done anything to make the government let him go; it was just that he was expendable, like everyone else. Since the Feds were running out of resources, he had finally been cut loose a few months ago. He and his remaining team had been working their way west, subsisting on the crates of MREs they had brought with them, and periodically shaking down the towns and villages they passed through. They were able to keep their vehicles fueled by trading contraband with the few remaining government fuel depots in the suburbs around the city. He still had eighteen men reporting to him after the botched shakedown near Hollis. Who would have thought a few farmers could cost him so many men?

Still, the remainder of his team had managed to stay clean and mostly presentable, maintaining their quasi-official appearance. With most of the towns they had passed, Richard had claimed to be with the Department of Homeland Security, and told the various inhabitants that he was searching for contraband weapons and enemy combatants from the resistance. Besides, whether people believed he was from the government or not, a couple dozen men with assault rifles and wearing BDUs helped convince them. The fact that they still had fuel and working vehicles helped sell it as well.

That strategy had worked fairly well, but as he passed out of the suburban outer ring outside of DC, the rural folk had been much less compliant. His recent experience with the farmers in Hollis had taught him that. When the final count had come in, that disaster had cost him five men. His new strategy was a roadblock that he called a 'military checkpoint', and using a road like this ensured they couldn't get ambushed in unfamiliar territory like that again. This was the first time he had tried it, and straddling the road allowed them a clear view in two directions. It had been working fairly well so far, and they had netted a good amount of food and some weapons. There had been no violence until they had to shoot at the couple today. Richard really hoped they weren't locals.

Chapter 19

The funeral was a big deal. While no one at Millwood had known Scott, they were devastated by what had happened. Lea was welcomed sincerely, but with a great measure of sadness. Gavin wasn't surprised by the way she handled herself. While still reeling from the experience with the raiders and grieving over Scott's loss, Lea remained stoic, handling herself with quiet dignity.

When she arrived at Millwood, Gavin rushed her to her room in the Big House and she let him help treat her cuts, scrapes, and bruises. He sat her in a chair and began applying poultices and tinctures to the worst of her wounds.

"I'll give you the tour of the farm later, baby. I just want you to rest now," Gavin said as he got her a pillow.

"I'm not a hothouse flower, Gavin," Lea said, even as she allowed him to put the pillow behind her back. "But I know what you mean, though. I don't want to see everything when I'm like this. Scott wanted to see this place, too. He…"

She broke off, eyes shimmering. She bit her lip. Gavin sat on the arm of the chair and held her gently. After a while, she asked, "Will you stay here with me?"

I'll stay here all day, but I won't sleep in here," Gavin said. "Scott was supposed to be our chaperone. I wouldn't dishonor him like that."

She smiled valiantly at him through her tears, and looked around the room she was staying in. The walls were lined with books. "Well, at least I will have lots of friends to keep me company at night."

Gavin's heart broke and soared at the same time.

I have to make this right, he thought, as his anger fought through. He embraced his amazing fiancé as he silently swore to extract justice from the men responsible.

Lea met Gavin's family that night, and she was solemnly welcomed. The next day, Bob and Stella helped her with the funeral arrangements.

They held the funeral two days after Scott's death. Pastor Dennis came for the ceremony, and Scott was buried in the family graveyard on the farm. Lea had requested that he be buried at Millwood. "My uncle, Ex, would want him to stay here," she said. "*I* want him to stay here."

The ceremony was quick and simple, and Lea finally allowed herself to grieve publicly, sobbing and leaning on Gavin throughout the ceremony. "Why him and not me?" she whispered to him at one point. It was all he could do not to break down. He stood holding onto her as tightly as he could, not having any words that could make her pain go away.

After the funeral, Lea went inside with Bob and Stella, and a small knot of local men formed to discuss what to do about the raiders. Gavin, Aidan, and Xavier had been talking and planning their next move since Scott was killed. After finding Scott's body, Gavin had scouted out their camp and position as best he could, determining that there may be more than twenty of them and that they were well-armed. He saw four Hummers straddling a crossroads on Broad Rock Road. They looked to have had been in that spot for a few days already. Gavin had to break off when he noticed movement in a line of bushes by the crossroads. While some part of Gavin hoped that they would decide to move on, a larger, fiercer part of him hoped that they had decided to stay in the area for a while.

Pastor Dennis was hungry for more information. "How can you be sure that they weren't with the government? And you said they had Humvees? I haven't seen one of those for years. How is that possible? How are they getting gas?" He sounded perplexed.

"I can't be sure, but they were wearing black fatigues and looked like Blackhawk men," Gavin said. "If that's the case, they might still be somehow getting fuel from what's left of the government. I didn't see any insignias on their vehicles, but I know Blackhawk used to favor black Humvees. Either way, even if they are Blackhawk or government, they aren't sanctioned to be where they are. A couple of locals in Scotville said that they charged tolls to a few people and shook them down for weapons. That sounds like trouble to me. Whatever they used to be, they're raiders now."

Gavin sighed. He doubted he would be able to convince many of these men to help him clean out the raiders. It wasn't like his family had been that social since the collapse. During the worst of times, when it seemed like the waves of refugees from D.C. would never stop, it had been every man for himself. The berms that his family had put up around their farm and the land's protective natural features had helped them close off and defend themselves fairly well, but had also kept them isolated. It had only been in the past couple of years as trade began between the farms that he even learned the names of his neighbors.

Xavier spoke up, saving Gavin. "We've gotta take these guys out. Lea is gonna be Gavin's wife and that was her cousin. That means they killed our family. The Outlaws can help out with this, that's six of us right there. We can take out their lookouts real quietly and surprise them. We could catch them in a crossfire from both sides of Broad Rock. We're gonna need more people though, because we're gonna do this one clean. Gavin said that Lea wouldn't want it any other way, and that Scott would have felt the same." Xavier crossed his arms and looked at the group of men.

Gavin noticed how the younger local men were looking at Xavier with fire in their eyes; there was no question they would help. Just a few words from Xavier, combined with the fearsome reputation of the Outlaws, had turned the tide.

The Outlaws and the Colliers had done whatever it took to survive and protect their community during the worst of the violence, often taking on larger groups to protect their neighbors. While the stories told about those battles were filled with cruel and brutal violence, they never involved harming locals. When things started to improve, Gavin and Xavier agreed that they wouldn't use those old tactics unless absolutely necessary and they hadn't needed to fight dirty for a couple of years. The old stories were still told just the same.

Now that Gavin thought about it, Xavier was probably the most social one at Millwood farm. He was always asking to have his friends hunt in the woods, and he would have neighbors over to work on his various projects. There must have been about fifteen locals there for the funeral and it looked like they would get a good turnout.

Gavin said, "We're going to meet up in the parking lot of Maybach's old store at midnight tomorrow, and we'll plan the final details of the strategy there. The main plan is to have the Outlaws be our point men and take out the sentries. We'll form two other groups and spread out to either side of the road. Any help you all could give us would be greatly appreciated." Gavin stopped and thought for a second.

"We know one of our neighbors has some kind of machine gun; we've heard it a few times recently," he said. "It would be really helpful if whoever owns it can bring it."

"Yeah, bring that shit!" Xavier shouted, smiling with glee. "I wanna see that bad boy!" That got a laugh and helped ease the tension. After a few more minutes of friendly banter, Xavier broke off with his brother, JB, and another Outlaw, discussing what weaponry they would use.

Gavin knew that Pastor Dennis would get a few more people that weren't there tonight, and that the people here today would bring friends and family also. He smiled grimly. It had ended up being Xavier who had gotten enough volunteers. Gavin was grateful for that. This was the first time something like this had happened in this area since the Crumble. Up until this, families had fought on their own, and some of them had died because of it. Many of the houses that were close to the main roads had been shot up or burned down. This was a sign of a community rebuilding itself in a new way.

Gavin had noticed that Mike was tailing him all day, and approached him after the meeting. "Let me guess, Aidan said you couldn't come on the raid, and you want me to try to convince him?"

Mike looked sheepish and sighed. "You're the only one who treats me like an adult, and I'm ready to help! You just gave me a gun, for God's sake!"

"Yeah, but that's all part of the process," Gavin said. "You start small and work your way up to things. When you're eighteen, you'll be ready, but not until then. Besides, we still need to have a few capable people guarding Millwood." Without responding, Mike walked away with his head down, and Gavin felt a little bad for bursting his bubble, but a whole lot better knowing he would be safe.

Simply reaching the age of eighteen is such an arbitrary way to mark the rite of passage into adulthood, Gavin thought to himself idly. *We can do better than that.*

Later that night, as he snuggled with Shiver before going to bed, he wished that it was Lea, who was sleeping in the guest room in the Big House. Before drifting away, he thought, *I wonder who owns the machine gun.*

Chapter 20

November 2008 - 'Quantitative Easing' is performed for the first time. The Federal Reserve starts printing money to buy mortgage backed securities, treasury securities, and bonds. It goes on for so long that they name the stages: QE1, QE2, and so on. The Fed builds up its balance sheet to more than $2 trillion, all the while keeping interest rates near zero.

"God, I love 'em young," Richard said as he saw the two women approaching on horses. His new idea was working out very well. Since the incident with the young couple, the next three days had gone without a hitch. They had recently caught a single woman, admittedly somewhat older, for the men to use. Richard had them stash her in the back of their fuel truck, and the men took her one at a time. Morale improved immediately. They had exacted plenty of food, fuel, and ammo through their toll system, and while the traffic had slowed somewhat, he figured they could stay at this location for at least another week before it was tapped out. There had been no retaliation for the incident with the couple, and after a few days he let himself relax. He had confiscated a large jug of local moonshine and was making it last. Not only was the moonshine stronger, but his men couldn't smell it on his breath as easily as the other stuff.

As the women came closer, Richard saw that it looked like a mother and daughter. The mother looked to be in her forties, and her face had the hard, worn look that was common among people who had survived the Crumble. The past decade had been lean for a lot of people. There was something familiar about her face, but he couldn't place her. No matter, he had dealt with so many refugees and rebels in the past years that he had probably run into her somewhere before.

Turning his attention to the daughter, Richard could see that she was pretty hot. While she was dirty from the road and had ragged clothes, she looked to be fairly young, around seventeen or eighteen. She had bright red hair and a cute face, with wide set eyes, and a small button nose. She had a great body. *Lots of women have great bodies these days though; scarcity of food and hard work will do that,* he mused. He had actually come to miss that particular body type that had evolved at the end of the twentieth century, slightly overfed females with a belly, great breasts, and thick legs. He hadn't seen a nice, plump young woman in a long time. As they approached, he put on his usual strut. He'd learned that body language helped in getting the upper hand in a situation. Looking confident went a long way.

"Where are you ladies headed?" Richard asked, feigning a friendly smile.

The girl squinted at him and looked around at his men. "I heard you guys were here. What are you going to do, search us? Ask us to pay a toll?"

Richard was put off by her reaction. Her mother was silent, and looked at him with something akin to disgust. The girl didn't seem intimidated at all. Richard looked at his men with their guns and black outfits and then back at the girl.

"Well, hello to you, too!" That got a mean-spirited laugh from his men. He knew that he had to put on a bit of a show. The women were still a few feet away from him, so he turned up the volume of his voice. "You know, in my experience, the people who don't want to get searched are usually the ones with something to hide. And when someone doesn't want protection, which tells me that they are the ones people need to be protected *from*."

"Is that what you are doing on this highway?" she asked. "Protecting me? Thanks, but no thanks. I'm just here to give you two choices. Either disband right here and now and go in peace, or be driven out."

At this, Richard let out a huge belly laugh, which was echoed by his men. Here was this little girl and her dried up mother, threatening him? He raised his rifle and pointed it at her.

"What the hell makes you think you can waltz up here and start ordering us around? You don't even know who we represent! Get off that damn horse, now!" Richard felt himself getting excited. He liked the feisty ones, full of spirit. He couldn't wait to get this one into his tent. She would be all for him, at least at first.

The girl raised her hand and pointed at Richard. For a reason he didn't understand, he stepped to the side just as a shot rang out. He looked at where he had been standing and saw a bullet hole in the Hummer behind him.

"Everybody, down! Longhurst, take your team and get that

damn sniper!"

Longhurst grabbed his gun and headed to where the shots had come from, his men following him. As Richard looked up again, he saw that the women had turned their horses around and were galloping in the other direction. As he motioned for his other men to fire after them, another bullet hit next to him, this time impacting one of his men in the shoulder. Cursing as he crouched down again, Richard knew he had a big problem.

Chapter 21

On the day of the raid, Gavin had an enjoyable afternoon with Lea, reaffirming the thunderbolt that hit him like a freight train just a month before. The pall of grief over Scott's death seemed to weigh less heavily, and Gavin took the opportunity to give her the grand tour. He spent the morning showing her the trails in the woods, and all of the various ways they produced food on the farm. BoBo and Shiver walked with them, Shiver walking with her nose to the ground behind Lea, and BoBo strutting around like he owned the place. As they were walking into the greenhouse, BoBo jumped up on Gavin, making his characteristic deep throaty bark that said he wanted attention. Gavin picked him up and rested BoBo on his arm. BoBo looked like the king of the world, his back straight and his chest out, his junk on display for everyone to see.

Lea scratched his chin and laughed. Gavin's heart soared to see that she was in a good mood. "He thinks he runs the place, doesn't he?" she asked, scratching BoBo's chin again.

Gavin smiled. "I've only had to kick his ass once, when he was less than a year old. BoBo and I started out on a funny note. I got him in 2023, right before I got really sick and had to spend some time in the hospital. That's happened to me twice."

Lea gave him a concerned look, and he realized that he hadn't told her the story. "Don't worry, I'm fine now. In fact, getting sick the first time was one of the things that woke me up to what was happening, so it turned out to be a good thing. It turned out that the machine itself was making me sick in a way. But that story is for another day."

Lea smiled up at him and gave him a hug and a kiss. "Good, I don't want to see you get sick again. You had better eat one of these oranges!" She playfully smacked him in the face with a leaf from one of the orange trees on the greenhouse. He smiled and they went back to browsing the greenhouse. Lea inhaled the wonderful smells and gazed at the beautiful blossoms on the citrus fruits, spending time examining each one. Gavin knew that she was mentally cataloguing each plant in the greenhouse by its medicinal properties.

"So what happened? You didn't like him because you associated him with being sick? And you kicked his ass? My poor little man!" She paused after reviewing a Meyer lemon tree and stroked BoBo's chest. He made little grunting noises.

Gavin put BoBo down, tired of carrying him. "He was still a puppy and wanted to play, and I wasn't feeling well at all. He cheered me up some of the time, but annoyed the hell out of me sometimes, too. Once he chewed through my IV and that was a real pain in the ass. But as I got better, he and I didn't seem to get any closer. When I got out of the hospital I started to do farming in a real way, and I'd just started raising free range chickens. I had been reading about how to do it, and I kept reading that dogs can be one of the biggest threats to your chickens, and that if you had a dog that got a taste for chicken, you either had to get rid of the dog or the chickens. I was really worried about that."

"Oh boy, let me guess." Lea leaned down and petted BoBo some more, as he grunted and preened for her. "He killed one."

"Yep," Gavin said. "I was petrified of having to get rid of him. He showed up with a dead leghorn hen in his mouth, like he was bringing me a gift. It broke my heart, but I smacked the hell out of him for that. I was scared to death that I would lose him, and I believed so strongly in what I was doing at the farm that I was scared of losing the chickens, too. I yelled at him and showed him the chicken for a good two minutes. When I finally let up, he was in the corner, looking at me sullenly. I felt terrible, and when I came back from burying the chicken, he was nowhere to be found. He didn't come back for hours, and when he did he was all wet and dirty. I took him and dried him off and said I was sorry."

BoBo was now shamelessly on his back for Lea as she scratched his belly. His grunts were reaching a crescendo and seemed to be timed with her strokes. "So he wasn't mad at you?" she asked.

"On the contrary," Gavin said. "It's funny; after that, it seemed like he respected me more. We've been the best of friends ever since." Lea laughed, and as they left the greenhouse, she looked longingly back at it.

"Don't worry, it's not going anywhere," Gavin laughingly assured her, throwing his arm around her shoulder.

They went on to spend the afternoon pruning blueberry

bushes.

"I know you think you know all about plants, my little healer," Gavin said, "but you don't know that I'm actually a botanical genius." He picked a random weed from under one of the bushes. "This one is Spermicus Receivus, and that purple one over there is Purplus Flowerus."

"Wow, you really are a botanical genius after all! So what's this one called?" Lea asked, pointing down at her feet.

Gavin thought for a minute and said very seriously: "This one is a new discovery. We are the first people in the entire world who found it, so we get to name it. I think we should call it… 'grass.'"

Lea doubled over laughing.

As evening approached they walked around the pool house, discussing the future. Gavin thought she was being extra nice to him because he was going on the raid later that night, and he milked it for all it was worth. BoBo, on the other hand, was unconcerned. Shiver had been sleeping at the pool house and BoBo gave her his full attention once he found her, although he'd stopped pestering her as badly as he had before. Shiver was putting on more weight and while at first she had been weak, she was now running around Millwood at full speed and becoming attached to the people, especially Mike and Lea.

Lea loved Millwood too, particularly the pool house and the library in the Big House. He had told her that he and Xavier planned to build an addition onto the pool house as they needed more space. He had decorated some of it already and knowing how much she loved Italy, had hung some of the artwork he brought back over the years. He told the stories behind each item as he showed her his art collection.

"Stella negotiated the guy down to half the price while I went to the ATM to get money to pay for it." He pointed to a small oil painting of an old woman bending down in her garden, the sky and landscape a riot of brush strokes and color. Lea gasped as she approached it, reaching her hand up to graze her fingers against the canvas.

"I knew the guy who painted this one; he is a charming old man who was always dressed up in a suit. He does carvings, too." He pointed to a simple, brightly colored painting of a boat on the water in a rough wooden frame.

"This sculpture was so heavy; I had to pay the airline extra to get it home!" Lea knelt down next to that one for a long time, stroking the curves and lines of the piece. It was a stone carving of a woman's face, her mouth slightly open in a beatific smile.

"I also knew this painter. He was a short, little guy with a soft voice, and he always wore short shorts and would try to give you his paintings for free," Gavin said. It was a dark but playful painting of a bunch of drunken Italian farmers leaning on each other outside of a bar.

"That one's my favorite," Gavin added, needlessly.

"That figures," Lea said with a snort, lightly elbowing him and smiling.

She walked around the room, taking it all in. "The colors are all so beautiful," she mused. "We need more color like this. I recently had an idea for a dress I want to make, and all these colors are giving me inspiration."

Lea pressed her hand into his and smirked. "Speaking of ideas... I like your stuff from Italy, but I'd like to see it for myself. So, prepper man, how does one prepare to go to Italy?"

At that moment, Mike knocked on the door, saving Gavin. It was time to start getting ready for the raid. He told Mike he would join him shortly, and then turned to Lea.

"So what is the plan for tonight?" Lea asked, for the third time.

"Well, we'll have to see how many people we get first. We're hoping to catch them from both sides of the road at the same time. With Xavier and the Outlaws, Aidan and me, and the other people I know are coming for sure, I think we will outnumber them. Plus, we know the area better than they do."

Lea bit her lip pensively, brushed her dark hair out of her face, and looked at Gavin.

"If you are worried about me, don't be," Gavin said. "We've all been through this kind of thing before, and Xavier and the Outlaws are total badasses. It's the other guys you should be worried about." He winked at her.

"That's exactly what I mean," she said. "I've dedicated my life to living things. I heal them. I try to keep life going; that's my job. We've talked about this before. Those bullets you use are so small, but they can kill a living being, someone it took years to raise."

Gavin thought for a moment. This was part of what had drawn

him to her in the first place. Her sense of humanity, even in the darkest of times, made her angelic to him.

"I know you feel that way, and I love you for it," Gavin said. "But you do know why this is necessary, right? We're trying to protect life. We hope that by doing this we'll get justice for Scott, but not only that, these guys are a menace. They have probably killed a lot of people already and if we don't stop them, they will kill more; maybe more of us."

"I know all of that," she said. "And I appreciate that you aren't doing this for revenge. Scott wouldn't want that. But I still hate it. I hope one day we can figure out how to stop doing this." Her normally stoic self gave way to quivering lips and teary eyes. "And I'm worried about you." She reached out and hugged him tightly.

Gavin stroked her head and held her, murmuring platitudes, but he knew anything could happen. It was just like she said. One bullet, no bigger than the tip of your little finger, could end a life in a heartbeat.

Chapter 22

One mile outside of Scotville, Virginia

The parking lot at Mayhugh's hadn't been that busy in years. It was too far from the town and too close to the road, and the owners had abandoned the place years ago. But tonight it was filled with people, standing in small groups and speaking in hushed tones.

Xavier and the Outlaws were nowhere to be seen, but Gavin knew that as soon as they showed up they would have to move pretty quickly.

Aidan stood with the largest group of men, with his familiar tactical vest and AR15. Pastor Dennis stood next to him, surprising Gavin by holding a large combat shotgun and wearing a bandolier around his chest. A couple of smaller groups stood close by, with Gavin counting sixteen in all. He surmised that, once the Outlaws arrived, they'd surely have an advantage in numbers. The people here tonight had seen violence before. These were the strongest and smartest of their little town, the ones who had survived. And now they were displaying just how tough they were. Many of his neighbors had unique weapons or fighting skills that they wanted to show off. Some of the local men had several knives strapped to their bodies, and others had done themselves up in camouflage paint and clothing. A couple of the younger people had taken it to an extreme, wearing all black clothing with black paint on their faces.

It turned out that the neighbor who owned the machine gun was Tucker Alton, who Gavin knew fairly well. Tucker's family lived north of Millwood and owned the tavern in Beulah, a town to the southeast. Gavin was sufficiently in awe of the weapon, an old Browning with two full belts of ammunition. "A .30 caliber World War II era M1919 Browning," Tucker said proudly. It looked menacing. Gavin, Aidan, and the Altons all agreed that the Altons would go with Tucker to circle west and set up on the other side of Broad Rock Road.

"I should have known it was you who owned this beast, Tucker," Gavin said with a smile as he caressed the gun. "You've been holding out on me!" Tucker and Gavin had been shooting buddies before and during the Crumble, and even now, they still managed to shoot together once per year.

Tucker laughed. "I can't reveal my secrets all at once! And I know you'll just try to trade me for it anyway, every time I see you you're trying to trade me pork for weapons!"

Aidan and Gavin laughed and bantered back and forth with Tucker and the Altons as they waited, defusing some of the tension.

"So what's the signal going to be?" Tucker asked a few minutes later, holding the Thompson.

Gavin and Aidan looked at each other and grinned. "A bunch of fucking shooting!" Gavin said, getting a laugh from Tucker. They all shook hands as Tucker's group departed for the other side of the road.

One of Pastor Dennis' group had some home-rolled cigarettes and Gavin took one, smoking with slightly shaking hands. Aidan sat quietly, staring off into the distance.

After about an hour, one of their lookouts heard Xavier's whistle, and he and the Outlaws came out of the night. Several tall black men with dreadlocks and tattoos walked toward the group in the parking lot, embracing and shaking hands with various friends. Gavin noticed that Xavier's penchant for swords had caught on; a couple of the other Outlaws now wore them too. Xavier was also a tattoo artist, and he had done many of his friends' tattoos himself, learning how to do that during a short stint in prison.

It still angered Gavin that his friend had been imprisoned for such a small offense. If Gavin had been caught with a joint in his car, he would have had to pay a fine and maybe perform some community service, but a black man, like Xavier, went to jail. Before the Crumble, many young, black men went to prison for small things while their white counterparts did not. The institutional racism of such a thing sickened Gavin, and was another reason he hadn't been sorry to see the machine's government arm erode and ultimately collapse.

The Outlaws consisted of Xavier and his brother JB, along with their friends, Derek and Lamont. There were a couple others there for the raid who Gavin didn't know well, but that core group of four men had been close since childhood and had formed a very effective fighting force. Each of them had experienced trouble with the law at one point or another, and in the early days, Gavin and Xavier had joked that his team should be called 'The Outlaws.' The name had stuck.

Xavier called Derek over, who was brandishing a new battle rifle, and had blood on his shirt. Gavin smiled at him.

"Was it quiet?" Gavin asked.

"Quiet, like a little mouse," Derek whispered and smiled back at Gavin.

"I got the other one," Xavier said. "I left his stuff on him, he's not going anywhere. Besides, I'm better with my .270. I've got that night vision scope on it that Aidan gave me."

"Nice," Gavin said. "So are you guys ready to do your thing?"

"You know we're always ready for this!" Xavier breathed. "Hey, you know something Bob told me the other day?"

"What's that?" Gavin asked.

"Did you know the original ninjas in Japan were actually farmers?" Xavier winked at Gavin and called the Outlaws over to him. They disappeared back into the night.

Chapter 23

January 2009 - After a sudden population collapse in 2007, salmon runs reach drastically low levels. This causes a complete shutdown of salmon fisheries in California. The National Marine Fisheries Service blames the majority of the decline on 'poor oceanic feeding conditions.' Scarcities of resources like this will become more commonplace as the wholesale environmental destruction caused by the machine accelerates.

No plan survives contact with the enemy. Gavin had read that once, or something like it. Despite what he'd told Lea, this would be the largest battle he'd ever been a part of, and the wait was the worst part. Most of the other times he'd fought it had been his family against small groups of people who were trying to attack and rob the farm. This time it was pre-planned, with many people on both sides, and Gavin felt none of the normal adrenaline rush that usually helped him get through violence. His stomach was sour and he felt like he wanted to cough his lungs out. His hands were shaking and he had broken out in a cold sweat.

As he lay in wait next to his brother, they kept their guns sighted in on the two enemy vehicles to the west, Aidan looked at him. "This is like what you were talking about when you went on that whole David and Goliath rant a few years ago. I hate to admit it, but you were right."

Gavin forced a smile. Normally he would laugh and tease Aidan, but right now it was all he could do to keep from puking. The camaraderie he felt while talking with the Altons seemed like days ago.

Aidan went on, as always seemingly oblivious to the impending danger. "These assholes think they're pretty great because of all the equipment they have, but in reality, they're Goliath and we're David, just like you said."

Gavin forced a laugh. "Ha! I seem to remember it took you a minute to catch on to that."

When it became apparent that the Crumble had progressed far enough for violence to begin reaching the farm, Gavin had brought Xavier and Aidan together and told them what he was thinking. As he often did, he began by telling them about something he had read.

"I just finished a book about David and Goliath. There were some good ideas in there, although the book wasn't great. I had expected more of the author."

Xavier and Aidan smirked at each other. Aidan said, "Enough about the book, nerd, and tell us how we're supposed to defend ourselves."

Gavin smiled and went on. "In the story of David and Goliath, the interesting thing is that it turned out that Goliath's strength and power were not the advantages he thought they were, and actually turned out to be huge disadvantages. In fact, the story of David isn't the story of an underdog at all, because *David* actually had all the advantages. *There is no way at all Goliath could have won that fight.* Think about it, Goliath was six foot seven, carrying a sword and shield, and wearing full armor and a helmet. David was wearing a tunic and sandals and he was small and thin, so he could move around a lot faster. David was a slinger in the army, so he was really skilled with that thing. All he had to do was keep out of range of Goliath's sword and hit him in the head with a rock. He could have missed the first five times and still won. The face and forehead were left open in Goliath's helmet so he could see better, and the forehead is exactly where David hit him. He knocked him out with the stone, ran up and grabbed Goliath's sword, and chopped his head off. Strength and power can actually become a disadvantage."

"So what are you saying?" asked Aidan. "We should learn how to use slings?" Xavier, on the other hand, was looking at Gavin pensively.

"You want us to use scouts, right?" Xavier said. "You want us to be able to move around and see who's coming."

"Exactly!" shouted Gavin. "But even more than that. When I was reading that story, I had an epiphany. Millwood, even with our land, food and guns, we aren't as strong as we think we are. *We're Goliath.* We are sitting out here like a piece of ripe fruit to be plucked. Not only do we need to be able to see what's coming, but we also need to have an advantage that's hard to see. So Xavier, I want you to convince JB, Derek, and Lamont to come stay here full-time. I want you guys to be our David. Your team will take most of the night watches. If you see a group coming, wait until they pass and then follow them in.

You can use my ghillie suit and I'm sure Aidan will loan you his too, and you can make a few more homemade ones. You'll have the night vision and binoculars and all of that, and you will have our best guns."

Xavier's eyes were gleaming. Gavin knew that Xavier was made for these times, a natural leader. When he originally thought of the idea, he had no doubt that Xavier would want to do it.

"What if it's a small group we think we can take ourselves?" Xavier was already thinking ahead.

"You know what I always say; use your best judgment. First of all, make sure that they're really coming towards us and that they're a legitimate threat. If we start taking people out on the road for no reason, then we're no better than the damn raiders. If they cross the berms and keep going, and if they're armed and trying to conceal themselves, I think it's safe to say that they bear us some ill will," Gavin said drily.

"Let's say a large group is coming, too big for you to take on your own. Remember, your team will most likely have to stay spread out most of the time. If that happens, like I said, use the suits to stay hidden, and sidle up behind them as they come in. Wait until they get to the dip in the driveway and start firing on them. When Aidan and I hear shooting, we'll come out of the front and attack from there. The bodies will go to that group of pigs we separated into the back field."

"Alright, I got you," Xavier had said, liking the idea. The passage of time showed that the strategy worked well, albeit with a few modifications. They ended up doing most of their fighting at night and in some of those chaotic battles over the years, they had all lost close friends. But they were able to defend themselves and as they got better at it, the pigs got very fat. They began to call that herd of pigs the 'cleanup crew,' and had to put them down a couple of years later when they started killing their own prey, afraid that they would go feral. No one wanted to eat their meat and they buried them instead.

"You know who would have loved this?" Aidan asked. "Xavier's cousin, Wood. I wonder whatever happened to him."

The sound of a gunshot ended the conversation, jarring the two men back to the present.

There was no way to know exactly where the Outlaws would be attacking, but the general strategy was to let them scout and engage the enemy, and for Gavin and Aidan's group to pour fire on them from the north, with the Altons engaging them from the southwest on the opposite side of the road. As Gavin and Aidan heard the first shots, they motioned to their group and ran up the crest of the hill they were hiding behind. As their team lined up in a row and flopped to the ground, they began peppering the vehicles with shots. The visibility was poor but that didn't last long, and Gavin saw figures running around, exiting the vehicles. It looked like a lot of them were actually sleeping inside the Hummers. One of the Outlaws hit a vehicle with a Molotov cocktail, and then another. Its gas tank finally exploded with a gratifying boom. Gavin started to see muzzle flashes from the raiders as they strived to return fire, but the Outlaws were impossible to deal with. Gavin could hear Xavier and Derek shouting taunts between their shots as they threw the enemy into disarray.

"Come on and fight, fuckers!" Xavier yelled as another Hummer went up in flames. Xavier was so unpredictable in battle. In fact, Gavin thought that Xavier himself didn't know until the last minute. They were constantly in motion and were experts at camouflage. They had gear for night, day, and all types of weather. They fought best at night, when confusion and terror became their allies. Gavin and Xavier had become experts in making Molotov cocktails, or just 'cocktails,' as they now called them.

Aidan paused firing for a moment. "Where's Tucker and them? I don't see any shots coming from over there."

Gavin took the night vision binoculars and looked in their direction, and he could make out muzzle flashes in the woods. It looked like Tucker and his group had problems of their own. He turned to look back down at the little cluster of Hummers. Two of them were now on fire, but the raiders looked like they were regrouping. A few of them were crouched under one of the two remaining vehicles, with the majority of their fire going towards the southeast, although Gavin did see a couple of them sighting in his direction, too. He and Aidan had the rest of the group spread out, moving every time they fired so they couldn't be targeted on by their muzzle flashes. Gavin did the same, scooting around on the top of the hill and jumping over its crest to take cover every time the return fire got too close.

The last Hummer's engine started. As it did, the machine gun finally opened up from the southeast. "Da-da-da-da-da-da-da-da" it blurted out, changing the dynamics of the battle in an instant. Along with the automatic, a cacophony of shots came with it. Gavin ran a few yards down the hill and met back up with Aidan.

"Tucker finally made it!" Aidan exclaimed. "Jeez, that sounds like a lot more than five guys."

The two of them crossed the crest of the hill again and looked back down. The last Hummer was getting away, but what was left looked like one of Dante's visions of Hell. The Hummers were all ablaze and the smell of burning plastic and cordite filled the air. The last raiders who made their stand were now in a tattered and torn heap of flesh. Xavier's whistle sounded again, and he and the Outlaws approached from the northeast. They all looked intact except Lamont, who was wearing a bandage on his head. Blood dripped down through it.

As Gavin and Aidan ran to him, Lamont said, "Don't worry, it's not as bad as it looks. You know how head wounds are. It's just a graze." With sighs of relief, the men shook hands and hugged, glad everyone had made it through.

As Gavin hugged Xavier, he laughed and said, "Man I thought you were on the other side of the road? You should have seen how much lead they threw that way!"

"Fuck yeah, man," Xavier replied. "Outlaws for life! We're not playing around with these people, know what I mean?"

As the men walked down the hill toward the carnage, the feeling of victory hung heavy in the air.

Chapter 24

Richard kicked himself as he heard the first few shots fired. He should have left the area earlier, but he had been lazy and complacent. He had figured they could stay one more night and head out the next morning. That damn moonshine had slowed him down. When the sniper hit one of his men after the strange encounter with those two women, Richard knew something was up. Longhurst had come back empty-handed from their search for the sniper, and the two women had gotten away as well. He had a feeling about the younger of the two; there was something about her that reminded him of the old days when his job had gotten so much harder. Those punk kids had started out with just sabotage, but they had quickly turned into nasty little bastards as he tried to root them out.

They'd attacked him and his men with every kind of homemade weapon they could think of. He had pulled nails and staples from his skin and washed paint out of his hair. The only reason he hadn't gotten any worse than that was because he had been lucky. He had lost good men, and toward the end of his career with Blackhawk, the kids had started to downright scare him. He took to sleeping with a gun and inspecting his car before starting it every day.

It's the damn locals, he thought to himself as he crouched against a tree. He'd been up sneaking a nip of moonshine and taking a piss, and his luck was with him again tonight. He immediately started crawling toward the lead Hummer, and tried to keep the vehicles between him and the hill to the north where the attack appeared to be coming from. All of a sudden, he heard breaking glass and a "whooshing" sound. His vision briefly went white and he felt blazing heat on his face. They had somehow hit the vehicle with a Molotov cocktail, and a dark figure ran past him, quickly throwing another. Richard shot at the figure with his pistol and saw it falter and dive to the ground. He fired twice more, but a shotgun roared behind him. He felt the dirt thrown onto his feet as the shot just missed him. Heart pounding, he scrambled to his feet and dove for cover under another Hummer toward the west, away from the flames.

From the shadows, someone yelled, "Come on and fight,

fuckers!" and Richard's blood ran cold. The shotgun roared again, this time from a different place, and another shadow darted past him. More clinking glass. *Shit*.

He rolled out of the way again as two more Molotovs sailed through the air, impacting close to the gas tank. A loud explosion filled the air, and Richard's heart soared as he saw Longhurst firing in all directions from one of the last intact Hummers, motioning to Richard. Richard ran to the passenger door, firing as he ran. As Longhurst put the vehicle in gear and they started to roll forward, Richard heard the sound of one of the back tires blowing out.

Caltrops, he thought. Caltrops were a cheap and effective tool for disabling vehicles that Richard had encountered before. They could be made at home with scrap metal, a pair of pliers, and a clamp, and the rebels had discovered their effectiveness early on. Richard hated the damn things. Longhurst sped up and got out anyway; they could change the tire when they got far enough away. As the Hummer jolted down the road on three good tires, Richard breathed a sigh of relief. They hit a bump and he felt a searing pain in his ribs. He looked down. He'd been shot.

Chapter 25

When Gavin, Aidan, and the Outlaws reached the carnage, everyone spread out to search for loot. "Stay away from the burning Hummers for a while," Gavin said. "We don't know what ammo could still cook off in there."

Any of the enemy who were wounded but still alive didn't stay that way for long. Xavier stood with Gavin and Aidan as everyone started putting loot in the pile. Gavin was hunched over the ammo while Xavier and Aidan looked at the guns and technology.

Finding three full cans of ammo, Gavin shouted, "We have .223! And .45 and 9 millimeter!" He felt like a kid in a candy store.

Xavier and Aidan were sitting Indian-style on the ground and looked up and cheered as Gavin called out the ammo he was finding. Xavier was peering into a new pair of night vision goggles and Aidan was examining a stripped down AR15. Xavier looked over to the woods with the night vision.

"Damn, this shit is thermal!" Xavier shouted with glee. "Yeah! And here comes Tucker and them now. Looks like he's got some more people with him."

Tucker approached from the woods carrying the Browning, and Gavin's mouth fell open. Tucker's little group of six had morphed into a group of more than fifteen people. As they got closer, Gavin could see that the new additions were a ragged bunch. They were thin with old, torn clothing, and they all appeared to be in their late teens and early twenties. One of Tucker's men looked to be wounded in the leg, and the new people had two wounded as well. One young man carried another girl who didn't appear to be moving at all. At the head of the group with Tucker, Gavin could see an older woman about his age, much older than the rest.

Tucker brought the attractive, older women over to Gavin and Aidan. She looked to be in her late forties, and had dirty blonde hair that fell to her waist. She had a delicate face, with a pointy nose and chin. She was rail thin but looked strong, and her dirty clothing and haunted eyes made Gavin think that she had been out on the road for a very long time.

"This is Monique," Tucker said. "Evidently, her people had a beef with these guys, too. We got into a skirmish with them in the woods, but as soon as I saw them close up, I knew they weren't our enemies. They helped us finish off the raiders, except the ones in the Hummer who got away."

Gavin introduced himself and shook Monique's hand, his mind whirling with the implications. *Most of them are young, they are living on the road, and they're going after people associated with the government. What does that sound like?* Gavin thought to himself.

Another couple of her people had come to stand next to her, a girl with red hair and a tall boy with a Mohawk. Both looked to still be in their teens. They were introduced as Shelly and Raven.

"So you guys had a problem with this group, too?" Gavin asked. "They killed one of our friends and we were just trying to drive them out of our town. What did they do to you guys?"

"Their leader's name is Richard Spiegel, and we think he was one of the ones who got away tonight," Monique said. "We've been following him ever since DC cut him loose. He subcontracted for Blackhawk through the Department of Homeland Security for years, but a few months ago the government finally couldn't afford to keep the Blackhawk contractors anymore, so he took his most loyal men and went on the road."

"Spiegel has a lot to answer for," Shelly said. Her face had gotten red, and she was beginning to breathe hard.

Gavin could tell that there was a definite animosity there. It appeared that it was personal, at least for her.

Gavin decided to ask what everyone was wondering. "So, you guys are with the resistance?"

Chapter 26

Having no interest in discussions of the resistance, Tucker walked over to where Aidan and Xavier were sorting through the loot, leaving Gavin with Monique and her two companions. Monique sighed and said, "Whatever we were, that's not what we are now. The machine is dead, or just about, anyway. We're just travelers now. All we're trying to do is get Spiegel. We want to see justice served, but beyond that, we don't have an agenda anymore. We're just trying to survive."

As she spoke, Gavin looked over to her group. They were caring for their wounded as best they could, and it looked like they were going to set up a rudimentary camp right there by the road. The girl who was being carried earlier was laid out on a blanket and a boy knelt over her, weeping.

"You're going to stay here for a couple days and then try to follow them?" Gavin asked.

"If that's okay with you all," Monique replied. Gavin looked over at Aidan, who shrugged. Gavin could see a couple of the rebels starting a fire and another was bringing over a skinned rabbit. He knew that they were tough and could provide for themselves, but he felt bad seeing them like this.

Gavin never had anything against the resistance. In fact, he had always agreed with their professed strategy. They attacked the machine itself, and not the people who ran it. In the beginning, they weren't too high up on the government's hit list, as they only destroyed small parts of the machine. But they grew bolder as time passed. They started bombing dams, fracking operations, and critical transformers in the power grid. That was when the authorities took their gloves off. Gavin had heard awful stories of how the rebels had been treated, and from what he heard, the private, corporate militias made the government look humane by comparison.

"Why don't you guys come to our farm and camp there for a few days? We can feed a group this size for a couple of days with no trouble, and maybe we can even get a deer. That way you can take your best people and go after that guy, and leave the remainder to get some rest and bury their dead. My fiancé is a healer; she can help with the people who are wounded. When you get Spiegel, come back and pick them up and then you can be on your way." As Gavin spoke, he could see a few of the rebels' heads perk up, including that of the boy weeping over the dead girl. Shelly glanced at Monique and asked to have a moment in private.

While Monique talked in hushed tones with what appeared to be her two lieutenants, the looted bodies of the Blackhawk men were piled up for burning. Gavin was reminded of the cost as he heard the boy sobbing in the background over his fallen love.

Monique returned to Gavin and stood next to him, and they were alone for a moment while Shelly and Raven joined the rest of the group. In a quiet voice, Monique asked Gavin why he was helping them.

"I don't even know who you are, and all of a sudden you're our guardian angel. How do I know we can trust you?"

Gavin tensed, thinking of why his heart went out to these people. He felt his anger rise.

"Listen to me," he spat. *"Fuck that fucking machine!* It almost killed us all. And not only humans, but all life on the planet. I didn't do anything to support your efforts beyond writing slogans on bathroom walls. I protected my little piece of the world from it, but not much else. I was *part* of it. So let me help you now." He looked at her.

Monique was silent for a moment, and she looked back at him with tears in her eyes.

"Thank you." That was all she said, and that was enough. The two of them parted ways and Gavin walked back to his people.

Everyone was still in awe of the equipment they found on the men and what they managed to salvage from the Hummers and the raiders' bodies. Gavin was pleased to see that Aidan and Xavier appropriated some of the best items, including a new bulletproof vest and the thermal goggles. The ammo and new weapons were parceled out, as was the fuel. Tucker was only interested in fuel, and he took the lion's share of that.

The rebels decided that Monique, Shelly, and Raven would continue to go after Spiegel, and the rest of the group would take up Gavin's offer to recuperate at the farm. As Monique gave the good news to the rebels, they gave a cheer that made Gavin smile. Gavin and his friends packed up the loot as their new guests said goodbye to

Monique, Shelly, and Raven.

After somberly loading the rebel girl's body onto Aidan's horse, a larger group than what came left for Millwood.

Chapter 27

June 2009 – Greece begins a large-scale crackdown on immigrants, arresting hundreds of migrants across the country and evicting them from their run-down dwellings and makeshift camps. Youth unemployment in Greece is at twenty-five percent. The housing bubbles in Greece and Spain are impossibly large, especially the latter. Greece and Spain's governments, like many others, have been complicit in borrowing money to fund a lifestyle the society can't afford. Now the bill is coming due.

15 miles Northeast of Scotville

Richard came in and out of consciousness. He looked around and found that he was in an abandoned house, one of the awful particleboard "McMansions" that had become so popular in the early 21st century. Most had been abandoned when the suburban lifestyle became untenable. This particular house, a monstrosity of cheap materials on a tiny lot, had been trashed before the occupants left; there were holes in the drywall and old clothes all over the floor. Nevertheless, Longhurst had managed to get him on a flat surface, and it looked like he had been able to get the bullet out and sterilize and suture the wound with the field medic kit they carried. *Good old Longhurst*, he thought.

Longhurst had been his right-hand man ever since Richard covered up a rape for him. At that time, Richard had been leading a team of Blackhawk contractors cleaning squatters out of foreclosed apartment buildings. Longhurst had liked the look of one of the female squatters. He grabbed her, took her into an alcove, and forced himself on her. Unfortunately, another member of their team who didn't share their 'rape and pillage' philosophy had seen him. The worst part about it was that this freaking Boy Scout, a guy named Jebson, had reported it directly to Richard's superiors instead of him, preventing him from squashing the complaint right then and there. Richard knew that things could happen in the heat of the moment during these operations; the men were under a lot of stress and had to be allowed to blow off some steam every once in a while.

In a stroke of luck, a supposedly secret drug sweep was scheduled to take place the following day, and Richard had planted a bag of meth in Jebson's locker. In doing so, Richard had killed two birds with one stone. One, it would get rid of a Boy Scout that Richard didn't need hanging around, and two, it would save a good man from losing his job.

But what he didn't realize was that it would gain him an ally for life. Longhurst was socially awkward, but highly intelligent and capable, and no one had really gone to bat for him like that before. After the rape complaint was dropped, Longhurst approached Richard.

"Jebson never did a drug in his life, so what gives? I'm not trying to find fault in a good situation, but I want to know what happened," Longhurst said.

Richard looked at Longhurst and let a bit of the truth out. "You've worked for me for a long time. I know what you're capable of and I respect you. Jebson, he's not a team player. He got what was coming to him. Plus, he's new and I don't know him. I don't even need to ask you what happened. It's tough out there, and as long as you don't make us look bad or let your work suffer, I'm not going to worry about the details of how you spend every minute of your day."

Longhurst gave Richard a long, intense look, and said: "Boss, I'm your man. I just want you to know that I will be there for you every step of the way. I am your man."

While Richard marveled at the fact that he was still alive, he was also thankful that Longhurst was, after all this time, still his man.

Chapter 28

Shelly's eyes were so tired from looking at the ground that she was starting to see spots. She took a break from her search and leaned up against a tree, closing her eyes for a moment. She could hear Monique and Raven nearby, walking around, peering at the ground like she had been doing.

They had lost the Hummer's trail fairly soon, as they knew they would. The blacktop on most of the roads was still fairly serviceable, and after a few miles of following the tire tracks, they came to a point where a large accident had occurred years ago. Several trails led off the road in different directions, as these were used instead of the considerable work of clearing the road. Most communities liked to have their roads blocked off, anyway. Working vehicles brought trouble with them, and nowadays, most travel was done by bicycle or on foot. Horses were a rarity for the first few years, but they had now become the dominant method of transportation for organized communities.

When the power went off, cars were still able to travel for a while, but after a couple of years, even the rich had stopped driving, at least outside of the cities. Nowadays, only the government and the raiders could still get fuel and working vehicles. People didn't want to see either one, as both groups took what they could and gave nothing in return.

Despite Raven's tracking skills, they couldn't pick the Hummer's trail back up, no matter how hard they looked. The entrance to the trails was a muddy mess. After more searching, the small group decided to camp there for the night. Raven took first watch. Lean and twitchy, he seemed to need little sleep and had taught himself some valuable skills from books they had found over the years. Besides tracking, he could fashion a weapon out of almost anything, and while his traps weren't that effective, they caught animals some of the time. Traps built by other members of the group had invariably failed miserably.

Shelly looked upon Raven with great affection, despite his oddities. Raven had first met Shelly when he was a young boy. At the time, he had been no more than 10 years old and was emaciated from malnutrition. On the day they met, he saved Shelly's life. She'd been following the highway west out of D.C., cleverly walking off the road in the woods parallel to it. This had kept her hidden. Looking back years later, Shelly's memories were still fuzzy about how she had gotten out of the city. She was only nine at the time, and was being bused to a fancy school in D.C. from her family's home in the Arlington suburbs, where there was still power. Whenever she tried to remember the day the world ended for her, all she got was a series of painful flashes. She could remember that her school bus got caught in traffic on the way to school, and that after several hours, it ran out of gas. The bus driver had no idea what to do and eventually left to find help.

At that point, her memory went blank, and in retrospect she figured that was a blessing. Piecing everything together years later, Shelly knew that she must have found a way back to her family's house in Arlington because she still carried supplies that she could have only gotten from home, like her father's hunting knife. But she had no memory of what happened when she got there. The next thing she remembered was meeting Raven. An older man had found her walking in the woods by the road and chased her down. She remembered a flash of the worst body odor she had ever smelled, and seeing the man's dirty face looking down at her. The next thing she knew, the man's eyes opened wide in surprise and pain as a small, dirty boy ran up and plunged a knife into his back.

The two of them had managed to survive until Monique found them days later. Neither of them had ever talked about what happened to them leading up to the events on that day, but they both had an ingrained hatred of authority, especially for federal authorities and contractors. To this day, whenever Shelly saw anyone wearing the black paramilitary clothes favored by security corporations like Blackhawk, she could still feel a deep, seething hatred and anger. The same went for Raven.

"This is good," Raven said, and Shelly sighed and tossed her pack to the ground. Raven always picked the campsites and it seemed like he had taken forever to pick this one. Even Monique, normally so stoic, grunted a bit as she got off her horse. This chase was getting to all of them. They had started with a band of rebels and were down to just three. Though Spiegel was a monster, he was a cunning one. He would fight to the very end, and Shelly hoped that all three of them would come out alive when it was done.

Chapter 29

November 2037
Millwood Farm

It was two weeks after the raid when Gavin and Lea prepared to leave Millwood for Ramsey. There was so much to do with settling the rebel group into a few empty stalls in the barn, and making sure they got the medical attention they needed. While Lea still checked her young rebel patients daily, by this time all their wounds had healed under her capable care.

They attended the funerals of the community members who had been killed in the raid, and further strengthened their relationship with their neighbors in the process. Although Gavin was charismatic, he was an introvert, which sometimes proved to be an odd combination. Lea, however, turned out to be quite the social butterfly. She was welcomed by the neighbors even during the sad occasion of a funeral.

Gavin mused on another change in society; death was now part of life again. So many people had been lost in the first few years. Death happened more often now, and often in full view. People had been forced to become more accepting and understanding of it. Before the Crumble, people had distanced themselves from death; it was hidden and sanitized, which had made the fear of it loom larger in their minds.

As for the wedding planning, Lea wanted to have it at Doc's house in Ramsey so her entire family could be there. They set the date far into November, right after Thanksgiving. Most of the people from Millwood also planned to make the trek to Ramsey for the event.

On the day before they left, Lea and Gavin were packing when Xavier walked up to pool house door.

"Hey Gavin, what's good with you?" Xavier said as he approached. "Hi, Lea!"

"What's up?" Gavin was pleased to see that Xavier had his son, Devante, with him. Devante was the best runner they had, and was becoming a real asset to Millwood. Out of the thirty-odd people that lived at Millwood, more than ten of them were kids, but each contributed in their own way.

"The north watch just saw a group coming towards us. Devante said it looks like they are some of the locals from Farrington, and they are coming from the right direction," Xavier said.

"Did you see them yourself?" Gavin asked Devante.

"Yes, sir," Devante said. "I'm pretty sure they're from Farrington, they had that look about them. But I didn't see any extra horses, so I don't know what they want."

As Gavin and Xavier exchanged knowing looks, Lea interjected. "Does anyone want to clue me in? What is Farrington?" She looked at Devante. "What does 'that look' mean?"

Devante looked up at his father and Xavier smiled at Lea. Putting his arm on his son's shoulder, he said, "Tell Lea what you mean, boy."

Devante was still shy at thirteen, but was proud to be asked. "They look like they used to be rich but they're not anymore. They have lots of nice clothes but they are real old now. Their horses are better than ours, though. I love their horses!" Devante's eyes shone.

"I have to admit," said Gavin, "They do have some nice horses. Devante, was Chris Orlund wearing his bright red hunting jacket?"

"Yeah, he's wearing it," the boy said.

Gavin and Xavier cracked up.

"It's like he's wearing a target on his back! It's definitely Chris and them!" Xavier shouted as Gavin mimed looking through a scope. They could see a red fleck out there even now, as the group came into sight on the road.

Lea pursed her lips. "Maybe he just likes fashion."

Gavin smiled at her. "Maybe he does. Maybe he does."

As they walked to meet the group at the end of the driveway, Gavin and Xavier filled Lea in on their odd relationship with their neighbors to the north.

"We trade with them from time to time, and I grew up right next to Farrington; we're only about five miles away, but we never really felt like we were a part of that crowd. Most of our friends growing up were from Beulah and Scotville."

"Why not?" Lea asked, looking at Xavier. She knew Gavin well enough now to know that his stories often were *too* good. She'd started asking Xavier and others on the farm for their opinions too, which were often more unvarnished.

Xavier didn't disappoint. "They're soft. Know what I mean? Gavin knew this stuff was coming, and he always said Farrington was gonna be the last place to fall because they were so rich. He was right about that. When the electricity started having problems, they started coming here trying to get food, wanting to trade gold and stuff like that. We didn't need any of that right then, and even if we did, we didn't know how to make for sure it was real. But when they started bringing horses to trade, we became *good* friends then." He looked at his son, who walked beside him. "Maybe you could be getting one of those someday."

Devante beamed at his father, puffing his chest as he walked.

"They have the best horses around," Gavin said. "Back in the day, this whole area raised racehorses, and Farrington was at the center of it all. They were so rich, but their wealth was inextricably tied up with the machine. It was hard for them in a lot of ways; maybe even harder than it was for us. It would be tough to rule the world one year, and then have to start raising chickens so you have enough to eat the next year."

Lea looked thoughtful, and they could now see the group from Farrington clearly. Gavin looked closely at Chris Orlund, their red-jacketed leader. Old, pale and thin, Orlund had the kind of aristocratic face that some of the older Farrington families had. Despite his advanced age, Orlund had become the de facto leader of Farrington.

"Why does he wear the red jacket, anyway?" Lea murmured at Gavin as the group dismounted and approached.

"He used to be the leader of the fox hunting club," Gavin said.

Lea stared at him.

"That was a big deal back then," Gavin said with a smile. He put his hand out and walked to meet Chris, shaking hands and clapping him on the back.

"Chris, this is my fiancé, Lea."

Chris clapped his hand over his heart in mock alarm. "Oh my Lord, you finally found someone to put up with you?" He and Gavin laughed and clasped each other's shoulders, and then Chris bowed to Lea and kissed her hand.

"My lady, it's a pleasure to meet you," Chris said with a flourish.

Lea grinned and kissed him on the cheek. "It's nice to meet

you, too. Why doesn't everyone come up to the house and rest a bit? Gavin, could we give them some of that cider in the pool house?"

Gavin was dumbfounded. They had never done that before. In fact, they had always done their business with visitors while standing in the driveway. All at once, it dawned on Gavin how unfriendly they must have looked to these people. They were so used to being careful that they had forgotten to be hospitable. Xavier always stood by with gun in hand as they transacted their business and they'd never offered them so much as a sip of water in the years that they had been trading. They did business with nearly everyone like that. Everyone else did, too.

He looked at Xavier and then back at Lea, who was beaming at him. *Spunky*, he mouthed at her. "Absolutely, and I don't think we've ever shown you guys the Big House or the gardens in back, how about a quick tour?"

Lea linked her arm with his, and they started going back up the driveway.

Chapter 30

July 2009 – HR 2749, a bill which gives the FDA sweeping powers over small farms and consolidates the power of large corporations like Monsanto and Cargill, passes Congress on its second attempt. This is just one of many ways that the government's tentacles have gripped daily life in America. Security checks, 'free speech' zones, smoking restrictions, seat belt laws, traffic cameras, and gun bans in cities all make up the slow creep of totalitarian control.

Monique groaned as she squinted at the dawn. Shelly and Raven were huddled together, as usual. It always struck Monique how close the two of them were; Shelly didn't allow herself to be touched by anyone but Raven, and almost every morning they could be found sleeping next to each other, like brother and sister. Monique figured that she would let them sleep for a while longer since she had taken the last watch anyway. She started a fire and began heating water in a coffee can. She pulled a small pouch out of her jacket, wrinkling her lips as she removed a teabag. Her last one. As Monique stared at the fire she felt a deep exhaustion in her bones. The exhilaration of the early days had long since vanished.

Her involvement in the resistance had begun with the loss of her husband, Victor, from Gulf War Syndrome. The U.S. Government had never even admitted that her husband had the syndrome, nor took responsibility for what happened to him. The chemicals they exposed him to in Iraq caused his early symptoms, and before much more time had passed, he was diagnosed with Hodgkin's Lymphoma, which ultimately defeated him. He fought the whole way with an inspiring strength that made Monique love him even more.

She grew up in a military family, but had always stayed away from soldiers. The lifestyle was still ingrained in her, however, and after majoring in Information Technology in college, she found herself designing software for a military contractor. Ironically, she didn't meet Victor through work, but through a family friend who told Monique that Victor had been unlike most soldiers that she knew. From their first date, she instinctively knew that she loved this man with all of her heart. And her friend had been right – he was no ordinary soldier.

Outgoing and gregarious, Victor played the drums for various bands and had a wonderful group of civilian friends. He was an MP, which he was extremely proud of, and fond of accosting cops on the street, telling them he was an MP and then asking for directions or tips about the surrounding area. One of Monique's most cherished memories was when the two of them had been visiting Memphis. They had gone for dinner and she was expecting a quiet night back at the hotel. Victor had other plans.

"This is so boring. Where is the real Memphis?" He had been moody all day as they had done the typical tourist thing, visiting landmarks and attractions. Seeing two police officers on the street outside the restaurant, Victor had approached them with his winning smile. "Hey guys, I'm an MP, how are you doing tonight?"

The cops immediately warmed up to Victor, and in a couple of minutes, they were laughing and talking animatedly with him. After a few more minutes the conversation ended, and they shook hands and exchanged hugs. Hugs! Monique never ceased to be amazed by how much people loved Victor. He walked back to Monique. "They're getting off soon and said they would show us around."

Thus began a wild night, one of the best in Monique's life. They met the cops at a rundown bar and had a few drinks, listening to great Blues music, and after a short time it was like they had all known each other for years. One of the cops was meeting his wife, who worked at another bar nearby, and Victor and Monique tagged along. Three bars later, their group had swelled to almost ten people and Victor was the star of the show. The music seemed to get better at each new place they went. Victor told stories about his first tour in Iraq, somehow making them all funny and accessible for everyone, and he knew the Blues so well that he could talk to anyone about it. And since it was Memphis, everyone talked about the Blues.

It was at the last bar of the night, maybe three or four in the morning, when Victor looked at the old Blues musician breaking down his equipment. "That's R.L. Burnsides. I can't believe it!" Victor exclaimed, rushing forward to meet the man. Monique had heard him mention the name before and knew that this old man had been a big influence on Victor's music.

"Mr. Burnsides, I'm a huge fan! I have all of your albums; I loved 'Ass Pocket of Whiskey' the most. I can't believe I missed your show!" Soon, the tired old man was smiling ear to ear, posing with pictures of Victor, Monique, and their new friends. Burnsides didn't appear to get much attention anymore, and this group of excited young people must have made his week. Within a few minutes, Victor had helped to set his equipment back up and was sitting behind the house drum kit. Monique was amazed to see that the two of them launched into an impromptu show, with Victor knowing all of the songs and shouting back at R.L. when the song demanded it, or sometimes just for emphasis. The hour that followed was magical. More people on the streets heard the ruckus and came in, and it turned out that one of the two cops they had originally met was a passable bass player. The show was amazing, and by the time they called it a night, they had developed lifelong friendships with stories to tell forever.

Six years later, Victor died in an army hospital bed, wasted and emaciated. That was in 2024. U.S. soldiers had been dying in the Middle East for decades, and there was nothing to show for it. Victor was just four days shy of his thirtieth birthday when he passed away.

He had only been back a year from his latest tour in Iraq when he died. The loss affected Monique profoundly. She had always been the quiet one of the two, and her experiences with the military bureaucracy leading up to Victor's death and afterward left her in a state of numb shock, which was probably better than the seething anger she would have felt if she hadn't shut down. The people whom she dealt with were indifferent. He was just a number to them.

While she got great support from the soldiers in his unit, the inhumanity of the military organization itself scared her. He had given his life for these people, and for an unjust cause. Monique had already known all of that, but it occurred to her that if the military was in such a state, the rest of the country might be as well.

She became obsessed with research, surfing the internet, starting with websites dedicated to uncovering information about Gulf War Syndrome, and then progressing to sites about the military industrial complex, which led her to understand just how deeply corporate control had gripped the American governmental apparatus and its people. Monique knew the system was too far gone, and that a true Corporate Oligarchy had taken over the federal government. As the years passed and it wasn't overturned, she had to do something. Little did she know exactly what she was setting in motion.

"After all, it was my idea that started it," Monique said to herself.

Chapter 31

"Started what?"

Monique jumped and looked over to see Shelly sitting up and rubbing her eyes. She gently put the blanket back on Raven and walked over to the fire with Monique.

"Sorry, I didn't mean to wake you," said Monique. "I was just thinking out loud."

"Do you mean the resistance?" Shelly asked. "How is that even possible? We were just one small group and we never even talked to anyone else."

Monique stirred the fire and saw that her water was hot. She put the teabag in.

"That was my last teabag. I don't even know what we're doing out here anymore anyway! Before we had Spiegel to go after, what were we even doing? We're basically just refugees now. I started it and now I don't know how to end it. I don't know what to do."

Shelly looked at her with wide eyes. Monique had always been such a strong and sure leader, always focused on the next thing. The next supply of food, the next mission.

"Why do you keep saying you started it?" Shelly asked.

Monique sighed. "Not that it really matters now anyway, but do you remember those first memes about the machine that started showing up?"

Shelly laughed. "No, of course not! Don't you remember how you found me and Raven? We were just kids that were lost in the Crumble. We only became rebels because you fed us and took care of us."

"I know," Monique said. "When I found you two, we were already on the run, and I didn't want to leave you guys alone." She smiled. "But it turned out that you and Raven had a hate on for authority even more than I did!"

Shelly grinned. "So tell me great leader, what were the memes about the machine?"

"When my husband died," Monique replied, "I had no other family. I watched my kindly grandfather die too, in another hospital bed years earlier. I finally got some money out of the military after Victor's death, and I was always good with my money anyway. I became obsessed with the machine, and I gave myself a crash course in hacking. I made my PC at home look like one that belonged to a typical American sheep. I checked social media and mainstream news sites often, and did lots of online shopping. On my unregistered laptop, however, I worked out of my car and used Wi-Fi signals and masking software, which gave me the freedom to do what I wanted. I had a remote printer in the trunk and could download and print hacking instruction manuals, updated versions of things like *The Anarchist Cookbook*, and various other useful troves of information."

Shelly looked at the coffee can. "The tea is ready."

Monique poured them both cups of the precious liquid. Shelly sipped at her tea. "So what were you trying to do? Hack the government or something?"

"I didn't mess with the government much except to go after their hired trolls. I got pretty good at it, but more and more of them just kept coming. So I decided to work on waking people up instead. I never was so naive as to believe that I could wake up the sheep, so I targeted people who were on the cusp. I wanted to find people who had already put some pieces of the puzzle together and were ready to see the big picture. The only way I could have an effect was by changing the general mindset, so I started experimenting with memes."

"I think I did hear about memes once," Shelly said thoughtfully. She opened an MRE and sniffed it gingerly before taking a bite. "Mmm, not bad. But from what I remember hearing, I thought memes were pictures of little cute kittens and funny jokes?"

"Not these memes," Monique said with a chuckle as she opened an MRE of her own. "Not these at all."

Chapter 32

December 2009 – An Associated Press investigation uncovers confidential Monsanto contracts showing that the company squeezes competitors and controls seed companies to assure its continued dominance in the multi-billion dollar seed market. Monsanto's patented genes can be found in ninety-five percent of the soybeans grown in the U.S., and eighty percent of the corn. Despite the monopoly laws and the risk of one company controlling such a large part of the country's food supply, Monsanto has always received excellent treatment from the U.S. government. Michael Taylor, head of the FDA, and Clarence Thomas, a U.S. Supreme Court justice, both worked as lawyers for Monsanto in previous careers. Justice Thomas has thus far been unwilling to recuse himself from any cases involving Monsanto, and all Supreme Court judgments involving Monsanto during his tenure have been favorable to the company.

"What we do here is scrape up all the pine needles a couple of times a year, and then we dump them around the blueberry bushes because they need acidity. We also have a pole with a carving of an owl at the end of each row to keep the birds away," Gavin said. He was having a ball. He had forgotten how much he liked to give tours when he had visitors at the farm before the Crumble, and this group was the most attentive he had ever had. *Orlund is so interested it looks like he wants to start taking notes*, Gavin thought to himself with an inner grin.

"When I first started, I didn't treat my soil at all. I knew it wasn't very acidic and that blueberries needed that, but I figured if I tried out an assortment of varieties, I could see which ones flourished in soil with a high clay content and low acidity. We found the ones that did the best, and started cloning those."

"So which ones were the best?" Chris asked.

Gavin walked over to the fourth row of bushes. "See how these are fuller and taller? They produce more berries, too. This was my 'eureka' moment. And guess what the variety is called? Reka!"

"How do you spell that?" Chris asked, sending Gavin into a fit of laughter. Chris frowned at him. "What's so funny?"

Pulling himself together as Lea and Chris glared at him, Gavin apologized.

"I'm sorry, Chris. It's just that before the Crumble, people used to get so bored by this stuff. I'd have guests over and would give them a tour, and most of the time it was like I was speaking Greek. I guess that now, since our survival is our own responsibility again, these things get a lot more attention. It's just nice, that's all. I wasn't laughing at you."

Chris smiled. "No problem. I really am interested. Do you think you could trade us some of your clones?"

"Of course he will, won't you Gavin?" Lea interjected, prompting a grin from him.

"Of course I will!" Gavin exclaimed. Chris gave a great belly laugh.

"You should listen to the lady!" Chris told Gavin with a smile. "I haven't been right in thirty five years of marriage, and I wouldn't have it any other way."

"Amen to that!" Lea said. Gavin swatted her on the ass.

"Let's head back to the Big House and we'll pass the greenhouse, and then we can go see Mike's rabbit project. He can tell you about that." Gavin started walking the group back.

The visitors were quite taken with the operation at Millwood, and it was obvious that they hadn't had seen many of the farms beyond their immediate surroundings. It made sense; you didn't want to show anyone what you had, because you were afraid that they might come back and try to take it. But Gavin thought that some of these things now had to change. He knew that these people were peaceful and he had dealt with them for years, and they had managed to feed themselves well enough that he wasn't worried they coveted the farm's food. Besides, it had been Lea's idea and it didn't seem very smart to piss her off before the wedding.

As the tour ended and the visitors had admired the library in the Big House, they all sat around the dining room table and Lea went to get the cider. Aidan asked Bob and Stella to sit in at the meeting, and Gavin saw the wisdom in that. They had a stronger connection with Farrington from the old days than either Gavin or Aidan. Chris Orlund, still wearing his bright red coat, thanked Gavin and Aidan for the tour and told them why he had come.

"We've been hearing all about you two lately. We heard about your trip, Gavin, and my wife would love to get a puppy if you do manage to breed any. She loves Bichons." Gavin smirked at brother upon hearing this.

Chris continued. "We also heard about your raid on those Blackhawk men."

"They technically weren't working for Blackhawk anymore, but it looked like they had been employed by them at some point," Aidan said, boasting a bit. "They killed someone coming to visit Gavin and they had set up a roadblock on Broad Rock Road. We didn't think we had much choice."

"We agree," Chris said. "We've had raiders come through our area and we've always just hunkered down and tried to ride them out. Eventually they move on, but not before killing more of us and taking as much as they can get their hands on. We hid as much as we could and tried to fight them, but we've been basically powerless against the larger groups. We want to ask for your help. If we can combine our forces we might be able to stop these groups before they can do too much damage. Think of it this way – if those men didn't work for Blackhawk anymore, it means that they must have had to lay off a big group of their mercenaries. We could see more men like that. And of course, we would help you, too."

Gavin looked at Aidan, who was deep in thought. Looking up at the group from Farrington, Aidan said "How have you all managed so far? What is the biggest group you have taken down?"

Looking slightly offended, Chris said, "I think eight men are the most we've ever attacked."

"That's about the same for us." As Aidan said that, Gavin could see Chris relax a little bit, realizing that Aidan wasn't trying to start a pissing contest. Continuing, Aidan said, "If we could set up a network of runners, we could communicate a lot better. We did find some communication equipment on the Blackhawk men, but we don't have the energy to spare and don't want to get dependent on something like that. What we do have is Devante. That boy could run to Farrington in under an hour and still have the energy to run back. If we could get four of five more kids like that, we could really have something here."

Gavin had a wild thought and began to speak. He did this sometimes, just thinking out loud as he let his thoughts run their course. "You guys have great horses, and you all are really good with them, too. Have you ever thought of doing cavalry style fighting? You could make slugs for your shotguns. I know you all have those fancy 20 gauges with the designs on them. If I saw a bunch of guys all riding horses towards me really fast, screaming and shooting 20 gauge slugs at me, I would probably start running. The topography of our area would support it, too. You could try to trap groups on inclines or at the bottom of hills and charge down at them. You all remember John Mosby from the Civil War? They called him the Grey Ghost because he would wait for a nice misty morning. Knowing the area so well, Mosby could always find where the best pockets of the densest fog would be. He would wait, his whole group dressed in grey, and they would all charge their horses at the enemy, surprising and scaring the hell out of them."

Gavin finished and there was silence for a moment on both sides of the table. He saw Orlund puff up a little bit. "You know, there might be something to that. We should play to our strengths. I'm tired of crawling around on my belly trying to sneak up on everyone."

Aidan chimed in, "I bet that could work; there was a reason that cavalry was so effective for so many years. You all are probably the best suited to do something like that, you have the best horses and riding equipment, and your people are the most skilled. Most of us will be leaving around Thanksgiving to go to Gavin and Lea's wedding, so once we get back, we'll send you a runner and set up a big meeting in the spring. We can get people from Ramsey, Scotville, and Beulah, too, and we can coordinate and train together."

As the meeting broke up, Gavin could hear excitement in the voices of the people from Farrington. His parents chatted up the group as they walked back to the driveway to get their horses, asking about various notables who had lived in the area. This information would be very helpful, Gavin thought.

One of the women in the Farrington group offered to coordinate finding the best horses for the job, and another said they would see about uniforms. Bob promised to scour the library for information about cavalry fighting, and Stella was negotiating to trade a couple of the extra saddles they had at Millwood. Up until now, Gavin hadn't paid much attention to the two young men in the group, dismissing them as just muscle. Maybe they were, but it seemed as if the cavalry idea had gone over well with them.

Chapter 33

Mike pestered Gavin into letting him go with the first group to Ramsey for the wedding, and bothered him some more to let him take the rebel girl, but Gavin hadn't budged on that one. On the ride to Ramsey Mike was sulking and hanging back from the group, missing his new female friend. Xavier was riding point with two more members of his team behind him, followed by Lea and a few of the older kids from the Collier and Jackson families. Gavin and Mike followed next, with two more of Xavier's team taking up the rear. Aidan and Gavin hadn't wanted to take any more chances, so they would be sending two groups like this, each with extra protection. A couple of neighbors and the Farrington people had offered to help guard Millwood while everyone was gone, and there was still a skeleton crew there, made up of a couple of guards, the elderly who couldn't ride anymore, and the very small children and their moms.

"You know, this is the first time we have done anything like this, and that this is the farthest you've ever been away from the farm, right?" Gavin was hoping to get Mike out of his funk.

"Yep, so far it looks the same," Mike replied, still in his mood. "I thought it would be different somehow."

They were passing a landscape that Gavin now knew well; overgrown grass and weeds everywhere, and litter all over the ground. Most of the buildings were ruined, and the few places that had been kept up were visibly defended. Their caravan was large and well-armed, and they made no threatening moves away from the road. They were left unmolested when they passed defended areas, sometimes getting a grim nod or two as they passed. The few people they passed looked a lot like they did. Lean and scruffy.

"America had gotten so homogenized by the time the Crumble came that everything looked the same. Nowadays, one burned out McDonalds looks like the rest. One crumbling big box store here looks exactly the same as another, even as far away as California. I think that now that we've gotten our feet back under us, we will be able to start building our own houses and towns again. At that point, we'll start to see more regional variation. It will be your generation who gets to decide what kind of places they want to live in." Gavin hoped that Mike's curious intellect would take over now, and he could stop thinking about the girl for a minute. From what Gavin remembered of being that age, it would not be an easy feat.

"So, who used to decide? Who decided to build all of that stuff, if not the people who lived there?" Mike asked.

Gavin thought for a minute. "Corporations, mostly. I guess it's kind of hard to understand now, but the people who owned those companies lived far away in really nice places, and they didn't care about the communities they built in. So they just built whatever was cheapest."

"They look like crap," Mike mused. "Even the buildings I've seen that are intact from before the Crumble look like huge boxes with no windows or anything. And why are all of their roofs flat? That's probably why so many of them are messed up now, all their roofs must have caved in because of the water and snow."

"You know, you aren't the dumbest kid on the planet." Gavin loved to tease Mike this way. They messed with each other a lot, one way they showed affection for one another. Mike had heard Gavin call it 'breaking balls' once and loved it, saying the phrase until it drove everyone crazy.

"Well, you know I learned everything from you, and you are about as smart as, say, Meatloaf, so that's a compliment coming from you!"

Meatloaf was their Duroc boar, a big friendly beast, but not the brightest bulb on the tree. Gavin grinned and playfully smacked Mike on the back of the head.

"You know," Gavin said, "You have a really good point there, but you are missing one vital piece of information. We had cheap oil, so not only did it power all of our vehicles, but we used it for just about everything else, too. We made fertilizer with it, plastics, and most importantly for this discussion, industrial roof sealant. That stuff was cheap enough that it was easier to just build a flat roof and seal it up every few years. Most of those buildings were only meant to last about twenty years anyway."

"I can sort of see that, but it still doesn't make sense," said

Mike. "If the company only cared about making money, wouldn't it lose money when it had to build a new building a couple of decades later?" Mike's curiosity was again piqued, and Gavin had no easy answers for him.

"It's hard to explain. The whole system was complex and twisted, things like that made sense at the time. Part of it was just how people thought; it was a culture where everything was disposable. And corporations were only designed to think about three months at a time, maybe a year. The people who worked for the corporations, all the way up to the CEO, were only rewarded for short-term results. When I was working in the corporate world, I was rewarded for the gains I earned for the company in the short term. No one was ever rewarded for doing something that would help the company, much less the world, twenty years down the road. Your generation needs to figure out how to reward people for doing things that last. I have no idea how that will work, though." Gavin knew that he didn't have the whole answer and Mike had always respected him for being honest.

"So what the hell am *I* supposed to do?" Mike asked.

"What do you mean?" Gavin said.

"I've been hearing my whole life about that time, and I completely missed it. I was only five when we came to the farm, and I hadn't even turned eight before the power went out for good. All the people who remember it seem to have a strong opinion about those days, though. Some of them say it was so wonderful! People had plenty of gas to drive cars everywhere, and they flew around on airplanes all the time, and the TV and movies, and the food, oh God the food they talk about!" Mike laughed and rolled his eyes at Gavin who was always talking about how he missed real pizza (their attempts at Millwood had never gone well).

"But then some others, like you, talk about why that time was so bad," Mike continued. "You say that the way people lived was wrong and unsustainable. You always say, 'your generation will do this, your generation will do that.' But how do we know which is the right way? Should we try to get technology working again, or become better farmers? I don't want to be your age still hanging out with Meatloaf. Know what I mean?" Although he was still using his sharp sense of humor, Mike seemed to have fallen into his depression again, and as Gavin momentarily thought back over recent weeks, he'd seemed down in general. Maybe this wasn't just about the girl.

"Well, lots of that will be for you to decide for yourself, but that's not a very good answer to your question. Let me think for a minute."

Gavin thought of telling Mike how good he had it compared to most people, which was even truer these days. But he had told him that many times before, not wanting him to take their life at Millwood for granted. Gavin knew what he really wanted to know. He himself had agonized over that very question many times since the Crumble. What could mankind look forward to now? What great achievements still lay on the horizon, now that humanity had made such a mess of their nest? *What a mess we made*, Gavin thought.

He suspected that many parts of the world now had problems with radiation from the failed nuclear plants, and sometimes Gavin wondered if his area was one of the lucky few that hadn't been affected. He still kept his NukAlert hanging on a peg by his front door just in case. Although he didn't think there was much of a risk at this point, old habits die hard. Fukushima alone had devastated the area surrounding Japan, and as time went on, the accident became more and more difficult to contain. The west coast of the U.S. had been affected, and Gavin wondered if they could eat the fish from the Pacific even now, so many years later. The Russian army had finally flown in and taken control of Fukushima, and the world breathed a cautious sigh of relief. But even setting the nuclear incidents aside, the damage done to the planet by humanity was incalculable.

"You know why I always loved science fiction, and why I still read those books today, even though it doesn't seem like any of that is possible anymore? It's because I believe that the destiny of humanity is to populate the stars. But before we can do that, we need to become better ourselves, or we won't deserve it. I think that fossil fuels were an important test for us, and we failed that test spectacularly. We were like kids in a candy store. We ate too much all at once and made ourselves sick. Hopefully for us we can learn from this lesson. So one answer to your question is to go to space! But in all seriousness, I bet that there are lots of other answers like that one, too. There are a lot of things that need to be done, like healing the land and finding technology that we can sustain under these conditions. We know how to make a culture that will last ten thousand years. We know how to farm without draining the land of its nutrients now. That will give us the time to figure everything else out."

Mike was grinning at him. "Alright. So, you said we were being 'tested.' Who is testing us? God? You never talk about that and you never go to church with us. Do you even believe in God at all?"

Smiling back at him, Gavin was just glad he had engaged Mike with something. He had wanted to tell Mike what he had said to Lea about Italy, but he risked upsetting Aidan if it hadn't been cleared with him first.

"I will tell you what I think about the religion issue, but it will have to be some other time. It looks like Xavier has found a good spot to spend the night."

Mike was still smiling as Gavin rode away.

Chapter 34

Shelly, Raven, and Monique were at a loss. They had formed a grid of the surrounding area and started searching for Spiegel's Hummer. They were operating under the assumption that, since Spiegel had been wounded, he would hole up somewhere close by. That big black vehicle would be hard to hide, so they based their search on that. They started searching the nearest cluster of houses they could find; a row of townhouses right up against the highway with a big concrete wall behind them as a sound barrier.

While they had discussed splitting up to make the search faster, Monique ultimately decided against that strategy because it was unsafe. Places like this had mostly been abandoned, but a passing group of raiders might decide to squat in one of the houses. They searched street by street, following the grid pattern they had decided on. Most of the houses were in terrible states of disrepair, and Monique wondered how quickly these places had emptied out after the Crumble.

She had seen her first ghost town in the mid-2020s, even before the grid went down. At that time, she and her group were dedicating themselves to making sure that the remains of the machine died faster. They were aware of what was happening to the world around them, and the time had come for them to help move things along. When the government and its corporate masters still had control, the machine had been like a wounded beast. It tried to take as much money from the populace as possible, and as things got worse, they squeezed the shrinking group of people who still earned and paid taxes harder and harder. So Monique and the rebels hacked into the tax records, wreaking havoc, and destroying traffic cameras, corporate property, and any other parts of the machine they could get their hands on. Unsurprisingly, they became a target of corporate thugs and soon had to live on the run.

After one particularly successful raid, they were passing through a suburban development, having found on a map that it was part of a shortcut that would take them away from major roads. As they walked through the streets, they noticed that everything was quiet. While a few of the houses had gardens in front, most had been abandoned.

Shelly said, "It looks like a tumbleweed is going to roll out any second."

Monique chuckled, surprised at Shelly who rarely joked. "I would have thought that was before your time, kiddo."

Shelly looked into the distance. "My dad used to love Westerns."

It hit home for Monique that day, what had been done to the American people. What they had done to themselves. They allowed themselves to be fooled into signing up for an unsustainable way of living. Monique looked around where they were walking and saw nothing but row after row of houses. There were no schools, apartments, farms, churches, or stores of any kind. It was just houses, as far as the eye could see. They were forced to drive to make money, to get food, and to do just about everything else. Their entire way of life was based on the idea that oil and gas would be cheap forever. Structuring their towns and cities this way destroyed the very communities that built them.

Monique and her group had made it through the ghost town without incident, but that memory had stuck with her. It had turned out that their work wasn't done yet, and they lasted a couple more years until the bastards put Spiegel on them.

Spiegel had been the worst of their pursuers. Monique scowled at the memory, and not just for the fact that he had been such a challenging adversary. It was also for the fact that back then, they were fighting for a cause. Now, the years of being pursued by Spiegel had sapped their will to fight, and besides, the machine had finally collapsed under its own weight. In the past couple of years, after they realized that Spiegel had finally been cut loose and they weren't being chased anymore, they were left with little to do but to stay on the road and try to keep themselves fed. When they had happened on Spiegel's little roadblock, going after him had given them something to fight for again. But killing Spiegel was personal, not for any noble cause. Even if they could find and kill him, what would they do then? Who would they be then?

Chapter 35

The next time Spiegel woke up, Longhurst was nowhere in sight. Spiegel hoped that he had gone in search of food, as the two boxes of MREs didn't look appetizing at all. Out of sheer necessity, Richard got himself up and went over to try and eat something. He was sore all over, and as he bent over to retrieve an MRE from the box, he felt light-headed and almost fell. He was simultaneously cold and sweating. *Now is not the time to go into detox*, Richard thought to himself as he tried to choke down the cold meal. The heating units for the MREs had been in one of the other Hummers. *That goddamn machine gun*, he thought. He was sure that was what turned the tide.

Richard vomited. The pasta and meatballs were still intact, and stared back at him listlessly from the floor. He went and lay back down.

He was still sleeping when Longhurst came back in, carrying several bottles.

Chapter 36

January 2010 - The United States Supreme Court holds that 'The First Amendment prohibits the government from restricting political contributions by corporations, associations, or labor unions.' Regardless of the constitutional interpretation of this issue, this decision effectively hands the reigns of the government over to the large corporations.

Ramsey, Virginia

The townspeople of Ramsey and Doc's family were distraught by the news of Scott's death, but they somberly offered their hospitality to the visitors at Millwood and all felt welcome. Despite the sad news, everyone was so relieved to see that Lea had survived, and they were so happy to see Gavin and his family that within a few days, everyone was bright and joyful. So much so that Gavin felt guilty and vowed to make a special toast to Scott at the wedding.

Gavin couldn't wait. He'd been proud of how respectful he was of Lea's boundaries, but as they continued to grow closer, they both felt the need to express themselves physically. Gavin was no spring chicken; he could control himself, so he and Lea had taken to chastely sleeping together. She had more trouble with it than he did, however. She was feeling the same connection that he had, and was eager to express those feelings with him. One night, after a make out session where it got so hot and heavy that Gavin had to pull away, Lea said, "I know you want to be respectful of my family, but you could have tried to convince me at any point. You could just have said, 'they will never know.' Why haven't you?"

Gavin was stunned. He had assumed she would be the one who wanted to wait more than he did, and he really wasn't clear on what was going on with Lea's family. He had no idea what he was doing, he was just winging it. When he had asked to court Lea he had assumed that no sex was part of the deal.

"Uhhh," he stammered, "well, you know... it's out of respect for your religion and everything, and I just want to be respectful."

"I'll admit, I do go to church with my family sometimes, and I do believe in God." She took the tie out of her hair and shook her hair loose. "But I've always been a practical woman." She shrugged off her top. "If we conceive this month, our first baby will be born towards the end of summer. That's as good of a time as any to have our first child." She removed the rest of her clothing, so like always, Gavin winged it. And it was beautiful.

"Ah, so *that's* where you hide your backup knife," Gavin sighed some time later. She smiled at him, playfully punching him in the shoulder and kissing his cheek.

Chapter 37

It was still a week before the second group from Millwood was to arrive. Gavin and Mike were spending their days helping Doc's family and the locals in Ramsey with their projects and chores, when Mike cornered Gavin again about religion. He and Lea were helping Ann jar squash, and Gavin was doing the peeling.

Although Gavin was on top of the world since he and Lea had taken their relationship to the next level, he was careful to conceal it. Mike seemed to know, however, and had been smirking at Gavin a lot. Gavin struggled not to laugh at his nephew's silly faces. Lea was standing facing the window in Doc's kitchen, and Mike looked at Gavin, looked at her ass, and then looked back at Gavin, raising and waggling his eyebrows up and down. Gavin quickly left the room to keep everyone from seeing him. He held onto the back of a couch in the living room, silently laughing. It was when he came back in that Mike asked him.

"So you promised me to tell me your thoughts on religion. Now seems like a good time, judging from that huge pile of squash sitting over there." Mike looked at him wryly. Lea and Ann both looked up.

"Well, I don't want to offend anyone. Lea and Ann, I know you two are Methodists. I want you to know that no matter what I think about religion, I believe that there are lots of ways to get to God, and I respect yours one hundred percent. Lea, you already know that. I will support you in everything you do, and that if you want me to be involved in that part of your life, I definitely will be."

Lea smiled coyly at him and went back to her work. Ann leaned on her cane and looked at Gavin. "I have seen a lot in my time and I have learned a few things. I know that preachers are human beings just like the rest of us, some good and some bad, and I know that God is unknowable. I have done the best I can in my life and I will meet God with a clear conscience. But I also agree that there is more than one way to get to know God. I would love to hear yours." With that, she went back to wiping the lids of the jars while Lea put the lids on and put them in the boiling water. Now that autumn was in full swing, they had been able to move the kitchen back indoors, which was a relief, as there was less to carry back and forth.

Gavin picked his peeler up again and looked at Mike. "Let's start by saying that I do believe that there is a soul. I believe that when we die, some part of us remains. I have always been fascinated by religion. I read about all of the major world religions when I was young, and as I got older I became interested in Paganism. Lots of these various religions had similar threads running through them, like the father-type gods and the tricksters. Similarities like that could be found all over the place and I was fascinated by it. I began to think that there might be some truth to every single religion. At the same time that I was looking into this, I also got into some pretty far out stuff online, and read about a few experiments with consciousness and how it could affect the outcomes of certain events. Of course, I take all of that stuff with a grain of salt, but I couldn't help but conclude that there are still many things that we don't understand about human consciousness and what it can do.

"I was thinking one day years ago about *Star Wars*. The storyline of the Jedi in the movie was very similar to what actually happened to the Shaolin monks in China. Those monks have a fascinating history, and they could do some pretty remarkable things with their minds and bodies through meditation and training. They could slow or speed their heartbeat at will; they could endure intense cold, heat or pain, and so on. They were also great fighters, though they tried to avoid violence. Over the centuries, they could sometimes be convinced to fight in various wars and uprisings when they thought the cause was just. At different times in their history, they were betrayed and attacked, and their temple was burned down more than once. At one point in their history, almost of them were killed off, but a small group of just a few monks survived and managed to keep the order going in secret. They always survived. In fact, I bet that they are still surviving today. If anyone could, it would be them. Those guys were tough."

Lea rolled her eyes at him. He had told her about *Star Wars* before but she had obviously never seen any of the movies. Mike had seen them, though. A few years back, Aidan had gotten a portable DVD player that he could charge with a solar panel, and those were the first movies they watched. Mike had loved all three of the originals. It

146

had turned out that neither Gavin nor Aidan owned copies of the new ones. *Hmmm*, Gavin thought. When they got back, he would have to dig up the DVD player and show them to Lea. Gavin looked at Mike. "So does that story sound familiar?"

"Yeah, that is just like the Jedi! The Jedi were monks with special powers, and they all got killed except Obi-Wan and Yoda, and they were all that were left of the Jedi order until they trained Luke!" Mike said, eyes shining. He *really* loved those movies.

"So the Jedi use 'the Force,' and the Shaolin monks call it 'Chi.' Lots of the eastern religions incorporate the idea of Chi. What they are really talking about is Life Force. It is the spark inside all living things that gives us life, and it connects all living things in a great web. We don't understand that and we can't measure it scientifically yet, and maybe we never will. But if you believe that such a thing exists, so many things start to make sense.

"When you die, the spark inside you doesn't. The Life Force inside you survives forever. When that spark leaves your body, I think it can do lots of different things. It can live on as pure energy, or if it wants to, it can join with other sparks. It can infuse life into another being if it wants to live again. It can merge itself with the larger spark that I believe is God. That is how Nirvana, Heaven, reincarnation, and most other religions can be explained under one roof. It would explain why so many people think they see ghosts – maybe that is because that particular spark hasn't left our world yet. And like I said, God itself is the source; the biggest spark of all, made up of the same stuff inside each of us. Every living thing is made from the spark of God. I don't think that God is a he or a she, but rather, a vast force of living energy."

Lea and Ann were quiet. Gavin had already explained an abbreviated version to Lea, and she'd only said, "I believe that. I've always believed that."

Mike was intrigued, though his mind worked like that of a seventeen-year-old boy. "So those monks were like Jedi? They could hold their hand over fire and not get burned? What else could they do?"

Gavin laughed. "They would get burned if they did that, but probably not as badly as one of us, and they could block out the pain. They could place a spear under their belly button and then balance on it, all four limbs unsupported. They could smash bricks on their heads, and do the most graceful martial arts I've ever seen. I think that they were able to do all of that because they taught their minds to harness the power of their inner God spark. When they enhanced their consciousness through meditation, they were using that power."

Mike was fascinated, eyes blazing. "Did any of them ever come to the States?" he asked.

"There was a temple in New York City," Gavin answered, "but I doubt anything is left there now. I do remember that they were building a temple in upstate New York, called The USA Shaolin Temple. I actually donated money to them once, I loved the idea. It was in this little town called Fleischmann; I remember it because it was sort of an unusual name. There was a rumor that two Shaolin masters who defected from China were hiding up there, but I never knew if that was true." Gavin was affected by Mike's excitement.

"So the Godspark, that's what God is?" Mike asked, intrigued.

"Yes, to a certain extent," Gavin replied. "I think that life itself is God and vice versa. But there is more to it than that. Think about the law of gravity, or the law of inertia, or any of the other natural laws. Consider the elements, and how DNA was formed, and how it can mutate, especially when faced with changes in the environment. Who made those rules? How are they enforced? That's God, too. If it weren't for those rules, nothing could exist. *Who made the rule that life could evolve?* Where did the *first* amoeba come from? Who created matter? Who created energy? No one could have done that but God. Maybe the Pagan archetypes are aspects of God, too; the same ones that show up all over the world. Maybe they're like the hands and feet of God. Or maybe human beings made those archetypes with our consciousness, our stories and imaginations. Who knows? But I do know this; there is magic in the world that we don't understand, and a lot of that magic is locked away inside our own minds and bodies.

"Now, we must learn to balance that magic with our technology. Why use a computer when we have a better one inside our own skulls? Why record a song when so many of us could learn to sing it beautifully, and each one uniquely? We gave so many parts of ourselves to the machine that we forgot something important. It's better for us to rely on the spark of God that each one of us has inside. That can't be taken away. It will last as long as we live, and even after that."

Gavin took a breath.

"The Godspark!" Mike said excitedly. "That kind of makes sense. That really makes a lot of things fall into place. Now I know why you carve that guy with one eye all the time; that must be the Norse god, Odin. Those carvings on your walking stick must be runes. I guess Norse mythology was your favorite of the Pagan religions then?"

"Good Lord, man, how much time have you spent in the library with my dad?" Gavin asked. He was amazed that Mike had been able to put all of that together so quickly. He never talked about Odinism with any of the family because Aidan was very clear in the fact that he wanted to raise his kids Christian. As the 'cool uncle,' Gavin knew that he had an influence on Mike, so he had always kept that to himself. But now Mike was old enough to not be unduly influenced, and Gavin enjoyed talking about it.

"I know you joke that Bob's stories are boring, but I like them," Mike said. "I know all about history because of what he taught me. Of course, I also know more about The Romans than I ever wanted." Mike rolled his eyes and smiled.

Bob had always been fascinated by Roman history. He and Gavin shared that interest, although Gavin and Mike both teased him about how obsessive he was about it. While in Italy, Gavin and his father would read about the history of the surrounding area and visit ruins and historical architecture. He shared his love of Italian food with Stella as well, so their trips to Italy were joyous occasions.

Bob and Stella now spent their free time on their hobbies, when they were not busy teaching the children. Bob had dedicated much of his time to expanding and cataloguing the library, and he was in his element; the history section was second to none. Stella focused on creating new recipes and running the kitchen, which fed the whole farm for dinner every night. If it weren't for her, mealtime would be a much less flavorful occasion. She also used her business acumen to negotiate some of the trading deals that Millwood did with its neighbors, as she was a better negotiator than Gavin would ever be.

Gavin joined in poking fun at his father. "I bet he told you all about the Punic Wars, and specifically the battles between Hannibal and Scipio Africanus?"

"Oh my God!" Mike laughed. "He talks about that all the time!"

Gavin retorted, "And I bet he hasn't even told you about the Spartans and the battle of Thermopylae?"

Mike looked confused. "Umm, well I know about Greek history, so I know about Athens and Sparta and all that, but I don't think I know that story."

"Oh man, I knew he would skip over Thermopylae just to spite me! The Spartans were way cooler than the Romans. Let me tell you about it. It was three hundred men against an army of hundreds of thousands!" Gavin and Mike then launched into an epic discussion about history. Lea and Ann chatted amongst themselves and they eventually finished the canning.

As Gavin and Lea were getting ready for bed that night, she looked at him and said, "You love him, don't you?"

"Who, Mike? Yeah, he's a great kid," Gavin responded, taking off his shirt. He was thinking more about the upcoming night's events than anything else.

"I can tell you this, Gavin Collier. You will make a great father. And Godspark or not, I love you."

He swept her into the bed.

Chapter 38

Monique's ragged little rebel group hadn't made much progress, although their lot was somewhat improved. Monique thought about the group they had left back at the farm, wondering how they were doing and wishing that she had brought a couple more people with her to go after Spiegel and Longhurst. Monique shrugged. The ones she left at the farm were all hungry and exhausted, and they needed rest and food.

After two days of searching the area, Shelly and Raven found a row of townhouses hidden behind a stand of pine trees. Upon further inspection, they found that these houses hadn't been ransacked too badly, and they found some useful items. They found a can opener, some old camping gear, and even a still-sharp paring knife. Monique hoped that if they made it back to Scotville, she would at least be able to bring some useful gifts with her. One of the houses had evidently been home to a teenager or young man living at home with his parents.

The house looked like a Normal Rockwell painting, with cross-stitched Bible quotes on the wall and the dusty remains of a potpourri mix in a bowl by the front door. One of the upstairs bedrooms, however, was a gold mine. There were posters on the wall of goth bands that Monique had never heard of, and the closet was full with a collection of swords and knives. While some were too decorative to be of any use, most were well made and not too rusty. Monique was overjoyed. The second in command at Millwood, the tall black man with dreadlocks named Xavier, had worn a sword on his back at the battle. She hoped that bringing back this gift would help to at least partially pay for the hospitality of the people from Scotville and Millwood farm. Raven took a new knife for himself and so did Shelly, although they both left the best one for Monique to take, which she duly did.

That night, Raven's traps bore meat and they made a stew with what they had. As they sat by the fire in the dark, Shelly and Raven oiling and sharpening their new knives, Monique almost felt content. Her belly was full and the weather wasn't bad yet. She thought that November would be ending soon, although she wasn't sure exactly when, and she stopped herself when she started to worry about what they would do for the winter. That would come when it came.

"So Raven woke up the other day and interrupted us. You were telling me about memes." Shelly was sitting next to Raven, who was quiet as usual.

Monique considered her two charges. Their faces were dirty and their clothes ragged; Shelly and Raven were lean and hard. That was what she had turned them into. But they were alive. She had taught them to survive, at least.

"Remember the rallying cry?" Monique asked.

"Fight the Machine!" Raven vehemently whispered, surprising Monique. He was normally so quiet.

"Exactly," Monique said. "There was nothing more we could do. Some had been able to partially disconnect themselves from the machine as they started producing their own food and re-creating their local economies, but it wasn't enough. Most young people were thoroughly brainwashed, but a few of them did have an inkling of what was being done to them. One day, I created a meme with a picture of a self-checkout aisle next to a red light camera. Over the top it said: 'Break the Machine!' I don't remember exactly what it said now, but it was something about how every time corporate technology gets better, our lives get worse. Every time a machine takes someone's job, it further dehumanizes the consumer's experience, too. The only person who profits from it is the one at the very top. It didn't matter what mine said though, because the meme I created was just the seed."

"That was enough to start the resistance?" Shelly asked, eyes narrowed at Monique.

"I posted mine and nothing happened. I posted it on a bunch of different sites, though, and on one of the hacker sites I used, I saw another meme show up a few weeks later. It had three pictures. The first was a picture of a voting booth and the text said: 'Voting didn't work.' The second was a picture of a student protest in Greece, and the text read: 'Protests didn't work.' The third was a picture of a smashed ATM machine, and text read: 'Maybe this won't work either, but at least we get to break shit!' At the bottom, in bright red letters, it said: 'Break the Machine!'

"That's when things really took off. The alternative news sites started reporting small events of sabotage, although the corporate media was silent, of course. Several months later, a video began circulating on the independent sites. It was grainy and looked old, but that may have been by design to make it more difficult to identify. A man of indeterminate height stood against a backdrop of plain white drywall, covered from head to toe in nondescript, military-style clothing. He wore a ski mask and wraparound sunglasses, and was holding an assault rifle. When he began to speak, his voice had been modified, making the deep sound so familiar to fans of horror movies.

'We have a message to the largest governments and corporations around the world,' the man said. 'You have taken everything from us. You have taken our money, our homes, and our way of life. In China, you took millions of us from our ancestral farms and destroyed them with your machines and your poisons. When we had no other choice, you took us and made us slaves in your factories, working day and night to make your electronic shit. In India, you did the same thing. Millions were forced to poison their farmland to feed your machine, and thousands of farmers kill themselves every year, horrified at what they've done to their own land.

'In Europe and the Americas, you bled us dry with your stealing and your lies. You stole from us in a thousand different ways, and smiled in our faces as you did it. You replaced us with machines. For those of us who were left with no meaningful work, you fed us with a poisoned tit of ignorance and moral degradation. You poisoned us with your processed food and your electronic bullshit, and filled a once proud people with sloth and wickedness until they were brought to their knees. You ruined lives just so you could have another yacht in the Hamptons, or more political power.

'In Africa, you killed us by the millions and looked the other way while we killed each other, fighting over the few resources left to us. You took our gold and our oil, and while you lived like kings, you stepped on the backs of millions to get there. All around the world, you have killed off entire peoples, and destroyed entire ecosystems, all to feed the greed of your machines.

'We cannot wait any longer for nature to stop you, or for the machine to run out of juice. If we wait that long, there will only be ashes left for our children. We cannot try to wake up others any longer, there is no time left. Our message to the machine is this: Stop. Stop fracking, and stop deep water drilling. Shut down the most dangerous nuclear plants. You know the ones we're talking about, the design that was used at Fukushima. Those plants cannot survive disasters and they must be shut down. Stop using the resources we have left for frivolous things. And most importantly: Stop your war machines! The United States war machine uses more energy than all of its citizens combined.

'If you don't stop, we *will* stop you. While many agree with us, we know that only a few of us will fight. But that will be enough, because *you are weak*. We know where your critical infrastructure lies, and we will fight to destroy it. We know you can barely maintain your decaying and rotting system. You'll never find our leader because there isn't one. You'll never be able to buy us off, because all your money is worthless. Our children can't eat your goddamn money.

'We also have a message to the sheep around the world. We mean you no harm. We don't blame you for not understanding what has been done to you. In fact, we all were once like you. If we're forced to act, please understand that we do not intend to hurt you or cause you pain in any way. We have no choice. If our children and grandchildren are to even have a chance at being able to survive life on this planet, then we must act now.'"

Shelly and Raven were both silent, eyes wide.

"How can you remember all of that?" Shelly asked.

"It was burned into my brain the moment I saw it," Monique said. "The next day, I went out and started recruiting."

Chapter 39

March 2010 — The Affordable Care Act is signed into law. This legislation, which was written by insurance lobbyists and wasn't even read by the people who passed it, was intended to provide affordable health care to those who couldn't afford it. In reality, it increases the cost and complexity of the already bloated insurance and healthcare industries. Despite the fact that a few million people are able to sign up for subsidized healthcare, many more lose their own healthcare or are forced to pay significantly higher premiums.

By the time Aidan arrived in Ramsey with Bob, Stella, and the rest of the second Millwood contingent, the town was in a cheerier mood. For Scott's family, however, as the shock of his death wore off, grief had taken its place. Gavin saw it firsthand with Lea's family.

Lea had her mother's looks, and Gavin had been taken with her when they first met.

"I'm Romina," Lea's mother said, smiling sweetly at Gavin and clasping his hand.

"Romina! I love that name. Is that Swiss?"

"Hungarian," Romina answered, still smiling at Gavin and batting her eyelashes. Lea nudged her mother.

"Mom!" Lea exclaimed. "He's mine!"

Romina's eyes twinkled for a moment, and then Gavin saw her expression change, as if she'd just remembered something unpleasant.

"Gavin, this is my husband, Harry." Romina gestured to the next room, where her husband was sitting on the couch. Realizing that Harry had no intention of getting up, Gavin walked over and shook his hand. His grip was limp, and his palm felt cool and oily. Gavin stood awkwardly for a few minutes with Harry, trying to make small talk. Thankfully, Romina quickly called them in for dinner.

"We loved Scott," Lea's mother said as they sat down at the table. She'd prepared an egg and potato frittata sprinkled with fresh herbs, served with a squash and zucchini medley. Gavin complimented her cooking, and received a lascivious smile in return. "He played at the diner a couple of times a week," Romina continued. "Harry and I used to go there a lot. Scott was something else with that guitar."

Gavin looked at Lea's father, nonplussed. Harry was on his second glass of 'tea' already, clearly mixed with moonshine.

"Heh, yeah, he was a good 'un, that boy," Harry grunted, taking another sip. "My brother didn't bring him up right far as I could see, but he turned out alright. A little soft with the guitar and long hair, though, just like his father."

Lea gave her mother a concerned look, reaching down to hold Gavin's hand under the table. She clutched it fiercely.

"Harry, why don't you go in the back and lay on the couch for a while? I'll clean up and bring you some of that peach cobbler we have, alright?" Romina bustled him out of his chair and into the next room, making sure to bring his 'tea' along.

Lea looked at Gavin sheepishly. "Now you know why I didn't bring you out here the first time you visited," she whispered.

Gavin squeezed Lea's hand harder and brushed his other hand against her face. "I love you Lea, and that includes your family. I love your mom, and I can see where you get your looks. And your dad…"

"Go ahead, you can say it," Lea said.

"It's not like that," Gavin said as she leaned her head on his shoulder. "These last years have been hard on everyone. I'm not one to judge how people cope with it." He mimed smoking a joint and winked at her. She grinned at him and punched his arm.

"Aaah, finally a smile!" Gavin said. "So, what's your uncle like, anyway? I've heard everyone talk about him and I feel like we've been avoiding meeting him."

"He's supposed to come tonight," Lea said as her mother came back into the kitchen. Gavin stood and offered to help clean up, but Romina shushed him.

"You stay here," she said. "Ex will be here soon and he'll want to talk to you."

As he and Lea and Romina made small talk, the peach cobbler came out of the oven, and it was triumphant. Just as he started to relax, a loud knock sounded at the door.

Lea got the door and a man resembling Jesus walked in.

"Freddie Exley is my name, but everyone calls me Ex," the man introduced himself. He was a tall and lanky fellow with dark eyes, long hair, and a neatly trimmed beard. After shaking Gavin's hand and kissing Lea and Romina, he sat down across from Gavin at the kitchen table, looking directly at him. He hadn't even bothered to say hello to his brother, who was still laid out on the couch.

Lea and Romina conferred quietly and then announced that they were going out to the garden to take in the cool autumn air. The two men sat alone, one of them grieving for his lost son and the other, consumed with guilt for being the cause of it.

Gavin spoke first.

"Ex," he said, "I've been looking forward to meeting you and I want to extend my condolences for the loss of your son. I only knew Scott for a short time but he was a wonderful guy, and very talented. I know enough about music to recognize that he had a special gift with the guitar. That night at Lea's and my engagement party, he was basically playing the history of American music. He started with Elizabeth Cotton and Robert Johnson, and by the time I realized what he was doing, he was already in the 1960s, weaving the Beatles and Arlo Guthrie in with Jimi Hendrix... I don't think anyone else realized what they were hearing that night, but for me, it was like hearing a master class in guitar. He was just doing it because he could; for the love of it." Gavin choked up as he saw the pain on Ex's face.

"I wish I had been there that night. I *would* have come if I knew..." Ex looked away, clearing his throat. Eventually, he looked back up at Gavin, this time with a distant look in his eyes.

"Listen, Gavin, Lea told me you blame yourself. You should know that no one else feels that way. In fact, I think I'm more to blame than anyone. I should have never let him go alone with her. Scott could handle himself in a bad spot, but we should have sent more than just the two of them. We forget sometimes that even though things are getting better, the world is still a much more dangerous place than it once was. I also heard that you killed the raiders that did it?"

Gavin took no pride in it, but confirmed that they had. Ex looked at him thoughtfully.

"Most men would boast about something like that, but I can see you have as little taste for violence as I do. The reason that I let Scott go alone with Lea was because I got caught up in the happy news of your engagement and wanted to believe that this wedding was the start of something better. A lot of people felt that way. Most of us haven't gone more than a few miles from here in a long time. I got caught up in the excitement." Ex sighed and looked away.

Gavin could hear that despite the man's grief, he maintained hope for the future as well. He wanted to encourage this. "You were letting him be his own man, risks and all. He would have been a part of this new world we're building."

Ex smiled at Gavin. "Scott was so excited to see your place. I think it was just because of your pot and guitars though," he said, chuckling at the memory. "My wife says that he isn't really gone and that his spirit lives on, and I guess that's true. It doesn't make me miss him any less." Ex wiped tears from his eyes and collected himself. "But we can't let his death break us. We need to keep moving forward."

"We're taking steps to prevent this kind of thing from happening as much in the future," Gavin said. "I swear, if any more of those bastards come within twenty miles of us, we'll attack in force. We can help you guys do the same thing. We have some tricks and we are getting organized. I would love to get you and the rest of your family involved in that."

Ex thanked him again, and they moved on to discuss books, and of course, Lea. Having known her for only a short time, Gavin got as much information out of Ex as he could without seeming rude. It made him love her even more as he heard Ex glowingly speak of her early days, and how inquisitive and bookish she had been. Later on, Lea and her mom joined them again, and they all told stories and laughed into the wee hours of the morning.

Shaking Ex's hand as they parted ways, Gavin knew that he had met a kindred spirit; a friend for life.

Chapter 40

The sun was out again, but Spiegel could barely tell. It had been three days since he was shot, and while he had started to heal, he still felt terrible, worse than he'd ever felt. He had pulled the shades shut in the dilapidated room as best as he could and then hung a moldy blanket over the top. He had barely moved from the moldy bed at all, for fear of reopening his wounds. Now that Longhurst had brought the alcohol, Spiegel could at least control his tremors and appetite. He had been able to eat and keep food down a couple of times. Spiegel sat up in the bed and looked over at Longhurst, who was sharpening a knife in the corner. It seemed like that was all Longhurst ever did, either sharpen knives or clean weapons.

The pain lent Spiegel an uncomfortable clarity of mind, and as he reviewed the choices that led him up to his current predicament, he felt nothing but scorn for himself. His team was gone and so were all of his supplies, and while he still had Longhurst, he couldn't understand why. He had saved the man once and he had been loyal ever since, like a trained attack dog. As these feelings came forth, Spiegel intensified his drinking, hoping to get some respite. *Longhurst brought plenty of bottles*, Spiegel thought to himself as he dropped a now-empty bottle of Triple Sec and picked up a dusty, and still only half-empty, bottle of cheap tequila. He screwed off the cap and took a swig, grimacing at the taste.

As Spiegel looked back on his past, he thought that he wouldn't do things much differently. His actions had made him feel alive, and despite the sick feeling after the rush wore off, he went back to violence again and again, like a drug. As the rules loosened, he pushed them even further while his superiors looked the other way. He had ruined lives. He had disfigured and killed people. They hadn't even done anything to him personally; they had just done things to piss his bosses off. Spiegel knew that the people above him were even worse than he was. So if he did what they told him to, what did that make him? He looked at Longhurst with undisguised contempt, taking another long swig from the bottle.

"We were all following orders, weren't we? You and me both. I did what they told me and you did what I told you. And what did it get us? We're stuck in this shithole house. We got our asses kicked by a bunch of punk kids and townies!" Spiegel laughed crazily and looked at Longhurst again, who had finally stopped sharpening. He turned his head and stared at Spiegel.

"Thank God, that sound was driving me crazy," Spiegel said as he took another drink. "You know, I never knew why you stayed with me, but I think I get it now. It wasn't because I saved you that time, was it?"

Longhurst didn't say anything, didn't even change his expression.

"It's because you need someone to follow. You're like a machine, and what good is a machine if it doesn't have someone to run it? You were like a gun; I just aimed you and pulled the trigger. But no matter how vicious we both were, we still ended up here. How do you explain that?" Spiegel coughed and took another drink. The tequila tasted even worse than before; worse than rubbing alcohol.

God damn it, Spiegel thought foggily. *I can't do this anymore.*

"You know something?" Spiegel asked, with a chuckle. Raising his voice now, he stared into Longhurst's eyes. "We deserve each other. A wounded drunk and a degenerate rapist. You must be weak. Isn't that what they say? That it takes a weak man to hurt a woman?" Richard laughed again, took a drink, and then spat the tequila out in Longhurst's direction.

It was oddly satisfying to finally see Longhurst's expression change. He looked at Richard with undisguised hatred, raising his knife and getting up from his chair.

Knowing now that he'd said those words on purpose, Spiegel counted it as a blessing when the knife descended and began to twist.

Chapter 41

April 2010 – The Deepwater Horizon oil rig in the Gulf of Mexico explodes and spews oil into the ocean for 87 days before it can be capped off. It will prove to be the largest oil spill in history. The spill kills off a significant amount of life in the Gulf of Mexico, and shows the difficulty of getting at this new so-called 'extreme oil'. The rig at Deepwater Horizon was attempting to extract oil from three miles under the ocean, which is a new and dangerous process.

Monique heard Raven's sharp *"tsst-tsst"* at the same time she saw the black Hummer. It was covered with a camouflage net, but the color was hard to disguise. It was hidden next to a house like any other in the subdivision, although when she looked more closely Monique could see fresh bloodstains near the front door, confirming her suspicion that at least one of them was wounded. Her heart was racing as they hurried out of sight of the house. Monique was surprised that Raven was the first one who spoke.

"I've been saving some stuff," he said as he pulled off his pack. "I have a couple of cocktails left and some flares." He pulled a small tear gas grenade out of his pack. "I saved this, too. Since they like to burn people's houses down with these."

Monique had seen this feral gleam in Raven's eyes before and didn't attempt to dissuade him. Shelly obviously agreed; she had a branch in her hand, and was wrapping it in cloth to make a torch for lighting the cocktails.

"You and those cocktails," Monique joked. "Sometimes I think you have a death wish, carrying those things around."

Raven gave her an odd, haunted look. "You know I always keep them sealed," he said quietly. "I wouldn't want you guys to get hurt."

"I've lost my taste for this," Monique said. "The machine is dead, and thank God. These men are nothing but remnants. Let's get this done and get back to the rest of our people."

Monique hugged them both and grabbed her gun. "You two, let me start firing, and then come in with the cocktails and the flares.

Concentrate them at first until you are sure the house has caught fire, and then all we have to do is keep up the pressure and wait them out."

Monique brazenly walked up to the front of the house and started placing shots at the upstairs windows, quickly moving each time she fired. *Shoot and scoot*, she thought. That strategy had saved her more than once. She saw a gun barrel poke through one of the upstairs windows and immediately threw herself behind the Hummer. While the shooter probed at her position, Shelly ran up and lobbed a cocktail at the front porch, then scuttled back to the mound of brush where Raven was hiding. The shooter directed his attention toward the brush, allowing Monique to stand behind the Hummer and fire at the window again.

With Monique covering her, Shelly tossed the second cocktail at the upstairs window. It bounced off the edge of the window and fell harmlessly to the ground, rolling back toward Shelly. She kicked it toward the house and ran back again, when Raven quickly popped out and blasted it with his shotgun, bursting it at the base of the house. The front porch had caught on fire and the second one had done damage as well, but Monique knew it would take a while for a fire to really get going. Shelly and Raven tossed several flares at the upstairs window until one finally made its way in, but it was thrown back out again.

Monique kept waiting for the other shoe to drop. Where were the rest of them? She knew that Spiegel and Longhurst were in the Hummer, but she hadn't been able to see if there was anyone in the backseat. Was there was only one person capable of fighting?

"Hey, in there!" Monique shouted. "If you come out the front door, we'll give you a quick end!"

She was answered by a volley of shots from another upstairs window. *Did he move?* She wondered. *Or are there two of them?*

Out of the corner or her eye, Monique saw Raven stand up and start toward the house. Shelly tried to pull him back, but he pushed her away. Horrified at the look of hollowness and hatred in Raven's eyes, Monique shouted, "Just wait them out! Wait them out!"

Ignoring Monique's loud pleading, Raven walked to the window where the last shots had come from, firing up at it with his shotgun. Monique and Shelly provided cover fire, and Raven tossed his tear gas grenade up into the window, making it on his first attempt. Just as he was raising his hand in victory, his face crumpled and he looked down. The sound of a gunshot rang in the air.

Raven looked down at the blooming wound in his chest, and his knees buckled underneath him. While Monique looked on in horror, her finger managed to find the trigger again, and she fired back at the dark shape in the window. Her shot connected and the shape was flung unnaturally backward. Smoke started to rapidly curl out the window. It was over.

Shelly ran toward Raven, sobbing and screaming his name. Monique couldn't let go quite yet however, and she stood in front of the house with her rifle raised until the entire structure was engulfed in flames. She went blank, only coming to her senses when she heard the Hummer pull up next to her. Shelly, whose face was streaked with tears and ashes, had commandeered the Hummer and put Raven's body in the backseat. Monique numbly got in.

"He wanted this," Shelly said. "He told me last night he didn't think he could ever be normal again. He said some people just weren't cut out to be farmers. He never knew any life other than this. I tried to convince him, but he wouldn't listen!"

Monique was weeping, too. "Let's get the hell out of here," she said. "We'll bury him where we can be near him, and never look back."

They pulled out and began to slowly make their way out of the subdivision. The house next door had caught fire as well, and Monique wondered if they hadn't just set a fire that would take out the whole neighborhood. *Good riddance*, she thought as she smelled the burning wood and plastic. At least the land would be free again.

As they made their way back to the farm, Monique tried to pick her way through the crumbling roadways, and made slow progress. Turning off the exit for Scotville, they passed a man with a shaved head, riding a horse in the other direction. He smiled and waved at them, and his bright grin reminded Monique of Victor's. Maybe his smile looked like Raven's, too, but she wasn't sure. Raven hadn't smiled much.

Suddenly, the pain and the grief of all the preceding years crashed down on Monique. She didn't know what she wanted anymore. She didn't want to fight any longer, but the waiting comfort of the farm held nothing for her either. She just wanted to be with Victor again, just to lay with him for a while. The pain of his loss, and the loss of so many others suddenly felt physical, like she was missing a limb. She began to sob and pulled the Hummer to the side of the road, slumping over the steering wheel, overwhelmed with grief. She opened the door and stumbled out, as Shelly ran around to the passenger side, not knowing what to do.

"Just put me in the back with Raven," Monique stuttered through her now-chattering teeth. "I can't do it anymore. You're in charge now."

Shelly helped Monique into the back with Raven's blanket-covered corpse, and got into the driver's seat. Monique lay with Raven's body for the rest of the ride, not saying another word.

Chapter 42

Ramsey, Virginia

It was the day of the wedding, and Mike looked so handsome, he almost stole the show from Gavin. Gone were the scruffy boy beard and cargo pants. Mike's hair was freshly cut and he was wearing a tuxedo. Ex had taken quite a liking to him and had offered some of Scott's clothes, including the tux. All the men were standing around the back of the church, a beautiful brick building on the outskirts of the Ramsey town proper. It would be a Methodist affair, of course; Lea's family was quite devout and took such things seriously. Gavin honored and treated their traditions with the respect they deserved.

"We could have had this kid in *GQ* magazine back in the day," Aidan joked. Mike took it all good naturedly, blushing a bit. He seemed a bit depressed, though; ceremonies like this made him think of his mother. As the men joked around and smoked, Gavin realized that this was probably the first time Mike had hung out with the men like this. Mike was Gavin's best man; Aidan and Gavin both agreed that he would enjoy the role more than Aidan. As an added bonus, the attention from the local girls had pulled him out of his recent sour mood.

Mike was standing next to Gavin. "You don't seem to be as excited about this as Lea does. Are you okay?" His voice was full of concern.

"I'm just nervous as hell!" Gavin said. "I love Lea and I want her to be my wife, but I'm not into all this ceremony. I'll play the part and try to look like I'm enjoying the process; but the whole time, I'll be thinking that all I really want is to have her back at the farm all to myself."

Mike laughed. "Yep! That must be love. I know you don't like crowds, and this time the attention will really be on you both. I know you're nervous, but you'll be fine. You always are."

As always, the kid was perceptive. "That's why you are the best man; you know these things. I'll perk up once it's over, we'll have a few drinks and maybe play some guitar."

The highlight of the wedding was how beautiful Lea looked. Gavin hadn't seen her for the past twenty-four hours, as per tradition, and he didn't see her at the wedding until he was already standing at the altar with the priest.

I hope she shows up, he thought wryly to himself, as he nervously smiled at the priest. A hush fell over the crowd, and Lea came through the doors, escorted by Ex instead of her father. *No surprise there,* Gavin thought. His mouth dropped open at her beauty.

Her normally straight hair had been done in a cascade of small curls, and she had makeup on, which he'd never seen her wear before. The makeup was applied with such subtlety that it only enhanced her appearance. Her dress was homemade; a simple, formal white gown with a short train. A lace corset completed the outfit, fitting seamlessly with the overall design.

Gavin was so in awe of her radiance that he forgot about the large crowd and the attention. As she came to stand next to him, Ex shook his hand and hugged Gavin, going to stand below the dais. Lea beamed at him, but Gavin could tell she was nervous as well. They had written their own vows. When asked, Gavin looked deeply into Lea's eyes and recited his vows from heart. For him, the crowd, the church, and the whole scene faded into the distance. Lea was all he saw.

"I vow to love you, provide for you, and protect you," Gavin said, tears in his eyes. "I'll nurse you when you're sick, and challenge you when you're well. I will listen to you and respect you. When we're rich, we will help others, and when we're poor, we'll lean on each other. I'll share your joys and your sorrows, as you'll share mine. I vow to make you feel beautiful, useful, and loved, for every day of my life. I love you, Lea."

Lea's lips quivered, and her eyes filled with tears. She clasped his hand as the priest prompted her to read her own vows. She held a piece of paper in her other hand, but she didn't have to look at it.

"I vow to care for you, nourish you, and make you feel ten feet tall. I vow to trust and respect you. I'll be your partner, and will take the risks you take. I'll win with you, and lose with you. I'll even submit to you... most of the time." Gavin smiled widely at that one, and could hear a few chuckles in the crowd.

"I will heal your wounds and help you protect us," she continued. "I'll cheer you up when you feel depressed, and I'll bring you down to earth when you're getting too cocky. I vow to love you with all my heart, and to be your woman, for every day of my life. I love you, Gavin."

Gavin wept freely as he slipped the ring onto her finger, a beautiful diamond that had belonged to Stella's mother. It was the happiest moment of his life. Lea's eyes widened at the size of the ring which Gavin had not yet let her see, wanting to surprise her.

As Gavin and Lea exited the church, they went to sit at the head table of the reception dinner. Folding tables covered with white tablecloths had been set up on the church lawn, and a bonfire burned merrily in the center. Since the wedding was held in the evening and after Thanksgiving, the town had gotten a jump on the Christmas decorations. A large spruce had been brought in and was hung with lanterns, and a group of carolers sang in the background. The tables were resplendent with the feast. *Ramsey pulled out all the stops on this one,* Gavin thought to himself. *I haven't seen anything like this in years!*

The carolers finished, and an acoustic band began to play in the background, starting with slow songs as the guests ate their meals. A whole pig had been roasted, and the tables creaked under huge racks of beef and lamb ribs, and mounds of crispy potatoes and greens. Ann and Stella had combined forces and made a beautiful butternut squash ravioli; but the stars of the show for Gavin were the cheeseburgers and fries, always his favorite. He and Lea wolfed down their meals, quickly moving to the dance floor. They were on their third dance when Gavin heard a clinking noise. Mike was standing at the main table, tapping his fork against his glass. Gavin took Lea's hand and led her to the table to sit with Mike.

"Ladies and gentlemen, for those of you who don't know me, I'm Mike, Gavin's nephew. I'm also honored to be his best man." The crowd applauded, causing Mike to blush.

"Let's take a moment of silence to remember Scott Exley. We know he is still with us in spirit, and we'll never forget him." The crowd was silent for a long moment, the heavy breeze being the only sound. After the moment passed, Mike spoke again.

"I first want to congratulate Gavin and Lea. Lea, in the short time we have known you, we've come to love you. And Gavin, we've known you for a very long time, and now that you have Lea, we might even start to *like* you." That got a great laugh.

"In all seriousness, though, we love you both with all of our hearts. We'd take a bullet for you. In fact, some of us have." The crowd laughed again and Xavier stood up and lifted his shirt, pointing to one of his many scars.

"This one was for you, brother!" Xavier shouted, to more laughter and applause.

"The two of you represent change. It's a word I have been hearing a lot lately, *change*. This world has seen tremendous change already, and I wonder what the future will hold for Gavin and Lea's kids, and mine." Mike had developed a deep and loud speaking voice and the people were really listening to him. Gavin was mesmerized, having never seen Mike in this element.

"Life is a journey, and for me, this trip to Ramsey has been a pit stop. It let me get out of my daily routine and look at the whole picture. It's recently been presented to me that a choice must be made about the world we want to build for ourselves, and those who come after us. We know that we don't want it to be like the old one, but we don't want to lose what we learned during those times, either.

"I see two communities coming together here tonight. We're surviving, and we're doing more than that. We're *flourishing*. We have the luxury of thinking about more than just staying alive now. We can decide, as communities, which steps we want to take towards our future. We can clean up the damage to the land and the water. We can build new things that can be sustained and don't poison the air, water, or land. If we work together, with each other and Mother Nature, we can achieve anything! I look out on the people here and I see the best of us, the ones who can survive anything. It's time to remake the world in our image." The crowd was silent as Mike finished his speech.

"Thank you all so much for welcoming me into your family. I love you Gavin and Lea, congratulations again."

Mike hugged Gavin and Lea, and then stood arm in arm with his father. The crowd stood to applaud, and Xavier came over to slap Mike on the back and shake his hand.

"Did you know he was going to do that?" Aidan asked Gavin.

"I thought you knew!" Gavin exclaimed. They were both dumbfounded.

As the moonshine and brandy flowed, Gavin relaxed with his new bride. After several more dances, they sat together at the table, watching the merriment. Gavin watched Mike dance with a Ramsey girl, and the candles began to blur in his vision.

"What's the matter?" Lea asked, her hand resting on his thigh.

"It's not bad, it's just that I'm so happy," Gavin said as he embraced Lea. "I don't think Mike has ever had a chance to do anything like this before. It's really special to me, too. And it's all because of you. I love you, baby, and I'm so happy you came into my life. You're the best thing that's ever happened to me."

Lea was in his arms and beaming back at him, her skin flushed and her hair hanging around her face. She made the white wedding dress look like the sexiest lingerie on Earth.

"I love you, too. And it's the same for us here in Ramsey, we haven't done anything like this, ever. I guess my marrying an eccentric out-of-towner is a big deal or something. And not only that, but you're actually not a bad dancer!" She winked at him.

"I think it's clear that I'm a phenomenal dancer," Gavin said drily. "I was a little worried that you wouldn't be able to keep up, but you did okay."

Lea chuckled, eyes twinkling. She leaned in to whisper in his ear.

"So take me on my honeymoon, prepper man," she said softly.

"Goodnight everyone, thanks for coming!" Gavin said, abruptly standing up. He took his new bride away from the crowd, which was met with hooting, hollering and ribald jokes as the couple exited. He walked out with Lea on his arm, who was flushed and radiant from the excitement.

"Let's make an honest woman out of you," he whispered to her.

She grinned, kissed him, and punched him on the arm.

Gavin and Lea walked out into the night, and entered their new life together as man and wife.

Chapter 43

July 2010 – The Dodd–Frank Wall Street Reform and Consumer Protection Act is signed into law. This bill, like so many others, is ill-conceived and overly complex. Not only does it not fix the problems it is intended to, it also creates a whole slew of new ones. It fails to break up the banks deemed 'too big to fail,' so the government remains hostage to them. Meanwhile, it attacks regional and community banks with overwhelming and incomprehensible new regulations. As always, the consumer gets screwed, absorbing the new regulatory costs in their banking fees.

December 2037
Millwood Farm

Christmas was always a joyous event at Millwood. Bob and Stella had everyone hopping, making sure that all of the decorations were up in the Big House. The atrium was laid out with a series of tables in a row, creating one long dining table for everyone to sit. One of the most difficult jobs in the winter was keeping the greenhouse warm with the homemade woodstove, but no one at Millwood regretted it when Christmas came. Lemons and oranges sat in bowls in the kitchen. There were fresh herbs in many of the dishes, lending them a milder flavor while also being more nutritious. Stella's famous lemon cakes and cookies were set out in little trays. Gavin was also trying a new recipe for cranberry orange glaze that would go on the pork chops.

BoBo and Shiver spent all day getting under everyone's feet in the kitchen, and begging for small morsels from Stella, who had always had a special soft spot for the Bichons.

Since this was Lea's first Christmas at the farm, a special effort was made to make her feel welcome. Stella encouraged her to make her own special recipes, and Gavin was looking forward to trying Lea's venison chili. Aidan, Bob, and Xavier weren't much in the kitchen, so they spent Christmas Eve morning hunting wild turkey in the woods, although Gavin suspected that they were more interested in the Wild Turkey in their flasks than actually shooting any.

The Colliers loved to give speeches at the holiday table, and over the years, the Jacksons had joined in. As they all sat at the table, stuffed from the meal, many of the speeches welcomed Lea and gave thanks for everyone's safety and continued prosperity. Mike was uncharacteristically subdued, speaking only briefly. He didn't seem unhappy anymore, just distant and deep in thought. When it came time for Lea to speak, she seemed nervous, but managed a big smile as she stood up.

"This is a new tradition for me. My family hasn't ever given speeches like this before, but if I know Gavin, he'll have convinced my uncle Ex to start the tradition soon enough." She smiled down at Gavin, who was holding her hand as he sat next to her.

"Meeting Gavin, and then meeting all of you, has changed my life," Lea continued. "It has indirectly changed other lives, too. Getting to know Gavin and falling in love with him has made me think a lot about the life that we live now. I can't remember very much about how it was before, but I know that a lot of you older people do, and I'm sure you miss some parts of it. So instead of focusing on the next grand achievement, which I'm sure is on the way, I want to say how thankful I am for the little things. The relationship that you all have with this land and the animals and plants on it, and the love you have for each other is so solid. It doesn't depend on things like cars, cell phones, or electricity. It's just us. We're the masters of our own happiness and fulfillment, and everyone here is a part of that. So I just wanted to say how thankful I am to be here with all of you." That got a loud round of applause and Gavin looked up at Lea in continuing awe and affection.

"Oh, and one more thing. We should be thankful for the love a mother and father have for their child." She leaned down as if to kiss Gavin's cheek, and whispered in his ear. "I'm pregnant."

Gavin shouted loudly and then just stood there, silently hugging his wife.

Chapter 44

May 2038

Spring was in the air and Gavin was exhausted. He and Xavier were chopping wood side by side when Gavin paused to take his hat off and wipe his forehead with a handkerchief.

"Why is it that people always think farmers love the spring and summer?"

Xavier chuckled. "Yeah, right? Shit man, you know I love the fall! That's when we get to chill a little bit and roast a pig, and get our drink on. Know what I mean?"

Gavin laughed, too, as he put another log on the stump. "So true man, so true."

They were preparing the farm for the new season, getting the fields ready for planting and moving the livestock into their new enclosures. The broody hens were segregated into groups of ten and placed in individual stalls, each with their own rooster. They would hatch the next batches of chicks. Gavin's collection of chicken breeds had grown, so he now had four separate stalls dedicated to his breeding program.

Before the Crumble, he had started with Americaunas and White Leghorns, and over the years he traded for two more breeding flocks, adding Dark Cornish and Freedom Rangers to the list. Gavin and Xavier had discovered the drawbacks of free ranging chickens in the early years as more and more of their flocks were lost to foxes. They quickly figured out how to modify designs they saw online to make moveable chicken coops, or "chicken tractors," as they called them. They were made to be as light as possible, and long and narrow to go up and down the rows of fruit trees and bushes as they were pulled to new pasture each day. They controlled the pests and weeds, and added fertilizer.

"It's a win-win scenario," Gavin had told Xavier when he proposed the idea. "When we add the bees, they pollinate the fruit. The fruit that drops feeds the chickens, and they feed on the insects and worms, too. Their chicken shit fertilizes the blueberries, and then it starts all over again. Mother Nature is just doing what she would normally do, anyway; all we're doing is coming along for the ride."

Doing his best Elton John impression, Gavin began to sing: "It's the Cirrrrrrcle of Life…"

Xavier smiled and rolled his eyes, not an altogether unusual response.

When they were done chopping wood, Xavier took a break, and Gavin went back to the pool house to join Lea. They laid out the seed collection on a large table, and he and Lea had a wonderful time looking through all the seed varieties. Decisions were made on tomato varieties, with Gavin picking his mainstay Roma, and some old durable Italian varieties like Principe Borghese and San Marzano. They also picked some delicious melons, pumpkins for the pigs (and people), and squash and zucchini. The greenhouse allowed them to get a jump on the spring, planting certain seeds as early as February.

"You're missing a lot of what I need," Lea said as they went through the collection. "I'm going to need Comfrey, Aloe, Chamomile, Arnica, Yarrow…"

"Whoa there, Dr. Quinn, Medicine Woman!" Gavin said. "I've never heard of half of that stuff. I thought I knew a lot about plants, but you take the cake." He paused with a glint in his eye. "You are soooo spunky!"

Lea playfully slapped him on the arm. "I knew you were going to say that! Don't worry, I already talked to Stella and she knows a woman in Farrington who grows a lot of herbs. And I can find some of it in the woods. Besides, you aren't completely bereft of good seeds. You do have some Chamomile."

"Bereft?" Gavin said. "I love you, Lea. I knew I loved you the first time you said 'accolades.'"

"You mean it wasn't just for my body?"

Gavin took her in his arms and showed her that he loved that, too.

The next day, Gavin went up to Xavier's house and worked on the root vegetables. Xavier traditionally handled the planting boxes where the carrots, potatoes, onions, and garlic were grown. They had found that using the deep boxes filled with compost was the only way they could grow large quantities of root vegetables in their hard Virginia clay soil. The compost pile got a lot of attention, much to the chagrin of all the kids on the farm, who had to turn it over and carry horse buckets full of compost and compost tea to all the plants in need of fertilizer on the farm.

Gavin and Xavier also took on the important task of deciding which pot seeds to plant. Aidan didn't smoke and focused on the staple crops, like corn and wheat, so he didn't have much interest in that area. He was happy when it sold at the farmer's market, though. Lea would take a hit once in a while, and she did need it as medicine for her patients sometimes, but Gavin and Xavier had the true passion for it.

Gavin's seed supply had been terrible when the Crumble finally progressed far enough for him to feel comfortable growing. While gains had been made in marijuana legalization in the west, the Crumble was already in full force before the eastern states or the federal government would consider legalization.

"We gotta do Blueberry again," Xavier said. "It took us so long to breed that one the way we wanted it. I can't really work like I want to during the day with anything but that."

"You and me both, buddy," Gavin said. "When we smoke Northern Lights at lunch, I feel like I need a nap. What else should we grow? We have that new strain going pretty well, we could take clones from one of the mother plants in the greenhouse by now."

"Oh yeah, I wanna try that this year," Xavier said. "What are we gonna call it?"

"I was thinking XG," Gavin said with a grin.

"Ah, yeah!" Xavier said as they got to planting.

Millwood always looked beautiful when spring was in full bloom. There were pink and white blossoms on the cherry and pear trees, and the bright yellow of the forsythia bushes showed up in cheerful spots of color all over the landscape.

Gavin loved the trees on the property, and enjoyed showing Lea the forest trails. She would walk with her bow and he'd bring his squirrel rifle. Every now and again they would get a tasty addition to the dinner pot. Lea was quite adept at finding rabbits that Gavin didn't even know were there, and rabbit stew was becoming a family favorite.

Lea often stopped to pick wild plants and herbs, giving Gavin a master class in herbal remedies in the process. Gavin showed Lea his favorite trees, slightly embarrassed by the fact that he even *had* favorite trees. But then he realized that he was still thinking in the old way.

Americans had spent so many years worshipping technology that it had eventually become perceived as silly to communicate with nature. Lea had favorite trees, too, and she told Gavin about hers.

"So this is your favorite tree?" she asked as they approached it. "It's amazing!"

Gavin's most cherished tree was on the back forty acres in the forest, and it was a huge beast, almost magical looking. Its branches hung low and its wood was strangely brittle. It stood several hundred feet in the air with a thick, smooth trunk, and thick leaves that looked like stars.

As Lea stood and put her hand on the tree, Gavin said, "Yeah, Xavier and I have made all of these trails ourselves over the years. I was following a deer trail one day and widening it when I came up on this giant."

Lea smiled at him and put her bow on her back. She began climbing the tree. "So do you know what kind of tree this is?" she shouted down at him.

"Actually, no," Gavin shouted up at her. He anticipated her response.

"I do!" Lea yelled back, climbing even higher. He wasn't surprised at all.

As Lea continued to climb, he sat beneath the tree in the clearing. And that's what he'd always called it, 'the tree in the clearing.'

He had first noticed it years before when he started making the trails in the forest. There were three species of wild vines that were making life a living hell for the poor trees, and Gavin and Xavier fought them for many years before finally declaring victory. One was poison oak, with its creepy hairy tentacles; one was a wild grapevine; and the other was a small vine made out of a white wood that looked sort of like Birch. The vines were the bane of Gavin's existence for years, and on every walk, he cut more of them. He loved doing that, and as the years passed, he could see how much stronger the trees were getting. He continued to forge deeper into the forest, cutting more vines and making new trails.

He was making a new trail one day when he came upon the tree. It was huge, one of the largest on the property, and it stood there alone in a wide clearing without a single vine on it. All around it, the other trees were still covered in vines and choked with weeds, but this one stood alone. Gavin was overcome with a peaceful feeling when he first saw it; it was a moment that would forever stand out in his mind. On that day, he stopped his walk and sat with his back against the tree for a while, before clearing out some of the brush and fallen branches around it. The clearing was surprisingly devoid even of that. Over the next few months he made a wide trail to it, and then another, until trails came off of that clearing like spokes from a wheel. It became a crossroads. Visiting that tree became a mainstay of his daily walks.

The twang of Lea's bow brought Gavin back to himself. He looked at the edge of the clearing and saw an arrow buried in the brush.

As Gavin walked over he yelled up, "I think you got something, baby!"

She dropped to the ground beside him as he bent into the brush. Sure enough, there was a large rabbit laying there, impaled by the arrow. Lea grinned at him as he pulled the arrow out, handing it back to her and putting the rabbit into his vest. "So?" Gavin said. "What kind of tree is it?"

"Maybe I'll tell you one day," she replied flirtatiously. Taking his hand and walking down the trail, Lea asked, "Isn't this where Mike has been having his meetings?"

"Meetings, ceremonies... whatever the hell they are," Gavin mumbled. Lea was quiet after that, always sensing when not to push him.

The weather had been kind to Millwood thus far, with nice breezes and plenty of rain, and Gavin looked forward to a long and fruitful warm season.

Early in the spring, Stella managed to get a bull in trade for some old saddles. In past years, Gavin and Xavier had just brought their heifers to a neighbor's bull to breed them, but now their herd had become large enough to warrant having one of their own. And judging by their experience with the neighbor's bull, they didn't think handling their own would be a problem. Unfortunately however, the bull that Millwood got didn't turn out to be as mellow and good natured as their neighbor's.

Xavier quickly named him "Mother" because that had been the first word out of his mouth upon seeing it. Of course, the word had immediately been followed by "Fucker," but they thought the whole word wouldn't be good to say around the kids. Stella had negotiated for the Farrington men to actually bring the bull to Millwood, and the look on their faces when they arrived, combined with Xavier's exclamation, told Gavin all he needed to know. The beast was huge and had a psychotic look in its eyes. The Farrington men were covered in sweat and dirt.

Gavin instantly wondered if the corral they had built for Mother would be enough. The Farrington men didn't seem concerned with that, however, and they unceremoniously deposited him in the corral and got on their horses.

"Wait!" Gavin said. "Rest and have some lemonade, we'll take it from here. Xavier said he wanted to talk to you guys, anyway. He thinks he might be able to make armor for your horses."

As Xavier walked over and started to chat with the Farrington men, Gavin sent Devante to the Big House to get lemonade. He stood and looked at Mother. Mother looked right back at him. BoBo had come out of the house and was giving the evil eye to the bull, but rightly decided to keep his distance. Shiver took one look at the beast and ran back into the house, probably looking for Lea, who was starting to show her pregnancy. Gavin had asked her to try to stay closer to the house until she had the baby, and joked that she and Shiver needed each other for moral support.

"Holy crap, would you look at that thing!" Mike said as he walked down from the woods with Shelly in tow. Seamlessly forgetting his first crush when she settled to a neighboring farm, Mike had become inseparable from Shelly. Gavin heard the story of how she and Monique had lost Raven, and his heart went out to her. The poor girl walked around with a blank mask on her face all the time. Gavin saw her demeanor improve only slightly around Monique, but she also seemed depressed. After the first couple months of being back at the farm, Mike had gotten Shelly to open up to him and she now followed him wherever he went.

Gavin was worried that he had created a monster with the religion discussion with Mike. Since they got back from the wedding in Ramsey, Mike had been checking out every single book in the library about religion. According to Bob, he had gone through the eastern religions first, moving on to Paganism and then to the western monotheistic religions. His work and school schedule were such that he still had time to devote to a passion, and despite Gavin and Aidan's misgivings, he had chosen that. Gavin assured Aidan that it was a passing phase.

"How do you think the library has all those books on the subject in the first place?" Gavin asked Aidan. "I went through the same thing. It will pass for him just like it did with me." A couple more months had passed by and it still hadn't yet.

Gavin looked at Mike as he approached the bull. Shelly hung back, being less comfortable around farm animals than Mike.

"Oh my God," Mike said. "That was really weird. For a second it felt like I knew what he was thinking."

"Let me guess," Gavin said. "He's pissed off."

Mike smiled and kept staring at the bull. It seemed to be calmer around him, so Gavin walked back a bit toward where Shelly was standing. Mike stared at the bull for a few minutes and walked away without saying a word, and Shelly hurriedly followed.

That night after dinner, Gavin passed by Mike and Bob talking, and Mike was kneeling down looking at a row of Carlos Castaneda books. "I haven't read these yet," Mike said. "What can you tell me about them?"

Bob grinned. "That's more of Gavin's hippie shit. A guy goes to Mexico and meets a Shaman named Don Juan, and he proceeds to take lots of drugs. The end."

Mike fingered the spine of the first of Castaneda's books and pensively flipped through it. Before Gavin could stop himself, he walked over and abruptly took the book from Mike's hands.

"I know this is like throwing gas on a fire, but I bet you haven't considered Octavia Butler because she isn't in the religion section. She is in science fiction."

"Who is Octavia Butler?" Mike asked, eyes lighting up in curiosity.

"She was a lesser known science fiction writer, but one of the greats. She didn't write very many books, but the ones she did were incredible. There was one in particular I remember where a group of people formed a new religion, and their god was change itself. The highest goal of their religion was to save humanity by spreading to the stars. At one point, she made the argument that only a religion could get mankind to colonize the planets around distant stars. Governments didn't have the will to expend the massive amounts of resources for such a distant goal. Individuals and corporations couldn't do it. Only a religion could take on a multi-generational project like that."

The last words were barely out of Gavin's mouth when Mike dashed up the stairs to the science fiction section. Gavin hurriedly followed with Bob yelling after him. "Make sure he logs that book!" Bob shouted, knowing it was a foregone conclusion that Mike would take it out. Bob went back to his desk, muttering about a book of New York maps he couldn't find.

Once Mike found the book, he disappeared and Gavin didn't see him again until the next day.

Chapter 45

December 2010 – The Arab Spring begins. In Tunisia, a young street vendor overwhelmed by government overregulation and corruption sets himself on fire, ending his life. In days, a vast protest movement springs up, accelerated by the proliferation of mobile devices and social media websites. The unrest soon spreads to surrounding countries, including Egypt. The mainstream media portrays the story as a popular uprising in the name of democracy, but the reality is far harsher. Those parts of the world can't afford to feed their populations anymore. The crowds in Egypt are chanting 'Bread, Freedom, and Justice.' Bread is the first thing they mention.

June 2038

Gavin had never seen so many people on the farm at one time. He sighed. It was the day of the "Big Meeting," as it had come to be known, and he and Xavier were directing traffic, sending people with horses to quarter them in the barn and store their bicycles in front of the Big House.

"Mike should have never given that speech at my wedding," Gavin muttered to his friend. "Now we have all these people trampling all over everything."

Xavier laughed. "You're grouchy now but you'll cheer up. Besides, it's good to see all these people coming out. That guy, Ex, is some character, too. If it wasn't for him I don't think there would be half as many people."

Ex had shown up with a large group from Ramsey, bringing many members of his and Lea's extended family. The first thing they asked when they arrived was to see where Scott was buried.

"Ex asked about the sword in the grave and I told him about what happened to your brother, Jake. I hope you don't mind, man."

Xavier nodded. "Ex is cool, and he's family now so I don't mind. He knows what we're going through too, with my brother and what happened to your cousin."

Xavier's older brother, Jake, was a great fighter who was killed saving Xavier's life in the early days of the Crumble. Xavier visited his grave often, polishing the sword marking the spot and pouring some liquor out for his brother.

Gavin's cousin, Jeremy, took his own life just as the Crumble began. Jeremy died in December 2012, when he was only sixteen years old. Gavin lived far away from him so they only saw each other a couple of times a year, but they were close, and often texted and called each other. As Gavin's obsession with the Crumble escalated, he wasn't there for his young cousin like he should have been. He wouldn't forget that, as long as he lived.

Gavin often wondered about what would have happened if Jeremy had lived to see what the world was like now. Like Xavier, Gavin kept Jeremy's memory alive as best he could, planting a teak bench in a stand of trees on a sunny south-facing hill. The bench had a little brass plaque on it, and Jeremy's name was still legible, even after so many years.

"He was really moved by the sword marking where your brother is," Gavin said. "And when he saw what I carved for Raven, he asked me to carve a guitar for Scott's grave, too."

"Yeah man, you're getting pretty good at that," Xavier said. "I used to only see you do faces, but that bird you did for Raven's grave looked real nice."

As the two men directed the last of the late arrivals to the meeting, they both walked up to the pool house deck, which made a natural stage. Gavin sat down next to a very pregnant Lea, who was holding Shiver with BoBo at her feet. Xavier joined Aidan, Ex, Chris Orlund, and several other notables who also sat on the deck. Gavin was the first to address the crowd.

"This all started when a seventeen-year-old boy gave a speech at my wedding. He managed to articulate what so many of us had been thinking. We want to move forward, but we don't know how, or what that would even look like. We want to build something new, but we're all scared to death of creating the same monster that brought us down before."

There were many nodding heads in the crowd, and many had craned their heads to look at where Mike was sitting in the front row. While Gavin expected him to shyly duck his head, Mike instead sat with his head held high and looked back at the crowd, smiling and briefly waving his hand.

"There are a few things that we can all agree on. We don't want extractive or destructive technology. We don't want centralized planning. We don't want *politicians*." Gavin spat as he said that last word, and several angry voices in the crowd muttered their agreement.

"The purpose of this meeting is to coordinate our efforts for the purposes of trade, communication and defense. Also, Mike and Chris Orlund are working on a special project that we'll all need to pitch in on." The crowd was quiet. This wasn't a surprise to them; they had been having informal meetings and discussions for most of the day.

"I'd also like to start organizing cleanup crews for each community. There is trash everywhere, from junked cars to plastic bags; the roads are strewn with the stuff. We did that. If we want our kids to have a better world, we will put our efforts into preserving what's left of nature. We made the mess, and that means we also have the power to clean it up."

Gavin finished speaking and the applause started slowly, getting louder and louder until it reached a crescendo. As it died down, Chris Orlund stood up and asked for everyone's attention.

"Hello, everyone. Most of you know me. I'm Chris Orlund, one of the leaders of Farrington. A few months ago, this guy here had another great idea." Chris touched Gavin on the arm.

"We've been practicing and working very hard, and we'd like to show off a little bit."

Xavier shouted from the back. "Let's see how tough you are!" Gavin could see that Xavier and JB were dragging several homemade scarecrows to the bottom of a hill a few hundred feet beyond the pool. They staked them into the ground in a ragged formation, creating a reasonable facsimile of a group of raiders. Chris stood proudly, pulling his red hunting jacket out of a bag and putting it on. The bag contained a bugle as well. Chris pressed it to his lips, sounding the famous hunting call often heard at the beginning of horse races.

Gavin was astounded to see a large group of riders emerge from the woods at the top of the hill. As the bugle call ended, he could hear the eerie rebel yell float down toward the crowd. The rebel yell may have sounded funny to some people, and the corporate media assholes liked to make fun of the 'dumb redneck' stereotype, but to hear it in this context made the hairs on the back of his neck stand up. The men on horses all wore red coats, and the loud cries of "Yee-Ha!"

became louder as the men thundered down the hill in a wide V formation. About halfway down, the men produced shotguns and pistols and began firing at the scarecrows. It was apparent Chris hadn't been kidding when he said they'd been training hard. Many of the shots connected, knocking several of the straw men down, and Gavin could see tufts of dirt fly as other shots came close.

By the time the Farrington men reached the bottom of the hill, only three of the scarecrows were still standing. Not stopping, several of the riders at the tip of the V produced swords and proceeded to cut down the remainder. Gavin looked over at Xavier, who was too engrossed in watching the display to notice Gavin's glance. *The swords must have been Xavier's idea*, Gavin thought. Xavier had gotten a new and better sword as a gift from Monique, and probably traded a couple of his old ones to the Farrington riders. Gavin remembered when Xavier had shown him the gift from Monique. He had the same look in his eye that he did years earlier, when Gavin bought him a K-bar knife for his birthday. Pure joy.

There is something about a sword that's scarier than a gun. While a gun implies violence, it's impersonal and used at a distance. A man carrying a sword has a more intimate relationship with his enemies than a man with a gun. Of course, a man with a sword *and* a gun is something else entirely.

Gavin was so amazed by the display of the Farrington riders that he initially didn't notice the cheers as they approached the crowd. When the riders dismounted from their horses, the crowd surrounded them, patting them on the back and yelling accolades. Chris Orlund smiled at the commotion, but Gavin noticed that he had a sharp gleam in his eye, as well. Chris had lost family and friends to raiders, and it looked like he was actually looking forward to the next time a group tried to plunder his town, or rape and kill his people.

Chapter 46

There are moments in life that one remembers forever, both good and bad. Gavin tried to file into his memory every detail of the day his son was born, even the little things, like Lea's hand clutching his as she went through her labor, and the calm instructions she gave to Stella and Shelly who hovered over her. He never wanted that day to fade from his memory.

While still not uncommon, the birth of a child was a rarer event than it was in the old days. Many said that they didn't want to bring children into such a hard life, but Gavin felt differently. He still had hope for the human race.

There were tears in Stella's eyes, and Gavin knew what she was feeling. They had all lost so much along the way. The cycle of life and death weighed heavily on Gavin's family at times like this. The birth was a bittersweet reminder of the fragility of life. But it was also a reminder of the indomitable human spirit. Life itself will always fight to exist, and to remain a bright, hot, shining light in the vast, dark void of space.

"Why the long face?" Lea asked between breaths.

Gavin looked at Stella. "You know, Jeremy would have loved this. I still can't believe he is missing it."

Stella took his hand, her thin hand strongly grasping his. "He isn't missing it. You're always the one who says his spirit lives on, and if that's true, then he definitely wouldn't miss this. Now breathe with your wife. Go, go!"

Stella was forever entreating Gavin to exercise more, sometimes waking him up early to go walking. "Go, go!" was her mantra. While Bob grumbled about it, he did admit that the consistent exercise and clean eating had contributed to why he and Stella aged so well.

As Gavin focused on his wife and helping her breathe, he looked down at the head of the baby as it emerged, red-faced and screaming right away. As he and Lea held their son for the first time, he knew he would forever remember Lea's glowing and exhausted face, and the joyous tears and smiles of his family. Both father and mother wept unabashedly. As an added blessing, there had been no complications and mother and baby were both fine.

"It's a boy!" Gavin shouted out the door. He could hear everyone let out a loud whoop, as they waited in an adjoining room.

"We got a future Outlaw on our hands!" Xavier shouted. Aidan and Mike cheered. The three of them lit cigars, and held a fourth one out for Gavin.

"Save that for me," he said, as he smiled at them and closed the door again.

"We did it," Lea said to him. She was quietly cooing to the baby. Her hair was a greasy mess, and her face was red and blotchy. Joyous tears streamed down her face. She had never looked more beautiful.

"You did it, baby. *You* did it," Gavin murmured as he sat next to her, embracing her and his son.

The following afternoon, Gavin and Lea were ensconced in the pool house, with Lea sleeping a great deal and Gavin happily helping take care of his newborn son. Mike and Shelly were with them to help with the baby, who had been named George after Stella's father. Mike and Gavin were sitting on the pool house deck discussing philosophy and religion, which Mike continued to obsess over.

Shelly sat with baby George on the lawn beside the deck, rocking him and looking at him like he was the most fascinating thing she had ever seen. Gavin marveled at the progress she had made, continuing to open up as she spent more time with Mike. Gavin had even caught her smiling a few days before.

Mike was waxing philosophic about what he'd recently been reading. "Once I finished the Octavia Butler book, I started thinking about what fiction could teach me. Bob had me pick up Robert Howard's Conan books after that. Conan's Cimmerian god, Crom, must have been modeled after the Norse gods. I liked Crom. He gave you everything you needed on the day you were born, and he expected you to provide for yourself after that. That started me thinking about prayer. Why would we pray to a god and ask for help and guidance, when we have the Godspark inside each one of us?"

Gavin, doing his best Arnold Schwarzenegger impression, said, "Crom laughs at the four winds. He laughs on his mountain!" He'd watched the Conan movies too many times in his youth.

Mike, used to Gavin's odd comments, just continued.

"It's like the word 'hope'. What exactly does that mean? Every time I hear about hope, it seems that it's about wishing for some positive outcome that you have no control over. Why would we sit there and hope for things to get better when we can go out and take control of our own destinies?"

Gavin was at a loss for an answer. Mike was touching on the edges of a whole new way of looking at things, and he wasn't sure he fully understood it. Weird things had started to happen around Mike; it wasn't just Shelly's change in demeanor. A few weeks before, Gavin had seen Mike on a hill in the back field, playing with a fox. Mike would crouch on his knees with his palms up, and bow his head toward the fox. The fox yipped and charged Mike, playfully darting aside at the last minute. Gavin had seen plenty of wild foxes over the years, but he'd never seen one behave like that. It went on for more than ten minutes, when Gavin finally got bored and went back to work.

Every weekend, Mike and Shelly would disappear into the woods, and lately some of the young people on the farm had begun joining them. Gavin had no idea what they were doing up there and asked Xavier if he had seen anything. Xavier only said, "Leave the boy alone, brother. Whatever they're doing up there, it's not so bad. They come back out looking all fresh and happy." Gavin hadn't asked about it after that.

Before Gavin could say anything in response to Mike, he looked up as he heard a commotion coming from the barn. Xavier was helping Derek down the driveway, heading toward the Big House. Gavin looked inside the pool house and saw Lea was still asleep. Shelly looked at them and said, "I'll keep an eye on George, you guys go ahead and see what's going on."

Mike and Gavin ran down and met Xavier and Derek. Derek was hobbling along, leaning on Xavier's shoulder.

"It's that goddamn bull!" Xavier said, fuming. "Derek was in the corral trying to replace a couple of fence boards, and I was trying to distract Mother on the other side. It was like he knew what I was doing, and before I could even yell at Derek to get out of the way, Mother had turned and flipped Derek over the fence. His leg is broken. You can see bone sticking out."

Gavin didn't see Xavier like this very often, and normally when he did, somebody got hurt or killed soon after. He was extremely loyal to his group, and by hurting Derek, Mother had become Xavier's enemy.

"Mike, go wake up Lea, and do it gently. She's worn out. Tell her what happened and she'll tell you what she needs." Mike ran back up the hill without another word.

He and Xavier helped Derek into the Big House, surprising Bob and Stella in the library.

"Let's get him onto the dining room table," Gavin said as they adjusted their grip on Derek. He hobbled toward the table, wincing in pain. He hefted himself onto the dining room table and Xavier cut his pant leg off. Gavin could see it was a terrible compound fracture, like Xavier said. Blood slowly leaked out of the wound and congealed on the table, and Derek's broken shin bone visibly protruded from his skin. Gavin gulped, getting a sour feeling in his stomach. He'd seen worse, but when his friends were hurt, he felt their pain as well. Gavin looked up and saw that Lea had arrived with Mike in tow, carrying her satchel and a wooden box filled with small jars. Her hair was mussed with sleep and she was clearly still tired, but her eyes were sharp and aware. He sighed with relief.

Xavier looked at Lea with tears in his eyes. "Can you fix this?" he asked desperately.

"Yes," she said calmly. "He may have a limp in the future, but if I can set it and stitch up the wound, I'll make sure it heals cleanly. I have some tinctures made just for this kind of thing. I need hot water and some clean rags." Gavin ran to get the supplies, and Lea went to work on Derek, first giving him a couple slugs of whiskey. Xavier stood by Derek, holding his hand and murmuring to him.

"You're gonna be alright, dawg, it's not even gonna be a thing. You saw how good Lea fixed up Gavin's shoulder. She's gonna do the same for you."

When Gavin returned, he saw that Xavier was holding Derek down while Lea set the bone. It was obvious Derek was in extreme pain, but he handled himself admirably. He vomited into a bucket a couple of times, and when the leg was finally set, he mercifully passed out.

"I'll take it from here, guys," Lea said as she began rummaging in her satchel. Xavier walked out and Mike followed him, leaving Gavin with nothing to do.

"Can I help?" Gavin asked, needing a purpose.

"Thanks, honey, but honestly you would just get in my way. I have most of what I need here, but I'm going to need some time in the kitchen to make a Chamomile tea wash and some plaster for the cast. Stella can help me with anything I need. Don't you have some farming to do? Go help Xavier and Mike. Where did they go, anyway?"

Gavin gasped. "Shit!" he exclaimed, smacking his forehead with the palm of his hand.

"What's the matter?" Lea asked, but Gavin was already out the door.

"He's going to shoot that bull!" he shouted back.

As he ran toward the corral behind the barn, Gavin thought that if he knew Xavier, he'd be out there with his rifle already. He hadn't heard a shot yet but he didn't think the bull was long for this world. It was a shame because Stella had negotiated the deal so well, and if they lost the bull they would be out the saddles she'd traded.

As Gavin ran, he expected to hear the report of Xavier's .270, but it never came. When he got to the corral, Xavier was standing there with the rifle slung over his shoulder looking at the bull. It took Gavin a second to realize that Mike was inside the corral, standing right next to Mother. He was about to scream at Mike to get the hell out of there, but Xavier turned back to look at him and put his finger to his lips.

Xavier whispered, "He begged me not to kill it. When I heard Derek might have a limp, I just lost it. I was gonna shoot it as soon as I saw it. But as I stood there taking aim, I looked up and Mike was standing right next to me. He put his hand on my arm and said I had to trust him. I believed him. And look, he does have some kind of a way with it."

Besides Xavier's whisper, it was silent by the corral. Shelly and a couple of the Jackson kids were quietly watching the display. Gavin was struggling. He thought he was going to lose his mind looking at Mike standing next to that bull, but the kid was almost eighteen and he had to become his own man. Being your own man meant that your decisions had consequences, and Gavin couldn't take that away from him. Gavin stood there silently as Xavier put his hand on his shoulder, calming him somewhat.

The next time he looked up, Aidan was there too. The look of concern on Aidan's face must have mirrored Gavin's, and all three men stood outside the corral, feeling powerless to do anything but watch. If the bull decided that Mike was a threat, he'd be lucky to get off with just a broken leg, considering he was in the middle of the corral with no quick way to escape. At least Derek had been wise enough to keep to the edges of the corral, which probably saved his life. A bull this large could kill a man without any trouble at all.

As Gavin watched, he realized that he had been holding his breath. His heart pounded, and he kept looking at Aidan, who had a grim expression.

Mike stood there looking at Mother for a long while. He would try to get closer and the bull would snort and stomp his feet, then Mike would stop and wait. Slowly but surely, Mike got closer and closer until he could reach up and touch the creature's nose. He waited for a few minutes before he tried to touch it, and the first couple of times he made contact, Gavin thought the bull would charge him. But while it shook its head and snorted the first few times it was touched, it still didn't make a move toward Mike.

After a few more minutes, Mike was patting Mother on the neck and scratching behind his ears. The creature pressed its head toward Mike's hand like a dog, shaking its head and nuzzling his shoulder. While Aidan, Xavier, and Gavin stood in disbelief, Mike climbed back over the corral fence and said plainly, "He should be fine now." Then he and Shelly walked back toward the woods again.

"So, who wants to test it?" Gavin asked, to quiet laughter from Xavier and Aidan.

"That thing is Mike's problem now," Xavier responded, as he walked back towards the Big House to check on Derek. Aidan also left, seemingly in a daze over what he had just seen. The Jackson kids got bored and wandered off, leaving Gavin alone with Mother, who was now contentedly munching on a clump of grass.

"Psst! Hey, Mother!" Gavin whispered. The bull looked up at him briefly, found him uninteresting, and went back to eating grass.

"Hey!" Gavin shouted. The bull again looked up again but went back to eating. Getting a long stick, Gavin poked at the bull's hindquarters trying to get a reaction out of it. After some more tentative testing, Gavin got up the courage to jump in the corral and walked up beside the bull, placing his hand on its back. He could feel its powerful muscles rippling and a brief tremor as he touched it for the first time, but the animal didn't otherwise react at all. Not wanting to push his luck, Gavin jumped out of the corral and walked back to the Big House to check on his wife.

Who knew I'd land myself a doctor? Gavin thought to himself with a smile.

Chapter 47

January 2011 – An investigative panel formed by Congress finds that Goldman Sachs diverted almost $3 billion from TARP bailout funds intended for the insurance giant AIG to its own coffers. Goldman Sachs is one of the most extractive and reprehensible companies on the planet, alternately known as the Vampire Squid or the Monsanto of the financial world. The U.S. Treasury Secretary at the time of the TARP was Henry Paulson, a former head of Goldman Sachs.

September 2038

It was fall again, and with a new baby in their lives, Gavin and Lea's nesting instinct had set in with force. They had the pool house cozy and warm, filled with firewood, knit throw blankets and rugs, and a giant box full of toys. Some of them were pre-Crumble, as Gavin had brought his old Star Wars action figure collection out of storage, but many of the other toys were handmade by people on the farm. Mike had collaborated with Xavier and Aidan to make a tiny wooden steam engine for the baby, which was intricate and beautiful.

Lea was entranced with the pool house; an old, stucco covered building sitting on a hill with a large stone deck on the north side. She had added her own touches, as well. Large, colorful throw rugs now covered the floor, and dream catchers hung above the bed. When Gavin brought out his action figures, Lea sat with George on the floor, playing with him and showing him various figures, to his squealing delight.

"These little dolls are so cute, Gavin," she said, as she began to nurse George.

"Action figures, baby. Action figures." Gavin said this seriously and solemnly, acutely aware of how many men had felt the same pain he felt right then. *Dolls! As if!*

Baby George was fussy at first and hadn't slept well, but as Gavin and Lea established a routine, he settled down just fine. One night after successfully putting the baby to bed, they were sitting on the deck drinking hot tea. Lea had Shiver on her lap and BoBo was sitting at Gavin's feet. Although Shiver hadn't conceived yet, Gavin thought that her body might need quite a while to recover from the hardships she'd endured in the wild. Gavin was pretty sure that she hadn't even gone into heat yet, as he would have noticed BoBo's increased interest.

Along with Mike, Lea had been having her way with the library, although her focus was on an entirely different section. Gavin thought she would have raided the books about medicinal herbs, but her knowledge of that subject was already encyclopedic. She had another subject in mind.

"Bob gave me another travel book about Italy, and I think you're right about how the Calabrian region would weather the Crumble better than almost anywhere. In the later books, there was a lot about agricultural tourism and sustainable farming. In fact, you could say that the food movement started with the Slow Food movement in Italy!" Lea was visibly excited.

Gavin smiled as she continued to gush about Italy. She was glowing with passion and he couldn't stop staring at her. Her excitement was infectious, and had reignited his own love for travel.

"So what have you thought about the trip so far? I want to know the plan!" she said, interrupting his reverie.

"It's in the hopper," he said, not yet ready to get into the discussion.

"The what?" she asked, grinning and swatting at him. She loved it when he was weird. *Thank God for that*, he thought.

"The hopper. Sometimes when I need to figure something big out, I let my subconscious work on it for a while."

Lea smiled and kissed his cheek. She smelled great, like lavender and something else he didn't recognize. "I know you have more of a plan than that. I've been talking to Bob, you know."

Gavin laughed, knowing that Lea must have swept Bob off his feet by now. "How much have you been pumping poor Bob for information?" he asked. "I assume he's already told you about the marina?"

Lea smiled coyly. "Well, at least I know now that you weren't full of crap when you said you had a 'place to start' for a trip to Italy. I told Bob what you said, and he spilled the beans. What was the name of the place your family owns? Port Walker Marina?"

"Port Walter. It's in the northern neck of Virginia, about 150 miles from here. It used to be less than three hours by car, but obviously we haven't been there for years. We still own it, whatever that means these days, but I'm assuming there are squatters there. The buildings were in pretty good repair and there were still about fifty boats in the slips the last time we able to visit, which was right before Christmas of 2025. The food riots had started by then and it was getting hard to travel. We were worried that the restaurant at the marina was going to get ransacked, so we went down there and put all the food outside and left a note that said, "NO FOOD INSIDE." We shut off all the electricity and got out of there. That was one of the last times we left the farm for a really long time. We had Xavier with us and he and I were both armed, with Bob driving, but we had a couple of close scrapes and shady situations on the trip anyway. It hit home for us on that day, how bad things had gotten.

"We did have good relations with the employees and the townspeople there, so it wouldn't be impossible to reestablish some sort of a beachhead. I think we can plan to start the trip two summers from now."

Lea's eyes were shining, but her practicality won through. "How? That's different than going to Ramsey. On the shorter travels, we have a caravan of people and we know there is a friendly place waiting for us at the other end, and we can make the whole trip in two days. This would be a lot harder than that, even if we did have a big group with us, because we don't know what's waiting for us."

"You're right as always," Gavin said, pointing to his temple. "You know I married you for more than just your body, right?" He smiled and reached for her, pulling her into his lap. "But my darling, don't you know me well enough by now to know that I always have a plan?" Gavin winked at her.

Looking down at the old pool, he saw that Devante was approaching with a message. Gavin sighed as Lea stood up. He followed suit, feeling his age as his bones creaked with the effort.

"Make sure George doesn't take over the world while I'm gone," he joked as he kissed Lea. Briefly reading the message, Gavin asked Devante to stay with him, and walked down the hill to the Big House. He let Devante ring the bell, which seemed to delight him, and he rang the bell three times, which was the signal for a meeting. One ring was for dinner and two was for visitors, and if Millwood came under attack it rang continuously. Gavin then went to the dining room and sat down next to Devante. Scanning the message one more time, he sat down heavily. He'd been expecting something like this and instead of feeling his familiar dread, or even excitement, all he felt was a deep fatigue.

After a short wait, Xavier, Aidan, and Mike came in one-by-one and sat at the dining room table. Xavier was the last to arrive, ruffling the hair of his son as he saw him. Gavin held up the paper and read the message.

"From Farrington: New group camped out on Stonewell Road. It appears to be more government mercenaries turned raider. Twenty or more men and five vehicles. We will attack at dawn the day after tomorrow and are asking for help from Millwood and Scotville. Thank you and God bless."

Stonewell Road had proven to be a problem for Farrington, because while it was a secondary road, it had several intersections close to the town and had been well traveled before the Crumble. Raider groups with vehicles used it often because it was still in relatively good repair, and it gave easy access to farms for groups that came from the slums and ghettoes that were once called suburbia. The raiders loved to attack farms because they were so isolated, and often bore troves of guns and food. The pickings were slim nowadays though; anyone who had survived the first few years of raids was very hard to kill.

"I don't see how we have any choice but to help," Xavier started the conversation. "Devante, go run to Scotville and give this message to Pastor Dennis, as fast as you can!" Devante took the message and its leather case back from Gavin and ran out the door. Gavin didn't envy the boy's five mile run that awaited him.

"I agree," Aidan said. "And Mike is ready, if he wants to go. I tried to convince him otherwise, but he's eighteen now and I can't stop him anymore." Gavin looked at his brother and felt his pain. He held the same fears for Mike, wanting to protect him from being hurt. He tried once more.

"Are you sure you really want to do this, buddy? I know I've said it a million times, but this is not some glamorous pursuit. It is terrible. We're now at the point where we don't have to fight for our lives every single day, and if you wanted to, you could choose to try to

194

stay away from violence. I know you have been doing some deep thinking about spirituality lately, and don't a lot of those teachings have a pacifist bent?"

Mike calmly looked around the room. "I have looked to each of you for guidance as I have grown up, and I appreciate what you are trying to do. Xavier, even you, the greatest fighter among us – you, too, have tried to treat me with kid gloves and keep me away from violence and death. I love you all for that. But each of you has seen it, and I have to know what it's like. Besides, violence is a part of nature itself, and can't always be avoided. Most importantly, I want to *help*. I'm a good shot and I've been steady in tough situations so far, so I know I can be a solid addition to the team. If I can help another one of our family survive, then I have to be there."

Each of the three men nodded at Mike, and Xavier spoke.

"You know the question I want to ask. If we're gonna be outnumbered, how about taking the gloves off? If we do, we're gonna save some of our people that way."

Aidan and Gavin gave each other knowing looks, Gavin silently stroking his chin.

"Does someone want to fill me in?" Mike asked. "Does that mean what I think it means? I didn't think any of those stories were true!" He had a shocked look on his face.

Aidan put his hand on Mike's shoulder. "Listen to me, son. Sometimes, in order to defeat a monster, you must become one yourself. We all swore to each other that we would only operate that way when it was necessary, and that if any one of us started to like it too much, the other two would pull him back from the brink. We *swore* that to each other. It's been more than two years since we've had to fight dirty like that."

Mike's mouth was gaping open, and his voice shook as he spoke. "So you guys rubbed your bullets in shit, and wounded people on purpose, just so their screams would fuck with the heads of the ones that were left? Is it true about the 'Outlaw belt?' You really did that to people while they were still alive? Jesus Christ, Xavier! Is that *true*? I always thought those were just stories the neighbors told to make us sound scary and tough!"

Xavier was quiet, looking at Gavin and Aidan. Aidan nodded at him. Gavin had a pained expression on his face.

"Look, man," Xavier said quietly. "This life we live now, it didn't come for cheap, know what I mean? You were still too young to know about what was going on, and we're all glad for it. But let me see you go up against fifty guys, and they are three miles away. They know where you live because they tortured one of your neighbors to death, and they heard about all the stuff you got. They're coming for you." Xavier sighed and took a deep breath.

"Let me see you deal with that!" he continued fervently. "Then try to tell me you wouldn't do everything you could to make that three miles seem like a hundred. I got my son here, man! I got my babies and my woman here. We did what we had to do. And if you've got to choose between your family and fighting dirty, I know what you're gonna do, too."

Mike was quiet for a long time after that, as the other men debated their course of action.

"Let's just soften them up the night before," Aidan finally said. "That should be enough. We can fight clean on the day of the actual fight."

Xavier and Gavin nodded, while Mike continued to stare at the table, ashen-faced.

As Gavin walked into the pool house later that night, he was surprised to see that Lea was upset with him. She was sitting in a chair with her arms crossed, using her foot to rock George in his homemade wooden rocker on the floor. She scowled at Gavin when he came in.

"What was that?" she asked.

"What was what?" Gavin replied, unsure of what she could possibly have to be upset about.

"So you get an important message from Farrington, and now that I'm a mom, I'm just a sack of potatoes? You didn't even ask me to come down with you. Or, at the very least, include me in a discussion before you go to your big 'man to man' meeting." Lea hadn't changed position, although her scowl had deepened.

Gavin sat silently for a moment, giving thought to her statements. She was right; she was his wife now, and should share in every decision. He felt like he'd just failed a test.

"I'm sorry," he said. "I've been single for so long that I'm used to doing everything on my own. Of course you should be involved with all the decisions. But you wouldn't have wanted to come to this meeting, anyway. It looks like we'll have to fight again the day after tomorrow, and I know you don't like violence."

"If you think it's for a good reason, then you know I'll support you. But this time, I'm going with you. I should have been at the last battle, too. I could have done a better job with the rebel kids if I'd gotten to them sooner. You've seen me with my bow. I could have done more good. At the very least, you need someone with healing experience there." Lea had a firm set to her jaw; she wasn't going to budge on this one.

Gavin saw red. "No way in hell are you coming! I forbid it! You don't get to have it both ways. You have a baby to worry about now! *Our* baby! I get some say in this, too. And besides, the rebel kids are all fine now. You did a great job!" He caught himself yelling, and George began to cry. He hung his head.

"Besides," he said more quietly, as Lea picked up George and started to nurse him, "I don't want you to see what we'll have to do to win. But you're right; we wouldn't be doing this if it weren't important. A new group of raiders is threatening Farrington. They sound well-equipped and there are a lot of them. These people are our neighbors; we have to help them." He sighed and sat on the arm of the chair next to her, stroking her hair.

Lea looked up at him. "The fact that you're so conflicted about it tells me that you're a good man, husband of mine. But if you think, for one minute, that I'm going to let you risk your life without me there to help you, you need to think again. We're partners. Bob and Stella can watch George for the day; they dote on him, anyway."

Lea looked down at George in his crib, and her face hardened. "And if these people threaten Farrington, that means they're close enough to be a threat to this little guy, too. So do whatever you need to do. I'll back you up one hundred percent."

Gavin looked down at his fierce, passionate wife, and embraced her, crushing her to his chest. "You know, I never told you the whole story about my cousin, Jeremy. I just told you that I had a cousin who took his life, but not what really happened."

Lea nodded, her head still pressed against him.

"All the way into my thirties, I led a charmed life," Gavin said. "Everything I touched turned to gold. No matter what mistakes I made, somehow things always seemed to work out. I got to the point where I expected things to always go well, and I got sloppy. I got selfish. I was so self-absorbed that I didn't love anybody except for my family. Like I told you when we first met, I'd had some long-term relationships, but I was too self-centered to commit." Gavin got up and walked over to the top drawer in his nightstand, taking out a book of pictures. He walked back to the chair and handed the pictures to Lea.

"That's Jeremy," Gavin said, as she opened the book. It was filled with photos of a younger-looking Gavin with a handsome, smiling boy with curly black hair. As Lea turned the pages, she saw Gavin get older, and Jeremy grew from a boy into a young man.

"He was my cousin," Gavin continued, "but he was like a little brother to me. I loved that kid so much. He was so funny and curious, and he reminded me of myself. He was so smart, and so funny and cool, that I figured the world would be his oyster, just like it was for me. But it wasn't. He put on a good show, and he seemed so cavalier and tough, but now I see that he was just putting on a front. He had family problems, and he was hurting inside, but I always thought he could handle anything.

"I was so goddamn selfish! I wasn't there for him enough. Many years ago now, on the night before New Year's Eve, I got a call from Bob and Stella." Gavin put his head in his hands.

"Stella was crying, and she told me that Jeremy had hung himself. My life changed forever that day. I would have traded all my luck, and my whole charmed life, just to have him back. But he wasn't going to come back. There was nothing my luck could do about it, and all of a sudden, my whole life seemed worthless to me."

Lea gasped. "I'm so sorry. I didn't realize how close you two were."

"I gave the eulogy at his funeral," Gavin said. "I just told funny stories about him; I had nothing else to say. What can you say about something like that? I still think about him every day, and I'll never forget that failure."

"I'm sure it's not like you say," Lea said quietly, stroking his knee. "You couldn't have known what would happen."

Gavin looked up at her, eyes wide and rimmed with red.

"Do you know what I was going to do for New Year's that year? I was planning to go to a huge party in Baltimore. There was going to be coke, booze, weed, the whole bit. I was dating this girl at the time, and I was supposed to have a threesome with her and her friend." His voice was shaking.

"Do you get how I fucked up now?" Gavin whispered, as Lea looked at him with sad eyes. "I was so consumed with my petty, hedonistic lifestyle that I hadn't even called or texted Jeremy for days, and he needed me more than he had ever needed me in his entire life. If I had just fucking *called* him that day..." Gavin broke down and sobbed. "Not only did I not reach him, but I couldn't even say goodbye. I could have been the one that got through to him. But then one day, in the blink of an eye, it all ended. His life was ripped away, and it wasn't just that. His *future* life was gone, too. I never knew the pain of losing someone really close before, not like that. I can't even fathom what it would feel like if I lost you... I'm not sure I could handle the agony. I can't even let myself imagine it..."

"Shhh... I get it, Gavin," Lea murmured into his ear. "I get it. And I promise I won't lay that 'it wasn't your fault' bullshit on you about Jeremy. I wasn't there, and I didn't know you then." She put her arms around him.

"But I know you *now*, Gavin," she said. "You're a good man. And I understand now why the idea of losing another loved one scares you so much. So let's say this. I want to be included in all decisions, like we agreed, and I'm definitely coming to help you at Stonewell Road. But I won't ask to fight just for the sake of being there. If it's a small engagement, I'll stay out of it, and deal with any wounded you bring back here. If you don't need my help, I won't risk myself unnecessarily. Does that sound fair?"

Gavin was still crying, now clutching the book of photos in Lea's hands. He looked at her, his face broken with the anguish of his guilt and grief.

"You're so fucking *logical*, baby. Thank you. That makes perfect sense. I love you so much."

Lea held Gavin's head on her lap as he wept for his lost cousin.

Chapter 48

Farrington, Virginia

Farrington was abuzz on the day before the attack. Gavin, Lea and the rest of the team from Millwood arrived in the afternoon with a larger group than they anticipated. Monique and Shelly had decided to join their core team, which surprised Gavin, who expected they would want a break from violence.

While Shelly had remained living at Millwood over the last months, Monique had chosen to relocate to the neighboring farm that had taken in the majority of the rebels. Millwood's southern neighbors were the Stanwell family. They had been trying to grow cotton and tobacco, but had never had enough of a labor force to do it properly. With the addition of the rebels, the Stanwells had managed to produce a large tobacco crop, although the cotton had still failed. Gavin was excited about the thought of having cigarettes again, but Lea had expressly forbid him from smoking around the baby and he quickly abandoned that fantasy, a remnant of his bachelor days.

Gavin hadn't seen Monique for a while and hugged her when he first saw her again, but she felt limp and cold in his arms. She seemed pleased with Shelly's transformation, but Monique still projected that lost, blank look that she and Shelly both had when they got back from chasing Spiegel. *Maybe Mike can help her with his Godspark magic,* Gavin thought wryly to himself. He took everything he had seen Mike do with a grain of salt, and attributed it to his charisma and force of personality, but if he could help Monique, Gavin didn't think it would matter to her if it were magic or not. He assumed that whatever effect Mike had on Shelly could only help Monique as well.

As Gavin and the team stood in the center of Farrington, he could see Chris Orlund on the other side of the town center. Seeing that Orlund had noticed them and was waiting for him to approach, Gavin took in the sight of Farrington and was reminded of how charming the place was. Much of Farrington's structures had been constructed before the modern habit of building monstrosities began, and because of that, the town was an exceedingly pleasant place. The streets were lined with mature trees, and the buildings all came out to the same place in the street, making every block feel like a town square.

The only incongruous element was the men on the rooftops with assault rifles and binoculars, but Gavin knew that with a raider group camped out so close by, Farrington was wise to be ready for anything. Gavin didn't think that a group of fifteen to twenty men would brazenly attack the whole town, but anything was possible.

Gavin smiled and leaned toward Aidan, speaking in a low voice. "You know, in the old days, a place like this would have been called 'quaint.' Now we call it, 'still standing.'" Aidan chuckled and rolled his eyes at Gavin, as he held out his hand out to shake with Orlund, who had approached the group.

"Hello, everyone!" Chris Orlund beamed as he took in the large, armed group that had come from Millwood. In addition to Shelly and Monique, Xavier had brought three Outlaws, and of course Aidan, Gavin, Mike, and Lea rounded out the group, each in body armor and carrying assault rifles. Gavin had his trusty M4 at his side, as always. Lea had her bow and a large backpack full of medical supplies.

After he had hugged Gavin and kissed Lea on the cheek, Orlund approached Xavier, who was standing next to Aidan.

Addressing both men, Orlund said, "Thank you guys so much for what you did last night. I just got a report from one of our scouts, and it seems that a few of the raiders have jumped ship already. One of their vehicles is completely burned, and they're definitely on edge now. I don't think any of them got any sleep last night!"

Aidan smiled and looked at Xavier, who had a fierce gleam in his eye. The Outlaws behind them stood tall, always glad to hear appreciation for their skills. "We're going back tonight," Aidan said. "I figure we can keep them up for another night, and maybe chase away a few more."

"What exactly did you do to them?" Orlund asked. "Some of those old tricks we've heard about?"

Xavier walked up to Orlund and put his hand on his shoulder. "Don't worry about it, Chris, we're gonna handle it so you don't have to. Let's just say that they're afraid of what they can't control. They don't know what we're gonna do. We just try to scare them away. We make it so they would rather take their chances on the road alone than to stay in that camp another night." He grinned at Chris.

Orlund clapped Xavier on the back. "I'm so glad to have you all with us. I figure you guys will want to sleep for a while before nightfall. I have rooms for you." Orlund sent them off with one of his grandchildren. He turned to Gavin, Lea, and Mike, who had stayed behind.

"We are so glad to see you guys. Lea, any puppies yet?" As she shook her head in the negative, Orlund shrugged and said, "Well, I hope they are trying! My wife keeps asking me about it. I hope you get to meet her soon!" Chris smiled, and then faltered, remembering why they were all there.

"Anyway, back to the situation at hand," he continued. "Scotville has sent some people too, and with what we have been able to round up here in Farrington, plus what the Outlaws are doing for us, we should easily outnumber these guys two to one. Let me show you what we have ready," Chris said, linking his arm with Lea's. He led the group toward the town stables, which were in a beautiful old stone firehouse.

As they approached, Gavin could see that the cavalry concept had taken off even more since the demonstration at the big meeting at Millwood. The town stable was filled with what Gavin could only describe as war horses, and the tack for them was equally impressive. Gavin knew that Xavier had been working with some of the Farrington men to make armor, but he didn't expect it to be so well crafted. The breastplates were obviously welded together from reused pieces of metal, but the work was good and they had been polished to a shine. The craftsmen even managed to forge a rough-hewn coat of arms in the center of each individual breastplate. There were piles of mail and more pieces that Gavin didn't recognize, and he couldn't wait to see what a fully outfitted horse looked like.

"Chris, this is amazing!" Lea said excitedly. Gavin added some compliments of his own, but Mike just stood there for a moment, his mouth hanging open.

Mike had been quiet up until now, doing what Gavin and Aidan had taught him. In a new situation, it was better to listen before speaking, but he was obviously excited by what he saw.

"These are modern day knights!" Mike exclaimed. "I've never seen anything like this. I can't wait to see what these guys can do!"

Orlund smiled a wolfish grin, and pointed over to the corner, where a lanky boy was sitting on a stool. "Did you hear that, Sir Justin? You're a knight!"

The kid smiled back and said, "I like the sound of that. I could get ladies to wait on me hand and foot, and have a man servant to carry my armor and take care of my horse..."

Laughing, Chris said, "Enough of that! You will work like everyone else. Now, Sir Justin, get back to mucking the stalls!"

Smiling as he turned away, Chris said, "That's my favorite grandson."

That night, Chris put Gavin and Lea up at his house in a beautifully decorated guest room. Lea looked glum as she watched Gavin put his gear on and check his weapons.

"Are you sure they really need your help tonight?" Lea asked him. "I'm not going to ask to go on this one," she said with distaste.

"I'm just going for a few hours," Gavin said. "I need to get some sleep tonight, and you should do the same. And don't worry about George. Everyone at Millwood will be fighting to see who gets to take care of him."

She stood and kissed him. "Come back soon, and be careful."

"Don't worry," Gavin replied "These guys are guerrilla fighters. Tonight we aren't in much danger. Tomorrow, when we have to attack in force, is when we take the biggest risk."

Gavin rode Buck again, and he quickly made it to the Outlaws' meeting place. It was dark already, and Aidan and Xavier stood together, waiting for him.

"It's gonna be harder tonight," Xavier was saying to Aidan. "They've got their lookouts in a lot closer to their camp, and they circled some of those big trucks around the easiest ways to get in. JB and Lamont are over there already. They're gonna start a diversion, and the three of us will go and see if we can find another one who is by himself." Xavier motioned to a tree behind him, where three crossbows sat. "Load up with those, but keep your other guns, too, just in case."

The three men put on nighttime ghillie suits made with black, gray, and dark blue twine. They grabbed their crossbows and made their way to the edge of the camp. They didn't wait long before the diversion began, marked by loud shouts and the flames of Molotov cocktails. Several shadowy figures emerged out of vehicles and started firing their weapons toward the commotion. Aidan looked through the new thermal goggles he'd gotten from the raiders in Scotville.

"I think I see one," he said. "It's hard to use these things, and it was a pain in the ass to get it charged up, but it looks like someone is hiding behind the gray truck on our right."

As soon as the words left Aidan's mouth, Xavier was already gone. Gavin could see a faint outline as Xavier circled around the truck. A quiet "thunk" sounded as Xavier's crossbow fired, followed by a brief yelp. A short time later, Xavier came back, dragging a struggling raider with a bolt in his back. As he approached, Gavin saw that Xavier had his hand clamped over the man's mouth.

"Gavin," Xavier whispered, "Put that gag on him, and Aidan, get his legs."

The raider they had captured smelled terrible, and was as thin as a rail. He snarled at them, biting at Xavier's gloved hand. He reached for the knife at Xavier's waist, and Aidan punched him in the throat. The captive raider slumped to the ground, as Xavier shook out his hand and removed his gloves. Gavin grabbed the raider's legs, whispering, "This guy is about to have the worst night of his life."

Xavier snorted quietly. "Worst and *last*," he said.

The three men quickly dragged their captive away.

Chapter 49

March 2011 - A catastrophic triple meltdown occurs at the Fukushima Daiichi nuclear plant in Japan, caused by an earthquake and the resulting tsunami. Experts predict that this disaster will vastly exceed the damage done at Chernobyl. This is what happens when corporations sacrifice safety standards for profits and growth. The planetary economic system is based on the concept of infinite growth; a fiction that seemed to be a reality as long as the cheap energy kept flowing. Natural limits are now starting to impose themselves, however. With almost no energy resources of its own, and now significant ecological and health-related problems from the Fukushima disaster, Japan may be the first country in the world forced to de-industrialize.

Stonewell Road – Eight miles from Farrington

The next morning was foggy and gray, and the temperature had dropped. It was just the kind of weather the Grey Ghost would have loved. Gavin and the Millwood team were serving as the distraction in the overall strategy because they were the best at staying unseen. Everyone in the group had donned their ghillie suits and they had spent the early morning hours sidling up as close as they could to the raider group, staying hidden in the woods running along Stonewell Road.

"These guys are too stupid to leave this crossroads. It looks like there are only twelve of them left, but that's going to be the core group; the toughest ones," Gavin said, handing the monocular to Xavier. "So far, I'm seeing only four men on watch; it looks like the rest are still trying to sleep, even after last night."

As was their traditional strategy, Gavin stayed with Xavier and the Outlaws and Aidan led the second group, consisting of him and Mike, Lea, Shelly, and Monique. Gavin liked it that way; Aidan's team was made up of sharpshooters, which would keep her out of harm's way. Xavier looked through the monocular and passed it back to Gavin, grunting. "Did you see that fifty? I can't believe I didn't notice it before. They might have just mounted it this morning."

"What?" Gavin asked, looking back through the monocular

again. Sure enough, atop one of the raider's vehicles there sat a .50 caliber heavy machine gun, with a wide section of armored plate to protect the operator.

"Fuck!" Gavin spat, keeping his voice as low as he could. That rifle would tear through the Farrington riders like tissue paper, right on their first outing. Looking at Xavier next to him, he could only see his eyes, nose, and a loose dreadlock. The rest of his body was obscured by the ghillie suit. Xavier's eyes told him all he needed to know.

"We need to do this shit Rambo-style," Xavier said with gleaming eyes and a wide grin. "Signal Aidan to start shooting. The most important thing is to keep them away from it, but we should try not to destroy it. That bad boy is gonna be mine."

Gavin whistled at Aidan to start firing, and he and Xavier began sneaking closer with the Outlaws. Gavin managed to pick off one of the men as he started toward the .50 caliber, but as more raiders emerged from the vehicles they were firing at everything that moved, and that included Aidan and Gavin's groups. Gavin could see some of the men squinting around, not being able to see who was shooting at them. Gavin was thankful for their skill at making ghillie suits as he sidled closer. As they reached the edge of the woods, Xavier pushed himself off his belly and onto his knees. He dropped his rifle and drew his sword, looking at Gavin.

"Cover me!" Xavier said quietly as he started moving toward the road.

Xavier ran into the midst of the scene, still in his ghillie suit and brandishing his samurai sword. Gavin saw one of the raiders look up at him in shock, not even getting a chance to bring his weapon up before being skewered through the chest. Xavier managed to pull that trick once more before he ran out of targets close enough to reach. Another raider approached, firing twice at Xavier as Gavin frantically ran toward the scene. Xavier fell, clutching his neck, as Gavin cut down the raider with his M4.

"Xavier!" Gavin shouted, as the bear of a man got back to his knees. Xavier had his hand clapped to his neck, and took it away for Gavin to look at it.

"How bad is it?" Xavier asked, breathing heavily, but calm.

"It's not too bad," Gavin answered, as he pulled a bandana

from his vest and tied it around Xavier's neck. "It's a graze, and a pretty deep one. But it looks like it missed anything major. This should hold you for now."

The other Outlaws were firing on a large group of the enemy that had managed to group together behind their circle of vehicles, and were pouring heavy fire in the general direction of Aidan's group. Gavin assumed they had withdrawn by now, but his heart felt like it was going to explode with worry about Lea. He shook it off and focused.

The bugle sounded. While the machine gun wasn't present today, Gavin thought the sound of the bugle was just as musical. The Farrington knights thundered toward the cluster of rebels, firing too early to be effective but throwing the enemy into disarray. Gavin saw the opportunity and yelled, "Move in on the vehicles!"

Gavin and the Outlaws began firing and darting forward in random directions, taking out one more raider who made a run for the fifty caliber. This allowed Xavier to break cover again, and he made it up to the top of the vehicle and took control of the weapon. Blood leaked from the wound on his neck, but not at a worrisome rate. Xavier appeared to have forgotten all about it.

Gavin and the Outlaws managed to sandwich the raiders to the south, between them and the Farrington men coming at them from the other direction. He could hear more gunfire behind his back, and knew that anyone trying to escape to the north would be met by the Scotville group. As the knights got closer, their effectiveness increased, which took the pressure off Aidan's group. Gunfire came from the woods, and Gavin saw two more of the enemy fall, one with an arrow in his chest. *That's my woman*, Gavin thought.

The Farrington riders were using two different styles of shooting, with the older men shooting one handed while the younger ones seemed to be able to ride with just their legs, using both of their hands on their shotguns. They wore all-gray uniforms, and they were shouting out their rebel yell again. Gavin could see that they were using a mixture of slugs and buckshot, devastating damage. They were also shouting off their numbers in the group and firing in sequence, so none of the raiders could duck out from cover for even a moment. A loud clank sounded above his head and Gavin looked up.

"How does it look?" Gavin asked. He jumped up next to Xavier as the shooting reached a lull.

"I think I've got it now, it took me a minute to figure out how to load it and where the safety is. I have only seen these things in pictures. You want first shot?" Xavier grinned.

"Yeah man, Jeez! Sit down for a minute. That graze is starting to bleed more." Gavin switched places with Xavier and aimed the huge rifle at the cluster of raiders.

Tightening the cotton in his ears that he always wore during battles, he pulled the trigger for the first time. The rifle was designed for a much longer range, and the sound of the report made Gavin's head ring, despite his ear protection. "Thud-Thud-Thud-Thud-Thud-Thud" went the sound, big brass casings spilling out the side. Seeing the devastation it had caused, he and Xavier whooped loudly. Half of the raider group lay in a tattered mess and the vehicle they had been hiding behind would never move on its own again. Gavin shot once more, finishing the job. Their cheering was more subdued this time as the destruction began to sink in.

A few final shots rang out as the Scotville group mopped up the remaining raiders trying to escape, and Gavin was relieved to see that Lea, along with the rest of Aidan's group, emerged from the woods unharmed. Gavin's heart soared. Lea's face was dirty and grim, but determined. For a moment, the five ghillie-suited team members looked like a family of Sasquatch emerging from the woods.

Gavin walked toward them, opening his arms and smiling. As he did, he saw Aidan's eyes widen, and everyone in the ghillie-suited group began to raise their weapons, as if in slow motion. Lea knelt and pulled out an arrow, drawing her bow. She aimed at him, and he instinctively threw himself to the ground. She fired two arrows, and Gavin heard a choking noise behind him. Aidan and Mike fired a couple of shots as well, running towards Gavin's prone form.

Gavin got up and dusted himself off, finally looking behind him. A raider lay on the ground less than ten feet from away, a long machete in his hand. Two arrows protruded from his neck and shoulder.

"Are you okay?" Lea asked as she reached him.

"I'm fine. I owe you one, baby," Gavin said shakily. "Remind me to thank you properly later," he said, quickly kissing her.

The Farrington riders had reached them. They looked grim as

they saw the devastation, and young Justin looked ashen-faced and shaky, his left hand pressed to his chest. Blood poured from his hand.

Lea saw him the same time that Gavin did, and they both rushed to grab him as he fell off his horse. Mike followed close behind.

"Tell my grandfather I'm sorry," Justin mumbled, as the color faded from his face. "I wanted to be a knight."

His hand had been hit by a large caliber bullet, his pinkie was completely gone, and the second hung by a thread. A jagged wound ran down a large part of his palm as well.

Lea immediately took charge. "Mike," she said, "hold him on his back and comfort him. Do whatever you can to calm him down. Gavin, I need my bag, I left it right at the edge of the woods. And leave me your canteen; in fact, I need all the water you can find."

Mike calmly spoke into his ear, and Justin closed his eyes and started breathing more normally. Shelly sat nearby, waiting to see if Mike needed her. Monique had gone to sit away from the scene.

As Gavin retrieved Lea's supplies, he glanced at Monique. She was facing away from him, rocking back and forth, visibly in shock. He shook his head and walked back to the group.

"We're going to save your hand," Lea was telling Justin. "You'll still have enough fingers that you can do anything you want; even be a knight."

The next hour was difficult, but not for Gavin. He could do little but watch and hand items to Lea when she requested them. The time passed quickly, and Gavin was mesmerized by watching his wife at work. She lamented her lack of anesthetic at first, but Mike had calmed Justin to the point where he was in a sleepy, dreamlike state. After applying a poultice to help the blood coagulate, she methodically cut off pieces of flesh from Justin's hand, cleaning the wound as she did. She managed to create a roughly straight flap of skin to cover what was left of his palm, and stitched it up.

Lea looked up at Mike. "This next part will really hurt. Is he ready?"

Mike whispered to Justin again, who gave a slight nod. "Go ahead," Mike said.

Lea produced a pair of clippers and cut off Justin's dangling finger, quickly stanching the blood flow as she did. Justin moaned and shifted his position, but otherwise didn't react at all. She stitched that wound, as well.

As Lea finished with Justin, Gavin looked up to see that Xavier sat next to them, holding his neck wound tightly. Pastor Dennis sat with him, clutching a bleeding leg. As Lea got up and looked at them, she said, "Xavier, I'll get to you next, and Pastor Dennis, can you make it to Millwood? I'm going to need a better setup than this to get that bullet out of your leg. It doesn't look like you're bleeding too badly." She paused, and smiled at them. "Don't worry, you'll both be fine," she reassured them.

Gavin left her with Xavier and went to see how Aidan fared with the cleanup. He stood by one of the undamaged trucks, supervising the loading of the new weapons and supplies, including the .50 caliber.

"We're getting a bit too good at this," Aidan said. "And am I the only one who is a little freaked out by Mike? Do you remember the first time we had to kill someone? I thought I would never stop puking. And you were even worse, you didn't come out of your room for two days. I mean, it's not like he is jumping for joy or anything, but he's already together enough to help someone else? How is he doing so well?"

"I think he's so concerned with others that he processes his own pain through them. He's really a remarkable kid," Gavin said.

"He's not a kid anymore. He's a man now," Aidan said. "He's eighteen and has fought in a battle; if that doesn't make him a man, I don't know what does."

"True," Gavin mused, as the two brothers stood shoulder to shoulder, surveying the scene. Bodies were being disposed of and gear looted. "Did it start drizzling during the battle and I didn't notice?" Gavin asked.

"Huh," Aidan said, looking up. "Looks like it did."

After a few moments of silence, Aidan looked behind them and noticed that Xavier stood by the truck with his neck newly bandaged, inspecting the .50 caliber and taking an inventory of the ammo. "It looks like Xavier has himself a new toy."

"Well, I don't know if it's been decided how the loot will be divvied up, it may not be his to keep," Gavin said.

Aidan smiled and said, "Do *you* want to be the one to take it from him?"

Gavin laughed, looking to see whether Lea was finished. "Okay brother, I'm going to intercept Lea and take her and Mike back home. No need for them to see the cleanup..."

Aidan nodded knowingly. "Xavier and I will take care of it, little brother."

Gavin walked back to his wife, escorting her and the remainder of the group toward Farrington. Aidan turned to survey the scene behind the line of vehicles where he and Gavin were standing, seeing the results of what the Outlaws had done the night before. More than half of the vehicles had been burned, and three human heads lay in the center of camp, with various threatening epithets carved in their foreheads. Two more dead raiders lay near the edges of the camp, each one at the end of a trail of blood. On both bodies, the intestines had been pulled out through a hole in the belly, and wrapped around the waist. The raiders had been carefully kept alive during the process, and then allowed to escape back to their camp, so they could share their excruciating final hours with their fellows.

The reign of the infamous Outlaw belt lived on.

Chapter 50

October 2038
Millwood Farm

Gavin was worried that his beautiful farm was going to become a junkyard. Several old vehicles that had been stripped down for metal and parts over the years still littered a back field, and with the Hummer that Shelly and Monique had brought back, the addition of yet another vehicle was a concern to him. Although, at least the Hummer still worked, and it even had some gas.

The last few days of fog and drizzle had lifted and it was as beautiful as a fall day could get. The trees were more colorful than usual this year, with hues of yellow, orange, and red covering the rolling fields and woods. The day was crisp and dry, and they had a brush pile burning. The smell of smoke mixed with the fall air made Gavin smile. Each turning of the season was important to him, but this one was his favorite. Fall was when Mother Nature put on her slippers, curled up with a good book by the fire, and prepared for her winter's rest.

"We need to get rid of some of these," Gavin told Xavier, breaking his reverie. The two men worked to unbolt their new rifle from the roof of a late model Ford pickup, which they would ultimately junk as well. "Even though these raiders seem to still be able to find gas, we haven't had that kind of luck. I think we need to focus on just one vehicle and get rid of the rest, or at least use up all the metal and get rid of them that way. Let's give all this stuff to Chris Orlund. He can use them for the project."

"Yeah, I got you. Let me think about that," Xavier mused. "Maybe we can use the rest of the metal for armor. Did you hear Ex found a boiler and brought it to Beulah? Chris was over there last week looking at it. I think they are really gonna be able to pull it off. I've seen Orlund with those books, and the steam engine looks pretty close to the drawings so far."

"I haven't been over there yet, I can't wait to see it! The steam engine is definitely a huge accomplishment that will help everyone, and it gives people something to look forward to again. It's funny, you would think it would be easier to find an old one rather than build a new one. But you roll the dice every time you go on the road, and plus, Orlund said that once we build this one, it will make it a lot easier to get another one."

"Hell, yeah," Xavier said with a smile. "And Orlund already says you and me get to go on the first trip!"

Gavin grinned and clasped his friend's hand.

Getting back to the task at hand, Gavin said, "Let's get out the welding gear and start to at least cut up some of this stuff into smaller pieces."

"Why is it so quiet today?" Xavier asked.

"Cider day," Gavin replied. "Don't you remember, we got out of it this year since we did the whole thing last year."

Xavier grinned and laughed. "Oh yeah! Hell yeah! I forgot about that. Thank God we don't have to mess with that old press this year."

Gavin laughed and slapped his friend on the back. "Yep, and Lea specifically said she wanted to help make the cider today. Wait until she sees that bulky thing they have to deal with!"

Years ago, Gavin and Aidan had found an old cider press in an antique store, and while they had oiled it and fixed as best as they could, no one seemed to be able to quite get the hang of using it.

Just as Gavin was ready to head to the tool shed with Xavier, he saw Monique approaching with Justin at her side, coming from the front entrance and heading up to the woods.

"Start without me buddy, I'll be back later," Gavin said as he headed to intercept Monique and Justin. They stopped and waited for him as he approached.

"Hey!" he said, approaching and hugging Monique and shaking Justin's hand. Gavin looked at his left hand, which was covered in a fresh bandage. "How is the hand healing up?" Gavin asked.

"It's doing pretty well, but it hurts like hell," Justin replied with a grim smile. "Lea said she doesn't see an infection though, so that's good news." Lea had converted a room in the Big House into a permanent medical area. She had already done one surgery; the removal of the bullet from Pastor Dennis' leg. She also used it for the follow-up appointments, prescribing a variety of herbs and natural remedies to reduce infection and speed the healing process.

"That's *great* news!" Gavin said. "So, are you guys going up to the tree in the clearing?"

"Yeah, Mike just invited us and we thought we would check it out. He said to meet him at a big tree in the center of the trails, which one is that?" Justin asked. Still a bit pale, he looked a lot better since the last time Gavin had seen him after the battle at Stonewell Road, and Lea had told him he was dealing with his injury as best he could. Justin was also missing the cockiness that he'd had when Gavin met him in the stalls the day before the battle.

"I'll show you. I kind of want to check this out myself," Gavin answered. He led them up to the trails, talking along the way.

"Did Mike tell you what they do at these meetings?" Gavin asked.

Monique responded, as Justin looked lost in thought, holding his bandaged left hand to his chest. "Well, they really didn't tell me much at all. But Shelly really seems to like Mike, so I thought I would come and check it out. I don't know what he told Justin; I just met him on the way in."

Before Gavin could ask Justin, they had arrived at the tree. Mike was sitting with his back rested against it, surrounded by a small circle of people. Shelly sat to his right, and Renee and a couple of the older Jackson kids sat with a group of three of the former rebels who were living on the Stanwell property next door.

"Hey, buddy!" Mike cried as he got up and hugged Gavin and their visitors. Looking at Gavin with a grin, he said, "I'm glad you guys could make it. Have a seat and we'll start."

Gavin sat in the circle with mild trepidation, although he respected Mike and was willing to listen with an open mind.

Mike sat back down. "Let's start by talking a little bit. Normally we are silent for a while first, but I'll explain to the new guests what we are doing."

"We believe that God is life itself," Mike said softly. "There is a spark inside each of us that gives us life and connects us all together. We call that the Godspark, and we believe that each individual spark is a piece of God. If we can harness that power and focus our minds, we can accomplish incredible things. What we do here is use meditation exercises to strengthen our minds. As we learn more, we'll try to strengthen our bodies as well, and our connections to each other and the earth. And isn't that where our strength comes from? Our minds, our bodies, Mother Nature, and the people we love and care about?"

Mike leaned over past Shelly and touched Justin's leg. "Do you mind if I talk about what happened on the day of the battle?"

"No, that's fine," said Justin, carrying a slightly defeated air about him, hiding his bandaged hand below his leg.

Mike said, "After the battle at Stonewell Road, Justin was seriously injured. His left hand may never work quite the same way, even when it's fully healed. That has been really affecting him. He feels like he's less of a man now, and less useful."

Justin nodded, head hanging down.

"Does anyone have anything they want to say to Justin?" Mike asked, looking at the small circle of people.

Gavin looked around and decided he was best qualified to address the issue. He looked at Justin, who stared at the ground. "Look, man, I won't sugarcoat it. If this had happened to you five years ago, you might be dead already. And if you had a handicap like that five years ago, that might have been the difference between life and death for you. But all of us have been working really hard to make sure that the violence of those years doesn't come back. Now, you can do anything you want. We need all kinds of trades, not just fighters. We need bakers, and farmers, architects, and builders. We need engineers," Gavin said.

Gavin patted Justin on the shoulder. "From what I saw, you did very well in a stressful situation; you held it together when it counted. I saw you on your horse, charging and firing with everyone else. You did yourself and the men on your team proud, and you didn't fall off your horse until the fighting stopped, even with your wounded hand. Now you know something about yourself; you have balls when it counts. Everything else is secondary. Whatever you choose to do, I know you'll do it well."

Mike smiled and looked at Justin, who now sat slightly taller and had brightened up a bit. "Now let's try an exercise."

The next hour was illuminating for Gavin. There were times when it sounded a bit like mumbo-jumbo and it was obvious that Mike was still finding his feet, but some of it was remarkable. Mike had done a mental exercise with Justin and the group, where Justin imagined the essence of the Godspark inside of him, reaching out to heal his wounded body. The rest of the group was asked to imagine the same thing. As Mike led the exercise, he made the spark larger and larger in all of their minds until Justin was exploding with power, his damaged hand glowing. By the end of the exercise, Gavin was so enthralled by the moment that he was almost certain he saw a powerful spark of light shining from Justin's body.

After that, Mike led a long period of silence that must have lasted ten minutes, where the group members closed their eyes and imagined each other's Godsparks, and tried to detect other sparks around them, including that of the tree they sat under. Gavin knew from his walks just how calming nature could be for a person. Regardless of any metaphysical benefits, the effects of slowing down and listening to the sounds of nature were good for the soul. Mike tried a few more meditation exercises after that, and at the end there was a lively discussion about personal issues, morality, and of course, farming.

After the meeting, Mike lounged by the tree with Gavin for a while before they walked back down.

"So how did it feel to have some of your own ideas spouted back at you?" Mike asked with a grin.

"Actually, it was kind of disconcerting at first, but I think you might be on to something with this. I can't pretend to understand what you are doing exactly, but I'm sure you have a plan."

Mike laughed and there were crinkles around his eyes as he smiled. "I learned from watching you," Mike said. "I'm just making it up as I go along!"

Chapter 51

July 2011 - Standard & Poor's downgrades the U.S. credit rating for the first time in its history, taking it from a AAA to an AA+ and throwing the markets into turmoil. While the nominal reason for the downgrade was the debt ceiling debate and a broken Congress that couldn't pass any significant legislation, the escalating debt of the U.S. government no doubt played a part in the decision as well.

Shiver finally went into heat and BoBo lost his mind; Gavin couldn't get him to sit still or shut up. Shiver wanted nothing to do with him for the first couple of days, so Gavin decided to do something about it, especially because he knew BoBo was coming on too strong.

"We need to lock her up in the Big House for a day or so and let her calm down," Gavin said to Lea. "BoBo is on top of her every second and she can't relax. She needs to, you know… feel her womanhood." While Gavin was normally an excellent wordsmith, there were still times when words failed him.

Lea said, "So that's your scientific opinion, Mr. Genius Prepper with decades of dog breeding experience? 'Let her feel her womanhood?'" She cracked up laughing, all the while holding Shiver as BoBo jumped in the air at her.

Laughing with him, Gavin said, "Well, do you have any other ideas?"

And so it was decided that Shiver would be sequestered for a short time. Bob and Stella took charge of her, and Gavin was amused by watching BoBo stalking all of the doors around the big house, trying to gain entrance. After a few minutes, Gavin got bored and went back to work, forgetting all about the dogs. He went to help Xavier and Derek catch a pregnant sow that was ready to birth and get her settled into a private stall. This sow was a first time mother, so she would get special attention. He and Xavier talked about it as they herded her into the stall and got her settled in. She was already showing redness around her genitalia, which told them she was just a few days from having her litter. As they shoveled sawdust into the stall, Derek went off to get a water trough. Gavin looked after him said to Xavier, "Derek is looking good. I don't see a limp at all."

"Yeah, he's good," Xavier said. "He was real happy about that, too, I can tell you. That woman of yours is something else, I'm glad we have her."

"Don't I know it! I have no idea how I got so lucky," Gavin said. "I'm going to suggest that she start training a couple of new apprentices here."

Laughing, Xavier said, "Good idea. And I like that word, 'suggest'. It sounds so... polite. We can *suggest* that our enemies eat their own guns."

Laughing too, Gavin said "Now that you mention it..." he leaned into the stall, and as he was often wont to do, he started talking to the pig.

"Listen, honey, I *suggest* that you don't lie down on all your piglets within the first three days and squash them. If you do that, then you will become sausage. If you turn out to be a good mom, however, you will live a very long time." Gavin patted her on the rump and hoped she understood.

"How long do you think it will take before we stop seeing all these bad mothers?" Xavier asked. "It's because of all that stuff you used to talk about, industrial farming and all that, right?"

"Yep, exactly," Gavin said. "Industrial farming messed up a lot of these livestock breeds because it was so automated. They bred out important genes needed for survival. These Durocs are a prime example. They were raised in industrial settings for so many decades that they almost bred out the motherhood gene. All the moms were placed in these tiny corrals where they couldn't lie down or turn around, and that way they didn't lose a single piglet. It made them more money in the short run, but turned into something evil in the process. The artificial breeding methods meant that the bad mothers and the weakest pigs couldn't be weeded out. It was also torture for the pigs, which were smart enough to know what was happening to them. That's why nowadays, when we get a good sow, like Tookie, who doesn't kill her piglets, she lives out her whole life and has as many litters as she can comfortably have. And that's also why more of her daughters have been good moms, too. It runs in the family. I figure that if the machine had around eighty years to screw up agriculture, we can probably fix them in twenty." He smiled at Xavier as they went back to work.

Hearing the dinner bell that night, Gavin was reminded of Shiver's confinement, and realized it would be over as soon as people started coming in for dinner. *Oh well, at least she had some peace today,* Gavin thought. As he got closer to the Big House, he could hear Aidan's loud laughter from the kitchen. Gavin jogged up to see what was happening.

It was chaos. Stella was berating Bob, who had evidently let BoBo into the house by accident. Lea had put George in the bassinet in the dining room, and was now frantically trying to separate BoBo and Shiver, who were stuck together. Shiver was barking and whining, while BoBo, on the other hand, looked quite calm now that he had gotten what he wanted. Aidan was just standing there, chuckling.

"Baby, that's okay, you can leave them like that. It happens sometimes, they will only be stuck together for a few minutes," Gavin said, smacking his brother on the arm for not telling Lea that earlier.

Poor Shiver's eyes were dilated and she had a thick length of drool coming from her mouth. She was trembling slightly, fulfilling her namesake once again. BoBo's face, however, was a happy and satisfied one. His eyes were glazed over and his tongue was hanging out. Gavin and Aidan both doubled over laughing at the sight, tears streaming down their faces.

"Good God, what did BoBo do to her?" Gavin gasped. "Lea, how come you have never looked like that afterwards?"

Aidan was sucking in great gulps of breath as he continued to laugh, and Lea gave Gavin a mock glare, although he could see she was barely containing a smile. She was still squatting down beside the two dogs, holding and petting Shiver. "My poor thing, what did that big bad boy do to you? We girls have to stick together!"

Gavin and Aidan finally stopped laughing, only to start up again as they overheard Stella and Bob, who had moved to the dining room. They were setting up the dinner table, still fighting.

Bob's voice was the louder of the two. "Damn it, Stella, how was I supposed to know someone would open the kitchen door? Besides, that little bastard was going to find a way to get in eventually!"

Stella could be heard only distantly, but when Aidan and Gavin heard her say, "And look what he did to my little baby!" they could barely handle it.

"You two are silly," Lea said as Shiver and BoBo finally separated. She scooped up Shiver, and headed to the dinner table. As she passed Gavin, she pointed at his chest. "And you, Mr. Man, you had better take good care of this little baby, too."

Gavin promised that he would and solemnly kissed his wife, following her to dinner.

Chapter 52

October 2011 — In one of the largest bankruptcies in U.S. history, the investment firm MF Global files for Chapter 11 bankruptcy protection. Soon after, federal regulators begin an investigation into hundreds of millions of dollars in missing customer funds. The CEO of MF Global is none other than John Corzine, a former head of Goldman Sachs. At the final accounting, $1.6 billion in customer money is lost.

December 2038

The Christmas season of that year was one of lifetime memories. The winter snows came early and so did the cold, but Gavin had never been so happy. He took such great joy in his beautiful wife and baby son that sub-zero temperatures and twelve feet of snow wouldn't have dampened his mood. Millwood's help for Farrington at the battle of Stonewell Road had further cemented their relationship, and the Colliers and Jacksons were invited to the Farrington Christmas Ball for the first time.

While Gavin had never gone in for such displays of pomp and circumstance, Lea had been very excited when she heard about it, and Gavin wasn't surprised to see that Shelly shared her enthusiasm. Shelly continued to blossom as she and Mike grew closer, though it wasn't just her demeanor and attitude that changed. While she hadn't seemed to care much about her appearance at first, as time went by she began adding small touches to her outfits, like flowers and brightly colored fabrics, and eventually started wearing bright and colorful homemade dresses. Shelly and Lea had become close friends in recent months and were now starting to make some very beautiful outfits together.

The two of them had retrofitted a room in the hayloft to make their clothing. On their most recent trip to Ramsey, Lea had retrieved one of Ann's old Singer sewing machines, powered by a foot pump. With Gavin and Mike helping to make scissors and various tools they needed, they were up and running very quickly. When the news had come about the Farrington Ball, both women were so excited they were jumping out of their skin.

Mike and Gavin stood and watched Lea and Shelly working on a gown for the event, and as it was right before dinner, Gavin was smoking a joint. Mike never partook, taking the advice that Gavin had given him when he was younger.

"If you want to try it, don't do it until you turn eighteen and your body and brain are fully developed," Gavin had told him when he got old enough to ask about it. "If you start smoking before that, it can have a negative effect on your brain development."

"And then I might turn into a pothead like you?" Mike had asked, teasing Gavin.

"You know, there might be a little truth in that," Gavin said. "I started before I was eighteen and actually smoked a lot, and sometimes I wonder if I taught my brain to want it all the time by starting smoking so early. Either way, don't try it until you're grown, and maybe not even then. At that point, it's up to you."

Mike had recently turned eighteen, but he hadn't asked about it, and Gavin definitely wasn't going to offer it to him. He looked back at the two women, marveling at how lucky he was to have such a beautiful wife, and also being struck again by how much better Shelly looked.

"Shelly has seemed happier lately, more animated somehow. I think it's more than just her friendship with Lea. What's going on with you two?" Gavin asked Mike.

Sometimes Mike could be inscrutable, and this was one of those times. He leaned away, looking up at the entrance to the woods. "It's hard to explain. She was really damaged when she got back here and she talked a lot about that guy, Raven, at first. I was just start trying to learn about meditation and some of the techniques I found in books, and I thought they could help her. The first time that we did the inner fire ceremony, it was amazing. I really felt something otherworldly when we did that, under that tree of yours. It seemed like that's when she started to get better. It's so great seeing her like this, and like you said, Lea has really helped her, too."

Gavin wanted to ask if Mike was sleeping with her, but he held his tongue. That was Mike's business. Instead of mentioning that, he took the opportunity to tease his nephew instead.

"The inner fire ceremony? Oh man, you are getting pretty fancy there, boy. The next thing is we will all start calling you the great lord

Methusaleth Poonabi and you'll wear robes and a pointy hat!"

Mike grinned and punched his uncle in the shoulder. "It was all your idea! Does that make you L. Ron Hubbard? Bob showed me a picture of him once and he was wearing this weird captain's hat. We need to get you one of those."

The two of them laughed and broke each other's balls, and after a while, Lea and Shelly had their first dress assembled enough to do a showing. Both men were duly impressed, and fawned over the clothing and the beautiful women in their lives.

Chapter 53

December 2011 – Monsanto is declared 'Worst Company of 2011.' Besides its interest in genetically modifying crops, Monsanto may be best known for its Roundup herbicide. Not only do farmers use Roundup on vast tracts of cropland, but homeowners use it on their lawns as well. The overuse of Roundup has led to 120 million hectares of 'super weeds' around the world, which are not only impervious to Roundup, but are significantly more difficult to deal with in general. Monsanto's pesticide products have created 'super pests' as well, mutated insects that are resistant to Roundup. Monsanto's response to the problem is to create a 'super pesticide' intended to kill the new mutations.

Farrington, Virginia

On the night of the ball, Gavin and Mike decided to use a vehicle instead of horses, something that the family hadn't done in at least a couple of years. The Hummer that Monique and Shelly brought back had a half tank of gas and a full jerry can in the back, and the F150 from Stonewell Road had an almost full tank when they got it. The inside of the Hummer had been stripped for materials, but it still had the seats, and was able to fit everyone: Gavin and Lea, Aidan, Mike and Shelly, and Xavier and his wife, Samantha. Xavier drove, with Gavin in the passenger seat. Gavin held a 12-gauge Mossberg pointed out the window, returning the term 'shotgun' to its literal meaning. Aidan stood out of the sunroof in the back with his rifle. Despite the fact that Farrington was just a few miles away, they knew better than to take any chances.

Gavin and the men had brought out their best clothing, with Gavin wearing a studded brown leather vest over a pre-Crumble shirt, and a pair of black cargo pants that Lea had made for him. As always, he wore long boots, with his pants tucked into the tops. Earlier that day, Gavin had looked for his old duster in the pool house, eventually asking Lea where it was.

With a twinkle in her eye, she reached behind the couch and pulled out a large package wrapped in newspaper. He didn't know how she and Shelly had done it, but they had recreated his old, worn out duster in dark brown suede with leather cuffs and toggles for the buttons. Gavin had loved it immensely and he wore his gift proudly.

The rest of the men looked equally well-turned out, with Aidan in his best suit, Mike in his tux, and Xavier in an all-black outfit that Gavin suspected concealed at least a couple of knives. Mike hung his head out of the window, not having ridden in a car for a long time.

The women, however, stole the show. To Gavin's eyes, Lea was the most beautiful of all, but he knew that each of the other men likely felt the same way about their own dates. Lea wore the last dress that they made, and Gavin could see the progression of Lea and Shelly's skill as he looked at the different dresses. By the time they got to making Lea's, they had learned from their mistakes and it was obviously the nicest one. Despite that, Shelly was wearing the first dress they made and it, too, was beautiful.

Lea's dress was a similar blue to the one she had worn on the day of their first walk together. But this dress was much nicer than that one had been, and could compete with any of the pre-Crumble dresses that Gavin remembered seeing. The neckline was modest but showed a bit of cleavage, and the shoulders had beautiful flowers embroidered on them in black thread, with the design flowing from both shoulders to meet in the middle of Lea's back. The dress had a slight Asian flair and Lea had accentuated the look by pinning her hair up with a pair of chopsticks.

As they passed the scenery on the way to Farrington, Gavin saw it from a different point of view. It was beautiful; none of the burned-out buildings he had seen on the way to Eastchester were present on this trip. In the fading light of the day, Gavin saw small and large homesteads, thinking of the people that lived on each property. The remains of fall gardens dotted the landscape, and smoke puffed from a few chimneys already, despite the fact that the temperature hadn't yet dropped below freezing. Hoop houses and greenhouses abounded, as did livestock. The larger farms had sentries posted, often hidden, and they protected the smaller farms as well, ringing bells or blowing air horns when trouble approached. *My people are doing well,* Gavin thought happily to himself.

They parked the Hummer and noticed that besides the prerequisite bicycles and horses, there were several other motor vehicles there, ranging from pickup trucks to motorbikes. The Farrington Christmas Ball was held at Chris Orlund's house, which was right outside the Farrington city limits. Gavin had seen it from the road, but never been inside.

As Gavin stepped out of the vehicle, he stumbled, and Xavier caught him.

"It feels weird, right?" Xavier said. "I almost threw up about halfway here, can you believe it? I guess our bodies forgot about it was like to go so fast." The two men laughed.

The front door of the house opened to a long hall that was beautifully decorated with sculptures and horse paintings. There were candles everywhere and a roaring fire, with a string quartet playing Mozart in the background. The women went to stand by the musicians, mesmerized by the beauty of the music being played. Gavin could see Lea's shining eyes in the candlelight as she listened to it for the first time. He imagined that she had probably heard guitars and fiddles by themselves before, but doubted she had seen anything like this. Even before the Crumble, it had been unusual to see a string quartet, with all the players combining the sounds of their haunting instruments to transcend what any one of them could do alone.

Mike and Gavin were briefly left alone as Xavier and Aidan went to find some of Orlund's famous ale. In the center of an adjacent sitting room, Gavin noticed a crowd of Farrington residents, all dressed in their finest. They stood around a large painting, and when Gavin came close enough to see what it was, he went and grabbed Mike. He pulled him over to the painting.

"Do you see what this is?" Gavin asked. Pointing at it, he said, "When you gave that little speech at my wedding, you started a ball rolling. You got people thinking about *doing* something again. This image here represents one of the results of that."

The painting was of a beautiful steam engine sitting on a set of tracks with the town of Beulah in the background. While it was clear that some of it was jerry-rigged, the craftsmen whose efforts had gotten the project along this far obviously took great pride in their work. 'The Pride of Colton County' was written in elegant cursive script underneath the picture. It was signed by Lloyd Goetting, who Gavin knew was a local painter and a friend of Orlund's.

"Wow, cool!" Mike exclaimed. He paused, and smiled. "Why

didn't they just take a picture? I know they can still develop photos in Ramsey."

Gavin put his hand on Mike's shoulder. "It's Farrington, man. It's Farrington. They love to do stuff the fancy way."

Mike laughed, and took a closer look at the painting. I can't believe they are this far along; it looks like they are almost done! That machine shop in Beulah has been an even bigger help than we thought!"

"A steam engine will give us a closer connection to our allies, like Ramsey and Beulah, and to go further out to connect with other peaceful communities," Gavin said. "It will let us travel and trade faster and more safely. And as long as we don't overdo it, and don't kill the trees we get our wood from, we can use something like that without doing significant damage to the environment, and without stripping our forests. This will be a big step for us."

As he and Gavin stood with the group around the painting, Justin approached, shaking their hands. His hand looked much better, with just a small bandage on it now.

"Isn't it great?" Justin asked, his eyes filled with excitement. "I've been going with granddad on his weekly trips to Beulah, and they have been teaching me to weld and work with metal. I think I want to be a blacksmith. We stay the night in Beulah since it is almost fifteen miles away, and I've been helping out in the mornings. I can still do all of the work, even with my hand like it is. The other fingers still move really well. There isn't a blacksmith in Farrington now, except for a couple of the old farriers that only work on horses. I could make wrought iron gates, weapons, and tools, it would be great! All I have to do is find someone who can teach me and show me the right equipment to use."

"Couldn't you trade with the machine shop?" Mike asked, always thinking.

"They don't have what I need. They're just welders and machinists over there, not blacksmiths. In fact, they'll have used up almost all of the welding fuel they have left on making the steam engine, so after that we will *really* need a blacksmith." Justin looked pensive.

"It looks like you guys need to go on an adventure," Gavin said as he nodded at them. "I know Mike has been looking for certain kinds of books that we don't have, on Buddhism, martial arts, and meditation stuff. Maybe the two of you could mount another expedition like I did to find Shiver." Mike looked very intrigued at that idea, and Gavin left him and Justin to talk as he went to find Lea.

He found his wife still standing by the string quartet, holding a glass of ale with an enraptured look on her face. He took her by the hand and began to slowly dance with her, joining a few older couples nearby.

As they danced, Lea got a distracted look on her face, looked away, and bit her lip.

"Don't worry about George; he's fine," Gavin said. "Bob and Stella have him, and Renee is there, too. You can relax. You don't have to feel guilty about enjoying this."

Lea smiled at him. "You know me too well. I just missed him for a minute. I know it's crazy. I've already been away from him for longer than this, but all the same…"

Gavin kissed her lightly on the lips. "I wouldn't have it any other way." They danced quietly for a while, her head on his shoulder.

"This is so beautiful," Lea said, as she held him closer. "By the way, what was that painting you and Mike were looking at in the other room?"

"It's the first stage of my plan," he said. "This has been in the works for a long time; we first started talking about it at the Big Meeting at Millwood. There have been lots of different people working on it, but the machine shop in Beulah, and Chris Orlund, have done the lion's share of the work. I've been waiting to tell you so I could surprise you." He looked into her eyes.

"We've nearly built a working steam engine, and we've already stacked up enough wood to make a trading trip to Ramsey. Xavier and I will be going on the first trip." Gavin paused. "And you too, if you want. But the first trip to Ramsey will just be a test. Not only will we be able to see your family more often, but we'll be able to take it farther and farther. All the way to Port Walter Marina."

Lea's eyes widened, and she squealed quietly, burying her face in his neck.

"I love you, Gavin," she said into his beard, kissing him several times. "That is the best surprise I could have asked for. You built a train for me!"

Gavin chuckled. "I'd love to take that credit, and what a sweeping romantic gesture to claim! But it wasn't just me. In fact, I didn't actually do very much, and there were a lot of other reasons to build it besides going to Port Walker..."

"Shush, prepper man," Lea said. "Take the compliment."

"I love you," he sighed happily into her hair. "Wait until you see Tropea."

He wanted to do every single thing he could to make her happy, no matter what it took. He looked into her eyes and softly sang her a few bars of one of his favorite Sublime songs.

If I had a shotgun, you know what I'd do?
I'd point that shit straight at the sky and shoot Heaven on down for you.

Lea loved it and gave him a long kiss, prompting Aidan to yell from the bar, "Get a room!" After they had danced for a while longer, Gavin took Lea by the hand when the quartet took a break. "Let's see what kind of spread they have here."

And what a spread it was. The beef was in long supply as Colton County was thick with cattle farmers, Chris being one of them. A great rack of ribs had been roasted and the scent of the seasoned meat made Gavin's stomach rumble. There were delicate quail wrapped in bacon and stuffed with squash and nuts, and several large chicken pot pies. There were stewed greens and candied carrots, and a tray piled high with crispy zucchini slices deep fried in hot lard. When he saw the large plate of fried chicken, Gavin moaned, "Oh, this is too much! Good God, look at the desserts!"

Gavin's lifelong weakness for sweets culminated in the pastry. There was nothing that he loved more than the taste of a pastry flaking apart at the bite, and the dessert table almost made him weep. All of the various fruits and honey that the region produced were represented. Apples, pears, figs, grapes, and cherries were all used in a multitude of baked concoctions, and Gavin even saw some of the lemons and oranges Millwood had traded to Farrington last year represented in two delicious marmalades.

"It's one plate per person, and fifty cents in silver for any additional plates."

Taken aback for a moment, Gavin turned around to see Chris

Orlund's smiling face. Laughing, Gavin joked, "I'll gladly pay it! This looks incredible!"

"Don't let Chris bother you. He likes to tease the guests." A lovely older woman approached, wearing a shawl and a long pre-Crumble dress that was a riot of color. She was slightly on the plump side and had gray hair that framed her face. Gavin had never met her, but immediately figured out who she was.

"You must be Belle! Chris has told us so much about you!" Gavin gave her a hug and looked over at Chris.

"How did you get such a great woman, Chris? Did you keep her from us because you were afraid someone would steal her away?"

As Belle beamed and playfully touched Gavin's chest, Orlund smiled at his wife and said, "I don't know, I'm just lucky, I guess."

Gavin said, "Belle, I know there is something you have been asking about for a long time, and I have an early Christmas present for you." He leaned over and whispered in her ear. "We're going to have a litter!"

Belle clapped her hands loudly. "Oh Chris, we're going to have a little baby again!" she said through tears. "Gavin, did you know that Chris and I used to have a Bichon? We can name this one Tia 2, so we can always remember the first Tia." Belle continued to gush about the puppy throughout the rest of the night, and to anyone who would listen.

Later on, Gavin and Chris had a quiet moment as Chris showed off his setup for raising quail. Chris had brought out his special stash of bourbon and they sat sipping it together, looking at the quail as they nested in the enclosure. Chris said, "Sorry about my wife earlier. She isn't normally overly emotional like that."

"That's cool man," Gavin said. "I wasn't put off by it, and I don't think anyone else was either. It was actually kind of nice for me. I went to a lot of trouble to make this litter happen, and it's great to know that people appreciate it."

Chris didn't respond at first, quietly looking at the quail. "We were one of those cliché couples that treated their dog like their child, you know? Especially my wife. Once our kids were grown, she and I had an unspoken agreement. I was allowed to be eccentric with all of my antiquated hobbies, and she had the dog. I loved that dog, too. Tia was spoiled, but you know how Bichons are. They are so affectionate and sweet that it's hard to spoil them too badly.

"When things started getting bad, Belle lost her part-time job and spent even more time with Tia. We had enough money from my earlier career and the money I had from my family so I didn't have to work full-time, either. I spent all of my time with my antique farm tools and horse carriages. I ignored her. When the world started to really go downhill, I wasn't like you. I didn't understand what was happening. But my parents had gone through the Great Depression and taught me to be prepared and thrifty. I got most of my assets into hard currency before my money had lost too much of its value, and when I realized what was happening, I actually got quite excited. I'd always had a nagging feeling that technology was a mixed bag for humanity. I felt a kinship to an earlier and simpler time, when craftsmanship still mattered and the world was more civilized."

"I had always wondered that about you," Gavin said. "I knew you were into all of that vintage stuff and you had a lot of pre-industrial tools and things like that, but I didn't know if it was because you knew what was coming or just because you liked that kind of thing."

"Yes, there was definitely a deeper reason for my interest in that," Chris said. "As time passed, I ignored Belle even more, taking her for granted. I focused on learning old time farming techniques and acquiring more tools, and I quickly became a leader for the community as others saw that we needed to reorient our way of life. It wasn't yet bad enough that we had stopped driving, and one day, Belle took Tia to the groomer. On the way back, she had her tires shot out and was robbed. They killed Tia just for fun, laughing and calling her a 'foo foo dog.' They took everything Belle had in the car and beat her up, saying she was lucky that she was too old; otherwise they would have raped her, also. She had to start walking back. She used the groomer in Springfield, so it was more than thirty miles away. She was on the road for two days. She was heavier back then, and she barely made it home." Chris paused and blew his nose into a handkerchief.

"I thought I had lost her and called her phone a million times, but they had obviously taken that, too," he continued. "I borrowed my neighbor's truck and was out looking everywhere for her. I also had search parties out on the roads between us and the groomer, and when I got back on the second night, a woman from one of the search parties was helping her onto our front porch. I immediately thanked God, and I swore I would never take her for granted again. Belle looked so bad when she first got back. She was dehydrated and pale, and there were huge bruises on her face. I thought I still might lose her until I got her to eat and drink again, and after a few days she got a little better. But she has never been quite the same, and she's missed Tia ever since. Right when I thought I'd lost her, that's when I remembered how much I love her." Chris put his head in his hands, crying softly.

Gavin put his hand on Chris' shoulder and patted him on the back. "It's okay, man. That's all behind us now, and you're one of the people who made it that way. We're coming back, and the world we make will be better than the old one. Look at what we have done! Look at the steam engine, it's going to be amazing. It signifies a turning point for us. And I bet that a lot of it is for Belle, right? Like you having this party every year. Wouldn't you rather we were sitting here working on that old scythe in the corner than milling around in fancy clothes, talking to people?"

That finally got a laugh. Chris wiped the tears from his eyes. "Thanks, Gavin. That puppy is really going to make a difference for us. I have to admit that I'm pretty excited myself!"

"And speaking of coming back, how in the hell did you find a string quartet?" Gavin asked.

"That's a story in and of itself," Chris said with a wink. "Let's just say that it's a lot easier to find an actual cello than a cello *player.* Getting that guy all the way here cost me a head of beef, but it's worth it to see how much people enjoy it."

"Count me as one of those, man, I love it. I could listen to them all night, and Lea is even more entranced than I am."

Chris gave him a hug and a smile, and they rejoined the party. Gavin could see that the gathering was starting to degenerate into debauchery, which was when things got a lot more fun. The laughter was louder, the conversations were more animated, and people had loosened up. He went to the Hummer and got the items he had brought. Walking back through the front door, he brandished his guitar and a bottle of whiskey, yelling, "Who wants a shot?"

Lea came up, joined by Justin and Mike. Gavin looked behind him and saw that Belle was holding a large jar of apple moonshine. "Oh baby, you are speaking my language now," Gavin said to her and he started pouring shots. Xavier produced a large cone joint wrapped in tobacco leaves, and it started to make its way around the room.

As the night progressed, Gavin cozied up to the string quartet, chatting with them in hushed tones during their break. Shortly thereafter he brought his guitar over. "Ladies and Gentlemen, for your entertainment, I present the Colton County Players!" Gavin shouted.

He launched into 'Wagon Wheel.'

> *Headed down south to the land of the pines,*
> *Thumbin' my way into North Caroline,*
> *Staring up the road and I pray to God I see headlights.*
> *Well, I made it down the coast in seventeen hours,*
> *Picking me a bouquet of dogwood flowers,*
> *I'm hoping for Raleigh so I can see my baby tonight.*

As the chorus approached, the bassist dropped his bow and began to pluck out a bass line. The viola laid down an upbeat background melody.

> *Rock me mama like a wagon wheel,*
> *Rock me mama any way you feel,*
> *Hey, hey, mama rock me.*
> *Rock me baby like the wind and the rain,*
> *Rock me baby like a southbound train,*
> *Hey, hey, mama rock me.*

As the song continued, the violin and cello joined in too, and the violinist got loud applause when he played a solo melody over the chorus. It seemed like everyone at the party was singing along by the time the last chorus rolled around, and Gavin and the quartet played it one final time for emphasis. The makeshift group played a couple more songs, finishing with a slow version of 'Hallelujah.' Belle and Lea sang the chorus with Gavin on that one, giving the song a tremendous fullness of melody.

When he finished playing, Gavin led the group in a couple of Christmas carols accompanied by the quartet, and ended by giving a toast.

"To a time when life is more real, although sometimes more

difficult," Gavin toasted. "It makes us appreciate each other all the more, and best of all, the music includes the sound of our own voices. Salud!" The crowd raised their drinks and cheered.

As the night finally wound down, Samantha drove the group home, as she was the only sober one. Aidan sat in the front this time and Gavin and Xavier drunkenly standing out of the sunroof. Xavier looked at Gavin, saying, "That was lot of fun, man; I don't normally see you drink like this."

"It's not often we get out these days, brother, and I'm sure Bob and Stella will be happy to see us back. The kids are probably driving them crazy. But you're right; it's fun to do stuff like this once in a while. As long as we don't get too drunk to shoot!" Gavin guffawed drunkenly.

Xavier laughed along with him. "I hope these motherfuckers *do* come right now! I'm ready!" They both laughed again.

Sadly for Xavier, but fortunately for the group, the trip home was uneventful.

As Gavin sank into bed with Lea, she nestled her head into his chest.

"You were the life of the party tonight," she said. "Anyone who saw you like that would think that you loved it." She smiled and nudged him playfully.

"It's a funny thing," Gavin said. "I do love it. But it tires me out in some deep way. And liquor helps me, too; it makes it easier for me to feel comfortable in a big crowd like that. I'm good with people, but the desire to be around them a lot isn't really in me. But I *did* have a really good time tonight. Maybe it's because of you." He stroked her hair, tucking it behind her ear as he liked to do, and kissed the top of her head.

"I love you, Gavin," Lea whispered as he held her in the spoon position. "I love my gift, too. And I was kidding when I said you built it for me; of course it's for the whole community. It's not that. It's the fact that the first thing you thought of doing with it, was get us closer to Italy. Nice job, prepper man," she murmured.

"I love you, too." Gavin shut his eyes, in a blissful state. As she arched her back into him and sighed, he lazily caressed her, thinking that the night might not be over just yet. *The hangover tomorrow will be worth it*, he thought contentedly.

Chapter 54

January 2012 – The smog situation in Beijing finally gets a response from the Chinese government. Fearing social unrest, the authorities will begin releasing more data about the smog, including hourly air pollution counts. Citizens of China's capital city wear masks whenever they are outside, and they rarely see the sun. Cancer rates and respiratory illnesses have skyrocketed. The U.S. embassy in Beijing reports unhealthy levels of pollution 80% of the time.

January 2039
Millwood Farm

Christmas came and went for Mike, and this year was like the last. He gave no great speeches and was uncharacteristically quiet. The food was incredible like always, and the gifts this year were remarkable; everyone had gotten so good at their individual crafts. Gavin's carvings were like nothing Mike had ever seen, and were progressing to smaller and smaller pieces. Aidan loved Christmas and every year he asked for a Santa to add to his collection. This year, Gavin gave him a Santa carved out of a block of ash wood, with smile crinkles around his eyes and a bulbous, red nose. He gave an intricate bottle holder to Bob and Stella, and a decorative wooden dagger to Xavier. For Lea, he made a portable herb carrier the size of a cigar box, with several rows of small drawers with spaces for labels. The whole thing had intricate designs carved on it. A lid snapped shut over the top of the drawers, making it secure while traveling. Lea clapped her hands with glee and hugged Gavin for a long time. For Mike's gift, Gavin handed him a package wrapped in newspaper.

As Mike opened it, he knew exactly was it was. "Wow, man! You're giving me your harmonicas?" Inside the newspaper was an old military ammo belt loaded with a harmonica in every key. Gavin had owned that belt, and the harmonicas inside it, for as long as Mike could remember.

"I was never that good, anyway," Gavin said with a smile. "Maybe you'll be better."

Shelly and Lea made beautiful knit wool scarves for everyone, in the brightest colors they could muster. Xavier always had a gift for working with metal, although he had no formal training. When Justin visited Mike's meetings at the tree in the clearing, afterwards he and Xavier would work together. They made some beautiful metal sculptures as well, and gave them to family and friends. Gavin received a sculpted metal boar—about the size of a fist—that he was particularly pleased with.

Mike was so pleased to see his family happy and prospering, especially Gavin. Mike hadn't experienced loss like the older people in his family. As he grew up, he was kept away from the hard times and the violence. Knowing the world as he did now, he realized what a luxury that was. Shelly had asked him about it recently, when she saw Gavin's mood change as he told a story about his old life.

They were out in the back field taking a break from repairing fencing. Gavin had the foresight to plant several locust trees for fence wood many years ago, and Mike and Shelly sat beside a pile of logs cut from fallen locust branches. It was a bright, clear day, with a biting wind. Mike had the collar up on his pea coat, and had a thick red and brown checkered scarf wrapped around his neck. Shelly wore another item of clothing that she and Lea made; a long, red coat with the collar and cuffs wrapped in fox fur. Mike had noticed earlier that they matched, and asked Shelly if she had done that on purpose; making him a scarf that would match her new coat. She'd only lifted the corner of her mouth, in her own abbreviated version of a smile.

"Why did Gavin get so sad when he was telling that story about the old days?" she asked Mike, as she kicked her feet against the locust posts.

"Gavin loved a woman back then, but he didn't marry her because she was with someone else. After the lights went out, he never knew what happened to her," Mike said. He knew what that was like, to just not know what had happened to a loved one. He often wondered where his mother, Janine, was now, or if she was even still alive at all. If she was, he wondered if she ever thought of him.

"Monique used to talk about that sometimes, too," Shelly said. "Back in the old days, everyone had friends and family spread far and wide because it was so easy to communicate and travel. Monique's family was from California, and she used to cry sometimes because she knew how bad it had gotten there. She lost touch with her family and never knew what happened to them either." Shelly looked sad thinking about it. She had gotten so much better than when she first arrived at the farm, but she was still prone to bouts of depression.

"I wish I could say something to make them feel better. I wish I could do something to *make* it better," Mike said passionately. He was gifted in many ways. His education had been excellent, as had his childhood. As he grew up, he would sometimes feel bitter about not having his mother in his life. But the more refugees Millwood took in, the more Mike came to know of the outside world through their stories. He began to understand that the rest of the world didn't have it nearly as good as his family and community. In fact, it appeared that he was extremely lucky to have been raised where he was. At Millwood, he had a life and family that others would be envious of, and he knew how lucky he was.

Mike decided at an early age to use his gifts to help others as much as he could, and it now drove him to the point of obsession. He felt that he alone had the power and responsibility to fix the whole world, and it weighed heavily on him.

"But you've already made some things better," Shelly pointed out. "Look at how much better Monique is doing. She will never get to the point where she is happy all of the time and neither will I. But I don't think we're supposed to be happy every single day. Our struggles define us. When Monique and I lost Raven, we were supposed to mourn him. That was a good thing. He meant a lot to both of us. But once you started teaching me about the Godspark, I started to see that balance is a good thing, too. Even when times are bad, it's still okay to feel happy sometimes. These ceremonies have been helping people, Mike." She looked at him in a way he hadn't seen before, and then leaned back to pick up Shiver, who had been sitting on a log. Shiver was showing her baby weight but wasn't yet so big that she had to be confined to the house.

"I feel like we've hit a plateau, though," Mike said as he stood back up and grabbed a fencepost. "I need to know more. I want us to start conditioning our bodies, too, not just our minds. I know I said we need to find more books, and that's true. I've already found some very useful stuff in the library, so more books would definitely help. But what we need most of all is someone who can really teach us about these things." Mike became excited when they talked about the future like this.

As always, Shelly fed off his enthusiasm. She grabbed the other side of the post, helping him carry it to where it was needed. "Cool! You should show me those books sometime. And what do you mean, find someone to teach us? Like a priest or something?"

"I'm not sure," Mike said. "We need to do this expedition with Justin and see what's really still out there. We might be able to find other communities to trade with, but honestly, I'm looking for something more than that. I need to find a new teacher. I need to find someone who knows things that none of my teachers so far have taught me. It may be very difficult to find such a person, so we might end up on the road for a while."

As soon as he mentioned leaving Millwood and going on the road, Mike immediately saw fear in Shelly's eyes. This caused some trepidation in him. He had never been out on the road without a large caravan, and he knew that she had, many times. The fear in her eyes told him that he needed to be scared, as well.

As he and Shelly worked, a white owl landed where they had been sitting and sat for a while, watching Mike.

"That's weird," Shelly said, looking at the owl. "I've never seen one so close. And aren't they only supposed to come out at night?"

"Nah, I see them all the time," Mike said casually. "I like this one; he comes to watch me sometimes. I call him Marvin."

"Isn't that right, Marvin? You're my buddy!" Mike looked at Shelly with a grin, wanting to show off a bit. "Want to see something cool?"

Shelly nodded, biting her lip.

Mike put out his right arm. "Come here, boy!" He let out a soft whistle.

Shelly's mouth dropped open.

Chapter 55

February 2012 - It has been reported that China is 'hand-pollinating' its pear trees in certain regions this year. While the process is expensive and labor intensive, it's the only way they can grow pears, as pollution has killed all the wild bees in those areas.

Gavin couldn't sleep, so he snuck out of bed. His day had been frustrating. An ice storm had come in very quickly, causing a frantic and familiar scramble at Millwood. He and Aidan raced around the farm with their tools, shoring up any buildings that needed it and scraping off snow and ice that weighed down roofs and eaves. Mike and Xavier brought all the animals indoor and bedded them down with sawdust and hay. They had gotten everything done, although the day had been a demonstration of Murphy's Law. A couple of tools had broken and one of Aidan's boots lost one of its strap-on spikes somewhere, prompting Gavin to tell him that he should have used screw-on spikes like he did. It was an annoying kind of ice that had a thin sheen of water on top of it, so Aidan wasn't the only one having trouble with traction. Gavin did smugly note, however, that everyone using his screw-on spikes did just fine.

Besides that, Mike told everyone at dinner that he was mounting an expedition in the spring to look for books and tools, and that Shelly and Justin Orlund were going with him. That would mean more work on the farm for Gavin. *Me and my big mouth,* he thought wryly. But what he was really worried about was Mike. He loved that kid so much and worried about his safety even when he was at the farm, much less going on a dangerous trip. *I made a trip like that and almost died,* Gavin thought. He needed to clear his mind.

He suited up in his winter gear, and picked up a very pregnant Shiver from her mat by the woodstove. He placed her in the crib with George so they could keep each other warm, although Gavin was more concerned with how cute it looked than the baby's warmth. Lea had fashioned canvas bags that hung on the sides of the crib. The bags held hot stones that had been sitting on the woodstove, and they warmed the baby all night long. He threw a couple more logs in the woodstove.

After briefly considering his sleeping wife and child and reminding himself of how lucky he was, he walked out to the pool house deck and marveled at what he saw.

The storm had finally passed over, and the stars shone more brightly than he had ever seen. There was a full moon and it lit up the snow and ice-covered landscape, making it reflect a bright white light back up toward the sky. The trees were coated down to even the tiniest branches, and they shimmered in the distance.

Gavin's eyes were drawn back to the stars again. In the old days, he had always figured that his view of the stars wasn't obscured by the lights of the cities and suburbs because he lived in a fairly rural area, but now he realized that hadn't been true. This must have been like what the ancients saw in the sky at night. *That's why they had names for all the constellations and were such good astronomers,* Gavin thought. *Because it looked like this!* He saw the few constellations that he knew, and named them, and couldn't stop looking.

How could a civilization that couldn't even *see* its own stars ever muster the will to go to them? Gavin had spent a lot of time living in suburbs and cities after college, before he moved back to the farm. During that time, he'd noticed that he could barely see the stars at all in places like that. And now he knew the truth. Before the Crumble had turned out the lights for good, even out on the farm, he could barely see them. Now they were right in front of him. They blazed away amazingly and he stood there, star struck.

Chapter 56

April 2012- A recent study shows a significant link between the serious bee population decline in the U.S. with a class of pesticides known as neonicotinoid. While many are quick to blame Monsanto, Bayer is actually the leading maker of neonicotinoid pesticides. Many critics point to several converging factors putting pressure on bees in addition to the neonicotinoids, with monoculture farming leading to less forage, and general pesticide use weakening their immune system. Many beekeepers in the U.S. reported losing half of their hives between 2011 and 2012.

Mike was quite amused at his uncle. Gavin had seemed dazed and exhausted at breakfast, and Mike asked him if he was okay. "All I can say is watch the stars, man," Gavin said. "I can't explain it, but tonight, just go out there and take a good look. It's all been up there this whole time and I didn't even notice!" Mike grinned at Gavin, used to his odd moods.

Gavin had taken the day off and was napping in the pool house with Lea, and Mike went with Shelly to the library. It was another snowy day, and Bob and Stella were already there, lounging by the fireplace. Stella sat with BoBo by her side, and Mike assumed that the very pregnant Shiver was up in the pool house. Mike didn't see his father, and assumed that he had ensconced himself in his room, as he often did on winter days like this.

Shelly sat down and started on a Jodi Picoult book Stella recommended to her, and Mike listlessly wandered past the shelves in the front room of the library, already knowing the titles he would see. He was relieved when Bob called him over to his desk. Bob had a book of Virginia maps, and he patted the chair next to him. As Mike sat down, he saw that the page Bob had opened showed maps of the northern neck. Bob looked the part of a college professor, with his distinguished white hair and glasses. He even wore a cardigan sweater with leather patches on the elbows and dark green corduroy pants, completing the image.

"I've been thinking about your trip, and I have an idea. You are looking for books, supplies, and old time tools like anvils and blacksmithing equipment, right?" Bob asked.

Always respectful of his grandfather, Mike nodded, although he kept his own counsel about the larger purpose of his trip. "I think we need to get to a larger city. I know that makes it more dangerous, but we'll have a better chance of success."

Bob nodded and looked thoughtful. "That makes sense. You should follow the train tracks and go to Fredericksburg first. That's halfway to the northern neck, and besides helping Gavin prepare for his attempt to go to Italy, we could really benefit from a trading relationship with that area." Bob stopped talking and mopped his head with a handkerchief.

"It's funny," Bob said. "We're sitting here talking about going to *Fredericksburg* like it's a walk in the park. But the last few times Stella and I left the house, hell, that must have been ten years ago now… it was downright scary out there." Bob put his hand on Mike's shoulder and looked him in the eye.

"Promise me you'll be careful, and that if you need to act, *do not hesitate*." He gripped Mike's shoulder harder. "Do you understand?"

Mike solemnly nodded at his grandfather.

"Ahhh. Good, then," Bob said as he refocused on the map, clearing his throat.

"You can check the tracks as you travel," Bob continued. "You'll be paving the way for the steam engine to do the same trip this coming fall. Stella and I still own Port Walter Marina down there, and if the steam engine makes it, we could reestablish those connections. The people down in the northern neck were a tough breed, and excellent farmers. If you don't find what you're looking for in Fredericksburg, you could travel even farther towards Port Walter and check the communities on the way to the marina. If anyone had any working blacksmiths right now, it would be the people in the northern neck."

It made sense to Mike. Fredericksburg would be a perfect place to start. He and Bob were planning his route when Lea came running in.

"It's starting!" she gasped, out of breath. She ran back out before anyone could say anything.

Bob smiled, looked at Mike and said, "You two go and see; Stella and I have seen it before. I'll draw some routes on the map and we can look at them after dinner."

Shelly put down her book down and already had her jacket on. Although she wasn't smiling, Mike could see that her eyes were alight with excitement. "Are you ready?" Shelly asked impatiently. Mike quickly shrugged on his pea coat and they raced up to the pool house. When they got in the door, they saw that they had already missed the birth of the first pup. Shiver was panting and lying on her side as Gavin held her head. Lea was holding the freshly born puppy and had a growing look of concern on her face.

"It's not breathing!" she said, and brought it over to Gavin.

Mike's heart stopped. Gavin had so much of himself invested in these puppies. It wasn't just about the puppies themselves; it meant something more to Gavin. Mike took Shelly to the couch and they sat down, staying out of the way.

Lea had a book from the library about raising dogs, and it was turned to the birthing section. As Gavin shakily took the puppy, Lea grabbed the book and frantically flipped the pages back and forth.

"I can't find anything about this!" Lea shouted, her voice breaking. "Gavin, what do we do?" She rushed over to Gavin, who had tears in his eyes as well.

As Mike watched, feeling powerless, Gavin cupped the puppy in the palm of his hand. Shiver and Lea looked on with trepidation. He cleared off the amniotic sack and the mucus that covered its nose and mouth, putting his pinkie finger into its little mouth to open it. He held it in his hand, slowly blowing puffs of air into its nose and mouth. It seemed like this took forever, and Mike crossed his fingers, worriedly looking at Shelly.

"It just took a breath!" Gavin shouted through his tears. Mike breathed a heavy sigh of relief. With shaky hands, Gavin placed the pup with its mother, who began to nuzzle it. The next pup was starting to emerge, and Gavin asked Mike to hold Shiver's head while he helped the pup out. This one was larger and more vigorous, struggling right away. Gavin cleared away the sack and placed that one next to Shiver, too. Once Mike was in place and keeping an eye on Shiver, Lea grabbed Gavin and kissed him for a long time.

She had two more pups over the next hour, and later than night, she had another that was stillborn. When that one was born, Mike hoped that Gavin could revive it, too, but Gavin took one look and sadly said, "That one is already blue and cold, we won't be able to do it this time." He tried anyway, but turned out to be right. All in all, they had four living puppies, although the first one, the runt, didn't seem as vigorous as the rest. Shiver was exhausted, but seemed satisfied with herself, and she nursed the pups happily.

"I know how she feels," Lea said. "It felt so great after I had George; I had just lost twenty pounds in a day. Towards the end of the pregnancy, it's hard to get comfortable because you are carrying so much weight."

Shelly had picked up George from his crib, and said, "That's true; this little guy was heavy even when he was still a newborn, and he's getting bigger by the day! He's going to be eight months old soon, right?"

"That's true," Lea replied, stroking George's forehead as Shelly rocked him. "My little man is growing up so fast! He's sitting up already and trying to crawl. He's going to start driving us crazy soon, he has so much energy!"

Mike lay down next to Shiver and took each of the puppies in his hands, holding them up to his face. They smelled great, and he could feel their warmth on his face. He stayed like that for a while, and as Shelly and Lea sat together with baby George, Gavin came over and lounged next to Mike.

"It's awesome, right?" Gavin said. "I forgot about how they smell. It's not like anything else in the world. I can't wait until they are old enough to give Doc his puppy, and to give Chris and Belle theirs. These little guys will all have good lives."

Mike now had three of the puppies perched on his chest, having placed the runt back so he could nurse Shiver on his own. Despite his small size, as the minutes passed by, the runt grew stronger. When he found Shiver's nipple for the first time, he had gone at it like crazy, making Mike more optimistic for the little guy's future. Even just a few hours old, they already nuzzled into his neck. "I can only imagine how cute they'll be when they open their eyes," he said. "They are already cuddly now, but with their eyes still shut, they look like blind little mice."

Laughing, Gavin agreed. "It's dark already, let's leave the pups alone for a minute and go outside." He and Mike suited up and walked out past the deck and over to the same hill where the Farrington knights had done their display at the big meeting. From there, they could see a huge expanse of sky as they looked down into the little valley below. "Look up at the sky. Try to open your mind and just take it all in."

Mike looked up, not seeing anything that he hadn't seen before. "Is this related to this morning when you were babbling about the stars? Have you been playing with your Star Wars toys too much again?"

Gavin cracked up and leaned over, holding his sides for a moment. When he straightened, he playfully smacked Mike on the back of the head. "Be serious. When I was out here last night I had this incredible experience. I felt like I was seeing the night sky for the first time. You don't remember when it used to be obscured by all the background lighting and pollution, but I do. The funny thing is that it took me years to notice how much it had changed; I guess I was so caught up in our daily life here that I never took the time to just go out and stare up at the night sky. So I just wanted to tell you that this is something that was very important to our ancestors. Don't take for granted what this looks like."

Mike looked up again, really trying to take it all in. He could see the constellations that Bob and Stella had taught him, and as his eyes wandered over the whole sky, it suddenly hit him how small they all were in comparison to the giant cosmos they resided in. They stood there for a while, silently.

As they walked back toward the pool house deck, Gavin asked, "How come you haven't asked to go on the Italy trip? It's come up a few times and I'm surprised you don't seem more interested."

"I am interested. It sounds really cool," Mike said. "But that's your and Lea's dream, not mine. I need to follow my own path for a while. Besides, it's so far away still, maybe by then I will have figured out more about what I want to do. I still might decide to go."

"Well, you know you're always welcome to change your mind. I could use you at my side." Gavin patted his shoulder.

Mike thanked Gavin and gave him a hug. As he looked at his uncle on the walk back up the hill, he saw that Gavin's Godspark was pulsing with gold and silver.

We may be small fish in a giant pond, Mike mused. *But our power is limitless.*

Chapter 57

October 2012 – Hurricane Sandy makes landfall in New Jersey. At the height of the disaster, almost 3 million people lose power and there are long lines for fuel in every affected area. Significant infrastructure is destroyed. Like her predecessor Katrina, Sandy will ensure that not everything she destroys comes back. While reconstruction will occur, the resources don't exist to rebuild everything, and not all of the affected areas will fully recover.

April 2039

Mike and Shelly were panting raggedly as they ran down the train tracks looking for cover. Everyone in their small group was running for their lives as bullets cracked behind them. Mike paused to fire back at their pursuers, giving Shelly time to scramble further ahead. They were the rearguard, and the rest of the group had managed to get ahead of them, shadowing the train tracks in the woods and heading east. They had walked into an ambush, and Mike hated himself for the fact that he hadn't seen it. They were sending scouts ahead, but their ambushers not only had the advantage of terrain, but excellent camouflage, as well. Mike didn't know who the hell they were waiting for, as his group had been shadowing the tracks for five days already and hadn't seen a soul.

Their pursuers didn't seem to care about Mike's opinion, though, and they were savvy enough to see the scout for what it was, not making a move to show themselves until the whole group was in range. Mike must have appeared to be the leader because his shoulder got grazed by the first shot, although not deeply enough to concern him. He immediately yelled, "Run!" and he and Shelly turned and started returning fire with their rifles to cover the rest of the group's escape. As he and Shelly fought together, they covered each other's retreat. They fired back at their pursuers to cover each other while they leapfrogged to different spots of cover. She had been with him at Stonewell Road, too, and they knew each other well enough now to fight together very effectively. Shelly was solid under pressure and he appreciated that a lot. Mike saw a large ruin of a concrete building ahead and instinctively knew that the rest of his team had stationed themselves there for a counter attack.

He could see their pursuers getting closer as he and Shelly broke into an all-out run, zigzagging back and forth. Just as he passed the building, he saw that Justin had several cocktails ready, and that the others had their weapons out. He and Shelly dove for cover and heard breaking glass and a whooshing sound as Justin threw the first one, followed by the sound of screaming. He looked up and saw that their pursuers were a mix of young adults and ragged children wearing homemade ghillie suits, carrying an assortment of artifact weapons. Their weapons may have been old, but they still worked, as evidenced by the bullets impacting the ruined building in front of them. The first cocktail had scared them though, and Mike covered Justin as he threw a second one.

This one impacted at the feet of one of their pursuers and the results were devastating. It was a boy who looked to be younger than twenty, and the gummy, flaming substance splashed all over his legs. The branches in his camouflage suit caught fire, creating an inferno over the lower half of his body. He let loose a high-pitched, blood curdling scream. After a minute, Mike yelled, "Shoot him!" as loud as he could. A couple of the members of his group stood and fired, ending the boy's misery.

We can't keep doing this, Mike thought. He ran to Shelly and started pawing through her pack, ignoring her quizzical look. He found what he was looking for: a white t-shirt. He quickly wrapped it around a rock and threw it towards the enemy. "Parley!" He yelled. "By the rules of the white flag!"

The firing stopped. "What do you want?" A deep voice yelled from behind a tree.

Mike yelled as loud as he could. "We want to stop fighting! Send your leader to talk to me one on one and we can negotiate!"

There was silence on both sides for a long while, and then the same voice yelled, "Only if you come to us, and come unarmed!"

Shelly immediately looked at Mike, but he was already standing up and walking out into the open. As he came into sight of their pursuers, he held out his gun belt in one hand and his rifle in the other and dropped them both on the ground. As he got closer, he saw their leader finally come out of hiding behind the tree when he saw

Mike had dropped his weapons. *Coward,* Mike thought. Their leader had let his team go into danger while not being willing to do it himself. He saw that the man still had a pistol strapped to his waist.

As Mike got closer to him, he could see something else; something he hadn't seen in a very long time. The leader of the group's physical appearance was unremarkable; he was just a heavily tattooed thin man in his early twenties with long stringy hair. But when Mike looked at his Godspark, he saw that it was gray and lifeless. It was as if there was a hole in the fabric of his life force. The man's eyes gleamed with a feral intelligence.

The man sauntered closer to him, strutting for the benefit of his group, and Mike struck.

He lunged and grabbed the pistol at the man's waist, tossed it away and wrapped his hands around the man's tattooed neck, looking into his eyes. At first, he only saw surprise. Mike had been taught that when violence was necessary, you had to strike quickly, unexpectedly – mercilessly. As Mike switched his grip to one from behind, he squeezed his throat harder with the inside of his elbow. The man's eyes changed to panic while he pounded at Mike's face, trying to free his throat from the iron grip of a hand that had done hard farm work for years. He fought for a long time, and as the light finally died from his eyes, his last look was one of cold hatred.

By this time, the two of them were on the ground, with Mike crouching over his enemy's body. He slowly stood up, feeling that intense focus leave him and the world return. His heart was pounding and he was breathing raggedly. The emotions raging in his mind threatened to cripple him, and he pushed them down, taking a deep gulp of air.

As he looked out at the audience that had assembled, he couldn't tell which side was more shocked. Justin and Shelly stood out from behind the rock with looks of amazement, still aiming their rifles at the remaining group. The rest of Mike's group peered around the corner of the building with hard looks on their faces, holding their weapons and ready for the confrontation to begin again.

Mike looked back toward the ragged band that had been pursuing them, and yelled for Shelly and Justin to lower their guns. He started walking toward the group of dirty kids with his hands in the air. They had a defeated and dumbfounded look about them, and only a few of them still held their guns half-heartedly aimed at him.

"Shoot me right now, or let me speak," Mike said forcefully, making eye contact with each member of the group. They all sullenly lowered their guns.

"That man I killed... I'd never met him before. But I *know* he was evil. I don't know how he treated you, but I suspect that a lot of you already knew that, too." That got him a couple of nods. One of them spit towards their leader's dead body.

"My name is Mike Collier, and I come from a place where we help each other, and fight to protect our friends. If you're willing to be our friends, you can join with us. I know we've just been fighting, and that we killed two of you, including your leader. I'm sorry about that. But if you trust us now, we'll do the same for you. We won't ask you to give up your weapons. All you have to do is come over and introduce yourself to me, and you can join with us. We can help each other." Mike could see that although some of the Godsparks of these people had been tainted, none of them were altogether dead. These people could still be helped.

As soon as he finished talking, a couple of the older and more disreputable looking ones grabbed what they could and disappeared into the woods. The rest stayed, however, leaving eight thin, ragged young people who looked between the ages of ten and sixteen. One by one, they came and told Mike their names. He hugged and welcomed them, trying to share some of his spark with each one.

As if I have any clue how to do that, Mike thought to himself wryly. He tried anyway.

Many of them had animal names like the rebels sometimes used, and now they had an Owl, Lion and Wolf to add to their roster. He welcomed them all, and went back to his pack and handed them all some of the food that he had been intending to use for trade. He gave them a big chunk of salty Virginia country ham with a loaf of hard bread, and showed them how to make sandwiches. Their faces shined while they ate, and he even saw a few of them visibly drooling as they devoured the hearty food.

After the now-larger group found a campsite for the night, Shelly and Justin made introductions and ensured that the new group settled in with the old. Some of the new additions were bruised and battered, having lived a hard life. The girl named Wolf had a nasty cut on her leg that Shelly rubbed salve on. When night fell, they all sat around a fire. The silence was deafening.

"Well, this is awkward," Mike said, getting a few chuckles. "I know we aren't going to mesh well at first, and there may be some squabbles. But do me a favor. It's been a long day. Let's wait for the morning before we tackle how we're going to work together. For tonight, let's just tell each other stories. And no sad stories, either. Tonight, let's each one of us tell the best story we know."

Justin started, telling the story of the battle of Stonewell Road. When he got to the part about how he lost his fingers, he held up his healed left hand and wiggled his three remaining fingers for everyone. *That's a good story to start with,* Mike thought, while Shelly rubbed the salve on his shoulder wound and some cuts he'd gotten on his face from the man's punches. Having broken the ice, Mike asked one of the new additions to tell a story next. He sent out the sentries for the first watch, and excused himself from the group and walked off into the woods.

When Mike had gotten far enough away, he sat on a log and put his head in his hands. He felt a clammy sweat on his forehead and his heart started pounding as he relived what he had seen in that man's eyes. He put his finger down his throat, but nothing would come up, and he started shaking as he sunk off the log and onto the ground. He lay like that for a while, shaking like a leaf and retching. His mind was running a mile a minute and wouldn't stop. After a few more minutes of this, he was mercifully brought back to reality by a hand brushing the top of his head. Sitting up quickly, he saw that it was Shelly. He struggled to pull himself together.

"Sorry about that," he said. "I was just having a little moment there." He looked at her, seeing concern on her face. "Is everything okay?" he asked. "Are there any problems with the new group?"

"No, they're fine," Shelly said. "Why do you do that?" She looked at him sternly.

"Do what?" Mike asked.

"You always take everything on yourself. You don't have to do this all alone, you know. I know I haven't always been the best friend to you, and I know I'm not touchy-feely like you and your family, but you have to let me help you in some way."

As he and Shelly had gotten closer, Mike had tried to initiate physical contact with her, but quickly stopped when he felt the strong barriers she had in place. She stiffened at any contact with another person, although she would now tolerate a little more than she used to, and they had held hands a few times in recent weeks.

"That's not true, Shelly. You've been the best friend I could ever ask for. I know something bad happened to you that made you not like to be touched. I would never ask you to do that when I can see it's so hard for you." Mike sat slumped on the log next to her, suddenly exhausted.

"Put your head on my lap," she said. So tired that he didn't even think about how much of a breakthrough it was, he just flopped to the ground and lay against her legs and placed his head on her lap. He closed his eyes as he felt her lightly stroke his temples.

"I still don't get it," she said. "You talk sometimes about how you have a responsibility to help people, and that because of the great gifts you have been given, you owe something to the world. I can see that. Your family is well off and you had a great education, and you always had enough to eat. You're obviously very smart. So I understand why you would want to help people."

Shelly paused as he coughed and adjusted his position, and went on. "But sometimes it seems like you think you have to do it all yourself. I'm sure you aren't the only smart, resourceful, and well-educated guy left on the planet, so what am I missing? And what exactly happened today? If you really knew that man was evil, then he deserved to die. But how did you know with such certainty? I can't help you unless you tell me what's going on in your head." Shelly continued to rub his temples and moved on to stroking his hair, which felt wonderful.

Mike was quiet for a long time. Shelly was accustomed to his silences, and kept stroking his hair.

"Are you sleeping?" she asked softly, after nearly ten minutes.

"No, I'm just thinking," Mike said. "I've never talked to anyone about this before, and before I say anything, you have to promise me you won't think I'm crazy."

Shelly laughed, a rare occurrence in itself. "Mike, I could never think that. Besides, I have seen you do things I can't explain, so I'm open to hearing whatever you have to say."

Mike took a deep breath. "I can *see* the Godspark. Or at least, I can see *something*. I've been able to do it since I was a kid. It's why my mother left us."

"How can that be?" Shelly asked. "I thought you were really young when she left, like five or six?"

"I was six," Mike said sadly. "I had been seeing these auras in everything, and for most people, they glowed and changed all the time. When I looked at them closely, it was like looking at a shower of brightly colored sparks. I was too young to think it was strange; in fact, I loved it. One day, I was sitting with my mother, and I kept trying to see her spark, but it was all gray and lifeless. I looked at her and said, 'Mommy has no spark!'

"She looked at me, and at the moment I looked back, it was like looking into the eyes of a monster. She had let her mask slide off for a second. I remember it so clearly; she quickly covered it up and laughed about it, but for a moment there, I truly saw her for what she was. I think she knew that, somehow. She left us a few months afterwards." Mike's voice was quavering, but he set his chin and continued.

"I must have unconsciously suppressed it after that, because it didn't bother me again for a long time. But when I hit puberty and my voice started changing, it began again. I'd blocked out some of my early memories by then, so at first I thought my eyes were going bad. I started seeing smudges of color around everything. I didn't say anything about it, and learned to live with it. As time passed, I started to learn more about how it worked. I couldn't turn it off, but I learned how to turn it *down*, which was a blessing. The only objects that had the color around them were living things. Over time, the blobs of color sharpened and they started looking like auras, which made me feel a lot more comfortable. At least that was something I'd heard of, something I could research. I didn't find much in the library and didn't want to tell anyone about it, so I never pressed it further. When I started looking closely at them, I realized that what I was seeing was made up of millions of tiny sparks. That's when I remembered what happened that day with my mother."

"Is that why you killed that man today?" she asked. "Was there something wrong with what you saw?"

"Exactly," Mike said. "His spark was dead, like a gray void in the air. I instinctively knew that he was evil, and that's why I did what I did. Your spark represents who you are at your very essence. When

Gavin told me about his theories on religion, it all clicked into place for me. I finally had a name for what I was seeing. I thought maybe if I could teach other people how to see it, too, they could help me find a way to use it. That's why I've been so driven. This gift has been given to me, and I need to find a way to become worthy of it."

"So that man was evil... like your Mom? What are you saying? If you saw your mother now, would you kill her too?"

Mike lurched forward, hacking and dry-heaving, his hands on the back of his neck. Shelly put her hands on his shoulders and pulled him back toward her.

"It's okay Mike, you don't have to be perfect, I'm sorry. I know you don't have all the answers."

They were quiet for a while longer.

"So that's why you never told anyone?" Shelly asked softly.

"If I tell my dad and Gavin what I am, I'll have to tell them the whole story. Then my dad will know that's why Mom really left." Mike took several deep breaths and leaned back into Shelly.

"Besides," he said, "I didn't want people to think I was nuts. Maybe I was a little embarrassed." Mike looked up at her and asked, "And what about you? Do *you* think I'm crazy?"

Shelly didn't say anything, but instead, leaned down and kissed him. It was a brief and dry kiss, but Mike was astonished. He looked up at her with wide eyes.

"So what does mine look like?" she asked softly.

"When you first came to the farm, you were barely glowing at all. Your spark was a dark green, with flecks of purple and red. But that's not what it looks like anymore."

"What does it look like now?"

"You're a bright, strong silver. You glow fiercely now, and there are gold flecks all throughout. The other colors are still there, too, but they are muted. The silver is so bright now that it's almost all I can see."

"What does it look like when you close your eyes? What do *you* see when we all sit around that tree and shut our eyes?" she asked earnestly.

Mike shut his eyes. "We are all luminous beings, not this crude matter." He held up his hand and she clasped it in hers. Tears flowed down from Mike's closed eyes as he looked at Shelly, seeing her true essence. "I wish you could see it," he whispered. "But I finally feel like I'm not alone anymore."

She leaned down and kissed him again. They just kissed that night and nothing more, but Mike wasn't disappointed. Every kiss was a little better than the last. After each one, her spark pulsed ever more brightly, until it lit up the whole night.

Neither of them saw it, but a white owl perched on a nearby tree watched over them.

Chapter 58

April 2013 — Unknown snipers attack and disable a Silicon Valley power substation in California. It will take several weeks to order the necessary parts to get the substation back online. This illustrates the fragility and vulnerability of the U.S. power grid, and also shows something more insidious. The national mainstream media utterly fails its customers, not bothering to report on the incident until ten months later.

May 2039

Wood Jackson rode his horse out of Williams City, exhausted and hungry. His last job had ended when his boss had to sell his horse farm and move in with his son and daughter-in-law. He kept his eyes open, searching for any farms that looked like they had horses, hoping to find work.

Still grieving over the gruesome loss of his friends more than a year ago, the Tolson family, Wood's thoughts wandered back to the days when he had tried to convince them to learn to fight. Wood had started helping the Tolsons in his spare time in the mid-2020s, working out their racehorses and taking care of the barn and fields. Wood was handy, too, and he had quickly become indispensable to the Tolsons. After less than a year, he had moved into an outbuilding and began working for them full-time.

Wood adored the job; it gave him the freedom to do what he loved. He was an accomplished horseman and had dealt with all types of racehorses. He had a soft and gentle manner with the creatures, belying his nighttime hobby, MMA fighting. First introduced to mixed martial arts by his cousin Xavier, Wood took to it like a fish to water. It gave him a way to keep in shape and alleviate stress, and he was good at it.

While Wood was living with the Tolsons, he passed the time fighting, raising horses, and chasing local women. The pay wasn't much, but he got a cottage for free and felt fulfilled. He could do what he loved. One day, nearly a year after he started living with the Tolsons, Wood drove to the 7-11 for a soda. When he pulled into the parking lot, a young woman in the car next to him made the motion to lower his window.

"Excuse me, sir, could you spare some change for me to buy some gas to get home?" the woman asked. Her car was old and rusty, and there was a baby in the back seat, nestled among old fast food bags and trash.

Wood was bemused. While it had happened a few times before, it wasn't that common for him to be asked for money. A six foot three black man with short dreadlocks and a whip thin physique, Wood wore tattered clothing and was driving a 2009 Chevy Blazer. He didn't exactly look rich. He gave her his trademark smile.

"Honey, I think you're asking the wrong guy. I'm as broke as you," he joked as he turned to walk into the store.

"How about something else?" she asked.

Wood stopped. He turned back to her, looking at her closely now. "What are you talking about?" he asked.

"You know, whatever. I'm down for whatever. I just need to get some money so I can get home," she said, with a hint of hollow desperation in her voice. "I can make you real happy, baby."

Wood looked at the baby in the backseat with a frown, and turned back to the young woman. "Honey, I have never needed to pay for it, and I ain't starting now." He grinned and winked at her, and handed her a ten dollar bill. She thanked him profusely, and he walked away with his thoughts churning.

When he got back to the Tolson place, he went to their house and knocked on the door. Brandon opened the door, a pudgy and useless nineteen-year-old. "Dad, Wood is here!" Brandon shouted as he walked away. Wood waited outside a minute until Brandon's father, Jonathan, came to the door.

"Come on in. Brandon didn't invite you in?" Jonathan asked.

Not wanting to get into their family affairs, Wood asked, "Can we sit down for a minute? I need to talk." As they sat down at the kitchen table, he got right to the point.

"I saw a woman selling her body at the 7-11 today," Wood started. "I have never seen anything like that before. She was just a young kid with a baby of her own already. I've noticed some other things lately that have really got me thinking. It seems like things are breaking down. The roads are getting worse and I have seen a lot of people walking lately. Last week, when I was in Williams City, I drove around the back of the Super Saver store to cut through and it looked like there were a couple dozen people living out of their cars back there. They had little tents and awnings set up and they had a grill going."

"Oh yeah, they have been there for a while. I saw them about a month ago in the same place," Jonathan said. "What are you getting at?

He thought for a minute. "Did you know my real name is Darryl?" he asked. "Everyone always called me Wood because I was tough and stubborn as a kid. My mom would always say, 'This boy is like a damn piece of wood!' And it's true, you know. I don't like change. I don't like to do things I don't want to do. But today, I got a really strong feeling that we are seeing some big change, and we're gonna have to change with it. If things are that bad out there, people are going to start getting desperate. They're going to want to take whatever they can to feed their families. If they see anybody that has something good, they are going to try and take it. Do you see what I'm saying?"

Jonathan's eyes wandered back in his head, and Wood knew him well enough to know what his response would be.

"You think people are going to come and rob us? This is real life, not a zombie movie," Jonathan said. "I don't think that will happen; it's not *that* bad out there. The stock market is on the way back up and the economy is showing signs of improvement. They are drilling that big field in the Antarctic and that will bring oil prices back down. And I just heard in the news today that there is a vaccine for that new Ebola strain. The power hasn't flickered in more than a month. Besides, the government isn't going to let anyone starve; they can always sign up for public assistance."

"Yeah, but I'm sure that girl today was already on benefits, too, and it looks like it wasn't enough. That small Coke I bought today cost me almost four bucks. She must have thought she was broke enough to sell her body, anyway. And it's not even the end of the month yet," Wood said.

Jonathan smiled at him in a slightly condescending way, making Wood's hackles rise. "Don't worry. I don't think everything is going to fall apart tomorrow, buddy. You know I have a shotgun, so even in the worst-case scenario, we're protected. Besides, you're a good fighter, right? You can just beat them all up!" Jonathan smiled and stood up, and Wood knew the meeting was over.

Two years after that ominous conversation, Jonathan Tolson and his family were killed and their home was ransacked and burned to the ground. A group of hungry locals had come by and asked for money and food, and Jonathan had scared them off with his shotgun. When they returned in force that night, Wood was two hundred yards away, working with a horse. He could only watch and listen in horror. There were at least ten people circling the house, yelling and shooting. He thought he heard Jonathan get off a couple shots with the shotgun but he wasn't sure.

Wood took his favorite horse, Easy Daisy, and circled around to his cottage for his stuff. Once he packed up, he slipped off into the night, crying silently. The smoke from the burning house was suffocating, even as he got further away. He went back the morning after to scrounge for supplies, and he'd found Jonathan in the burned rubble of his home. While so badly burned that he was barely recognizable, Jonathan somehow still clung to life. As Wood knelt by him, trying to make him more comfortable, he somehow managed to croak out a few words.

"My family?" he whispered.

Wood sadly shook his head.

"You were right," Jonathan said hoarsely. "You were right."

Those were his last words.

Wood had been on the road with Easy Daisy ever since. He'd never worked at the same place for longer than six months, never finding another place he liked as much as the Tolsons'. Now he was again on the move, looking for work and a place to stay.

Wood saw that he was approaching what appeared to be a flourishing and well-defended ranch, and he carefully rode his horse up the driveway with his hands raised, hoping for another safe place away from the chaos of the world.

Chapter 59

June 2013 – Edward Snowden begins leaking a series of classified U.S. government documents, eventually showing that the NSA has been spying on the phone calls and computer use of American citizens, as well as spying on allied governments in foreign countries. Orwell was right. If the technology exists, the government will abuse it.

June 2039
10 miles west of Beulah, Virginia

Aidan and Gavin were on their yearly supply run, going to visit Jimbo "The Ammo Man" and their old butcher for supplies, like sausage casings and any spices, they didn't grow themselves. Both men were in a light-hearted mood and bantered back and forth as they rode, but Mike's absence cast a slight shadow. Inevitably, the conversation would turn back to Mike, as they speculated on his safety and whether he would find what he was looking for.

"What do you think he is doing right now?" Aidan asked.

"I'd like to think that he was sitting on a silken sofa with Shelly feeding him grapes, but I get the feeling that he's dirty and tired, and sick of eating salted meat and peanut butter," Gavin joked. "But, we taught him well. If anyone could survive a trip like that, it's him. Justin and Shelly are solid, and although I haven't gotten to know the rest of his group very well, the ones that used to be rebels are so tough it's scary."

Aidan checked around the area with his monocular, keeping watch, even though their route was through friendly territory. "It looks like the Reeds have finally got their goose breeding program going. They must have finally tamed enough of the wild ones that they started calling other ones down to stay." Geese had a way of doing that. If given safety and a food source, they would eventually decide they liked the spot and call down some of their wild brethren as they passed overhead. The Reed family had been trying for years, and as Gavin raised his own monocular and looked, he saw that Aidan was right. The pond at the family's homestead on the other side of Beulah was filled with healthy and squawking Canada geese. Herding dogs sat around the perimeter, protecting them from predators.

"It looks like goose liver for everyone this Christmas," Gavin said, licking his lips at the thought. Like so many other natural processes, the machine had bastardized the production of foie gras, as well. The process of extracting it industrially was a horror show, where the geese were force-fed and confined until their livers were overloaded with fat, and then slaughtered when they couldn't grow any larger. After the Crumble, people had reverted to the ancient ways of raising geese, letting them pasture naturally and only slaughtering a few from the flock in the late fall, when they had naturally foraged and fattened up for winter.

"Mike is going to love that," Aidan said. "It's one of his favorite things."

"You know, we can pick up the geese this fall in our brand new carriage," Gavin teased his brother, gesturing to the beautiful two-wheeled carriage behind his horse. On the first leg of their trip, they had gone through Farrington and brought Chris and Belle their puppy. Belle had wept until it looked like she would run out of tears and Chris got a little choked up. The pup was a little ten-week-old female, and she had a loving and energetic personality. Gavin had already taught her to respond to her name.

"Tia!" he whispered, and she immediately looked up at him. "She even knows her name!" Belle said, prompting a new round of tears as little Tia licked her face. Chris offered silver and Gavin refused as Aidan scowled at him. "You're our friend and neighbor, Chris. It would mean a lot to us if you would take Tia as our gift."

Chris hugged them both, and as he walked them out, he asked them to stop by his shed. He opened the door and a beautiful antique racing carriage sat inside. "This is my gift to you," Chris said with tears in his eyes. "You made my wife happy again, and there isn't enough money in the world to pay for that. I want you to have this."

And so, Gavin's horse pulled the carriage on the next leg of their trip. They passed the Reed homestead and approached Jimbo and Mazie's little schoolhouse. Gavin and Mazie had gone to school together and knew each other well. Gavin was very fond of Mazie. They had dated briefly in college, before they both realized that their equally dominant personalities made them romantically incompatible.

They stayed great friends, however, and when Mazie met Jimbo, Gavin and he also became friends. Jimbo was a bit reserved, but over the years they discovered a shared interest in guns and self-sufficient living. Jimbo also turned out to be a skilled gunsmith and ammunition maker, something which Gavin knew he would desperately need in the future.

By the early 2020s, Gavin had known it wouldn't be long before he wouldn't be able to buy ammunition anymore. Inflation, intense regulation, and scarcity had made the market all but dry up, and what was left was incredibly expensive. After a Herculean search, Gavin showed up at Mazie and Jimbo's with his pickup truck full of gunpowder, ball, and various gunsmith supplies.

Jimbo was normally fairly reserved, and the look of surprise on his face had been priceless. "What's all this for?" he asked. "This is more than I could use in five years!"

"That's exactly what I'm thinking," Gavin said. "Just think of this as 'vendor management.'"

While Jumbo liked being self-sufficient, he didn't share Gavin's views about the Crumble.

"Ahh, this is for when the zombies come," he had joked. To his credit though, he had agreed to take the supplies and hold onto them in the event of an emergency. That decision had paid off for the entire community in spades, as Jimbo became the premiere ammo man in the county. Of course, he always gave Gavin hundreds of rounds of ammo in return for small packages of pork, never forgetting Gavin's gift to him.

Jimbo and Mazie were now quite well-off, with a pastured chicken operation that produced several hundred meat birds per year. Mazie also had a greenhouse operation of her own which put Millwood Farm's to shame. She had exotic fruit, like bananas, kumquats, blood oranges, and various unusual lemon varieties. The small amount of citrus fruit that could be grown in the area was prized, as it offered a great supply of vitamin C, as well as increasing the variety of foods available. Most of the citrus went to jams and jellies, as it was too precious to eat raw.

As they got off their horses, Mazie came out from one of her greenhouses. She was aging slightly now, but was still beautiful. She had thick and curly black hair with wide, welcoming eyes, and a curvaceous figure. When they were young, Gavin teased her that she was the sort of woman the cartoonist Robert Crumb would have loved. She gave great big hugs to Gavin and Aidan, and Aidan went off to find Jimbo. Mazie pulled Gavin to the greenhouse, going through the same ritual they always did when they saw each other. The first thing was to look at each other's plants and gardens. He was ready to step inside the greenhouse, but she instead directed him to a small stand of trees she had planted nearby.

The plants were odd looking, almost more vine than tree. Their look didn't appeal to Gavin, who didn't like vines and crawling plants because they offended his orderly nature. "What are these?" he asked, dropping to a crouch next to one and inspecting it.

"These are Arctic Kiwi trees," Mazie said proudly. "I have been looking for something like this forever; a citrus tree that can grow outdoors in our climate. I finally found these at one of the old nurseries in Williams City, and I had to pay through the roof for them. But if they work out, we may have a way to produce citrus without having to use the greenhouses." Mazie smiled at him sweetly. "You don't like them, do you?" she asked in a singsong voice she used to tease him with. "Do they offend my little obsessive-compulsive man?"

Gavin put on the caveman voice that he sometimes used around her. "Caveman not like vines, can't control them," he grunted. "Caveman rip vines out! Rarr!" As they laughed, he had to admit that he was, in fact, impressed. She planned to build trellises for them as they grew, and was hoping to see her first fruit sets the following spring.

After Gavin and Mazie had caught up for a few minutes, Aidan returned with Jimbo. As they walked over, both of them were laughing while Jimbo finished telling a story about an aggressive rooster. Jimbo mimed a kick, gesticulating wildly.

After hugging Jimbo and saying hello, they all went into the schoolhouse, which was more spacious than it looked from the outside. The center of the great room was dominated by a small library and a woodstove, with the kitchen on the north side. They had an open loft upstairs where they slept. Mazie got Aidan a bottle of Jimbo's latest batch of honey wheat ale, but Gavin stuck with water, bringing a joint out of his pocket and lighting it with Jimbo. "No wonder we haven't seen you guys for a while," Jimbo said. "It sounds like you have been busy."

"We're sorry we didn't make the big meeting!" Mazie shouted from the kitchen. "That was the weekend we went to get the kiwi trees!"

Gavin jokingly forgave them, and they discussed recent news and passed the joint around. The steam engine was nearing completion and wood was being brought from all over to fuel its first trip. Millwood had contributed the largest load, using some of their last gas to bring a load to Beulah. Others in the community had brought wood in by horse-drawn carts, bicycle, or even by hand. Everyone who had items to trade with Ramsey managed to contribute wood.

Xavier had been in Beulah for the last week, helping them attach weapons to the engine for defense, and attaching a railcar behind it that would carry the wood and trade items going on the first run to Ramsey. Colton County would be trading pork, citrus, beef, and various vegetables for some of Doc's medicinal plants, heavy bags of deer corn for the livestock, and honey. The honey was the most valuable of the trade items by far.

The U.S. bee population had been almost killed off completely by the end of the Crumble as the large agricultural conglomerates genetically poisoned the crops themselves, killing the bees that tried to pollinate them. The pesticides used by industrial farming also made the bees' navigation systems go haywire. The insecticides and poison crops combined to weaken the immune systems of the colonies that didn't die outright, making them more susceptible to various deadly ailments. Honey was now an incredibly valuable commodity, and Gavin never had enough to trade. In the beginning, it was all he could do just to make sure that his bees survived, much less make extra honey.

One of his hopes for the trip to Italy was that the Italians would have large quantities of honey available to trade, as Italy had outlawed the neonicotinoid class of pesticides that killed the bees in the U.S. As far as Gavin knew, the Italians had never had a problem with bee population decline like the Americans had. From the news that Aidan found over the years, the Crumble was worldwide, affecting various regions in different ways, but affecting them all in some way. He often wondered how Italy had fared through the Crumble, and hoped his Italian friends were doing alright. *The Italians are probably doing better than most,* he thought. *After all, this isn't the first time their people have lived through the slow collapse of a civilization.*

Mazie came with Aidan's beer, and Gavin told her what he had been thinking about Italy and the honey supply.

"God, that would be great!" Mazie gushed. She saw the joint in Gavin's hand and smiled sweetly at him. He gave it to her.

"I also want olive oil!" Mazie said as she hit the joint. "I miss that so much. And coffee too... I bet they can get that easier than we could. Do you think you could bring back some actual hives? That would be a huge help for us."

"If my friend, Antonio, is alive and well, then I think so," Gavin answered. "He had more than forty hives the last time I saw him; that must have been twelve years ago now. *There* was a master beekeeper. I wish I could bring *him* back, too!"

Jimbo chimed in. "You know what I miss? Pepperoni and salami, stuff like that. I don't want to hurt Rick's feelings, but that stuff he's been making just isn't the same." Rick was the local butcher, highly skilled, but never able to learn the fine art of making charcuterie. His attempts to teach himself had been mediocre at best.

Aidan was looking at Gavin with dollar signs in his eyes, and Gavin smirked back at him. "Yet again, one of Gavin's crazy ideas might pay off, huh, brother?" Aidan grinned and started talking to Mazie about potential things she could trade for the items.

"Stop right there," Gavin said. "Don't negotiate with her; she's worse than Stella. Besides, we don't even have any of this stuff yet. Hell, we're probably a year away from even making the attempt."

Mazie smiled sweetly and threw a towel at him. Getting down to business, Gavin went out to the horses and brought in the items they had to trade, banishing Mazie back to the greenhouses. "I'm talking about ammo now little lady, so shoo! This is your man's business; you only get to negotiate the prices of your own stuff." She turned around and showed him her rear, haughtily walking off.

Jimbo laughed hysterically, saying, "I don't know many people that can do that."

"I'm just relieved it worked," Gavin chuckled. "If I had to negotiate with her for this ammo, Aidan and I would have ended up walking home because we'd have had to trade the horses, too. I don't know how you ever get your way; I admire you."

"I never get my way," Jimbo joked. "How do you think I ended up having to marry her?"

The three men laughed and ended up trading some cured bacon and country ham for the ammo they needed, and of course Jimbo got all of the spent brass they had collected. Gavin had also thrown in a dozen fresh fertilized eggs, as he knew Jimbo liked leghorns and wanted to start a flock. He could get one of his broody hens to sit on the clutch of eggs and would have leghorn chicks in no time.

The one thing Jimbo couldn't give them was .50 caliber ammunition, although as more brass was collected that problem would be remedied. He whistled when Aidan handed him the handful of spent shells they had already collected. "Oh yeah," Jimbo said. "This is the stuff right here. I need to come out to Millwood and try that baby for myself."

"You're always welcome there, buddy," Aidan said.

As they were loading the ammo onto the carriage, Jimbo admired Orlund's gift, and then stopped loading for a second. "Where's Mike? I would have thought he'd be with you guys."

Aidan looked worried now that he had been reminded his son was out in the world on his own, but Gavin was confident that Mike would be fine.

"He's on an adventure," he said.

Chapter 60

August 2013 – Youth unemployment in Greece reaches sixty-one percent. Protests and social unrest continue, as does the worsening of the Greek economy. This is what a slow motion collapse looks like. There are no jobs left for young people now that the machine has completely taken over. Greece is the canary in the coal mine, and the canary isn't looking too good.

Outside Fredericksburg, Virginia

This adventure sucks, Mike thought. They had found an old phone book in an abandoned post office on the way in to Fredericksburg, and Mike's heart soared at all of the listings they found. His first sight of the city, however, brought his mood crashing down. He surveyed the wreckage and burnt ruins, first seeing a tall sign that said "Central Park" in the distance, surrounded by a burnt and trash-strewn lot. It appeared that many of the signs had survived while the buildings hadn't, and colorful signage advertised donuts, chicken, and hamburgers over more burnt wreckage. There wasn't a soul in sight, giving the area the feeling of a ghost town.

Crossing his arms and taking a deep breath, Mike chided himself for his negative attitude. He looked back at Shelly, smiling at her as he did. Even if nothing came of the trip, the kisses with her alone had made it worthwhile.

Their group had been shot at twice but not chased again, and the new additions proved to be excellent scouts. The sparks of the newcomers had brightened as they meshed in with the little expedition, and their ragged and thin appearances had already improved as well. Wolf, the girl with the wounded leg, even looked better with more color in her face. The new group's clothing had also improved, and the boy named Lion now wore one of Mike's old t-shirts and a mesh hunting vest.

Mike, Shelly, and Justin were the leaders, and the three Jacksons and three rebels that had first joined Mike's meetings made up the core group. Five of their pursuers had joined them on that day, making a total of thirteen. Renee was the oldest of the Jacksons at twenty-two, and she adopted a mother role, making sure everyone was fed and clean. She was particularly motherly toward her younger cousins Carl and Vance, who were brothers only a year apart. Each of them was starting their dreadlocks, trying to emulate their idol Xavier. The new group quickly became as fiercely loyal to Mike as everyone else was. *It must be the food we're feeding them,* he thought humbly.

Mike looked back at the ruins of Fredericksburg, sighing heavily.

"There is another part of the city that didn't burn," he heard from behind him. He looked back and saw that Owl was approaching. One of the youngest of the new ones, Owl didn't talk much. His spark was muted, but clear, and he had big eyes rimmed by dark circles, which must be what gave him his name. He was lean and short, but made up for it with a thick shock of black hair on the top of his head. Owl was the youngest of the group, and said he was ten. Mike didn't believe him; he was too small for ten.

"Really? Where?" Mike asked excitedly.

Owl explained that he had come from Fredericksburg before joining up with the band in the woods, and that he knew the area well. He was orphaned very young and left the city soon afterward, but he remembered that the older areas of the city hadn't seen as much damage. "I passed through it when I was leaving the city," Owl said. "It actually looked like a pretty nice place. I was so scared at the time that I kept going, and I wish I hadn't. Later on, after Zack had found me, I thought back and wished that I had stayed in that little town. They might have taken me in. I should have at least tried."

Mike was taken aback by finally hearing their leader's name. *Zack,* he thought. *The name of the man I killed.* He had purposefully never asked and no one had mentioned him until now. It brought home how momentous a thing he had done in taking a life. He thought that if he ever had to kill again, he would try to find out what their name had been. He owed them that much.

Shaking off his reverie, Mike called Justin and Shelly to bring the maps over and Owl got down to the business of showing them what he knew, although it took a few minutes to show him how to read a map. They found an easy approach to where they wanted to go and had everyone pack up.

They were able to get closer to the old town area and scout it out the very same day, and Mike was amazed at what he saw through his rifle scope. This little section of Fredericksburg looked like Farrington in a lot of ways. There were sentries with rifles posted on some of the taller rooftops, and as Mike looked down on the little village, he could see people going back and forth about their daily business. Horses were corralled in a small paddock next to a tack shop, and several tables were set up in the street. One man was selling old glass jars, and another was selling spices. Mike's heart quickened. The buildings were mostly intact, and the town was beautifully built of brick and old stone, with a crisscrossing network of streets surrounding a large community garden on the lawn of what looked to be the courthouse.

Mike broke into a broad grin as he saw a building at the end of the block, right next to the dry-goods store. He handed his rifle over to Shelly and told her where to look.

"Wow, there are a lot of people down there," Shelly said as she looked through the scope, and then she barked a short laugh as she saw the building at the end of the street. "I see what you mean," she said.

The sign on the building said 'Drugstore,' and a large cannabis leaf was painted above the awning. A smaller sign below said 'Drugs and Books.'

"Gavin would love that store," Mike said with a chuckle. He looked down one last time, and turned back to the group.

"We should be able to keep our pistols," he said. "But I didn't see anyone down there with a long gun; that must be their rule. I think if we leave our rifles, we should be able to walk right in with no trouble."

Mike, Shelly, and Justin left their rifles with the rest of the group, and walked down to the town.

Chapter 61

September 2013 - Quantitative Easing continues. The Federal Reserve continues to print money, and has built up an absolutely unprecedented balance sheet of almost four trillion dollars. That's more than a quarter of the entire United States GDP.

July 2039
Beulah, Virginia

Xavier was sweating like crazy as he manhandled the final piece of the rifle nest atop the steam engine. Chris and Justin Orlund were down below, working on some final modifications to the engine itself. Xavier loved the sounds and smells of metalwork, and loved being around the machine shop. Since he had volunteered to help put the armor and weapons on the steam engine, he took the opportunity to spend as much time there as he could.

The gun nest could hold either two men with rifles, or one man with the .50 caliber. Xavier loved to travel when he could and he offered the use of his rifle for the steam engine's first trip, although he made it clear that he and the rifle were a package deal.

In his younger days, Xavier had visited New York and Washington, D.C., and also made several trips to North and South Carolina. He had visited Port Walter Marina several times with Gavin, and he was excited to hear the talk about trying to revisit the place, being the first to add himself to the list for the Italy trip. The marina was about 150 miles away, which used to be less than a three-hour drive. Now, they would need the steam engine to even consider it. Before the Crumble, Gavin had once asked Xavier why he loved to travel so much.

"It's the freedom you feel," Xavier had answered. "And you get so excited to see someplace new. It's like the first time I went to New York. I was walking down the street and right in front of me stood the comedian, Nick Cannon, do you remember him?" Gavin nodded. "It was totally out of the blue, and it wouldn't have happened if I hadn't taken that trip. I saw stuff on those trips that I would have never seen if

I stayed home."

"I got that," Gavin replied. "You know me; I'm more of a homebody than you. Hell, more than anyone," he chuckled. "But you still love to go to the marina though and you have already been there a bunch of times. Don't you get bored of going back to the same place?"

"Nah, because the more you go to a place the more you know about it," Xavier said. "Besides, it's fun to go down there. I like the boats and the restaurant. It's cool to see you play, too." Before the Crumble, there had been a restaurant at the marina where Gavin occasionally played his music.

Xavier looked up as he heard the Orlunds whoop loudly, and he heard the engine starting as they tested it. It didn't sound like any engine he had ever heard before, and instead of a growl there was only hissing and a soft squeaking sound. As they stoked the fire, it heated the water in the tank, which produced the steam that drove the great pistons up and down. It was an incredible sight to behold. Xavier finished welding in the last piece of the armor plate and noted that this was their last tank of acetylene. He hoped that Mike could get a lead on where and how they could secure more.

Listening to the engine get louder, Xavier had a thought and jumped down, walking over to the Orlunds. He motioned for Chris to come away from the engine so they could talk.

"That thing is pretty loud," Xavier said.

"I know, isn't it great? I can't believe it started up on the first try!" Orlund beamed. "Justin and I didn't think it would work the first time. We just guessed on what oil to use for the pistons..."

"I hate to interrupt you," Xavier said, "But that thing is *really* loud." Chris looked at him, not understanding.

"People will be able to hear it from really far away. We're gonna act like a magnet for any little bands that are out there and want to get something." Xavier was gratified to finally see understanding in Orlund's eyes.

Orlund narrowed his eyes, and it was almost like he was looking at Xavier for the first time. "I knew there was another reason Gavin liked you besides the fact that you're a badass," Chris said.

Grinning shrewdly, Xavier said, "That's alright. Sometimes it's not a bad thing if people underestimate you." Xavier had been blessed with a sharp mind and was a quick learner, often seeing insights and connections more quickly than others did. He found that it had passed on to his kids as well, with Devante and his other children excelling at their studies with Bob and Stella, and contributing to the farm in valuable ways.

"We're gonna need more than just the fifty," Xavier mused. "We're gonna need more space for guys up top, and maybe we can get a guy on each side of the cab with a rifle, too. Let me think about it a little while and get back to you."

As he and Orlund parted ways, Xavier stalked around the steam engine and the car behind it, thinking about how he would attack it. He noted the weaknesses that he saw and began to form a plan for further increasing the security. The wheels definitely needed protection, and the cab needed armor as well. There wasn't much time left to add modifications, as the engine would ready in less than two weeks. The engine loudly hissed away as Justin and Chris continued to work on their new toy.

Chapter 62

November 2013 – Protests begin in Ukraine. The government's refusal to sign a trade agreement with the European Union and fears of a move closer to Russia brings people into the streets of Kiev and surrounding towns and cities. Considering how brutally cold it is there this time of year, these people appear to either have a serious grievance, or to have been stirred up by an outside force. Spring 2014 in Ukraine should be interesting. Ukraine doesn't have any energy resources of its own, but it does have one thing. Lots and lots of oil pipelines, connecting Russia and Europe.

Mike saw his second lifeless spark in the old town of Fredericksburg. He and Shelly had split up from Justin once they realized it was safe, and they walked from shop to shop asking around for what they were looking for. Mike had passed an attractive young woman who had the same kind of colorless spark he had seen in Zack, and Shelly noticed his reaction and asked him about it.

"It was just like that other spark I saw," Mike answered. "I know it doesn't look like it from the outside, but there was something wrong with that woman, too."

"I guess you are going to have to get used to seeing them now that you are out in the world," Shelly said thoughtfully. "I wonder how many I'd have seen by now if I were able to see what you can. I bet Spiegel and Longhurst didn't have any color in theirs, either."

"Probably true," Mike said. "I need to learn more about what that means." They paused before they went into the next shop, a little butcher on the corner across from the courthouse garden. Mike put on his best smile and made sure to keep his hands well away from his sidearm. His mouth watered with the smells of the place. Besides the meat for sale inside, there was a table under a little tent outside where they were cooking sausage and hot dogs. Mike gave Shelly a piece of silver and said, "Get something to bring back for everybody, and get me a couple of Kielbasas if they have them. Those are my favorite." Shelly walked back outside and he looked at the young couple in their early thirties who seemed to run the place. The man was stocky and had a long beard with a hairnet covering it, and the woman had short blonde hair with a cute, compact face. They looked at him happily, having seen the sale they just made outside.

Mike introduced himself and learned that their names were Morgan and Aaron. He made small talk, admiring their meat selection. Getting around to his point, he said, "I'm actually on a search for some fairly specialized stuff, and I have been asking around about acetylene gas, blacksmith tools, stuff like that."

"There's a blacksmith shop right in town. It's just a couple blocks away, on Princess Anne Street," Aaron said. Mike knew that was the direction Justin had gone, and could imagine his excitement when he found the place.

Thanking the couple, Mike walked out of the store and saw Shelly holding a Kielbasa sub out to him. She wasn't quite smiling, but one corner of her mouth was upturned like he had seen happen a few times recently. *She's going to be fine,* Mike thought.

They saw that Justin was quickly approaching, eyes wide with excitement. "Awesome!" He said as he saw the large bag of sausages Shelly was holding, and then he looked back to Mike.

"I found a blacksmith shop!" he exclaimed. "The blacksmith said he would take me on as one of his apprentices in the fall because one of his is leaving to start his own shop. I showed him my hand, and he told me that I'd have to work harder because of it, but that if I didn't let it stop me, he wouldn't, either."

Justin paused and took a breath. Mike noticed that Justin wasn't trying to hide his hand like he'd been doing; both of his hands hung relaxed by his sides. "You wouldn't believe what they are doing in there," he continued. "They have great tools and some of the stuff he has made is just amazing! They also have small bottles of acetylene and said they would be willing to trade. We ought to be able to carry them back in our packs." Justin was almost salivating with excitement, and Mike could see his spark pulsing brightly. This was what Justin was truly meant to do.

Mike pulled Justin and Shelly over to a bench and asked them to sit down.

"Justin, I'm not going to be able to go back with you. I'm going to upstate New York," Mike said quietly.

Justin sat in stunned silence, and Mike glanced at Shelly, who looked pensive and surprised, but not as dumbfounded as Justin.

"Could you take a letter back for me?" Mike asked. "We can decide tonight who stays and who goes. Wolf should definitely go back with you; I don't like that infection on her leg. She needs to get that thing looked at and have some bed rest. In fact, the best thing to do would be to stop and drop her off with Doc Ball in Ramsey on the way home." Mike paused and looked at Shelly, speaking to her softly.

"I want you to come with me, but you don't have to. They will welcome you back at Millwood if you want to go back with Justin. I can barely explain why I'm doing it, and it will be really hard. But if there is a chance to find people who might be able to help me, I have to take it." He looked down at his hands and was silent.

"Of course I'll go," Shelly whispered, reaching out to hold Mike's hand. "I knew there was more to this trip than you let on. Wherever you go, I go, too."

That night around the fire, they handed out the sausages and discussed their future. Lion, Owl, Renee, and the three rebels decided to stay with Mike and Shelly, and everyone else opted to go home with Justin. They had traded what pork and citrus they still had for as many of the small acetylene tanks they could carry, with Mike having to throw some silver into the deal as well. Justin promised the blacksmith he would be back in the fall. The night was a slightly somber one, with the groups already having split up in their own minds. One group would go back to all the comforts of home, and the other would stay on the road and keep looking with Mike, for whatever it was he was looking for. To the new kids who were going back, it sounded like they had won the lottery. They sat unbelieving as they were told stories of fresh food, running water, and warm, soft places to sleep.

Renee had a soft heart and had become quickly attached to the youngest of the new kids, who cried as she told them that she would see them back at the farm soon. "Millwood is a better place for you than out on the road like this." She looked at little Owl. "I wish you would go back with them, too. You're too young to be out here with us."

Looking back at her with his big dark eyes, Owl said, "When Mike goes back, then I will go back with him. I want to see how this part of the story ends."

Laughing, Mike said, "You are a wise sounding little man, you know that?" He looked at Renee. "You know you can go back, too. You don't have to stay out here with us."

She gazed back at him, firelight shining off her dark eyes. "The people who are left are going to need me more. Besides, I agree with Owl. I don't know exactly what you're looking for, but I want to be there when you find it."

"You and me both, honey," Mike said through laughter. "You and me both."

That night, he and Shelly cuddled in their tent. While their physical relationship was still in its infancy, they were slowly making strides and she was comfortable enough to sleep next to him. At first it had been hard because it reminded her of Raven, but after a few nights, they settled into a routine. She would sit next to him and stroke his hair while they talked of the day before going to sleep.

"Aren't you worried about Justin?" she asked.

"He's tougher than he looks," Mike said. "Plus, we gave him some of the equipment we had, and he has one of the new bulletproof vests, although, of course, we kept more since we'll be out longer. Since Justin only needs to get them to Ramsey, they should be fine. We already blazed that trail anyway."

"I love how you have already thought about that," Shelly said. "You're always thinking about other people. Maybe the fact that you can see the Godspark isn't even your strongest magic." Shelly didn't even to ask him about his decision to stay on the road, or why they were setting out for a place so far away. Her hands wandered down to his chest and then his belly, lightly stroking him with her fingers. As she began to unbutton his pants, he gasped and arched his back.

"Be still, magic man," she breathed as she lowered her mouth to kiss him.

Chapter 63

December 2013 — The hoped-for rains in California haven't arrived. The state is in a severe long-term drought, a fate that will eventually afflict much of the West Coast. The Colorado River no longer reaches the ocean and the Ogallala aquifer, which delivers much of the underground water to the Great Plains, is rapidly depleting. Wildfires are getting worse every year. If it doesn't rain soon, parts of California will start running out of water within a year. California produces a significant portion of the food eaten in the U.S.

Beulah, Virginia

The heat of summer was really coming on by the time the steam engine was ready, and the Orlunds were worried about what the heat would do to some of their more tenuous connections and welds. The first trip to Ramsey was a big event, and their railcar was stacked with produce and meat, along with some homemade products. A small crowd was starting to assemble by the steam engine. The day was already getting humid and warm, and Chris was also worried about the effects of the humidity.

"That guy worries about everything," Xavier muttered to himself as he did a final check on his fifty caliber. Gavin stood next to him in his duster, holding his M4 and wearing an eyepiece that Xavier had made from an old pair of glasses and welding goggles. Two of Xavier's Outlaws, Derek and Lamont, stood with shotguns on platforms jutting out from either side of the cab. Orlund was in the cab and another grandson, Will, was with him, feeding wood into the firebox when necessary. Xavier looked back at the second car, admiring his handiwork. They had built a second rifle nest on a platform in the back of the railcar, and they had several boxes of cocktails and caltrops for any horses or vehicles that decided to chase them. That nest was well-armored as well, and manned by two men from the Beulah machine shop. Gavin had been happy to use up the last of their junked vehicles on the project.

"You got a name for her yet?" Xavier asked Gavin, pointing to his M4. "She's saved your ass enough times, she should have a name."

"I actually had the same thought a while back. I'm thinking, 'Vera,'" Gavin replied. "That's got a nice ring to it, don't you think?"

"Yeah, I like that. I like that a lot." Xavier smiled, a gleam in his eye. "And speaking of ladies, Lea didn't want to come this time?"

Gavin nodded. "She didn't think this trip was that risky, so she decided to stay home with George," Gavin said. "I think her exact words were, 'You boys have fun with your engine, and don't mess it up. We need it to get to Port Walter next year.'"

Xavier laughed. "Yeah, man, like I said, that's one hell of a woman you got there."

As he surveyed the completed project, Xavier had to admit that the steam engine looked pretty cool. It stood tall on its tracks, and the metal gleamed fiercely. While some of the modifications and jerry rigging were visible, as a whole, the steam engine looked very similar to the old pictures Xavier had seen. They had taken most of his security ideas, including the spikes and armor covering the wheels. Thick armor plate also protected the most vulnerable parts of the engine, and of course Xavier's rifle nests were the ultimate security.

If we get a blacksmith we're gonna be able to use up some more of those old cars, Xavier thought to himself as he looked at the growing crowd. These days, the landscape was littered with vehicles, hulking and rusting in front yards, driveways, and on the roadsides. There were so many that his kids would still be using them when he was gone.

Xavier looked over at Orlund, who was dressing in his finest red hunting jacket, a beige silk scarf, and white pants. Xavier thought that he would probably get really dirty, but he imagined Orlund wouldn't care too much. Xavier himself had worn his best clothing, a white button up shirt covered by a black vest, and baggy black jeans. He had his dreadlocks tied up in a knot on the back of his head and wore his signature samurai sword on his back. The significance of the day's events warranted clothing that reflected their accomplishments.

This was a proud day. Xavier was astonished at how full the train car was. It was filled with sides of pork, beef, tomatoes, and squash. There were four boxes of citrus fruits, three from Mazie and one from Millwood. And Xavier had contributed several of his smaller metal sculptures to the box for artisan work. Gavin had a few carvings in there, along with a birdhouse.

Looking out on the crowd, Xavier expected Orlund to be the one to speak, but he instead got the crowd's attention and handed it over to Gavin. Gavin stood on top of the cab.

"Ladies and gentlemen, let's have a round of applause for our conductor, Chris Orlund, and our protector, Xavier Jackson!" The crowd cheered wildly, and Xavier smiled and waved at everyone. Looking up at Orlund, Xavier saw that he was beaming, and waving at the crowd with his grandson, Will.

"This is a big moment for us," Gavin continued. "Many of the people here today have contributed to this project, and many more have goods on board. And today, as impressive as this machine is, our celebration isn't about the steam engine. It's about us. The people here are what are most important. We built it, and, even though Chris thinks he can find us one that was built back in the old days, to me, this will always be the best one. It's a symbol of our communities coming together again, and it's a symbol that civilization isn't dead yet. While there are some who believe that civilization cannot exist without harming the planet, I cannot believe that. We must find a way. And this is a first step. It will buy us the time for our children to find an even better way." Gavin paused as the crowd clapped and whistled.

"And now, allow me to introduce the mayor of Beulah, Wade Watts!" Gavin said. He stepped down and allowed the mayor to say a few words.

Xavier hoped that the mayor's speech would be quick, and that the trip would get underway soon.

Maybe there would even be a battle.

Chapter 64

January 2014 – Several of the world's largest oil companies report severe drops in income, with Royal Dutch Shell's earnings dropping forty-eight percent. Conoco Philips was alone in reporting an increase in earnings with a seventy-eight percent jump. However, the company does admit that the increase was due to 'non-core' assets it sold recently. The press release further states that production from continued operations is well below where it was a year ago.

Gavin hated battles. The engine had made it about twenty-five miles, almost halfway to Ramsey, when a piston came loose. Orlund stopped the train as the security force warily looked around. "Coming from the north!" Xavier shouted, and Gavin heard the .50 caliber crack off a shot. He scrambled over next to Xavier, seeing a convoy of vehicles approaching. This group didn't seem to be ex-government; in fact, they looked a lot like survivalists. Most of the men were outfitted in quasi-military camouflage clothing wearing ski masks, their vests bulging with equipment and their weapons black and menacing looking. There were a couple of light green pickups with large rifles mounted on the backs, followed by a dune buggy and a couple of horses. It looked like about fifteen men in all, more than the train could defend against.

Shit, Gavin thought. He had seen these types before, and they were tough to deal with. Some preppers thought they would be kings after the Crumble. Some of them had done so well that they decided it was because they were special in some way, and not subject to the universal laws of morality.

I don't care how many fancy guns you have, Gavin thought as he shouldered his rifle. *You don't get to take what isn't yours.* He adjusted his goggles and started firing on the enemy.

Xavier was yelling to the men in the second car, which faced the wrong direction. They grabbed the boxes of caltrops and cocktails and raced to the front of the steam engine. One of the men from Beulah ran out front and threw large handfuls of caltrops in case the vehicles made it to them, and another prepared the cocktails. Will and Chris covered them with 20-gauge slugs, alternating shots out of each side of the cab. Xavier told his men to go into the woods and try to flank them from the east, and the two Outlaws melted into the trees.

One of the approaching trucks was hit by the .50 caliber and flipped end over end in a spectacular crash, nearly missing one of the horses. Xavier whooped and shot again, turning the rider of the other horse into a red mist. The dune buggy and the other truck pulled up on the tracks and men spilled out of it, racing to the woods on either side as they were peppered with bullets. The survivalists had some pretty serious guns, and Gavin winced as he saw one of them return fire and make a hole the size of a fist in one of the armor plates on the engine. Xavier fired a couple more shots and disabled the other truck and dune buggy, but couldn't see anything else as the survivalists disappeared into the woods. Not wanting to waste ammo, he dismounted and stood next to Gavin.

"They've got nothing to lose now," Xavier said. "They can't get out of here, so we're gonna have to take them all out." Just as the words left Xavier's mouth, the engine started up again and the Orlunds yelled from the cab.

"Leave me here," Xavier said. "I'll go find the Outlaws and help them out. Pick us up on the way back." His eyes gleamed, and one of his dreadlocks had come free from its band and hung in his face. He drew his pistol, a black Ruger P series that matched Gavin's, and fired a couple of shots at their attackers as he ran toward the woods on the east side of the tracks. Gavin sighed, thinking, *better him than me.*

The train was starting to move again and Gavin shadowed it, keeping close to the engine for cover. As they approached the dune buggy, Gavin darted forward, pushing it off the tracks as best he could. The steam engine's guard pushed the rest of the buggy out of the way and it kept gaining speed, so Gavin hopped on. The train wasn't taking any more fire, and Gavin could hear shots in the woods as Xavier and the Outlaws did their jobs, holding the attention of the remaining raiders while the steam engine went on.

As the wind from the ride blew Gavin's hair back, they made it the rest of the way to Ramsey in less than an hour. There was a crowd waiting for them there, too, and loud cheering when they arrived. Gavin smiled sickly as the car was unloaded, full of worries for his friend.

Chapter 65

January 2014 – The government in Denmark collapses as the Socialist party leaves the ruling coalition in disgust over the sale of Denmark's state-owned energy company, Dong Energy. Despite the controversy, the Danish Prime Minister manages to push the deal through. Dong Energy's privatization gives Goldman Sachs an eighteen percent ownership stake, and unheard of management control. Protests are beginning on the streets of Denmark, with a significant majority of Danes opposing the deal.

The stay in Ramsey to load and unload the train was longer than Gavin would have liked, and he made it clear to everyone that they couldn't stay the night and had to go back to pick up Xavier and the Outlaws. Another hour had already passed when Ex came by. Gavin was glad to see that the unloading was complete. He motioned for Will to bring down a metal box with holes in the top. Gavin took the box and held it open for Ex to see.

"Aww, look at that cute little thing!" Ex said, grabbing the puppy from the box and cuddling it on his neck. It licked his face and nuzzled his ear, making him laugh. He put it under his arm. "Let me go bring this to Beatrice and Doc. I need to get Justin, anyway. He and a couple of Mike's group landed here a few days ago and they are going to need a ride back to Beulah. Mike wasn't with them, though. He sent this for you," Ex said, handing Gavin a letter.

As Ex hurried away, he called back at Gavin, "I'll be coming back with Justin. I heard you had some trouble and I want to go back with you, too."

Gavin felt a lot better when he heard that, but all the same, he just stood there for a moment, his mouth hanging open. First Xavier was in trouble, and now Mike wasn't coming back? He gripped the letter tightly in his hands, trembling a bit. Where the hell was Mike, and who were these new people Ex was talking about?

Gavin went to open the letter, but decided to wait until he got home. Justin could at least fill him in on the broad strokes and he could read the letter with Aidan and the whole family when they got back. Gavin's mind was swirling with questions and worries. He took a deep breath. The world would throw at him what it would; all he could do was control how he responded.

By the time Justin and Ex returned, Gavin had relaxed a bit. As Justin embraced his brother and grandfather, Gavin looked at the group that followed him and over the faces of the new ones. Mike must have found a few strays on the road and sent them back with the group. *That's cool. We're good with strays,* Gavin thought.

These kids looked pretty rough, and he assumed they had looked even worse when Mike found them. They were thin, almost to the point of emaciation, but they were clean and their eyes were bright. A couple of them were wearing Mike's clothing.

One of the girls had a large bandage on her leg, which explained why they were at Doc Ball's. Millwood would be a good place for them. Millwood and its neighbors had taken in many refugees over the years, healing them and feeding them. If the refugees were going somewhere, they would be on their way after they had rested and healed. If they had nowhere else to go, they were eventually placed on neighboring farms, or in one of the cottages at Millwood itself.

Gavin got everybody on the train and looked over what they had placed in the rail car. Large jars of honey sat in boxes, and there were several trays of plants with labels on them. Deer corn took up most of the space in the car, with huge bags of it filling up almost half of the space. Gavin had everyone in the group sit on the bags of corn in the car, and he took the spot up top with the .50 caliber. Ex and Justin took the ledges on the sides of the car in the place where the Outlaws had stood on the way there.

The engine started hissing and the train began to roll. He put his head back up top and looked at Ramsey and the crowd waving at them. He waved back and turned around, looking toward their destination. He was still worried about Xavier and the Outlaws, but as he thought about it more, he started worrying less. In fact, it would probably be better to worry about those poor survivalists.

This should be interesting, he thought.

Chapter 66

February 2014 – An anarchist group in Greece called 'The Popular Fighters' attacks a Mercedes plant and the home of a German ambassador. The group's statement said they were fighting against the 'German Capitalist Machine.' Some have called the anarchists a different name; simply, 'the Resistance.'

Xavier found the two Outlaws fairly soon after he left the train, using his trademark whistle to let them know where he was. The survivalists were advancing two by two toward them, firing as they went, and Derek and Lamont were on the run when they saw Xavier.

"Boss! We got trouble!" Derek shouted as he and Lamont kept running past Xavier. Wisely following them, Xavier could see that the survivalists were trying to flank them with two more men he hadn't seen before.

"They left those cocktails on the tracks," Xavier said as he ran, his sword banging against his back. "We need to circle around and get back to that spot. Let's split up and meet there in ten minutes." He took a hard right and began making for the tracks again, firing his shotgun wildly behind him as he did. He heard a yelp and smiled to himself. Lamont and Derek had parted ways too, confusing their pursuers. The survivalists appeared to be communicating with their hands, and Xavier looked back at them frantically making hand gestures at each other.

Xavier turned and saw that he had reached the end of the road. Two of the survivalists were standing in front of him with their guns pointed at his chest. They both wore ski masks to disguise their faces, although Xavier could see that one was black and one was white. As Xavier waited for the shot to come, he saw the black one turn to the white one.

"That's the last time you ever call me nigger, motherfucker," the masked man said, and shot his partner in the head.

"Wood!" Xavier shouted, rushing toward his cousin. Xavier didn't even need to see him with the mask off, having recognized his cousin's voice as soon as he spoke. Wood picked Xavier up off the ground in a bear hug and they fiercely held each other for a moment.

As they separated, Wood took off his ski mask and Xavier could see that he was a little thin, but otherwise looked good. His cousin was slightly taller than him and had grown a beard, which suited him.

"Where the hell you been, man?" Xavier asked, as Wood knelt beside the body, grabbing a gun and a pouch. Shots rang out in the background, and Wood said, "No time for that now. But I will tell you this: I don't think those guys like me anymore." Xavier led his cousin out to the tracks, taking shelter by the ruined dune buggy. Wood gave cover fire as Xavier went for the box of cocktails. Xavier lit two of his special timer cocktails, which he'd made with some recently acquired Tiki torch wicks. He placed them in the brush a few feet from the edge of the woods, hiding them as best as he could. He and Wood fell back a few feet from the buggy, trying to draw out an attack. Xavier saw three men burst from the woods near the cocktails, and he blasted the cocktails with his shotgun, sending flaming goo ten feet in every direction. One of the men was caught in the ball of flame, and his shrieks filled the air.

Xavier had seen this before, and it was a bad way to go. The survivalist had only taken the goo on one side of his body, but that was enough. He flung his hands up and tried to put out the flames, but his clothing had now caught as well. His flesh sizzled and melted into his clothing, and after a short time, he fell to the ground, no longer flailing. Xavier and Wood saw two more try to make a mad dash for the dune buggy, but they cut them down with ease.

"You got some nice tricks, cuz," Wood joked. Xavier grinned merrily, glad to have his gregarious cousin back around. Lamont and Derek circled around from the other side of the tracks, and they both started running as they saw who Xavier had with him. Xavier laid down shots toward the woods with his shotgun as the men briefly greeted each other.

The survivalists had been devastated. Xavier and Wood compared notes and estimated that there were only five or six men left. After a lull in the shooting, a loud voice came from the woods.

"Wood, what the hell are you doing? You're supposed to be with us!"

"Man, these are my family! Fuck you!" Wood yelled back as he fired shots into the woods. "Now that I have my brothers here I don't need you disrespecting me anymore!" Wood looked at Xavier and motioned for a cocktail. Xavier handed it to him after it was lit.

"Go ahead, call me 'boy' one more time. I fucking dare you!" Wood yelled as he threw the cocktail at a rock on the edge of the woods, setting the brush around it ablaze. He fired what was left of his clip toward the woods and the Outlaws joined in, creating a storm of bullets through the smoke of the fire. They threw the rest of the cocktails, shouting and taunting the survivalists.

"They're probably gonna try to flank us now," Xavier said as it became quiet. He sent Lamont and Derek to check either sides of the tracks, and minutes passed with no contact.

"I think they went away," Xavier joked. He looked over at Wood. "Sounds like you were having a real bad time over there, sorry to hear that, cuz," he said, patting Wood on the shoulder as they walked towards the brush.

"I wasn't with them for long," he replied. "When the electricity went out, I was in Williams City working for the Tolson family, taking care of their horses. The Tolsons didn't really seem to know what to do, so I stayed and helped them out, and that worked out well for a long time. They were nice people and they treated me good. One night, I was out with a mare about to give foal, and they got raided. They all got burnt up and killed, and there were too many people for me to fight. I took a horse and left, and I cried for days as I wandered around. I did some odd jobs around Williams City for a while, and found a few places to live, but nothing was ever long-term like the Tolsons again. It wasn't until a little while ago that I hooked up with this survivalist group out on a ranch. I started working for them doing security and helping with their horses. They had it really good out there and they treated me pretty well at first. But after a while, I started to notice little stuff, like I would be walking away and they would call me 'boy' and laugh when they thought I couldn't hear.

"There was one guy who was the worst. He started calling me 'boy', and towards the end, 'nigger'. One night, he pulled a gun on me and said, 'you people used to get real uppity about a certain word. But now there ain't anybody around, what you gonna do, call the PC police?' That happened about a month ago and it got worse after that." Wood paused and looked at the ruined trucks and buggy.

"What could I do? There were a bunch of white guys standing there with guns. I just laughed and played it off so I could survive, and the next day I approached the boss and said I wanted to leave. He told me that I owed money for the place I had been staying at and that I couldn't leave until it was paid off. He was armed when he told me that. That was when I started looking for my chance to get away. It seemed like I couldn't get a minute alone. There was always someone around. With that one guy, it got worse and worse. He'd say stuff like: 'Hey boy, go scout the north perimeter', or 'hey nigger, go check on that foal.' He was the one I shot today. When they heard the sound of the train, they set up a raid, and I offered to go because I figured that would be my only chance to get away. I'm gonna miss my horse, though, I had to leave her there."

"You never know with the crew we have here, cuz, we might be able to go get her," Xavier said as he hugged his cousin. They found two bodies and quietly looted them, then the four of them sat by the train tracks, waiting for their ride.

Chapter 67

February 2014 – U.S. Government officials shut down a little girl's cupcake business in a small Illinois town. While this particular item is picked up on the national news because of the human interest angle, it's endemic of a larger problem. Government 'regulators' shut down small businesses every single day all across the U.S., squashing any hopes of recovery and unknowingly doing the work of their corporate overlords. Farmer's markets, raw milk producers, small meat processors, community banks, and even tiny cupcake businesses are attacked by government regulators on a daily basis. This is what it looks like when the machine has full control.

"Lover boy!" Gavin shouted as the train pulled up next to Xavier and his group and he saw Wood was with them. Gavin had always called Wood 'Lover boy' because he adored women so much. In fact, for a long time, Wood had owned a car with heart shaped tailpipes. "Where have you been, man? We haven't seen you in years!"

"What's up, brother?" Wood grinned as the two men embraced.

After Wood quickly summarized his last few years, and he and Xavier talked about the day's events, Gavin said, "Thank God you were there! It sounds like we almost lost Xavier!"

"Nah," Xavier smiled. "I'm too pretty to die."

Everyone laughed as they got on the train. Gavin held out the goggles Xavier had given him and said, "I love these! I can see through them really well and they kept the dust out of my eyes."

Xavier smiled at Gavin and as the engine started he looked back at the car, seeing Justin and several people, but not Mike. Looking concerned, he asked, "What happened to Mike?"

Gavin held out the unopened letter. "It looks like his journey isn't quite done yet."

The ride home was quiet and uneventful, and it was past dark by the time they got back to Millwood. Everyone had been waiting up, and the Big House was full of people. Greetings were made; Justin and the newcomers were sent to sleep in one of the upstairs guest rooms that had bunk beds. Justin had wanted to make the trip back to

Farrington that night but no one would let him go. Wood greeted Bob and Stella who were overjoyed to see him again. He and Xavier took Ex out to a cottage where he could sleep.

Stella and Bob sat with BoBo and Shiver and the two remaining puppies, who they had named Princess and Boomer. Boomer was the runt, and Gavin had told Lea the name would give him confidence. Gavin hugged his wife and son for a long time, even though he had only been gone for a day. Aidan sat with worried eyes and everyone awaited the news of Mike. Gavin didn't make them wait any longer and began to speak.

"From what Justin told Ex, Mike has had a hell of a trip so far. His group was attacked on the way and Mike somehow stopped the battle. He brought in some of their attackers to his group, a couple of which are sleeping upstairs now. Supposedly he killed a very bad man in the process. It turns out that a part of Fredericksburg is functioning and peaceful, so they managed to get what they needed and Justin got an internship with a blacksmith over there in the fall. At that point, Mike decided to stay on the road and split the group up. Shelly and Renee are still with him, as are a couple of others they picked up along the way. He sent this letter back with Justin, and I haven't opened it yet. I figured we could all read it at the same time."

Gavin opened the letter, eyes already tearing up from missing Mike.

"Dear everyone," Gavin read. *"First of all, I have to apologize. I never intended to come back from Fredericksburg. I didn't tell anyone because I knew you would all try to convince me not to go. This trip is a search for something I can barely explain, and I know it will be dangerous. I really understand that now that I've been out on the road for myself."* Gavin cleared his throat and adjusted his glasses. He looked out on the sad faces of his family, and continued reading.

"We are human beings, and we're defined by the actions we take in our lives. We always need to strive, to grow and to move forward. Now we face a time of great change unlike any we have seen before. We can't grow the way we used to, and we can't strive for the same goals we once did. We need to find a new direction and a new way of thinking about the world. We don't need to grow anymore, just prosper. We don't need to conquer nature; instead we need to be a part of it. Our lives can be enriched in unimaginable ways.

"But there will always be one fundamental problem. What happened

to us with the Crumble was about something much deeper than just oil or money. The problem is that there will always be people among us who use violence to get their way, or employ lies and deceit to take from others. There will always be people who place their own desires over the needs of their community, and put their own welfare above that of future generations. We have to do better at finding these people, and we need to ensure that they don't get into positions of authority. Because no matter what we build, what kind of government we design, or what knowledge we learn, it will eventually be co-opted and used by the greedy and evil.

"Bob told me once that it's the sociopaths and psychopaths who ultimately come to dominate any large system. They hide among us so well, they are obsessed with power, and they're unrestrained by morals or compassion. Those are the people who broke our civilization. They have done the same thing many times before, all the way back to the days of Atlantis. If we don't figure out how to stop them, they'll just keep on doing it until humanity destroys itself." Gavin stopped and broke down, full of love for his nephew. Aidan sat quietly crying, and Gavin flipped the page, composing himself.

"I believe I can help with this problem, but in order to really understand, I have to find the Shaolin temple in upstate New York. I know that might sound crazy, and don't blame Gavin because he gave me the idea. I was determined to do something, and if I hadn't gone there, it would have been somewhere else. I'm well-equipped and strong, and I trust the people who are with me completely, especially Shelly. You all have taught me well, but now I have to do some more learning on my own. I don't know when I'll be back, but I promise to return when I have learned what I need to know. Millwood will always be my home. I love you all more than I could ever say."

Clearing his throat as he finished, Gavin saw that there was another page addressed to Aidan, who shakily took the letter and went upstairs. Gavin didn't even bother to tell anyone about the steam engine battle, knowing they would find out soon enough, and not caring at all at the moment. He sat down and put his head in his hands, leaning on Lea and the baby. After he sat like that for a while, Stella walked over with Boomer.

"I think he has a tick on his belly," Stella said, handing him the puppy. Gavin knew exactly what she was doing. He had always loved puppies. Even though he could see that Stella was just as heartbroken from missing Mike as much as he was, she was still trying to cheer him up. He took Boomer from Stella.

"Lea, can you see if he has a tick on him? I can't make anything out in this light." The puppy had rolled over on his back in Gavin's arms and splayed out his legs. Little Boomer gave a long yawn and licked his chops, snuggling in with Gavin comfortably. Lea rubbed the puppy's belly. "I don't see one, but he should probably stay with us tonight to be sure." Gavin put Boomer down and Lea and Stella started playing with him, making little noises and patting him on the stomach. Boomer put his little paws up in the air to playfully swipe at them, giving a cute little puppy growl. Baby George got in the act, smiling and gurgling and petting the puppy with his pudgy hands.

Shiver and BoBo barely looked up. Shiver was curled up asleep on a mat on the floor, and BoBo lay spread-eagled on his back on a stuffed chair next to her.

Gavin smiled as he watched the display. He would miss Mike every second of the day until he came back, and worry about him even more. But he looked back at his family, who he loved so fiercely that he would give his life to protect them, and knew that he owed them his full attention. As long as he lived, he would give them all of himself.

Gavin grabbed Boomer and raised him to his face, blowing a long raspberry on the puppy's belly. Everyone laughed, including baby George. He gave the puppy back to Stella and pulled his beautiful wife off the couch, embracing her.

"Do you know why I love you the most, Pocahontas?" he asked her.

"Why is that, because I'm smart and spunky? Or because I save your ass in battles?"

She paused, and looked at him with a gleam in her eye. "Or... is it just because I gave you an excuse to go to Italy?" Lea fluttered her eyelashes at him.

"No! None of that! It's because you laugh at my jokes! Rarrrr!" Gavin picked up his wife and swung her around. His family looked on, smiling and laughing.

Chapter 68

September 2014 — A new force in the Middle East has recently emerged, alternately being called ISIS, ISIL, or the Islamic State. This new group is different from Al Queda in many ways, but one way is particularly significant. ISIS can take and hold territory, where Al Queda could not. Their territory is increasing swiftly through Syria, Libya, and Iraq, and their stated goal is to create a new Islamic Caliphate.

September 2039
Southern Delaware

"Welcome to Delaware," Mike read on the worn sign as his ragged group walked past it. He had to squint to see the sign through the trees in the fading light. His group kept to the safety of the woods along the highway, traveling only between dusk and dawn. "Bob told me this is one of the smallest states in the whole country."

Autumn evidently reached this part of the country earlier, and some of the trees were already turning bright shades of red, orange, and yellow. Crickets chirped in the dusk, musically but incessantly. A light drizzle was falling, cooling the fall air even further.

"I bet it will seem pretty big to us," Shelly said as she munched on a piece of jerky. While they had been able to forage well so far, Mike knew she would miss the jerky when it was gone. Shelly had an inordinate fondness for anything salty.

"That flower in your hair looks nice," Mike told her, as he adjusted the rifle that hung on his back. She gave him the lopsided half-grin he'd come to love.

They had been on the road for more than two months, and were making slow but steady progress. They avoided people on the road, hiding in the woods whenever they saw anyone. They had entered a few small towns where sentries were clearly visible, and they had been welcomed at these places, and sometimes even invited to stay in the townspeople's homes. Once they were discovered to be travelers, they were constantly asked about news of the outside world. What little they knew seemed to be enough. Welcoming places like that were few and far between, however, and they spent many hard days and nights in the thin patches of woods along the roadways.

Above all else, they remained safe, and Shelly was stoic under the hardships of traveling, as was the rest of the group. But Mike knew that Shelly missed the life at Millwood. She had only been able to taste it for a short time, but the memory was always with her. She often talked fondly of the farm, and the dresses she and Lea had made.

Once I find what I'm looking for, I'll take her back there and never leave again, Mike swore to himself. His letter to his family had said he would only return when he'd learned what he needed to know. His greatest fear, one that kept him up every night, was that he would find the Shaolin temple and there would be no one there, or that they would refuse to teach him. Taking Shelly away from the first real home she'd had in years would all be for nothing.

Mike looked back at his followers, who walked behind him in a long, thin line. Shelly was directly behind Mike, followed by Renee carrying Owl on her back. Sarah, a young rebel girl, was followed closely by Lion, still proudly wearing his new vest. He fulfilled his namesake with a long mustache and beard, even at the young age of seventeen. Carl and Vance, the two young Jackson brothers, brought up the rear.

Mike asked Shelly to take the lead, as he often did, and placed his left hand on her shoulder as he walked behind her. He closed his eyes, having found that this was the best way to see the sparks that were emanating from other people. After walking this way for a few minutes, Mike raised his right hand in a fist, and then fanned out his fingers. Opening his eyes again, he saw that everyone had melted into the woods, and only he and Shelly remained.

"Come on!" she said, tugging at his hand as she motioned toward the thick underbrush, wanting to hide with the rest of the group. "You saw people, right?"

"Yeah, but it's too late. They're in the trees, all around us," Mike said.

Just as those words left his mouth, he heard the click of a hammer being pulled back on a pistol.

A deep, gruff voice calmly commanded, "Drop that rifle and put your hands up, boy. You too, young miss. You two look like you're far from home, but you're on the King's land now."

Mike placed his rifle on the ground and looked at Shelly, who was carrying a coach gun. She looked at him and then back at the man, raising her eyebrows.

"There are at least six more up in the trees," Mike whispered. He had turned slightly to get a look at the man. He'd never seen someone look so... nondescript. He was a middle-aged Asian man with a small build that belied his gruff voice.

Mike looked at his spark. It was hollow and gray.

The man whistled, and the rest of his group dropped from the trees. They all wore dull clothing to better blend in with the bark of the trees, and a few had their faces painted in hues of dark grays and browns. Mike saw that all of them had some type of tree climbing gear, and as he looked up, he could see small metal rings screwed in to various places in the trees.

The rest of Mike's followers were found and rounded up, and were all handcuffed with zip ties. Carl and Vance put up a fight, and their faces were bruised and cut for their trouble. The 'King's' followers, or the *tree people*, as Mike was thinking of them, stayed silent for the whole time as they did their work. Their sparks were muted, but untainted.

Well, at least the rest of them are human beings, Mike thought to himself wretchedly. *Why the hell is it always the damn leader?*

Renee had a look of fear in her eyes and little Owl was shaking. Mike gave a grim smile to them all, and said, "Don't worry, guys, this won't hold us up for long. Once I talk to the King, I'm sure he'll see reason. After all, I love his music!" Everyone in his group laughed, even Shelly. The leader gruffly told him to shut up, and pressed the barrel of his pistol into Mike's back.

As Mike and his group were hustled away, they were followed.

In the trees, a white owl flapped its wings and pursued the group, and a trio of red foxes followed on the ground.

Chapter 69

October 2014 – The Ebola virus makes landfall in the U.S. for the first time. Despite massive amounts of information in the media about each individual case, infection rates, and containment methods, there is no way to know what the ultimate impact will be. One thing is certain, however. This is prescient of things to come. When any given population becomes too large, Mother Nature acts to reduce it, and to restore the balance.

October 2039
Southeast edge of Millwood Farm

Xavier and Wood crouched in the brush, shivering in the cold autumn rain. They wore their ghillie suits over layers of rain gear and protective clothing, but the persistent rain soaked them to the bone anyway.

"I'm pissed we caught sentry duty tonight," Wood said. "But I'm glad to get it over with. I want to start scouting out those survivalists tomorrow. I know they still have my girl. She's such a good horse, I know they're not gonna put her down, no matter how much they might hate me for turning on them."

"Alright, I'll help you out. But are you sure you just don't want payback?" Xavier asked his cousin, as he looked through his scope. He was watching the south side of Smitten Road, the only main road leading to Millwood.

"Nah, I've got no more beef with them," Wood said. "I figure after what happened by the train tracks, we're about even. But I've got to get Easy Daisy back, man. She was the best horse I ever had, and I've had a lot over the years. I was gonna breed her."

Xavier nodded, and adjusted the hood on his soaked ghillie suit. "Yeah, I got you. You got your favorite horse, and this right here is my favorite spot, know what I mean? We can see everything from here." They were on the top of a hill on the very edge of the Millwood property, and they could look down over the entire approach up Smitten Road. An old stone wall was perfectly placed for protection. He handed the scope back to his cousin and raised himself off the ground slightly.

As Wood looked into the scope, he quietly slapped Xavier's arm.

"Look at this," Wood said as he handed the scope back to Xavier. Xavier looked and saw several black SUVs slowly coming up the hill. Just as Wood looked up and opened his mouth to say something, they heard the distant pop of gunshots. They both immediately pressed themselves closer to the ground, thankful for the protection of the wall.

"Shit," Xavier spat. "I bet one of them over at Moonshine Farm got spooked and started shooting."

"Yep, those trucks are firing in that direction," Wood said breathlessly, as he checked the clip in his rifle and flipped off the safety. The men in the vehicles were firing on the cluster of houses east of the road. Those houses, and the farm they sat on, were Millwood's close neighbors, Moonshine Farm.

Wood looked at Xavier. "What are we gonna do? I'm still new here; you're the boss man right now."

Xavier was already slinking over the stone wall and moving down the hill toward the action. The vehicles had stopped at the base of the hill, the third one obscured by the beginning of a forest on both sides of the road.

"Those are our neighbors," Xavier said, as Wood caught up to him. "And we don't need to warn Gavin and them back at the house, they'll be able to hear the shots. If we can distract whoever this is, then at least they can get their kids and old people away from the house."

"Yeah man, I got you," Wood said as he hurried behind Xavier, halfway between a crouch and a crawl. "Who are these fucks, anyway? They got a hell of a lot of vehicles."

"Probably more of the same that we fought in Farrington a while back," Xavier answered. "They used to be government, but they're hollow. You can tell by the black SUVs. Once you start blowing up their shit and killing a few of them so the others can see, they run out of steam pretty quick."

The two men reached the crest of a small mound of dirt that would give them cover, and Xavier began firing. His M4 spat again and again, and Wood could hear screams coming from the vehicles. He raised his rifle and looked through his scope, sighting in on the last

SUV in the line. As he did, his eye caught an unusual color. Khaki. He looked back at the first SUV in line, and zoomed in on the insignia on the passenger door. Department of Homeland Security. Behind the three SUVs, he could make out at least two khaki-colored personnel carriers, obscured by the trees.

"Cuz, fuck, man! It's the Feds! Stop shooting for a second. Look behind the trees!" Wood handed Xavier his rifle.

Xavier didn't use a scope on his AR-15, needing only his flip-up iron sights for targets up to two hundred yards away. He picked up Wood's rifle and looked through the scope.

"Shit," Xavier said woodenly. Just as he said it, a new round of shots erupted from the vehicles, plowing up the dirt into a flurry of flying mud in front of them. "Start running back up the hill, and let me cover you," Xavier said as he loaded a new magazine. Dusk had set in and it was almost dark, and the rain was coming down harder.

Wood acted quickly and started running up the hill, and despite Xavier firing back at their adversaries, he could see shots impact the ground around him. His heart was thudding in his chest by the time he got up to the stone wall, flinging himself over it. He turned and looked through his scope, intending to cover Xavier as he made his way up the hill. He aimed his .270 at the vehicles and let fly. He had a five-round clip, and timed his shots as best he could to buy time for his cousin.

Xavier was less than three feet from the stone wall, ready to vault over it, when a large caliber bullet impacted the rocks right in front of him, flinging shards into his face and chest. As Wood poked his head back up, he saw that Xavier's left eyeball was hanging down onto his face, with blood pouring from the empty red socket. Xavier briefly put his hand in the air as if to examine his injuries, and then his right eye rolled back in his head. As he swayed, Wood reached out and grabbed him, pulling him over the wall.

Wood grabbed his cousin's limp body and started dragging him down the hill. As he made his way back on the trail to the Big House, he began talking to Xavier, who was still unconscious.

"Don't worry, cuz, Lea will fix you up," Wood said in a cracked, hollow voice. "You're gonna be fine. And you need to hold on for me, cuz. Because I love you, man. And because we're gonna need your help. We've got to tell everybody." He paused and broke off a sob. He looked up and breathed a sigh of relief, as he saw that Gavin was coming to meet him on the trail.

"Tell us what?" asked Gavin, armed to the teeth and out of breath from his run. Aidan and the Outlaws were close behind. Lea was behind Gavin as well, and immediately ran to Xavier.

"How is he?" Gavin asked, as he hovered over Lea, his face pale with concern.

"I can't tell yet, but I'll do everything I can," Lea said in the clipped, efficient tones she used while she worked. She had placed gauze over the worst of the wounds on his face, and was examining another wound in his chest. She began pulling items from her bag.

Gavin looked back at Wood with fear and concern in his eyes. "Tell us what?" he asked Wood again. "What was all that shooting? More raiders?"

"No. Not raiders," Wood answered. "They're at the bottom of Smitten right now, just over that ridge." He frantically motioned behind him.

"Who?" Gavin asked impatiently.

"The Feds," Wood said. "The fucking Feds are back."

TO BE CONTINUED

Acknowledgements

To the Crumbleheads. As I started promoting the book, your overwhelming response to the first chapters, the FAQs, and pictures, drove me to make the book as good as it could possibly be, and worthy of your support. Thank you all. It means the world to me.

To my mentor, James Howard Kunstler. Thanks for all the advice, friendship, and encouragement. You have opened all of our eyes. Check out Jim's work at **www.kunstler.com**.

To Marc Harding, my longtime friend and head editor. Without you, this book would not exist. I aspire to write as well as you do. Check out Marc's excellent novels at **www.jmarcharding.com**.

To Thomas Chillemi, my story editor. Thanks for all your help and friendship over the years. You took a good story and made it great.

To Jaime Martinez Rodriguez, for the beautiful cover art.

To Michelle Paine Pellatt, who made me fall in love with Lea.

To my parents, Rod and Georgia. Georgia gave me the ideas for Gavin's journal and the FAQs, and Rod made me believe I could always do better. Thanks 'Bob and Stella,' I love you both more than I can say!!

To Leo West and Shawn Woodson, my brothers. Outlaws for life!

To the great thinkers of our time. Thank you to Greer, Ruppert, Orlov, Jensen, and Heinberg.

To Alessandro Carbone, the CEO of ATC Europa.

To Jacques Smith, Michael Santangelo, Terrence Johnson, Trent Porter, Sharon Taylor, Alison Cox, Bridget Harris, Linda Sandridge, Joyce Harding, Milton Harding, Jacques Smith, Katie Wolfe, Jim Favreau,

Natalie Lacaze, John Duvall, Brittany Wills, Katie Beam, Jen Aubin, Jake Hall, Morgan Garihan, Aaron Smith, Mandy Chillemi, Kyle Sullivan, David Wolf, Chris Handy, Courtenay Rucker, Robert Chambliss, Katie Porter, Natalie Martinez, Ben Witman, Leonardo Montoya, Sebastien Costantino, and Brian Ring. You all are the best friends a guy could ask for. If I missed anyone, I will mention you in book two. I love you all.

To Jim Longhurst, a great friend. I love your last name and used it for a bad guy, but that character is *not* based on you. You're one of the good guys!

To my publisher, Prepper Press. Derrick and Sarah, I don't know what I would have done without you. Derrick, your passion and knowledge have helped me immeasurably, and Sarah, your Jedi editing skills have helped polish ATC to a fine gleam. I'm so proud of what we've done, and can't wait for book two!

FAQs on the Crumble

Q: What is the Crumble?

A: The Crumble is the slow collapse of industrial civilization.

Q: When will it happen?

A: It's already happening. Depending on how you measure it, the Crumble began somewhere between 2005 and 2010.

Q: What caused it?

A: The same thing that has brought down all the world's great civilizations: too many people and too few resources. More people every year, and fewer resources every year.

Q: It took Rome hundreds of years to collapse. Why should I believe the collapse of industrial civilization will happen in my lifetime?

A: One word: Oil. Industrial civilization is utterly dependent on cheap oil, coal, and natural gas. We're running out of all three, especially when it comes to the 'cheap' part. That factor will make industrial civilization collapse faster than any that came before it.

Q: How long will it take?

A: There's no way to know for sure, but it's a good bet to expect the next 20 years to be characterized by a slow decline in living standards for people everywhere.

Q: Is there anything else causing the Crumble besides resource scarcity?

A: Yes. The damage that industrial civilization has done to the environment is starting to become apparent. Climate change is real, and much of the groundwater and oceans on the planet are already poisoned. We have driven so many species into extinction that the whole food chain is being affected. The drought in the American West and the smog in Beijing are just two examples of how environmental degradation is beginning to affect civilization directly.

Q: Can I see the Crumble in my daily life?

A: Depending on where you live, your own life may already be affected a great deal. If you watch the news and pay attention to your surroundings, you will notice it. More people walking, higher systemic unemployment, high inflation, and violence around the world in countries with oil resources or pipelines are just a few examples of how the Crumble is already affecting our daily lives. As the years go by, we will see it more and more.

Q: This is terrible news! What can I do?

A: Embrace the change. Prepare for a life after the Crumble. Grow a tomato plant on your balcony if you can, and if you have a backyard, try to raise chickens. Eat clean food. Buy locally.

Q: I already do all that. What else can I do?

A: Fight the machine!!

Q: What is the machine?

A: That's another FAQ!

FAQs on the machine

Q: What is the machine?

A: The machine is the unholy union of corporate money, government power, and technology. The machine is Monsanto and Goldman Sachs. It's hydraulic fracturing. It's Big Pharma. It's NSA surveillance and the military industrial complex. They're all part of a larger enemy. It's the biggest challenge we'll face in our lifetimes—the machine itself.

Q: Why is the machine a problem?

A: Because corporate power has subverted democracy all over the planet. The largest corporations have managed to buy off the governments of the world, and the people themselves no longer have any power. More importantly than that, however, the machine is quickly destroying the planet through pollution, resource depletion, and deforestation.

Q: Who is running it?

A: Many people believe the machine is controlled by "the elites"—a group of wealthy and powerful corporate and government figures. While it's true that they do have unimaginable power and resources, a small minority of people are beginning to believe that there is actually no one controlling the machine. The elites fight amongst themselves for power and resources, but the machine supersedes them all. Despite the fact that the elites use the machine to exploit us, at the end of the day, they're slaves to it just like everyone else.

Q: What does the machine want?

A: Just one thing. To feed. That's the way it was built. It must always have more resources, and it always has to keep eating and growing. It needs oil, water, and soil. It needs the production of human beings to feed it. The machine is like a large public multinational corporation. It has no morality or compassion, and must always feed and grow to survive, no matter which human beings happen to be running it.

Q: Are there manifestations of the machine in our daily lives?

A: Yes; any machine intended to replace a human being. Self-checkout aisles, automated ordering screens, and DVD rental machines are all examples. With every new automation, more people lose their jobs. The consumer's experience is often worsened, or at best, unchanged. Automations such as this only serve the machine, being solely intended to increase profits for the corporations.

Q: Since the human race is running out of cheap energy and industrial civilization is slowly crumbling, won't the machine eventually die on its own?

A: Yes. But because of how quickly it's destroying what's left of the planet, that may not be soon enough to save the human race. It's our responsibility to dismantle and disengage from the machine as soon as we can.

Q: How can we fight it?

A: By starving it. The less we depend on it, the weaker it will get. Every apple you grow is a blow to the machine. Every dollar you spend at the farmer's market is a dollar out of Monsanto's pocket. Every time you buy woodcarving tools instead of a new iPhone, you strike a blow. The more we can do for ourselves, the less we'll have to depend on the machine.

Q: How else?

A: By changing how we think about the world. When we worship technology, we worship death. We must remember to worship life again, like our ancestors did. Living things are more important than dead, or inanimate, ones. While human beings will always strive to build tools and catalogue knowledge, we must now learn to use technology as the tool it was intended and not as the end in itself.

FAQs on the New American Dream

Q: What is the American Dream?

A: James Adams coined the term in 1931, stating that the American dream is "that dream of a land in which life should be better and richer and fuller for everyone, with opportunity for each according to ability or achievement."

Q: What's wrong with that?

A: It's a lofty ideal, but it doesn't hold true anymore. The existence of the machine has stratified the elites and ultra-wealthy into unassailable positions. Even self-made millionaires like Oprah Winfrey or Bill Gates could never hope to amass as much wealth in their lifetimes as the world's most elite families. Social mobility for the middle and lower classes is virtually nonexistent. It's also understood that a "richer and fuller life" means increased material consumption. As our age becomes one of scarcity, society will no longer be able to afford a goal like that.

Q: What is the New American Dream?

A: To have meaningful work, a reciprocal and non-destructive relationship with nature, and to be an integral part of our families and communities. To have love and purpose in our lives.

Q: How can we be sure this one is better than the last?

A: The old American Dream brought us to a very difficult place. As long as the cheap energy kept flowing and the environment could withstand the damage, we could afford a dream of never-ending comfort and entertainment. But a time is rapidly approaching when the cost will be too high. Will we allow fracking in our communities so the machine can get a little more oil, even if it poisons our water table forever? If we trade our remaining fresh water for the last bits of oil on the planet, we will die. Besides, a life dedicated to material consumption and technology is meaningless.

Q: Does the New American Dream include a relationship with technology at all?

A: Yes. High technology has given us advanced medical care, instantaneous communication, and many other wondrous advancements. The generations alive today must learn how to balance our relationship with technology with new energy and environmental constraints, and only use what is necessary. Over the next twenty years, we must choose between tools and toys; between Angry Birds and dialysis machines. If we close our eyes and pretend we can keep both, then we may lose it all.

Q: So even with peak oil and environmental desolation, we won't have to go back to the Stone Age?

A: Not if we manage the next twenty years correctly. As for the environment, if we broke it, we can fix it, at least to a certain extent. If we can create a new sustainable culture to replace the dominant one, there will be an alternative in place when the machine crumbles. That's the essence of the New American Dream.

Q: There are already many movements like the one you speak of. What's different about this one?

A: Many of the existing movements, such as the slow food movement or transition towns, only encompass a part of the problem. The strength of our movement is in the big picture, and in the simplicity of our terminology and beliefs. We can't fight something we can't see, and to name a thing is to see it clearly. What are we going through? The Crumble. What is our enemy? The machine. What do we believe in? The New American Dream. Who are we? Crumbleheads!

Q: What is a Crumblehead? That name sounds kind of silly.

A: It's supposed to be. This doesn't all have to be prepping, guns, and doom and gloom. We believe in a positive outlook. Instead of saying, "what will happen to us?" we ask, "What changes will we make in the world today?" As for the rest, you'll have to wait for the next FAQ on

Crumbleheads!

Q: One last question: How come you don't capitalize the term "the machine?"

A: Because screw the machine, that's why.

FAQs on Crumbleheads

Q: "Crumblehead" sounds like "Deadhead." What's up with that?

A: That speaks to the last comment in the New American Dream FAQ. We're going to save the world and have fun doing it. We work hard but we aren't afraid to party a little bit. The Crumble isn't bad news: in fact it may be the only way that the human race can survive the next hundred years.

Q: The picture you paint of the Crumble doesn't sound like fun to me! How can we be optimistic about a declining standard of living and scarcities of food, water, and cheap energy? Where will we get clean air, water, and soil? How can we be upbeat about the fall of the greatest civilization the world has ever known?

A: We're optimistic because we're making positive changes in the world every day. We're creating the culture and the system that will last after industrial civilization has declined. When there are no more big-box food stores, we will grow and raise our own food. When there are no more big-box hardware stores, we'll make our own tools. But it's more than that. Before the big-box stores fall, we'll have already made them obsolete. We're going to take back the power ourselves. We can clean the air, water and soil ourselves too; Mother Nature can help us.

Q: That sounds implausible. Is that even possible?

A: Let's look at a couple of examples. Sunflowers and hemp can remove radiation from the soil in areas affected by nuclear disasters. When oil spills happen in other countries besides the U.S., they use biological remediation; in other words they ask Mother Nature to help clean up. (In the U.S., we still use chemical dispersants, which actually makes the spill much more toxic). As for creating a new system, we're doing it right now. Many of you have already begun building it.

Q: Are there any rules for being a Crumblehead?
A: Only one: we don't go backwards. We aren't throwing away our

culture; just fixing it. We're Americans for better or for worse. Even though it often seems our civilization is so sick that it can't be cured, not everything about modern civilization is bad. Modern civilization has created a culture where racism and sexism are unacceptable, and that's the right thing to do. Our culture is opening up to the fact that the war on drugs has been a destructive failure. We have a culture of helping those who are less fortunate. We've achieved a great many positive cultural and intellectual accomplishments, and we don't want to lose those advancements.

Q: This question is for Devon Porter, the author of After the Crumble. Aren't you a hypocrite? You rail against the machine but you're using the very same machine to disseminate your ideas.

A: That's an important point. While I've been able to remove myself from the machine in some small ways, I'm still very much a part of it. I hate what McDonalds represents, but I've eaten there a few times in the past year because it's convenient. (And I'll admit, I still think it tastes good; I grew up on the stuff!) I don't like to be dependent on the power grid but I still am. I drive a gas-guzzling truck. I could go on, but suffice it to say that like many of us, I'm not perfect. We don't need to feel guilty about that! We're children of the machine; cradled from the womb in its clammy, chemical covered hands. We'll do better every day, together. We'll use the machine when we need to, and we'll choose which parts of the machine to feed and which to starve. We'll teach those who are farther behind us and learn from those ahead. We'll never be smug about what we know and what we've accomplished. We're all in this together!

Visit **AfterTheCrumble.com** to follow the series.

About the Author

Devon Porter lives in Virginia and works in the corporate world. After spending his youth eating junk food and living in a techno-narcissistic haze, he almost died due to a serious digestive condition brought on by his unhealthy lifestyle. After several months in the hospital, upon his release he began researching the industrial food system, big agriculture, and the effect of processed food on the human body.

Shocked at the fragile and toxic state of farming across the planet, Devon began prepping and growing his own food. He currently raises chickens, blueberries, and pork, using natural techniques. After studying slow collapse theory, Devon came to the conclusion that the Crumble is happening now, and will continue to accelerate in the years to come. He believes that population pressure, resource scarcity, hyper-complexity, and environmental degradation will continue to intensify, until the creaking machine of industrial civilization is finally brought to a halt.

Devon has loved post-apocalyptic fiction and science fiction all of his life, and is honored to be included in the ranks of such great authors. His work shows that in this new post-industrial world we're entering into, we'll have new jobs to do, and new stories to tell. We can leave the planet a better place for our kids, and keep the bright beacons of hope, freedom, and knowledge burning during one of humanity's darkest times.

Visit **AfterTheCrumble.com** to follow the series.

Made in the USA
Lexington, KY
01 April 2015